A Blind Pig in Sugar City

A Fargo Novel

Joe Schneider

A Blind Pig in Sugar City

Copyright © 2022 by Joe Schneider

All rights reserved. Except as permitted under the U.S. Copyright Act of 1976, no part of this publication may be reproduced, distributed, or transmitted in any form by any means, or stored in a database or retrieval system, without the prior written permission of the publisher.

Any references to historical events, real people, or real places are used fictitiously. Other names, characters, places, and events are products of the author's imagination, and any resemblance to actual events, places or persons, living or dead, is entirely coincidental.

No payment has been received from any person, company or other entity in exchange for any mention or lack thereof in this book.

Cover art and design by Marc de Celle

Published by Fargo Press

First Edition, July 2022

ISBN 979-8-218-02991-3

*To my daughter Lara Lynne Hollenczer,
fellow print journalist, newspaper editor, and
co-author of one of my books. I loved that girl and
not a day passes when I don't think of her. I find
myself wanting to pick up the phone and
find out if her reaction to the daily
news matches mine.*

A Blind Pig in Sugar City

Chapter One

Congressman Drops His Trousers

"This is what you came to see. Keep your eyes on the screen," says the Capitol Hill policeman.

The *Washington Star* reporter watches closely. He can see two men standing side by side in front of urinals in a small bathroom. The black and white film is only 8 mm, which makes it grainy. But it clearly shows both men are sneaking looks at one another.

"They are definitely checking each other out," says Chuck Baker, the *Star* reporter.

The white man rocks back from the urinal, fully exposing himself. The black man watches intently. Then he steps back himself, revealing his erect member.

The two voyeurs watching the film grin at each other. Neither says a word, but they have the same thought: if they were judging a contest for length and girth, the Negro would have won hands down.

After a few strokes with his fist, the Negro wrestles his show piece back into his pants and moves over to the door. He locks it and returns to the urinals.

"Now watch this," says Tony Schober, the Capital Hill policeman. "It will blow your mind."

The distinguished looking white man, about 50 years old, wearing a summer suit, steps straight back from the urinal. He may not have won the big-dick contest, but that doesn't mean he's ashamed of his entry. The good-looking black man, wearing what appears to be a janitor's uniform, bends down on one knee in front of the white man and performs fellatio on him.

"Holy shit," says Baker. "I can't believe you got this on film. Do they know it?"

"Nope. But hold on," says Schober. "It gets even better."

The man in the suit is quickly satisfied. Without any conversation between them, he pulls himself together and zips up his slacks. The janitor rises to his feet and without a moment's hesitation the white man goes down on both knees in front of him. The Negro's pants are still undone. The white man reaches in and quickly finds what he is looking for. Once he wrestles it out, he takes obvious pleasure in examining it with both hands. Then he gets serious about returning the favor done to him. The white man apparently enjoys giving pleasure as much as he does receiving it.

After the Black explodes in his mouth, Congressman Jeff Walker of Pelham, Alabama, gets up off his knees and goes to the sink where he washes his face and hands. After he wipes them dry, he turns away and heads to the door. Without appearing to say anything, he unlocks it and leaves. The film ends.

"Good God," says Baker, trying to breath normally again. "That was unbelievable. You sure I can have this film? You won't get into any trouble?" Baker has been working at the *Star* for less than a month full time and he wants this film more than he has wanted anything in his life. But Schober is his closest friend. He wants Schober to say it's okay to take the film.

"If I thought I was going to get into trouble, I wouldn't be giving it to you," says Schober.

The young man attends law school at George Washington University during the day and works as a Capitol Hill guard during the evenings. The job helps him pay his tuition. His family has political connections; consequently, for three more years he can count on this desk job, "guarding" a congressional building during the late afternoons and early evenings. The way he looks at it, he is basically getting paid to sit and study.

"I checked this morning before I called you. The original has been duplicated and shared all over the Hill. I know at least a dozen people who have copies. I have no business having it. I wasn't part of the vice squad that filmed it. But this is too good to stay under wraps, particularly when the star of the film is Congressman Walker."

"I've heard the name," says Baker, "But I don't know him. Is he important?"

"Probably not to the average Joe College or budding young reporter," responds Schober. "But he's the ranking Republican on the Interior and Insular Affairs Committee. That makes him mighty important to several federal agencies and a lot of folks who get money from them. I suppose he's also considered a somebody to the people back home in Alabama who keep electing him to office every two years."

"I guess I should have taken a course in civics, or paid attention to what my stepfather does for a living," says Baker. "I don't have a clue about the Congress. All I know is that

Republicans are in the minority, Democrats are in the majority, and Lyndon Baines Johnson pretty much tells them all what to do."

"That would be my take on it," says Schober. "Anyway, I have a buddy who works for the committee that Walker sits on. I wasn't surprised to learn a Democratic staff member has a copy of the film. But I was blown away to find out a Republican staff member has it too. That means this isn't going to stay secret very long."

"Do you think one of the congressional aides will leak it to the press?" asks Baker, immediately worrying that he might get scooped on what could be the most important story of his career.

"I don't think so," says Schober. "Staff up here love to gossip. But they do a pretty good job of keeping their trash within their own dump. Besides, as much as the Democrats would enjoy this story getting out, the leadership would have to fire anyone who leaks it. That's why I didn't call you when I first got it. Then last night I heard something that really surprised me. The goddamn Beta house at GW has a copy. Can you believe that?"

"How did the Betas get their hands on a copy, for God's sake?"

Schober laughs. "Obviously, I don't know. But if I were guessing, I would say it happened because the good congressman is a big-time Beta from his Alabama undergraduate days. Every fall, you may remember, he helps the GW chapter recruit new members. Besides that, he personally writes fat checks to the chapter and helps it raise money from other alumni. I'm guessing an alum from a rival fraternity—some guy who works on the Hill—sent the Betas a copy of the film. Why would anyone do that? Probably to create friction within the Betas. Think of it this way: How many of the brothers will want to exchange the secret handshake with the congressman after they know he's gripped another man's privates? A Negro's, no less."

"It must have been a TKE or a Kappa Sig," says Baker. "It couldn't have been a Sigma Chi. Hell, we don't consider the Betas competition."

Schober grins. "It never seemed to me we were rushing the same student, that's for sure. I can remember during rush week we would send our losers over to the Beta house. All a rushee had to do was insinuate that he was considering a career in the Peace Corps and we would say, 'You really ought to consider the Betas; they're the serious do-gooders on campus.'"

"So that's when you called me, after you found out the Betas had a copy?"

"Yeah. I figure that between embittered Betas and gleeful Democrats, Walker's wang is going to be the star attraction in darkened rooms all across town this weekend," says Schober. "So, it's time my favorite journalist got a byline over this story. And with all the copies floating around, there's no way anybody is going to trace your copy back to me. If anyone does ask you where you got yours, I'm assuming you would have the common sense to know what to say."

As he said that, Schober pointed to the return address on a large, brown business envelope he is handing to Baker.

"But of course," says Baker, as he pulls the film out of the projector and shoves it into the House Interior and Insular Affairs Committee envelop that Schober has given him.

"One last thing," says Schober, as Baker is about to leave the small Capitol Police auxiliary room. Schober hands Baker an official-looking mimeographed letter.

"Stop by the Capitol Police main office downstairs. Ask for a copy of this memo. Don't show the guy at the desk that you have it; just reference the title and the date. It's essentially public information and he'll give you one if he knows you are aware of it."

Baker looks at the memo. It is from the Capitol Hill Police, addressed to Members of Congress and about a dozen key offices on the Hill. It says that for a two-week period, the Capitol Police would be conducting filmed surveillance of the common area within the men's rooms in all three House Office Buildings. This effort, said the memo, was in response to reports of homosexual encounters occurring in those rest rooms. Anyone noticing any suspicious behavior was told to notify the Capitol Police. The memo ended by saying the office hoped the surveillance would not be an inconvenience to anyone.

"I guess Congressman Walker doesn't read his mail," says Baker as he hands Schober back his memo.

"Do any of them?" responds Schober.

As instructed, Baker stops at the Capitol Police Office and picks up his own personal copy of the memo Schober had shown him. He asks for it by date and title and the officer behind the desk hands him a copy once Baker identifies himself as a *Washington Star* reporter.

Leaving the Longworth Office Building, Baker heads toward the old Cannon Office Building across the street. He wants to see the bathroom where the two men had their liaison.

Schober had said it was off the beaten path and he was right. Baker actually has a hard time finding it. The longer he looks for it, the more he realizes he's in need of a bathroom facility himself.

Since the brand new Rayburn Office Building opened last year, the higher-ranking Members of Congress who took up residence there seem to be pleased with the newest and by far largest such facility on Capitol Hill. It has four floors above ground and three below for parking. Three-room suites greeted 169 Members of Congress when it opened in early 1965, each equipped with toilets, kitchens, and built-in cabinets. In addition, the building houses nine committee rooms, a cafeteria, a *Star* office, a gymnasium, and a subway tunnel with two cars connecting the building to the Capitol. Members of Congress with the most seniority got first choice of offices in the Rayburn building.

But even those left behind in the ancient Cannon House Office Building benefited by the addition of the new Rayburn House Office Building. The freed-up space left by the departing congressmen meant the junior members who previously had been forced to occupy the cubby hole offices on the 5th floor had been able to move to choicer suites. By the summer of 1965, the only offices still open on the top floor of Cannon housed a few obscure select subcommittees and study commissions.

Baker finally finds the bathroom he's looking for, down a dimly lit hallway away from any occupied offices. Once he's in it he doesn't have any doubt it's the one in the film. As he stands in front of the urinals he feels as if he's on stage. He can't spot the camera and he wonders if it's still in play. He stares at the urinals. They stand against the wall, all white porcelain, from the floor up to his chest. Baker reaches for the fly on his zipper and then freezes. As bad as he has to relieve himself, he knows he isn't going to be able to do it there. He leaves and quickly finds a well-used facility on the ground floor.

Next he wants to go to Congressman Jeff Walker's office. Baker looks at the directory near the main entrance of the Cannon Building to find out where it is. He isn't surprised to learn it's in the new Rayburn Office Building. Walker certainly has the seniority for one of the Rayburn offices. Baker bets that even as a Republican in a Democratic-led Congress, Walker probably has one of the premier locations in the building.

As he walks down Independence Avenue toward the new structure, built out of white marble above a pink granite base, he fumbles with his new cassette recorder. He hates to be bothered with the thing, but since joining the *Star* he lugs it with him so that he can't be accused of misquoting anyone during an interview. It's a crutch, he knows, and hopes to soon outgrow it. Nobody else at the *Star*, as far as he can tell, uses one. But he is on probation, which means he doesn't have the luxury of accumulating three strikes before being called out. If he screws up once, he will be let go. All it would take to put him on the street is one prominent official denying what was attributed to him in the newspaper under Baker's byline. The tape recorder is his insurance against that kind of "I'm-more-important-than-you" arrogance for which Washington is famous.

He enters the Rayburn building, walks by a guard and up the marble stairs to the atrium. He turns right and walks down the hallway. At the end he has a choice to turn left or right. He turns right and walks down another hallway. At the end is an impressive set of doors and two flag stands. The one on the right holds the American flag. When he gets up to the other, Baker realizes it is the Alabama state flag. He has reached Congressman Walker's suite. Baker's first thought is, "My God, he must have a great view of the Capitol from his office window."

Just as he starts into the suite, the congressman comes walking out. Always sensitive to the possibility of visiting constituents, the congressman says: "Good afternoon son, how are you?" But he doesn't stop walking.

"Eh, Mr. Congressman, got a minute?"

"Sorry, I'm on my way to a committee meeting. Someone in my office will talk with you."

"Sir, I am Chuck Baker of the *Washington Star*, and I only have one question for you, if I could."

The congressman was halfway down the hallway. But he stops, looks at his watch, and sighs. He is thinking to himself. This is the 89th Congress, and it's sure to go down as one of the worst in the country's history. That fool Johnson and his congressional cronies are ramming through every damn piece of legislation they want and there's little the Republicans can do to stop them. At least those in the leadership like himself have an obligation to go on the record with their protests.

He turns back to Baker. "One question. Try to make it a short one."

Baker punches his cassette recorder and checks to see that it's running.

"Sir, today I saw a film of you and a Negro janitor having oral sex in a fifth floor bathroom in the Cannon House Office Building. Sir, do you do that often?"

Baker doesn't mean to be so flippant. He realizes as soon as he asks the question that he should have been better prepared for this interview.

"Turn that goddamn recorder off," Congressman Walker screams. "What film are you talking about? Who are you anyway? You say you're with the *Washington Star*? I know some people at the *Star*. I can tell you one thing, boy; you have just lost your job. You are through in this town. Do you realize who you are talking to? Now you get the hell away from me."

"Does that mean, sir, that you have not yet seen the film?"

"I don't know what you are talking about. Leave me alone or I'm going to call the Capitol Police."

And with that, Congressman Walker, the firebrand segregationist, the man who allied himself with Alabama Governor George Wallace, storms off down the hallway.

Baker clicks off his cassette player. This isn't the first time he's made someone furious while he's digging for a story. Baker actually rather enjoys the technique. The madder his subjects get, the more he believes they have something to hide. Congressman Walker's anger convinces Baker he probably doesn't realize his entire committee staff and the brothers over at the Beta house already know his secret. If Baker is half the reporter he thinks he is, tomorrow morning the rest of the country also will know the secret.

Out in front of the Rayburn House Office Building, Baker catches a District cab back to the *Star*. On the way he gives some more thought to the story. There are many different ways he can play it. He likes the angle about the dumb congressman who doesn't read his inner-office memo and consequently gets caught in a sting operation he should have known about. Then too, he could always feature the race and class angle. That's how the newspapers in Alabama are likely to play the story, Baker thinks. Their headlines will trumpet some version of "Republican Congressman Caught Sexually Servicing Negro Janitor." The *National Enquirer*, on the other hand, would probably run something like "Member of Congress Exposes Member."

But the *Star* isn't a tabloid; it does not rely on sensational headlines to sell copies. The *Star* is a sophisticated afternoon newspaper befitting the fact that its readership consists of the most highly educated readers in the country. As such, these readers want nothing but the facts, straightforward and objective. Then, depending on their political and ideological beliefs, influenced to a degree by their upbringing, they interpret these facts anyway they choose. Most *Star* readers, if asked to boil down the story into a succinct sentence, preferably employing an action verb, would undoubtedly end up saying: "White Congressman Caught Giving Blow Job To Black Janitor."

Baker realizes he needs some more facts. He hasn't talked to any Capitol Hill Police official. He has to get it on record that the police actually did the filming. He doesn't have the identity of the other man involved. Is the *Star* going to think that's important information to share? Probably not, figures Baker, but that doesn't mean his editors won't want to know who the guy is. Baker wonders how he can find the guy and get him to admit to being involved? Every good story presents its own challenges.

The cab drops him off in front of the *Star*, housed in one of the city's premier buildings. Baker pays the driver $2 and asks for half a dollar back. Capitol Hill and the *Star* are in the same taxi zone, which means the fare is $1.10. Baker thinks a forty-cent tip is sufficient, but concedes a DC cab driver probably doesn't expect to give any change back on the fare. Fuck it, he thinks: The day the *Star* reimburses its reporters $2 for a $1.10 cab fare is the day he'll increase his tips.

The *Star's* marble Beaux-Arts architecture dresses up what otherwise is a drab, rundown section of historical Pennsylvania Avenue, about halfway between the Capitol and the White House. The impressive building, which houses the *Star's* editorial, production, and advertising departments, dates back to the late 1800s. In the mid-60s it remains the grand dame of Pennsylvania Avenue. Around it, though, are boarded-up buildings. The once-imposing Central Post Office across the street, built to resemble a medieval castle, now sits barren and unapproachable, much as if a plague had checked in and never left.

Baker goes in the *Star*'s front door and up the stairs to the editorial department located on the third floor. His desk is shoved up against three others. Newspapers, government reports, books, and mail fill the other three desks and slump over onto his. The clutter reminds him of the lecture he heard the previous semester from a visiting professor from the University of Hong Kong. She had introduced him to the virtues of Feng Shui and the importance of clutter clearing. She had said clutter accumulates when energy stagnates. He had thought that was so profound he had even written it down in his notebook. Looking around at most of the desks in the newsroom, he figures she would detect a profound sense of stagnation.

Baker isn't bothered by the clutter. It comes with being a reporter. In fact, he's waiting for the day when he's a veteran journalist and stuff on his desk piles up and falls onto some new cub reporter's desk.

He sits down and threads the special three-sheet-with-carbons copy paper the *Star* uses for article writing into his Royal typewriter. He types: "By Charles Baker, Washington Star Staff Writer." Then he returns the carriage and sits and stares at the top sheet of paper, thinking about a lead sentence.

He nearly jumps out of his chair when the managing editor yells his name.

"Baker, goddammit, get your sorry ass into my office."

He realizes his face has turned red. He has never met the managing editor and he sure in the hell hasn't been in his office before. He looks around. The amused look on the faces of some of the reporters tells him he shouldn't expect this to be the managing editor's normal get-acquainted-with-the-new-staff session.

He doesn't know if he's supposed to bring along anything or not, but he picks up his cassette recorder and, being a reporter, he grabs a pencil and a wad of copy paper. He is walking down the hall when he realizes he doesn't have a clue which office belongs to the managing editor. All the senior editors have offices along the Pennsylvania Avenue side of the building. The offices feature large windows facing the large editorial bull pen that holds the reporters and copy editors. Most of the interior windows are covered by Venetian blinds that stay half closed all the time. He only realizes he's walked by the managing editor's office when a loud voice behind him yells, "Baker, get in here."

He turns around and stands face to face with Jim Harrison, the *Star's* longtime managing editor. He has on an expensive white shirt and a tie that Chuck recognizes from a Brooks Brothers catalogue. Harrison goes back into the office and Baker follows.

In the office sit two other men. One Baker knows. It's his immediate supervisor, the city editor, Larry Bauguess. He looks his usual rumpled self, with the sleeves of his J.C. Penny's white shirt rolled up and his tie loosened. The other gentleman wears an expensive suit and looks very much like an attorney. A rich, important, don't-waste-my-time kind of attorney. His entire wardrobe looks like it comes from a private tailor. He didn't pay for it on a newspaperman's salary, Baker knows.

Baker is conscious of the fact he is wearing his normal "uniform" consisting of a blue, button-down oxford shirt, khaki trousers, brown loafers with no socks, and a madras belt. He has on a brushed silk red tie he had bought at Garfinkles. He likes it. He owns four of them, all in different colors. His mother would say he needs a haircut. Hell, he would say he needs a haircut. He stands just shy of six feet and has the build of a defensive back. That's what he believes anyway; he has never played football, so he's not really sure.

"What did you do to piss off Congressman Walker?" yells Harrison.

Baker turns to Bauguess for support and gets nothing in response. Bauguess is staring at the floor. Baker realizes he's on his own.

"I asked him two questions. He didn't like the first and he didn't answer the second."

"What were the questions?"

"I told him I had seen a film of him having oral sex with a Negro janitor. So I asked him if he did that sort of thing often."

"Good God," said the attorney, who hasn't been introduced. He looks at Harrison. "No wonder the newspaper is facing a major lawsuit."

Bauguess says: "What, pray tell, was your second question?"

"Well, he didn't answer my first question. In fact, he acted surprised that I knew about the sex between him and the janitor. So I asked him if that meant he had not yet seen the film of the two of them."

"What did he say to that?" Bauguess wants to know.

"In response to the first question, he simply lost his temper. He said I was through in this town. He said he knew some people at the *Washington Star*, and, oh yeah, he wanted to know if I knew who I was talking to. In response to the second question, he just walked away saying he was going to call the Capitol Hill Police if I didn't leave him alone. So, I left him alone."

The three men sat there.

"May I say something else?" said Baker.

"On your way out the fucking door, I guess you can say anything you want," yells Harrison.

"I want to say two things, then," says Baker. "One, the congressman never denied having oral sex with the black janitor. I have everything he said here on my recorder."

Baker let that statement sink in for a minute.

"And two, I have a copy of the film showing him engaged in the sex act. Would you like to see it?"

The lawyer looks at Harrison. "You know, that would change everything. If in fact Walker actually did engage in a sex act, as your reporter alleges, then the congressman's threats are all bark and no bite."

"Well, let's get that film in here and take a look at it," says Harrison. "I'll get a projector up from downstairs. What kind of film is it anyway?"

After they watch the clip all the way through twice, Harrison turns on the lights and opens up the blinds to let the outside light into his office.

"Where did you get this film, Baker?" Harrison asks.

"From an anonymous source in the House Interior and Insular Affairs Committee."

"How anonymous?"

"As in I don't know—"

"How'd they get it to you?" Harrison interrupted.

Baker tries not to panic. He hadn't thought through how to keep his promise not to reveal his friend Schrober if the Managing Editor started to inquire about his source.

"Hey, Jim, he's my reporter, okay?" Bauguess jumps in.

Surprisingly, Harrison backs down. "Okay, Larry. Well, I'm guessing Walker hasn't seen this film or he wouldn't be threatening the publisher with a goddamn lawsuit. That sanctimonious son of a bitch is washed up as a politician. And for sure, he better not go back to Alabama, even if it's just to pack a bag."

"I guess my services are no longer needed here," says the attorney, and with nods from the two editors, he leaves. Baker still doesn't know who he is.

Harrison turns to Bauguess and says, "Alright, let's get moving on this story. I'll get the National Desk to assign a lead reporter to it right away. I'll see if they can free up someone to hop on a plane and get down to Alabama. I want someone on the ground there for the fall-out story. We'll need pictures of the congressman and the bathroom, and somebody ought to get a sidebar on the janitor too."

"Wait a minute," says Bauguess. "This story already has a reporter on it and he's from the City Desk. We don't need any help from the National Desk with this story. If you want to use the National Desk for your local angle in Alabama, fine, but we'll take care of the story here in town."

"Who is going to write the main story for you?" asks Harrison, "And don't tell me this kid here is going to do it because that dog won't hunt."

"How long have I been running the City Desk for you? Since when do you start telling me who I assign to local stories? If you don't like the way I do my job, then you can always find yourself a new editor. Until then, go breathe down the necks of some of the other desks in this newspaper. I know some that could use some serious help."

Harrison looks at his longtime friend and city editor and realizes this isn't the fight he wants to see end the relationship.

"Okay, do it your way. But it better be a goddamn good job or I'll replace both of you in a heartbeat."

Baugess doesn't respond. He just signals with his eyes that Baker and he ought to get up and leave the office. Baker starts to wheel the projector towards the door.

"Leave it," growls Harrison.

Baugess grabs Baker by the arm and leads him out of the office.

Standing in the hallway, Baker looks at his supervisor and says, "I just want to say thank you for standing up for me."

"It has nothing to do with you. I was protecting the City Desk. You think I want those pig fuckers from the National Desk wallowing in my backyard? You give them an opening and they'll be saying every story has a national slant. Next thing you know, some pencil pusher from accounting will question whether we even need a City Desk anymore. Then the goddamn National Desk will say it can incorporate our work into theirs. At that point, we're out of business."

"You want me to write the story?"

"You got it. Just don't fuck it up. Get me a draft as soon as you can. Make sure it includes a quote from the janitor. Get his name if possible. And I want him quoted saying if he knew who he was fooling around with. And get the Capitol Hill police to confirm that they did the filming. Now get to work."

Bauguess turns away and goes down the hall to his office. Baker stays in the hallway a moment to exhale. Then just as he turns to go back to his desk, he notices the blinds closing again in Harrison's office. Then the lights go off. Baker figures the managing editor is watching the film for the third time. Only this time, he is watching it alone.

The Capitol Hill Police are as bureaucratic and uncooperative as any large police force anywhere. Anyway, that's what Baker concludes after he calls their main number. He asks for the Vice Squad and gets switched to someone who doesn't identify himself but nevertheless demands to know who the caller is and what he wants. Baker identifies himself and says he has a few questions about a police sting the Capitol Police recently conducted to determine the extent of homosexual activities in the House Office Building. The officer says he knows nothing about it and hangs up.

Baker calls back and gets connected to the same officer. After identifying himself, Baker quickly says: "I have seen a film of two men, one of them a congressman, having oral sex. Care to comment on that?"

The cop on the other end of the line says, "Hold a minute."

Baker holds for nearly five minutes before a different male comes onto the line and in a gruff voice demands to know who is calling. Baker introduces himself all over again and asks who he is speaking with. He gets no response to his question.

"You say you have a film of two men engaged in a sex act in one of our buildings? Did you film this sex act?" asks the male voice.

"No, I didn't film it," says Baker. "I assume the Capitol Hill Police filmed it. The film was shot in the fifth floor bathroom of the Cannon House Office Building and one of the subjects is Congressman Walker of Alabama. The other subject is an unnamed Negro male who appears to be a Capitol Hill employee, probably a janitor."

"You say you have this film?"

"Yes, I have a copy. But I have been led to believe that numerous copies are floating around. Mine came from a fraternity house on the George Washington University campus. The Beta Theta Pi House, to be exact. I don't know where they got their copy."

A long pause.

"What do you want from us?"

"The *Washington Star* would like a confirmation that the Capitol Hill Police had been conducting a sting operation in hopes of catching homosexuals engaged in illegal acts in public bathrooms in House Office Buildings. We would like you to confirm that to catch men engaged in such acts you have filmed the common spaces within some of these bathrooms. Finally, we would like confirmation that this sting operation has in fact caught on tape Congressman Walker of Alabama engaged in a homosexual act with a Negro man."

"I don't think we are prepared to make that confirmation."

"Well, what are you prepared to confirm? Your office has already given me a copy of the memorandum that announces your intentions to conduct the sting operation and to film the common areas within the men's rooms. I have a copy of the film with the congressman and the Negro engaged in the sex act. Can you at a minimum confirm that this film is yours?"

Another long pause.

"We'll have to get back to you. Give me your direct line there at the *Star*."

As soon as Baker gives him the number, the phone line goes dead. Baker's heart sinks. Without the confirmation, he doesn't have a story.

He runs over to the City Desk and interrupts Bauguess' conversation with one of his other reporters. They both frown at him and continue to talk. Baker walks a couple of paces away and attempts to calm down as best he can. When the reporter walks away, Bauguess says, "What's on your mind?"

"I've got a problem. I had the Capitol Police on the phone trying to get a confirmation from them about the film. They wouldn't give me jack shit. I told them I had official confirmation of their sting operation. I said I had the film with the congressman on it. I said all I was seeking was confirmation that they had done the filming. But they said they would have to get back to me. Then they hung up. What do I do now?"

"You wait for them to call you back."

"What if they don't?"

"We'll deal with that problem if it occurs. Listen, the Capitol Police have to cover their ass like every other bureaucracy. They're not going to admit anything to a reporter before they are sure their patron saints are okay with that. So they've got to check with the guy who signs their checks, the House Clerk. He will have to check with the chairman of the House Administration Committee that has jurisdiction over him and the Capitol Police. The fact that the chairman and therefore the clerk are both Democrats probably ensures that they're going to be pleased as punch to expose Congressman Walker, no pun intended. So, I would guess you'll get a call back within the hour. If you don't hear from them in two hours, come see me. In the meantime, have you identified the Negro yet?"

"I'm getting on it right now," says Baker, already hurrying back to his desk.

But he doesn't have a clue how to get the name of the black man in the film. He doubts the congressman even knows his name, not that he would be likely to share it even if he did.

Baker picks up the phone and calls his best friend at his work number. Schober answers on the second ring. "Officer Schober at your service."

"Tony, it's Chuck. I've got a question for you."

"I'm all out of answers, buddy. I'm working for the other side this afternoon."

"Don't get cute with me now, for God's sake. I'm up against a deadline and I need a name. Did you guys ever identify the Negro in the bathroom with the congressman?"

"Oh for God's sake, leave him out of it. I thought you were after the congressman."

"I am, but I want to know if he knew who he was playing with. I don't have to use his name in the newspaper. I just need to know if this was a chance encounter or if they had done this sort of thing before."

"The vice guys talked to him. He told them it was the first time he had ever been with the congressman. I'm not sure our guys believed him. But he stuck to his story."

"Does he work on Capitol Hill?"

"Not anymore. We don't like our janitors to blow our congressman. He was asked to leave the employment of the U.S. Capitol after he was identified and interviewed. He asked if the congressman was going to be asked to leave too or if this just happened to men of color."

"Seems like a legitimate question."

"I don't know what the vice guys told him, but I know the question worried us. We began to think this janitor might attempt to blackmail the congressman. I mean, what does the janitor have to lose? We just fired him from his job. So if the white guy gets to keep his, why not lean on him for some cash? Anyway, the vice guys told the janitor in no uncertain terms what will happen to him if he attempts to contact the congressman. As far as we know, he hasn't done so."

"That makes it sound as if the Capitol Police have talked with the congressman about the sting operation."

"You didn't hear that from me. Talk to vice."

"I'm trying to. They're reluctant to talk."

"Keep pushing. This pimple is ready to pop."

"Okay, how about the janitor's name? I promise to protect his identity. I just want to ask him about the congressman.

"William Jefferson. He lives in Northeast Washington. For what it's worth, he freely admits that he's gay. He says everyone he cares about already knows, so he isn't worried about being outed. He is just upset about losing his job."

"Thanks buddy, I owe you."

"I know. I'm keeping a ledger."

William Jefferson answers the phone on the second ring. He doesn't seem surprised to hear the caller is from the *Washington Star*. Nor is he defensive about the subject.

"I had sex with that cracker, sure, and the Capitol Police have it on film. Don't do no good denying it now."

"Did you and the congressman know each other?"

"I never saw him before that day in the bathroom."

"Did you know he was a congressman?"

"Of course, man. He was wearing his congressman pin. One thing they teach us at janitor school is how to recognize those congressman pins. That way we'll know to bow 'n' scrape when the big shots walk by."

"How did you know he was a homosexual?"

"Shit, man, nobody using that bathroom unless they looking for some action. You didn't show up there if you didn't want to give or get. I knew as soon as he walked in what he was all about, congressional pin or not. The only question I had in my mind was whether he was going to give as good as he got, if you know what I mean. A lot of these white boys love it when a black man goes down on them. But they lose all interest when it comes time to return the favor. Not this dude. He loved the action both ways. I was hoping to run into him again real soon."

"Do you work on Capitol Hill?"

"Yeah, I did. I was a janitor in the Capitol. Good job, too. Now the man fired me. I guess he don't like a big black man getting serviced by a congressman. I guess they're afraid other brothers going to want some too." Then Jefferson started to laugh.

"Well, that's all of my questions. No, wait a minute. How old are you?"

"I'm twenty-nine, man. But I look younger."

"Thanks. By the way, you didn't ask me if I was going to use your name in the newspaper. Aren't you concerned about that?"

"Nah, you can use it, under one condition. You can say we had sex together. But you got to say the white guy did me. Don't say I did him. Okay, can you do that?"

"No, that wouldn't be truthful. I don't think we'll get into that much detail anyway. Why don't I just leave your name out of the story altogether?"

"Okay, that's cool, too."

Baker no more hung up the phone when it began ringing. The call once again demonstrates why it is big-ego reporters are constantly humbled by city editors and their seemingly bottomless reservoir of knowledge about how things really work in government, business, education, religion, and polite society. The Capitol Police Department is calling back.

"Mr. Baker, this is Chief of Police Cory Phelps of the Capitol Hill Police, at your service. I understand you have some questions about a recent operation of ours."

"Yes, I was told your department had filmed a scene in a fifth floor bathroom of the Cannon House Office Building involving a congressman and a Capitol Hill janitor. Is that correct?"

"That is correct. As part of an ongoing effort to crack down on homosexual activities that have reportedly been going on within the three House Office Buildings, we have been filming the common areas of selected bathrooms. One of those bathrooms is on the fifth floor of the Cannon House Office Building. And last Tuesday afternoon we caught on film a Member of Congress and a Capitol Hill employee engaged in a homosexual activity."

"Are you prepared to name the two individuals?"

"No, we have not gone public with their names. The Capitol Hill employee was identified and brought before his supervisor. He has since been discharged from his position for sexual misconduct. The congressman has been identified and his name has been given to the House leadership. It is up to them to determine what action if any is appropriate to take in this matter."

"Chief Phelps, as you probably know, copies of the film are circulating all over town. I have seen a copy. I know the congressman involved is Mr. Walker of Alabama. Sir, can you confirm his identify for me?"

"It is unfortunate that the film is circulating. Anyone caught doing that will be punished to the full extent of the law. That includes the media, by the way. I am not able to confirm the identity of the congressman. You will have to ask the House leadership for that information. Thank you, Mr. Baker."

The phone goes dead. Chuck is left listening to a dial tone.

Baker sits at his typewriter looking at his notes. Is he missing anything? He has the Negro's name and several great quotes from him. He has the Capitol Police confirming that they had done the filming. No confirmation of the congressman involved. But a confirmation of the fact that a congressman was involved and that his name had been turned over to the House leadership. Baker and his bosses had seen the film; no need for confirmation about the identity; they knew who the congressman was. Shit, he has a story.

By CHARLES BAKER
Washington Star Staff Writer

The Capitol Hill Police Thursday confirmed that they had secretly filmed a Member of Congress and a Capitol Hill employee engaged in a homosexual act in a Cannon House Office Building bathroom on Tuesday, July 21.

The Police will not release the names of the two participants. However, the *Washington Star* has learned that the congressman involved is Jeff Walker (R) of Alabama, ranking minority member of the House Interior and Insular Affairs Committee.

Walker is an outspoken segregationist and an ally of Alabama Governor George Wallace. Walker's campaign literature references his father's membership in the Klu Klux Klan and states that the congressman, while not a member, is in sympathy with many of the group's beliefs.

Walker's homosexual partner, a 29-year-old Negro, worked as a janitor in the Capitol.

When asked about the incident, Walker, 49, became highly agitated. He did not deny his participation.

When asked about his involvement, the janitor admitted participating in the homosexual liaison with the congressman. He said it was a chance encounter in the 5th floor bathroom of the Cannon House Office Building.

Although the janitor said he didn't know Walker, he said he knew he was a congressman because of the pin he wore in his lapel. All Members of Congress wear special lapel pins so that Capitol Police and other security personnel can recognize them as they make their way about the Capitol.

An admitted homosexual, the janitor said he assumed the congressman was one too when he came into the bathroom.

"I knew as soon as he walked in what he was all about, congressional pin or not. The only question I had in my mind was whether he was going to give as good as he got, if you know what I mean. A lot of these white boys love it when a black man does them a favor. But they lose all interest when it comes time to return the favor. Not this dude. He loved the action both ways. I was hoping I would run into him again real soon."

Chief of Police Cory Phelps of the Capitol Hill Police confirmed his staff filmed two men engaged in a homosexual act, one of them a congressman and the other a Capitol janitor, but he wouldn't identify them by name. He said he regretted that copies of the film had been circulating publicly and added that his office would prosecute anyone found releasing it to unauthorized viewers.

The Capitol Police had been secretly filming the common areas of selected men's' rooms throughout the three Congressional Office Buildings (COBs) for the past two weeks. The police action followed complaints of homosexual activity occurring in bathrooms within the COBs. A memorandum announcing the police intentions had been sent to all Members of Congress as well as other offices on Capitol Hill prior to the filming.

Chief Phelps said that the janitor caught on film has been fired from his job because of sexual misconduct. The name of the congressman involved has been given to the House leadership for whatever action it deems appropriate.

As soon as Baker finishes typing the story on the *Star's* special tri-carbon copy paper, he takes it out of his typewriter, rips off the back copy and keeps it for himself. He takes the other two with him to the City Desk and hands them to Bauguess.

The city editor leans back in his chair and puts his left foot up on a drawer that he has pulled out just for that purpose. He has a copy pencil in his hand. When he gets to the janitor's quote he winces.

"I like the janitor's comments. That's good stuff. But we sure in the hell can't print shit like that. We're not the fucking *New York Mirror*. Still, I'm going to try to get as much of it in as I can. Damn good quote, Baker."

Baker realizes the compliment doesn't require him to say anything.

Bauguess runs his hand through his thinning hair. He gets all the way through the piece and has only made a few marks on the two pages.

"I like it. It needs a little editing, but not bad."

The city editor slaps the story down on his desk and stands up.

"Here's what I'm going to do. I've got a guy who handles our congressional coverage over on the Hill right now. If he's any good, he'll badger the House leadership into telling us about our boy Walker. I want someone in the Speaker's Office to call the guy a homo. Then I want somebody to tell our readers what the consequences are for having oral sex in a congressional toilet. If I get anything worth printing, I'll stick his graphs into your story. In that case, you two will share bylines. You'll get listed first, though; it's still basically your story. If he can't deliver, your story stands alone. You okay with that?"

"Sure. Getting the House leadership to identify Walker, particularly if they say what they're going to do about the situation, will make the story a lot better."

Baker is silently kicking himself. He hadn't even thought about calling the House leadership to see if he can get anyone to comment about Walker. That was stupid of him. And he sure in the hell hates to think he has to share a byline on the biggest story of his career.

"Anything else you need me to do?"

"No, not today. We'll go with your story in tomorrow's paper. We've missed all the editions today. We'll just have to hope the goddamn *Post* hasn't picked up on our story. As soon as our first edition hits the street tomorrow, the shit's going to hit the fan.

"I'm assuming the guy Harrison is sending to Alabama will highlight the congressman's racist background in his story. If he hasn't got enough for a stand-alone, we'll work what he's got into a story that includes comments from his congressional buddies. I want you to do a feature on 'sex in the Capitol.' Has anything like this gone on before? That sort of thing. Do some background reading and talk with some Capitol Hill historians. Visit with some of the old Republican staff members too. If the Democrats are hiding any queers in their closets, you can bet the Republicans will be eager to flush them out. We'll run your feature on Sunday. Also, find out from your buddy, that Capitol Hill police chief, if he caught anyone else in his sting operation. We're focusing on the congressman. Hell, for all we know he caught two senators going at it. I would hate to read about them in the *Washington Post*. Now get out of here, we're not paying you any overtime."

"Okay." Baker turns away from the City Desk and looks at his watch. By God, it's 5:45 p.m., he realizes. He has to run if he's going to meet his stepfather for a drink at the Mayflower at 6 p.m. The ol' boy doesn't like him to be late. Baker heads back to his desk and grabs his blue blazer. At the last moment, he also picks up the carbon copy of his story. Maybe his stepfather will be interested in it. Heaven knows he hasn't been impressed by anything else Baker has written.

Chapter Two

Fargo's Illegal Blind Pig

Joe hates how she's toying with him. She's pretending to ignore him. A white whore who pisses off a drunken Indian has to be just plain stupid. Joe considers telling her that, but he doesn't want to scare her away. He sits there, sipping his whiskey, thinking about ways he could punish her. But the thought that dominates all others is how much he wants to fuck her.

Joe Running Deer has been drinking since late morning, ever since the bar opened. The passage of day into night is impossible to identify in the underground bar. The place has no windows and its door, which opens to a small vestibule, blocks any light that might slip inside when the heavy outside door swings open to the alley.

Anyone passing through the alley isn't likely to be drawn to the bar. The outside door was painted brown a long time ago and the weather hasn't been kind to it. An old, rusted metal sign screwed into it reads, "Deliveries Only." The door looks formidable, but not out of place, in that part of town. A buzzer next to the door hints that a push and patience might eventually fetch someone from upstairs—a run-down watering hole called the Silver Saloon, with an entrance on Front Street, Fargo's main thoroughfare. Just like all state-licensed liquor establishments in North Dakota, the Silver Saloon is closed for business on Sunday.

But the bar beneath it isn't a licensed facility and Sunday is its busiest day of the week.

During the summer months, three bartenders work Saturday from 11 a.m. until closing early Sunday morning and from 11 a.m. until 5 p.m. During those hours, thirsty customers push the delivery buzzer constantly. When they do, a panel slides open in the door and Henry, a large, fat bouncer sitting in the vestibule on a bar stool, growls, "What do you want?"

The waiting customer is supposed to say, "I'm here to see the blind pig."

Knowledgeable consumers of illegal liquor first learned to say that nonsensical ditty shortly after North Dakota joined the union in 1889. From the time settlers arrived in the Dakota Territories, liquor was an issue. Back then, self-righteous Scandinavians constituted the majority of rural settlers in the Red River Valley. And by arguing liquor was being sold to Indians, the Scandinavians convinced the Territorial authorities to ban its sale to everyone.

When North Dakota's application to statehood was approved in late 1889, the newly minted state constitution continued the prohibition against the sale and consumption of alcoholic beverages. Consequently, for the next 43 years, such beverages were illegal in the state. Then national Prohibition came along in 1920 and made the sale of alcoholic beverages a federal crime.

The laws against liquor had always seemed ridiculous to the Russian-Germans and other immigrants who followed the Scandinavians into the state. These new arrivals from across Europe found it absurd to be denied liquor when efforts to eke out a living on the prairie were challenging enough. They agreed among themselves there's nothing wrong with honest, mature, thirsty citizens enjoying an occasional cold beer or a shot of bourbon.

Despite its unpopularity with everyone except the Scandinavians, Prohibition was strictly enforced in more populated communities in eastern North Dakota. On the other hand, the law was loosely enforced—if at all—in sparsely populated parts of the state where the residents were primarily recently arrived immigrant farmers from the Ukrainian section of Europe. If they wanted liquor, they had to search out local "bootleggers." These were men who tucked liquor bottles in boots, pockets, and packs, and roamed through small towns and their adjoining fields looking for customers.

But even bootleggers had competition. Crafty North Dakota bar owners got around the law by insisting they didn't sell booze. Instead, they claimed they just sold tickets to see a blind pig or some other equally oddball attraction. Then when customers gathered, supposedly to observe the oddity, they were poured a free drink of their choice. In fact, as long as the customers kept purchasing tickets to remain in the presence of the blind pig, the liquor flowed.

During national Prohibition, when liquor—sold or given away—was considered illegal, drinkers across America flocked to "speakeasies." North Dakota, though, called their illegal saloons "blind pigs." A word like "speakeasy" made no sense to the state's many immigrants. It wasn't the kind of word a Russian-German or a Hutterite or even a Bohemian could readily understand or say. Blind pig, on the other hand, when translated, meant the same thing in any language. And spoken in English, it rolled off the tongue, even for a relative newcomer. North Dakota immigrants only had to learn to associate a blind pig with liquor; if this was a problem for them, it wasn't readily apparent. Of course, there were jokes told about Norwegians. In need of a drink, they would go out to search for blind pigs and then get frustrated and angry when every hog they found seemingly had perfectly good eyesight.

After Prohibition ended in 1933, blind pigs hung around in North Dakota because the state continued to ban the sale of hard liquor. But this ban ended in 1936 after voters said, "enough is enough." Finally, regular bars opened and blind pigs closed.

Except for one, in downtown Fargo. Oh, it had shut its doors after Prohibition ended in 1933, but then secretly reopened them again in 1960. The blind pig was located in the basement under the Silver Saloon on Front Street.

Its owners—a segment of Fargo's power structure—reopened the bar to meet a pressing civic need. Or at least that's how they justified it to themselves. They also acknowledged the bar made money, and they were businessmen, in the business of making money.

The place had no official name because it didn't have any need for one, being an illegal operation. No sign of any kind hung out front. No matchbook covers or cocktail napkins advertised its name. Most area residents didn't know it existed. Those few that did simply referred to it as the Blind Pig. Or Pig, for short.

The Blind Pig had been opened originally during Prohibition by the fathers of the current owners. The laws they broke and the shady deals they engineered made the original owners financially better off. Some even got rich. Now, years later, their sons had reopened one of the old, deserted Prohibition-era bars. They hadn't asked for permission because none was required; nobody could lay claim to an illegal operation.

But had they asked, their fathers would have said: "A blind pig only succeeds as long as the public tolerates it. The public tolerates it only as long as it attracts no attention to itself. If it operates without fanfare, though, it isn't likely to draw sufficient customers. Therefore, it isn't likely to be profitable. So why do it?"

But their sons knew something their fathers didn't: their blind pig was going to be small and insignificant and yet profitable. The trick was to have a large group of steady customers who would fill up the bar Saturday and Sunday from May through October.

Once the young owners had their illegal establishment up and running, they needed a password for their clients to use for admission. Unable to come up with a name they thought anyone would likely remember, the owners went back to the old standard: "blind pig." Sure enough, even the younger drinkers with no memory of Prohibition quickly picked up on, "I'm here to see the blind pig." Well, most of them, anyway. Every weekend, it seemed, two or three regulars stood out in front of the closed door shouting the name of their favorite pet or some farm animal. Management came to realize the bouncer at the door had to be flexible when enforcing the password requirement.

Mexican farm workers from the area's sugar beet operations dominate the place during the summer weekends. Those who speak little English usually just utter "pig." That's generally sufficient to get them through the door. The bouncer also swings it open if he hears "blinda cerdo." The weekend crowds are unlikely to know the significance of the password and its link to the state's storied past. Immigrant farm workers generally learn that it is often easier, and less stressful, to just go along with the host country's rules and routines than it is to try to make sense of them.

The Blind Pig traces its history back to the '20s. The underground space it occupied had been secretly dug out from under several two-story buildings that ran along a portion of Front Street, a block off the Red River. Chinese immigrants brought in from Moose Jaw, Canada, did the labor. They started out by digging a straight tunnel large enough for two men to walk side-by-side. The tunnel connected all the buildings along a four-block stretch of the south side of Front Street. Then the workers dug out four drinking establishments along the route of the tunnel. Each was capable of holding 25 to 40 customers at bars and tables. Side rooms provided storage for liquor and overflow crowds. Customers could enter any of the drinking establishments and then spend the evening wandering through the tunnel to any of the other bars without exposing themselves to the weather, the law, and the disapproving scowls of Scandinavian-dominated Temperance League members.

The Blind Pig in the tunnel under the Silver Saloon that reopened in 1960 looks pretty much as it did when it closed in 1933. It's dark, smoky, and smells bad. The bar is warm in the summer, but chilly in the spring and fall. In other words, it isn't any competition for a legitimate liquor establishment. But competition isn't a problem for the Blind Pig. It's illegal, attracts an undesirable clientele, and operates primarily when legitimate bars are closed.

The hole-in-the-ground establishment attracts only two kinds of customers. The first are the regular drinkers, the kind who want liquor every day and prefer to indulge their habit in the company of like-minded folks. As dependable as this client base is, they are too few in number to sustain an illegal bar on their own.

The second group of steady drinkers at the Blind Pig are Mexican farm workers. These men, and to some extent women, flood in during the weekends over the summer to drink large quantities of beer and tequila. They are the reason the Blind Pig makes a profit.

The immigrant farm workers come to the Red River Valley every year at the behest of the area's sugar beet farmers. These farmers grow their sugar beets throughout the fertile, moist valley. Historically, the farmers in the Red River Valley had grown enormous quantities of wheat and barley. Once harvested, these crops had to be hauled to large grain elevators owned by the milling interests in Minneapolis and St. Paul. There the farmers paid rent to store their crops until the railroads hauled them to the Twin Cities. But the trains wouldn't pull up to the elevators until the grain mills in the Twin Cities had purchased the contents. And the purchase price wasn't established until the mills were satisfied that they had driven the price to be paid the growers down as low as possible. Red River Valley farmers suffered every year from the realization that a lot can go wrong from the time they plant the seeds, harvest the grain, and sell the product.

A sugar beet has advantages over wheat and barley. It doesn't require storage in a grain elevator. It isn't dependent on the railroads to haul it, or the grain mills in Minneapolis and St. Paul to set the price for it. But it has one big disadvantage: beets rot quickly. They need to go promptly from the field to a processing plant or they begin to spoil.

As anyone residing in the Red River Valley can attest, nothing quite compares with the odor put off by a pile of large, ugly, whitish-brown root vegetables rotting in a field.

Farmers in the Red River Valley first started planting sugar beets in 1918. Then in 1926 they built a beet sugar processing plant in East Grand Forks, Minnesota; for years it was sufficient to handle all the sugar beets grown in the Red River Valley. But then the Red River Valley Sugar beet Cooperative decided to grow the business. Using their extensive political clout with both state and federal legislators, they fought to influence laws concerning transportation, labor, the environment, taxes, workers compensation insurance, and numerous regulatory issues.

The sugar beet growers got a boost when Fidel Castro assumed power in Cuba, then the world's largest producer of sugar. The sugar beet interests wrapped themselves in the American flag and asked why anyone would buy sugar from communists. Before long Congress legislated against imported sugar and created federal subsidy programs for American-grown sugar beets. The Red River Valley Sugar beet Cooperative couldn't have been more pleased.

Sugar beet acreage grew rapidly. The growers built another beet processing plant in the upper Red River Valley near Crookston, MN. A few years later they added an even larger one in Drayton, ND. The Red River Valley Sugar beet Cooperative promoted the idea of making the Red River Valley the "nation's sugar bowl." Merchants up and down the valley thought that was a sweet idea, but none more so than those in Fargo, the state's largest city. Beet sugar was driving the economy and many of the city fathers were getting rich from it. Before long many of them were calling Fargo "Sugar City."

Growing sugar beets and bringing in migrant workers has been a mainstay for the Red River Valley since World War II. Back then, during the war, Valley farmers faced a critical shortage of young men to do farm labor. Thankfully, the U.S. Department of Agriculture came up with the idea of importing Mexicans to help produce America's crops. Initially, the Mexican government opposed the idea, saying Mexicans were not generally well treated in the U.S. But after it declared war against Germany in 1942, Mexico decided it could support a program to help out an ally. Thus was created the Bracero Program, an agreement that provided Mexican workers to labor in American agriculture. In its first year, 36,000 Bracero men came north. In 1944 the number expanded to 63,432. About three percent of them ended up in North Dakota working in the sugar beet fields. These Braceros worked summers thinning and hoeing beets and then moved to other farms in adjacent regions to help with haying and the wheat harvest. But they returned to the Red River Valley in the fall to harvest the sugar beets. When they finished, they returned to Mexico—following the migratory patterns of the geese and a few of the wealthier residents of the Red River Valley.

The Bracero program continued long after the war ended, but North Dakota wasn't a player. Sugar beet farmers in North Dakota found it more advantageous to hire Mexican labors recruited by the American Crystal Sugar Company. By the 1950s as many as 30,000 Mexicans from southern Texas and Mexico arrived in the Red River Valley every summer to work in the sugar beet fields.

And work they did. Sugar beets are a labor-intensive crop. In the late spring and early summer, after the beets are planted, they have to be thinned and weeded by hand. Each row has to be done separately two or three times during the growing season. Most of this back-breaking work is done on hands and knees with a short-handled hoe. In the fall, the workers pull the beets out of the ground by hand, lop off the green tops with a machete, and then pile them on the ground. Next, the workers walk alongside a truck and pick up the sugar beets and throw them into the back. The truck then hauls them to the closest processing plant.

The Mexicans work long days and then return to the farms where they boarded to wash up, frequently with cold water at a farmyard pump. Workers cook their own meals, wash their own clothes, and sleep in huts that resemble chicken coops.

But on Saturday afternoons, the Mexican workers are paid for their labor, minus what the growers keep for their food and lodging. With what they have left, the Mexicans plan their weekend visit to Fargo. They have at least 24 hours to reunite with others from their home villages, spend time with their families, eat some Mexican food, catch up on their sleep, and get a glass of ice-cold beer. As much beer as they have the money to buy. And a shot of tequila if they wish. The Blind Pig under Front Street stays open late on Saturday nights and opens up again at noon on Sunday, just for them. All they have to do to get admission is push the buzzer and say, "blind pig."

Joe Running Deer isn't a regular at the Blind Pig, but he had no trouble gaining admission. He fits the category of an undesirable drinker, being a full-blooded American Indian. He doesn't know the password. But he was at the door when the place opened, and he surged in with the early crowd of Mexican drinkers. Later, as he sat at the bar, it occurred to him that the afternoon had come and gone: He knew that because the Mexicans had left. That meant the sugar beet farmers had herded their workers into trucks and hauled them back to the farms. They had to be fed and put to bed so they would be ready for another week of back-breaking work hoeing weeds in the sugar beet fields.

Stupid fucking Mexicans, thought Joe. No Indian would ever do that stoop labor.

When Joe was in the State Penitentiary in Bismarck, where the notion of prisoner rehabilitation has not yet gained a convert, he had a lot of time in his cell to think about things. One of the things he thought a lot about was totem poles. His eighth-grade history teacher, Mr. Jeff Snider, eagerly participated in the elementary school's decision to suspend Joe indefinitely. But Snider would be amazed to learn that his worst student ever had actually gotten something out of his totem-pole lecture.

Joe used to tell his cellmate, a Lakota Indian named Jerome Big Shell, about his vision for the totem pole he was going to carve. Jerome had no interest in totem poles. Indians on the Great Plains didn't carve totem poles. Besides, as a Lakota, he inherently disliked all Mandan Indians and after two years of sharing a cell with Joe Running Deer that prejudice had only intensified. On the other hand, he had no way to shut out Joe's story.

"Totem poles tell stories," Joe explained to Jerome, speaking slowly but not looking him in the eye, out of respect one Indian gives another, even though as a Mandan he believed he was talking down to a Lakota. "My totem pole will tell the story about who is on top and who is on the bottom of all people."

Joe sat back on his bottom bunk and with his hands he outlined the shape of his totem pole. It didn't make any sense to Jerome. But he could tell it was a large, tall totem pole.

"On the bottom of the pole are Mexicans and Colored people," said Joe. He would have said Lakota had his cellmate been a Chippewa Indian. He even thought about saying Chippewa to Jerome, but he had never heard Jerome say anything bad about them, so he decided not to mention any of the other tribes. In his mind, though, the Lakota would be squeezed in at the bottom right next to the Mexicans and the Colored. He bent down to show Jerome how low on the pole they were.

Then he stood up and reached for the top of the cell. It wasn't a high ceiling, and he could touch it with his fingers even though he was not a tall man.

"On the top are the Mandan Indians."

He lowered his arms. He told Jerome how his people thought of themselves as "The People of the First Man." Joe told Jerome it made him proud when he said it.

"The Mandan Indians are on top of the totem pole: The People of the First Man." Joe said it boastfully.

Jerome was about to say something and then thought better of it. He didn't want to get into a fight with Joe before dinner. If he did, they both would end up in the hole and not be fed for at least two days.

Joe went on to explain how he had been taught on the reservation that the Mandans were the first Indians to have settled in what is now North Dakota, back in the 15th century. His people were living in organized villages near the Missouri River when the first white explorers stumbled into that part of the country nearly 200 years later.

No question about it, Joe was pleased to be a Mandan Indian, Jerome could tell. He wanted to ask Joe why it was his tribe didn't feel the same about him. Jerome knew that the Mandans had thrown Joe off the reservation. When he got out of prison, he would have no home to go to.

Joe drank peacefully among the Mexicans. They sensed his hostility and left him to drink alone. He didn't understand their language and without any way of knowing if they were insulting him or his heritage, he had no reason to display his violent temper.

Hours passed and Joe noticed that after the Mexicans left, the town drunks had slipped into the Pig. The Mexicans spoke Spanish and the drunks spoke gibberish. Joe realized that the only place he could find compatible company would be in an Indian bar across the river in Moorhead. But that morning, Joe had come across a handicapped guy on crutches struggling to enter a hotel up on North Broadway. Joe approached him from the back, put his hand around in front of him, and lifted his wallet from inside his sport coat. Then Joe pushed him hard in the back, forcing him to concentrate on keeping his balance instead of turning around to see who had robbed him, then quickly ditched around a corner and down an alley. For the first time in weeks, Joe Running Deer had money in his pocket.

But before he even made it a half block, he was hit hard from behind, suddenly pinned face-down in the half-dirt, half-asphalt of the alley. He couldn't see his attacker. But he was big.

"I saw what you did," the guy breathed in his ear. Slick move, up from behind. Thought I'd try it."

Joe Running Deer grunted.

"So you're clever, huh? Let's see how clever you are. I'll even let you keep that money you stole off the cripple. But now you gotta do something clever for me..."

Joe was confused. Now, a half day of drinking later, his confusion was amplified by drunkenness. He couldn't remember what happened next, except he was in the guy's car. He was a big white guy. He'd seen him somewhere before. And he'd told him something about a lot of money in it for him if he did something... Then he stopped the car near all the Mexicans sitting around outside this stupid bar just before it opened. And that's why Joe wasn't doing his drinking in an Indian bar.

Short of throwing dollar bills into the air with an accompanying war whoop, nothing calls attention to an Indian flush with cash quite like one instructing a bartender to pour a shot of whiskey. Given their normal financial limitations, Indians tend to drink tap beer or Ripple wine. So when a brave orders a whiskey, particularly when he calls his brand, it's noticed by every Indian in the joint. Half the white clientele generally take note too, just because they become uneasy when Indians start drinking the hard stuff. The Indians, of course, are checking to see if the brother with the money owes them a round or two.

Joe Running Deer owed every Indian in the twin cities of Fargo-Moorhead at least a couple drinks and so when he bought whiskey, he never went near a bar that catered to them.

Then too, a drinker couldn't buy whiskey in Moorhead on Sunday. On the Christian Sabbath, its bars could only sell "weak" beer (3.2 percent alcoholic content) and wine by the glass.

Patrons eating restaurant meals in Moorhead on Sunday, on the other hand, could buy a "set-up," such as a glass of club soda or tonic water or just a glass of ice cubes. Thus equipped with the restaurant-provided set-up, the patron was allowed to mix it with liquor he brought into the establishment inside a paper bag. The paper bag-ensconced liquor bottles, however, were not to be raised above the table level. No sense in offending the sensitivities of the abstainers. For that same reason, drinkers had to lower their glasses beneath the table level to fill them. Patrons could order as many set-ups as they wished, of course, because the restaurant had no liability concerns when all it was serving was mixers and ice cubes.

Back in North Dakota, however, once the churches emptied their pews on Sunday, the towns rolled up their streets. Stores were not allowed to open because of strictly enforced "blue laws." Nor could liquor be purchased either at an off-sale or at a bar. Without the ability to serve cocktails, few decent restaurants even bothered to open in Fargo on Sunday.

That wasn't the case across the river in Minnesota. Its restaurants flourished on Sunday While a diner couldn't order anything but beer and wine, he had the option of BYOB.

Moorhead restaurants benefited financially from North Dakota's attitude toward liquor and took full advantage of it. As far back as the turn of the century, Moorhead restaurants and bars attracted restaurant patrons on Sunday. They even scrounged up business by employing "Jag Wagons." These horse-drawn wagons from Moorhead circulated through Fargo to pick up patrons and bring them back across the river for dinner and a few drinks. When finished, a Jag Wagon would drop their customers back home.

Some pundits still wonder if Moorhead could have survived had neighboring Fargo legalized liquor early on after Prohibition, allowing drinks to be served with a meal.

Joe Running Deer knew nothing of this history and couldn't have feigned interest if told about it. He grew up on the Fort Berthold Indian Reservation where liquor was always banned, but always available, even to high school boys. Liquor stores were prohibited on Indian reservations. But *hooch*, a name derived from some Indian tribe out of Alaska, was always available at bars just a short drive off the reservation. These highly profitable establishments were owned by white men who catered to Indian customers. They stocked strong beer and fortified wine; cheap whiskey, rum, brandy, and gin. Buyers received plastic cups with their bottles so they could pour everyone in the car a drink during the ride home. Then once the car plowed into a ditch, which was why towing and wrecking services were generally one of the most profitable businesses on Indian reservations, the custom was to just pass the bottle around until a ride came along.

When Joe was a boy his father and uncles would drive off the reservation to purchase liquor. They would fill their trunks with cases of Schlitz or Grain Belt beer, Ripple wine, and inexpensive bourbon and vodka and head back to the reservations to sell the hooch to underage drinkers or men unable to get to the liquor stores themselves.

One of his relatives introduced Joe to liquor. After a high school basketball game he bought a six-pack of Grain Belt beer out of his Uncle Floyd's car trunk. Later his grandfather would drive him around the reservation and give him wine in exchange for running errands. Joe didn't learn what a blind pig was until he was an adult and out of prison. Now he did most of his drinking seated in bars. But he was always comfortable drinking in a car and purchasing liquor out of a trunk. At least then he never had to hear anyone yell "last call."

The Blind Pig's bartender, Sam Bodini, had yelled "last call" at least 15 minutes ago. The bar was still about a quarter full. Nobody seemed to be in any hurry to leave. But Joe could see Sam wasn't serving any more drinks. The other two bartenders who helped him out when the Mexicans were jammed into the place had already left. So had the big guy who had been sitting at the door all afternoon. For all practical purposes, the place was closed. Joe had to score soon or do without. Now he was frustrated as well as angry. He knew he had a problem relating to women. He wasn't particularly bothered by it. He wasn't looking for a girlfriend. That is why he sought out whores. His friends Lincoln and Jefferson ensured him all the affection he wanted. He had a pocket full of money now, and yet this white whore was treating him like he was penniless.

Come to think of it, Joe realized, that run-in with the big white guy in the alley had something to do with fucking this blonde white bitch. Kind of. Didn't it?

What Joe didn't know, because it never occurred to him to even consider it, was that Sara Whitlow had a different perspective on the situation. She didn't think of herself as a whore.

While it was true she had been known to sell her body for money, that didn't mean she considered it a profession. A long time ago, when she was sixteen, she got caught giving a blow job to her high school journalism teacher in a classroom after school. Even though the sex had been Sara's idea, the journalism teacher got the blame. That was one of the more valuable lessons Sara learned in high school: Young girls who have sex with older men are always the victims, regardless of how aggressively the girls have stalked their prey.

Sara attended Fargo Central High School. It was blessed with unusually insightful female guidance counselors. Sara was a frequent topic of conversation when they met to discuss their hard-core cases. She was a spoiled child with an insatiable interest in the opposite sex. She had a figure that could qualify her for a picture layout in any of the men's magazines then on the market. And her parents were absent from her life and compensated for it by giving her practically everything she wanted.

Her class counselor didn't feel sorry for the journalism instructor, believing that male teachers had to be strong in the face of youthful temptation. On the other hand, she was privately thankful that Sara hadn't come on to her own husband, a chubby English teacher at the high school. She could only imagine how long his resolve would have held up.

Sara was able to ignore most of the guidance counselor's life's lessons, seeing as how they sounded much like the ones her mother peddled. But Sara was taken by one thing she said: *Don't ever give away sex for free.*

The guidance counselor hadn't used those exact words. She had said something to the effect that sex between two people was sacred and should be confined within a loving relationship. Sara, though, read between the lines. Sara knew what the guidance counselor really meant was, "If you don't love the guy, charge him for sexual favors." From then on, she did. She only gave it away free to men she loved. There were not many of them in her life.

In the Front Street basement dug-out bar where a drunk Joe Running Deer was going insane with lust, Sara happened to be married to a man who got his sex for free. He just wasn't around much to cash in.

During the summer, Sara's husband drove a long-haul gravel truck out on the interstate highway project. Everyone knew those truckers made good wages when they worked, and the trailer park where she lived had a lot of new cars in it to testify to that fact. He wasn't particularly generous with his paycheck, though, because he knew she would spend whatever he gave her. When he came home once a month, they shopped for what he said she needed to get by until he returned in 30 days or so. And then, he left her just enough money for cigarettes and incidentals.

The freeway was being built east to west, heading toward Montana. The road crews worked 14-hour days and slept in their pickup trucks or tents that they hauled along with them as they scrunched across the prairie, laying concrete. They were racing the clock and racking up the hours, knowing that when winter closed in, the entire operation would shut down for nearly six months, putting its crew out of work. But then that was the way of life for many working men in the northern prairie states. During late spring, summer, and early fall, they would work like dogs, sunup to sundown. The paychecks were fat and bills got paid on time. Then for six months of the year, while snow covered the ground and the wind chill could hit minus 60 degrees, they hunkered down. Local folks joked about how North Dakota winters ensured that the state never had a problem with vagrants or the homeless: "Keeps out the riff-raff."

The only money coming into the Whitlows and other seasonal employees during the long winter months was from unemployment checks and the little bit of savings they built up from their summer income. It was never enough. Proportionate to its population, North Dakota's suicide rate tops the nation. That statistic doesn't surprise anyone who has ever gone through a North Dakota winter unemployed and squirreled away in a mobile home. If that mix includes a partner who blames the other for the miserable way the two of them are forced to live, well, it becomes clear why domestic-dispute calls to trailer parks fill the police ledger about the same time *Rudolph the Red-Nosed Reindeer* starts playing on the radio.

Winter was still a good four months off as Sara moved among the usual Sunday afternoon crowd of drinking cronies down in the Blind Pig on Front Street. Sara was 30, still attractive, and knew this was the time of year she could call her own to do what she wanted when she wanted to do it. Once Bruce came home for the winter, she would be shut in with him for six months and it would be a living hell. She and Bruce had done it for eight years. By the time spring rolled around each year, they were barely talking to each other. She knew the only reason he didn't hit her when he said he wanted to was because he understood she would walk out on him and never come back.

Their home is a two-bedroom, one-bath trailer on wheels that haven't moved since it was bolted into place out on South 5th Avenue near the Fargo Slough. She never had enough money for the things she wanted. Her father, who had plenty, had written her off years ago. She could have worked, but her prison record pretty much dictated the kind of job she would have to take, and she wasn't interested in any of them.

Lately, Sara had begun to accept her plight in life, at least for a short while. She decided summers belonged to her. When Bruce came home on his days off, she still dropped everything and entertained him the way he wanted, which generally meant steaks, beer, and sex. Two or three days of that and he was back on the road for another month. But then, it was Sara's time.

She was careful to steer clear of the law. She had been arrested several times in her 20s for passing bad checks and she ended up in county jail for a year. Her parents were beside themselves with shame. "How could you do this to us?" seemed to be the only question her father wanted answered. Finally, on her 30th birthday, he made her a deal.

"You are our only child," he told her on one of his infrequent trips back to Fargo from *The District*, as he referred to Washington, D.C. "We are not going to live forever. As you undoubtedly know, your mother and I are worth quite a bit of money. We have a great deal of property here in the Red River Valley and a significant amount of wealth amassed in various bank accounts, both in this country and in foreign banks. If you want an inheritance, do not embarrass me."

"What do you mean by that?" she asked. "It seems everything I do embarrasses you."

"I'll be specific then. Stay out of jail. Keep your name out of the newspapers, unless you receive some good citizenship award. Don't become the town slut. Your mother would like some grandchildren, but if that involves your husband Bruce, then I'm not going to make that requirement part of the deal."

Thank God. Sara didn't want children and luckily neither did Bruce.

"He does want the inheritance, though, big time," Sara said to Terri Squires, her best friend and drinking buddy. "When he heard about the deal, he actually seemed to start treating me better. Of course, he wanted to know how big the inheritance was going to be. I told him I didn't know."

"Well, you must have some idea," said Terri. The two of them were sitting together at the far end of the bar in the Blind Pig, as far away from Joe Running Deer as they could get. "You grew up with them."

"All I know, it's a lot. Mom was rich when they got married. When they fought, which was all the time, Mom used to say her family's money was the only reason Dad married her. And she was an only child. They have a really nice apartment they own here. It's on the top floor of the new high-rise building on South 5th Avenue overlooking Island Park. It has to be one of the most expensive residences in Fargo. And they hardly are ever in it. I've never been in their home in Virginia, but I bet it's huge. Both places have live-in help."

Terri lit a Salem with her Zippo. Terri was about Sara's age. But that and naturally blond hair was all she had physically in common with Sara. Terri wished she had Sara's looks and figure. Some days she wished she had Sara's husband. Other days she simply wished she had a man in her life, any man. Raising two kids on her own wasn't easy.

It had been Terri's idea to come down to the Blind Pig this warm Sunday afternoon. The invitation had surprised Sara. Terri wasn't much of a drinker and Sara knew her friend couldn't afford to spend her money on liquor. But Sara was glad to have the company; no woman likes to walk into a saloon by herself, even on a Sunday afternoon.

"Did Bruce treat you better after he heard about the inheritance?"

"You bet your sweet ass he did," said Sara. "I think he looked at me and saw dollars and cents. But hey, I'm not complaining. Winters even got a little more tolerable. This summer he started talking about maybe spending this coming winter in Arizona. He says he thinks he might be able to get seasonal work out there. He says there are a lot of 'snowbirds' or something coming to Arizona and they have money to spend."

Sara took a long pull on her drink.

"We talk all the time about what we'll do after we get our hands on my parents' money. It shouldn't be too long. Christ, my old man must be pushing 80. Mom is quite a bit younger. I think she's about 62. She and I still talk on the phone a lot. Dad doesn't even know about it. I think once he passes, Mom will send me money. At least that's what she says. Right now everything is in Dad's name. She can't even get her hair done without his permission. But once I get my hands on his money, Bruce and I are going to move—maybe Arizona or even Southern California—to live the good life. No more goddamn trailer parks and head-bolt heaters for me."

Terri said, "Seems to me you just got to hold the marriage together until your boat comes in."

"I know I'm unfaithful to him. But I'm faithful when he's around. For God's sake, it's just him and me all goddamn winter. I never leave his side. Shit, we hardly ever leave the bedroom. I mean, what else is there to do for entertainment during a long North Dakota winter? I make him turn the television off first, though. I hate to have sex when I think he's still watching the goddamn TV. One time we were both going hot and heavy and all of a sudden, he burst out laughing. Seems some sorry ass comedian on Jack Parr's Tonight Show told a joke that really cracked him up. I popped his wiener out of the bun so fast he didn't know what happened to him. He was still lying there humping the mattress when I slammed the bathroom door shut."

Terri laughed out loud at the image of Bruce humping the mattress. Then she imagined for a moment just how appealing a sight Bruce would be lying face down on a mattress without any clothes, in obvious love-making readiness. Bruce was construction-worker hard, with broad shoulders, big biceps, and a thin waist. She could see his plunging bottom perfectly and she could catch glimpses of his large penis as it struck the mattress and slid off to the side. She grabbed a cigarette out of the pack in front of her and fought to get back into the conversation.

"But we're not talking about the winter months, are we?"

"The summers are mine; I've always believed that," said Sara, defensively. "I mean, if he was here with me, I'd feel different. But he's not. He's the one who decided to drive a gravel truck out by Dickinson all damn summer. Last year he was in Mandan and the year before it was Jamestown. I haven't seen him for an entire summer in years. You can't tell me he doesn't do this on purpose. You wait, next year that damn freeway is going to push on into Montana. Then he is going to tell me he's going with it. Isn't that crazy? I mean, building a four-lane freeway across North Dakota doesn't make any sense. But across Montana? Bruce says it's the trucking industry. He says it owns the Congress. Now Congress is willing to spend taxpayers' money to build freeways across the country so the truckers can put the railroads out of business. That's what Bruce says, anyway. What do I know?"

"Is Bruce suspicious that you sleep around when he's out of town?" Terri asked as she lit her Salem.

"Of course not. Geez, what a thing to ask. What are you saying? God, you make me feel like a tramp or something."

"Calm down, sweetie. I'm not judging you. I just know you have sex with other men. And didn't you tell me you always charge them for it?"

Sara took another drink of her Tom Collins. And then she sighed. She didn't know why she needed to explain herself to Terri.

"Give me one of your cigarettes, would you? Listen, this isn't as complicated as it may seem. When Bruce is around, I am a faithful, loving wife. During my time—the summer months—I screw around. I always have, and I don't give it away for free. But I am not a whore."

Sara lit her cigarette.

"It isn't like someone can call me on the phone and schedule time with me. I don't have a little black book of regulars or anything like that. I don't have sex with just anyone either. I have sex when I need spending money and that isn't an everyday necessity."

Terri said, "Okay, I guess I would say you are more promiscuous than professional. I certainly am not accusing you of being a whore, that's for sure."

"Well, thank you very much," Sara harrumphed.

"Anytime," said Terri, as she drained her glass of gin and tonic and looked around for Bodini.

"I've obviously thought about what I'm doing. I definitely see a pattern emerging. One, I do it sometimes when I really need some spending money. When that happens I get furious at Bruce. I blame him for forcing me to sell my body for some lousy spending money. Other times, I want to have sex because I am attracted to a guy. But even when that happens, and it doesn't very often, I am not about to give anything away for free, having established that rule a long time ago. Third, and this is the least often scenario, sometimes I run into a guy who really, really wants to have sex with me even though I can't feign interest in him. Once in a while, under those circumstances, I say to myself, 'Oh hell, I might just as well make him happy and take his money.'"

They laughed and Sara asked Bodini to fix them two more drinks. He said "no" in that tone of voice that bartenders use when they are trying to close their joints and go home.

Chapter Three

Grades Trip Up Reporter

On his way out the door, Baker grabs a last edition of the *Star*—the 4 p.m. edition that's sold almost exclusively from newsstands and newspaper boxes across the city. It has the biggest headlines of any edition, because it needs to convince a potential reader to dig into a pocket or purse for a loose quarter and buy it.

The *Star* is an afternoon paper. The regular edition comes off the press around noon every weekday, and is delivered across the city to subscribers, mainly offices, before 1:30 p.m. Throughout the country, afternoon papers find themselves losing the competition for circulation and advertising revenue to their morning rivals. But the *Star* holds its own in its marketplace. It has one big advantage over the *Washington Post,* it's main rival: Pulitzer-prize-winning writers and big-name columnists. Chuck Baker is thrilled to be a probationary reporter on the *Star* staff.

He tucks his newspaper under his arm and walks out of the building as if he owns it. He's feeling pretty damn good about himself. He likes being a journalist. He has wanted to be one for as long as he can remember. In both high school and college he edited the schools' newspapers. The awards he piled up for his writing and editing caught the eye of the editor of the *Washington Star* and Baker received an invitation at the end of his junior year of college to accept a summer internship. From all indications, the *Star* editors consider him a legitimate journalist.

Baker was told, when he was first hired in June of 1964, that if he made it through his year-long probationary period successfully he would be offered a full-time job as a *Star* reporter. But now that he's accepted that full-time position, he knows the *Star* management expects him to be a college graduate—and he realizes that requirement may well be the death knoll of his journalism career.

Although Baker has attended college nonstop for four years, he is more than a few credits shy of graduating. As far as George Washington University is concerned, he's dangling somewhere between being classified as a second semester junior or a first semester senior, with a lousy grade point average. Between the courses he has dropped and those he's failed, he probably faces another year of coursework.

Baker doesn't doubt he can grind through another year of college. The challenge is to bring up his grades. He needs to earn straight As in every class he takes from now on to bring his overall grade point average up high enough to graduate. Mathematically, that's possible. But anyone looking at his transcript is going to ask: "What are the odds of you earning nothing but straight As?"

The personnel office at the *Star* just assumed he was a graduate when he accepted his prized new position as a full-time reporter last month, and Baker said nothing to suggest otherwise. Not to worry, he said to himself. He will do his job, complete his courses, get his degree, and eventually everything will be copasetic.

As Baker leaves the building and walks up Pennsylvania toward 13th Street, he thinks back over his day. He makes a mental note to call his buddy Tony and thank him for all the help. The guy is a prince among men.

At the corner of Pennsylvania and 14th he walks by the old Willard Hotel, now boarded up and abandoned except for a few street people who camp out in its bowels without the benefit of either electricity or running water. Baker doesn't understand why the hotel is still standing. It's an eyesore. Maybe it survives because of its distinguished history. He remembers his surprise when he learned in high school that former presidents, including Ulysses S. Grant, made the Willard their "home" during their stint in Washington. The term "lobbyist" came into being as a way to describe people wanting favors from President Grant who would lurk in the hotel lobby hoping to nab a minute of his time as he was coming and going.

After he passes by the hotel, he turns up 14th Street for a block and walks by Garfinkel's, his favorite department store. Actually, it was his mother's, and all throughout his childhood he had been brought there to be outfitted for clothes and shoes. While in college he shopped there on his own. He figures he'll probably shop there his whole life.

Baker then turns left on "E" Street and heads toward the White House. He turns right on 15th Street and walks along the side of the East Wing of the White House. Although he has lived his entire life in the Washington suburbs and attended school in the District of Columbia, he has never gotten over his awe of being in the nation's capital. He thinks it's pretty damn cool to be able to stroll past the White House on the way home from work. He wonders how many young newspaper reporters in the country wish they could say that?

He picks up his pace as he walks through Lafayette Park in front of the White House and across "H" Street onto 17th Street. He's going to be late. He hits "K" Street and has to make a decision. He could turn left and go a short half block and be on Connecticut Avenue. A right turn there and a quick walk up two blocks will bring him to the front door of the Mayflower Hotel. But he thinks it may be faster to enter the Mayflower from the back entrance. Having decided on his approach, he stays on 17th Street.

Going into the Mayflower the back way enables him to step down into the wide hallway that runs the length of the hotel, lit by crystal chandeliers that bounce light off the large mirrors lining the walls. Strolling down the splendor of the hallway, it's easy to feel important, if only for the moment.

When he gets to the lobby he slows down, putting his sport coat back on over his sweat-dampened shirt. He certainly doesn't want to look like a tourist. Nevertheless, he can't stop himself from glancing up at the second-floor balcony. It encloses the lobby on three sides and exists solely to enable fashionable people to sit at tables and sip drinks while throwing bemused looks down at the little people below. He realizes, with a grimace, that by looking up he has just identified himself as one of those little people.

With his copy of the *Star* bulldog edition still in his hand, Baker heads for the Town & Country lounge off to his right. It's his stepfather's favorite watering hole in downtown Washington. As he pushes the door open, Baker again puzzles about his stepfather always arranging to meet with him here at the Mayflower. He works on Capitol Hill and lives in Arlington. The Mayflower isn't close to either. It isn't particularly handy for Baker, for that matter, but it's consistently the place his stepfather suggests they meet.

Baker suspects his stepfather likes the bar because of its history. He's mentioned more than once that the lounge is the place J. Edgar Hoover, the head of the FBI, and his "boyfriend" frequently meet for lunch. Baker always lets the comment go without a response. He isn't sure what his stepfather means exactly when he says it, but Baker doubts he's suggesting that the head of the FBI is a homosexual.

At least once in a while Baker wishes Pinks would choose Arlington for their occasional lunches. Pinks belongs to the Washington Golf and Country Club near his Arlington home. Baker's mom, Gloria, likes the club because she plays bridge there once a week, and she and Pinks meet friends there for Saturday night dinners. But Pinks says he seldom goes to the country club for a drink. He says the bar conversations revolve around golf and few things bore him more than listening to men talk about their putts.

The two men have been family for nearly seven years, but they are not close. Pinks entered Baker's family a few years after his father died and his mother decided to remarry. Baker assumes Pinks probably isn't thrilled to have a stepson as part of the relationship, but then for his part, Baker was intent to show the new man in the house that he wasn't a replacement father.

Baker grew up surrounded by memories of his father and all the way through high school kept a picture of him on his bedroom wall. Chuck was mindful of the fact his father had been a Marine who had served in the Pacific during World War

II and then died fighting in Korea. His stepfather, he knew, had somehow avoided military service. When Pinks was still courting Baker's mother, the 16-year-old pressed him on the subject. That's when Pinks insisted he had served his country: He had been the security director of a secret prisoner of war camp in North Dakota.

That was a story Baker always found hard to believe. Why would the federal government haul Germans all the way to North Dakota and lock them up for the duration of the war? But he never challenged Pinks' tale. On the other hand, he had attempted to find something written about such a prisoner of war camp, and never could.

After Baker's father died, his mother had gone to work for the Department of Agriculture as a secretary. The job didn't pay particularly well, but with benefits coming in from the Veterans Administration, they got by. She did her job well and became indispensable, especially to the political appointees who came into the department without a clue about how it functioned or the ways its programs operated. She frequently accompanied her boss, an assistant secretary for soil conservation, to Capitol Hill when he testified in support of the agency's appropriation request. She had usually helped prepare his testimony. And if her boss got into a jam when questioned by the congressional committee, she could be counted on to slip him a note with an appropriate response.

While on one of these Hill visits, she met an aide who worked for a senator from North Dakota. One thing led to another, and after an appropriate courtship, Chuck's mother had a new husband. They remained in Arlington, but moved into a larger house and bought a new car. His mother was happier than he had seen her in years, and this pleased Baker. He frankly couldn't see what she saw in the guy, but he was content to get along with him to make her happy.

His mother took Jerry Pinks' name, but not her son. He was in junior high school and old enough, he said, to decide if he wanted to be the "Pinks' boy." He was proud of his father's name and wanted to keep it. Pinks told her it wasn't important to him, so she bowed to her son's wishes. Pinks assured her that legally and emotionally, her son was now as much his as hers. Baker didn't think he said it with any sincerity, but his mother burst into tears and ran into his arms, so the comment seemed to have accomplished what he wanted.

Throughout his high school years, his mother established the rules, with Pinks providing her emotional support when needed. But young Baker wasn't a problem child. He was a popular student, active in theatre, journalism, intramural sports, and student government. His grades never warranted honor-roll status, but he tested well and his counselors believed he just needed to study a little harder to become a top student. Baker believed that too. Trouble was, he always had other things to do that he considered more important than studying.

That attitude toward study carried over into college, unfortunately. He enrolled initially at American University, figuring the academic rigor wouldn't interfere with the other things he wanted out of his college experience. But then he was expelled for his participation in a student protest against the university's plan to require universal Reserve Officer Training Corps (ROTC) for all freshmen and sophomore men.

The protest started out friendly enough, but some radicals in the crowd got carried away and torched an old wooden World War II era building on campus used by the ROTC program. Although Baker had nothing to do with it, he was photographed by police inside the building just as it burst into flames. He tried to explain that as a student journalist he was just an observer of the fire, not a participant. But his involvement in the protest was judged sufficient to warrant his dismissal.

The experience taught him a valuable lesson, one that isn't generally taught in Journalism 101: the greater his participation, the more likely a reporter will describe events as situational. That is, the situation causes the problem, not the people involved. This creates a quandary for journalists, because hardly anyone thinks participants can be objective. Observers, on the other hand, are considered much more likely to be neutral and therefore factual, or as the journalists themselves would say, they are "factual and neutral."

But the more a reporter steps away from a simple observation role to dig deeper into the facts of the story, the more he risks being labeled a participant. That is, they learn to understand most conflicts are backed by strong points of view coming from multiple perspectives. For example, when a group of citizens (e.g., immigrants or poor people) say the police are corrupt, a neutral observer would dutifully report the allegation. But to provide balance to their story, the reporter would quote the police as saying their critics are troublemakers, anarchists, and lawbreakers. On the other hand, the more the reporter actually becomes immersed in the conflict, the more likely he is to learn where the truth emerges, and the allegations being thrown around start to unwind. Some journalists are able to become active participants and still be somewhat objective observers. But not many.

Despite his forced departure from American University, George Washington University agreed to enroll him. He joined a fraternity, made friends, and moved onto campus. Then he got heavily involved in the campus newspaper. Before long, it became his passion.

School became secondary, as it always does when a student journalist has something more interesting to pursue. His grades suffered; at least every other semester he found himself on academic probation. By the end of his sophomore year, he realized he was in serious trouble.

Baker thought long and hard about his problem. He invested hours thinking about it. On occasion, a friend would try to straighten him out by suggesting he spend more time studying and less time worrying about his lousy grades. Baker intensely disliked that analysis. He would do almost anything to avoid studying. Finally, he came up with a strategy.

He told his college roommate about it first. They were at the fraternity house on a Saturday afternoon following a basketball game. They were drinking beer and killing time before heading off to Georgetown to cruise for girls who they believed assembled at the local watering holes just hoping they might drop by.

Saturday nights generally were spent prowling Georgetown unless the fraternity house had a mandatory event that night, which meant a member had to pay for it, whether he showed up or not. Baker was good looking and capable of picking up girls on his own. But his friend Tony Schober was the real stud muffin. He stood six feet two inches, had curly black hair and a smile that could light up a dimly lit room. He was bright, witty, and able to convince nearly anyone that one more beer wouldn't hurt. Guys liked him and girls thought he was suitable enough to meet their parents. He dated, but not seriously. Tony had his goals, and they didn't include early marriage. He wanted to go to law school and become a big-time lawyer. With fame and fortune secured, he then wanted to get into politics back home in New Jersey. Then maybe he would have time for a family. Before all that, though, he had time on Saturday nights to hang out with his pal Chuck.

"Tony, I figured out why I'm getting such lousy grades."

"You don't study."

"No, smart ass. Somehow, the university knows I can't memorize. I've never been able to memorize. I asked my mother about it. She says it's because when I was an infant I was taught to never crawl off my baby blanket. She says she thinks not crawling around screwed me up somehow."

"Yeah, I'll buy the brain damage part. That might explain why you never pick up a book and study."

"Will you get off that? I'm serious about this memory problem I have. And the university is on to me. That's why it forced me to take all those heavy-duty memorization courses in my first two years of college. They wanted me to flunk out. You see what I'm talking about? They required me to take a lot of courses in math and science and foreign languages. University officials knew I'd get low grades in those courses. Those bastards figured I would become discouraged and quit. And if that didn't work, they planned to use my low GPA as an excuse to bounce my ass out of here."

Baker took a big slug from the quart bottle of beer he was sharing with Tony.

"Dammit, I almost caught on to what the university was doing too late. God, I've failed every math and science course I've taken. Then when I take them over, all I get is a goddamn D. That's a lot of Fs and Ds, I've got to tell you."

"Sounds to me like you've definitely identified the problem," Tony said, taking the beer back from Chuck. "The university has got your number. You and all the other idiots who can read and write, but can't memorize. They want you out of here, that's for sure. So how do you beat the bastards? Are you going to hire somebody to take your tests for you?"

"Don't I wish. Don't think I haven't thought about it. But there's no way that would ever fly. The faculty really watch for that sort of thing. Particularly for us failing students. If I ever got an "A" on a test, I would be required to take it over again under the steely-eyed glare of at least two of those nerdy teaching assistants."

"Okay, so what's your secret?"

"I love its simplicity. I'm thinking we ought to let the pledges in on it. Listen to this."

Tony is belching, loudly, leading Chuck to wonder just how attentive his friend is to the scheme he's about to explain to him.

"You listening or what?"

"Sure, I'm listening, go ahead. You have a system."

"Okay. Here it is in two sentences: Don't keep flunking courses semester after semester. Space them out."

Tony looks at him. Then he grabs the quart bottle of beer out of Chuck's hand and takes a long pull.

"That's your system? You space out your flunks?"

"Here's how it works. I take as many of math and science requirements as I can during the fall semesters. It's a disaster waiting to happen, I know. At the end of each of these semesters, I'm on academic probation. The next semester I load up on social science courses. No memorization, just a lot of essay writing and junk like that. No problem for a journalism student. I pull down anywhere from a 2.5 to a 3-point grade point average. That takes me off probation.

Then I sign up for more math and science courses the following fall. Some of them will be new courses, but others will be repeats of courses I've flunked earlier. I'll undoubtedly flunk all the new courses I take, but I ought to be able to snag a D or even a C in the classes I repeat. At the end of that semester, I'm back on probation again. So, more social science courses the next semester. I do this until all my math and science requirements have been met. At that point, I'll have accumulated a lot of Fs and Ds. But I'll also have a lot of As and Bs to offset them. By my last quarter in school, I should have a GPA high enough to graduate. Maybe but just barely, but that's enough. That's how I intend to thwart the beast."

"Wait a minute. How many math and science courses do you intend to flunk and then take over again and get Ds in?"

"Well, I've had to take a year of botany and a year of zoology. Then a year of geology. Then a year of algebra and a year of calculus. The science courses are all five credits each. Most of the math courses are only three credits each. I don't really know how many Fs and Ds that adds up to. That's not what keeps me awake at night. I just have to make sure I have an equal number of social science course credits with As and Bs. Then I need at least one more course with an A grade to put me over the top. In other words, I'll have the necessary 2.0 grade point average plus a smidgen more. Not much more, that's for sure. But enough to get me a college degree."

"Wow. For every three science courses you fail, you have to take five social science courses and get As in all of them just to average out a 2.0, overall. For every one of those three science courses you took over and got a D, you have got to take five additional social science courses and get all Bs or better."

"It's a lot of work," Baker agreed. "But let me tell you, it beats the hell out of studying."

Tony graduated from GWU in the spring of 1964 and was accepted into the university's law school. But the two continued to room together. Baker wasn't sure why. Tony said his roommate's bad study habits didn't rub off on him and he liked the companionship.

"Besides," said Tony. "I need to stay here and hound you through your undergraduate degree."

This last spring, Tony asked Baker how things were going. It was the semester that should have been Baker's last. Tony knew his roommate hadn't been able to gather a sufficient number of As and Bs to offset his losers in math and science, and consequently didn't have enough credits to graduate.

Baker has an excuse for his situation, of course. He spent the past 12 months as editor-in-chief of the college daily. He approached it as if it were a full-time job. The rewards were great; national recognition for the newspaper, individual awards for himself, and the opportunity to travel across the country to speak to journalism groups about his exploits. All this left little time to attend classes or earn decent grades.

"How are you doing this semester?" asked Tony. "If you stay around another year, will you have the grade point average to graduate then?"

"That's the million-dollar question," says Baker. "I ask it myself weekly. That's why I went to meet with the University Registrar. Nice fellow. He looked at my transcript and said there was no way I was ever going to graduate from George Washington University. I said there's always a way. Then he sat down with his calculator and did the math. He said if I took eighteen credits each semester for one more year and earned all As, I would bring my overall average above the necessary 2.0 I need to graduate."

"There you go," says Tony. "Nothing to it."

"Well, there is one caveat," Baker says. "He said I had to get at least a 2.5 GPA this semester just to stay eligible for another year of college."

"Can you do that?"

"I don't know. That was the plan, get the high grade-point average in the spring, with the humanities. Oh, the humanities. I'm trying, ol' buddy. Four years of being a college student is long enough. I'm ready to move on with my life."

"I hear you. And you know something I think George Washington University is ready for Chuck Baker to move on."

Baker grabs a law book away from Tony and throws it at him.

"Hey, don't screw around. You ought to have more respect for the study of law. God knows, I'm probably going to have to get your sorry ass out of jail someday."

"That's a sobering thought," says Baker. "Anyway, if I can get through this semester, I'm in the home stretch. My last couple of semesters in college will consist of nothing but courses in things like sociology, history, political science, and journalism. I have no doubt I can get straight As and walk away with a diploma. That's the plan, anyway."

Baker knew graduating from GW would please his mother and stepfather. He suspected they were skeptical he was going to. He and his stepfather never discussed his grades. His mother asked about them occasionally, but never pursued the topic. Now he was on his way to see his stepfather for drinks and reassured himself the topic wouldn't come up, since it never did with Pinks. Maybe he could mention the article he just wrote. Perhaps that would please him. Well, you never know, Baker thought. Pinks and his boss were Republicans, but on the Senate side. Hard telling how much they would care about a Southern congressman.

As Baker walks in, he spots Jerry Pinks sitting at a table, smoking a Chesterfield and drinking a scotch and water. He looks every bit of his 63 years. He also looks upset.

That isn't unusual. Baker thinks his presence generally upsets Pinks. The guy is just uptight around his stepson, and Baker has given up trying to figure out why.

Pinks spent the first 30 years of his life in North Dakota before moving to Washington, D.C. to take a federal job. According to his mother, he went from that position to the staff of the then-senior congressman from North Dakota, Thomas Christenson.

He was in that position when he met Gloria Baker, a war widow with a young son named Charles. They dated, apparently fell in love, and got married. She went back to North Dakota with him once in the summer and thought the state had charm. Then they traveled back once in the winter. She vowed to never do that again. She even told him that if he ever suggested moving back to North Dakota, she would leave him. That was enough information for her son to digest: He was never going to visit, let alone live, in North Dakota.

"Hey Jerry, what's up," says Baker as he slides into a chair across from the older man. "I thought by now you would have ordered me a beer."

"I didn't know when you would get here. What kind do you want?"

"I don't care. Order me a Bud?"

While Pinks tries to catch the waitress' eye, Baker looks his stepfather over. He's wearing his usual "Hill Duds" as Baker calls them. Gray suit, white shirt, blue tie. Probably a brown belt and shoes, too, beneath the table. Baker tries to recall how long Pinks has worked for Tom Christenson, one of the Senate's longest-serving members. A long time. Pinks has watched his boss go from a nobody congressman to one of the most powerful men in the Senate. Christenson is the ranking Republican on the Senate Appropriations Committee. As such, he has designated Pinks as the Committee's Minority Staff Director. That means Pinks is one of the most powerful staff members on Capitol Hill—perhaps even the most powerful in the Republican Minority. When he got the job, he told his wife Gloria and his stepson that his major responsibility was ensuring the Democratic staff didn't hog all the bacon when the annual appropriations were distributed.

Baker knows enough about the appropriation process to understand that the majority party gets first crack at determining how the annual spending bill is going to be allocated across agencies, and then within agencies, across programs and projects. Smart administration heads are careful to make sure they address the priorities of the majority party members on the Appropriations Committee. The higher you rank on the committee, the better you get taken care of. As the ranking minority member, you generally draw a lot of attention, too. This is particularly true if your party is in charge of the White House. That isn't the case now, in 1965. Nevertheless, the Democrats in the White House want to keep the Senate Appropriation Committee's leadership happy, so the ranking Republican gets a lot of attention. His job—and consequently the job of his staff director—is to make sure the other Republicans on the committee get some of their needs met, too.

Another crucial part of Pinks' job is taking care of folks back home in North Dakota. Senator Christenson has been in poor health the past several years and isn't always capable of remembering who his friends are and what they expect from their senator. Truth be told, the senior senator from North Dakota has suffered several small strokes and is essentially being shielded by his staff and his wife from any decision making, both at home and in the office. Pinks goes to North Dakota at least once a month on behalf of the senator, to meet with various constituents, particularly those in Fargo, the state's largest city.

The Senate takes care of its own, and the senior senator from North Dakota isn't the first incapacitated member to serve in office. Until he drops dead or voluntarily gives up his seat, he will remain the ranking minority member on the Appropriations Committee. To demonstrate that he's still kicking, Senator Christenson shows up for critical votes; attends appropriation mark-ups; and maintains abbreviated office hours to sign letters and pose for pictures for the few visitors from North Dakota who stop by. Otherwise he is at home with his lovely and younger wife Pam who, with the help of aides, takes care of him.

Pinks never discusses his business with his stepson, but having lived together, it's hard for the young journalist to ignore the unusually close alliance between his stepfather and his employer. The Pinks live just a few blocks from the Christensons in Arlington, and Jerry spends many evenings and weekends over at the mansion, as he calls it. Other times he is on the phone with either the senator or his wife. In the den at the Pinks' home, the desk is covered with legislative drafts and correspondence concerning wheat, soybeans, and in particular, sugar beets. When he was home for Easter dinner, Baker noticed a map of North Dakota and what it will look like when the Missouri River grows in size behind the recently completed Garrison Dam.

When Baker has listened to Pinks talk to the senator on the phone, it sometimes seems as if his stepfather is telling the senator what to do. Of course, that could never happen. No staff member gives orders to his senator. But these two North Dakotans clearly have a different relationship than most other senators and their senior staff.

Baker looks across the table at his stepfather and thinks the *Star* ought to do an expose about the way he and the senator work the system on behalf of one of the smallest states in the nation. But politics isn't his beat, so he would have to convince someone else to write the story. Maybe he can write it himself, after his stepfather retires. He wonders if blood, even if only by late marriage, is thicker than printer's ink.

"Why are you looking so glum?" he asks.

"I'm looking so glum, now that you ask, because of this," says his stepfather, as he takes an envelope out of his pocket and drops it on the cocktail table in front of him. Chuck recognizes the return address and the logo. It is from George Washington University. It has to be his spring grades. Shit. Why did Jerry have them?

Baker opens the envelope and sees the computer-generated punch card with his grades. A letter accompanies the punch card. He looks at the grades on the punch card first, setting the letter aside. He took four courses last semester. He has a C in American History. That upsets him; he had been expecting a B. Then he sees he has a D in both English literature and second-year Spanish. Finally, he has an F in music appreciation. Fuck. He figured on a C in that carrot course. How do you flunk music appreciation, for God's sake? They must have been serious about taking attendance into consideration when putting together the grade. He sighs, sets the punch card down on the table, and picks up the letter.

It is brief, but pointed. He's out. The letter says he had been on academic probation spring semester. That meant his grades had to be high enough to get him off probation. But they aren't. In fact, they are even worse than the previous semester's grades. Therefore, the university says he's not making suitable progress toward graduation. At some point in the future, if he wishes, he can apply for re-admission. The letter closes by wishing him good luck with his future endeavors. Blah, blah, blah.

Baker looks at Pinks and asks: "Why did you get this letter and I didn't?"

"What difference does that make? The point is, the university has thrown you out. Focus on the matter at hand."

"No, I'm just curious. I'm over twenty-one years of age. The university sends my grades to me, not to my parents. So why did you get my grades?"

"You really want to know? I got them because a year ago you made an enemy of the president of George Washington University with that series of articles you did. Remember those? The ones about his raid on the library funds to support his effort to recruit big-time basketball players? That ring a bell? Well, let me tell you something, he sure remembers them. He had these grades sent over to my office by courier with a personal note. And guess what: He sent a copy of your grades and his letter to the editor of the *Star* too."

"Ah, fuck me."

"I think that about says it all."

"He sent a copy to the *Star*? Christ, I'll lose my job when they find out I got thrown out of college. I mean, they thought I was a graduate. That son of a bitch."

"I think the word for it is 'payback.'"

"Well, that bastard was playing sleight of hand with university funds. All I did was report it. I just did my job."

"I'm sure you did. But let me tell you something. There are some absolutes in politics. Some of these same absolutes must apply to journalism. For example, when you kick a jackass, be prepared for it to kick back."

"Well, I'm really fucked. I'm out of a job and now out of college. Shit. The next letter I'll get will be from the goddamn draft board saying Uncle Sam wants me to go fight in a jungle."

"You've always been a little reckless, Chuck. This is a perfect example of it. You of all people should not have gone after a university president. You were too vulnerable to take that risk. You caused him some momentary anguish, to be sure. But now he's caused you some serious pain. Don't they teach you anything in your journalism courses?"

Baker is seething. He doesn't want to get into an argument with Jerry Pinks about the righteousness of a journalist's quest for truth. And he doesn't want to concede that the president of GW has gotten the best of him. Above all, he still hasn't totally grasped the enormity of what has just happened to him.

Then it occurs to him.

"I wonder if I did the same thing today."

"What do you mean by that?"

"Oh, I wrote a story for the *Star* about a congressman having sex with a black man in a House Office Building. It will be in tomorrow's newspaper."

"For God's sake, Chuck. Have you lost your mind? Why in the world would you do such a thing? A member of Congress can get you fired."

"That's what he told me. Won't that be interesting? My termination papers and my dismissal papers might be processed at the same time." Baker felt a smirk starting to creep up the left side of his face.

"I don't see any humor in this. Spreading rumors about the sex lives of congressmen is the lowest form of yellow journalism, and I'm amazed that the *Washington Star* would publish such a story."

"Amazing you would come to that conclusion before you even read the story."

Baker tossed the carbon copy of his article on the table in front of him. Pinks looks at him and then picks it up. His eyes widen immediately.

"My God, Jeff Walker. Is this for real?

"Yes, Jerry, I saw the film myself. The film I saw is now at the *Washington Star*. Two of my editors and a lawyer for the newspaper saw it with me. It's for real."

"Oh my God, this is unbelievable. Oh my God. Jeff Walker and a Negro janitor. You say this is going to be in the *Washington Star* tomorrow morning?"

"I'm not sure this exact version of the story is going to be in. This is how I wrote it, but it will go through editing and some other stuff might get added. But yes, the story will be in the paper tomorrow morning."

"Sit here and have another beer. I've got to go make a phone call.

Jerry slid out of his chair and took the article with him.

Baker drinks his second Bud before Pinks comes back to the table. He is in a joyful mood.

"That is quite a story. You're to be commended for it. Were your editors pleased?"

"Yes, they seemed to be."

"Well, let's get back to you and your problem, shall we? What are your thoughts about serving your country?"

"I haven't thought about it. I mean, I have a student deferment. I realize that it isn't going to last forever. I figured that when I graduated, I would probably get drafted. I had hoped that if I did I could join a branch of the service where I could use my journalism skills somehow. I don't know, be a public information officer of some kind or other. I sure in the hell don't want to shoot anyone. I want dad to be the only hero in our family. Now I suppose I have to worry about being drafted right away."

"To be an officer, you need a college degree. To get that, you have to keep from being drafted. Right now, you're registered with a draft board in Virginia. As I understand it from the newspaper, Virginia's draft boards are grabbing up every college dropout that appears on their rolls. That means we've got to get you enrolled in college right away."

"I don't know where I'm going to go. I can't get into the University of Virginia. I've been thrown out of American and GW. I doubt if Catholic University will take me. The University of Maryland isn't likely to want me either and if it did accept me I doubt it would transfer in many of my credit hours. It would be like starting over again."

"Here's a thought. You've not going to like it. But hear me out. Your mother and I own property in North Dakota. That makes our children eligible for in-state tuition at its universities. More important, North Dakota colleges have to accept all applicants from state residents as long as they have a high school degree.

"North Dakota?"

"What if I can get you a job working on the largest newspaper in the state?"

"You mean while I'm going to school?"

"Sure. Go to school in the state's largest city; work on the largest newspaper between Minneapolis and Spokane; and graduate from a land-grant university. You'll lose some credits when you transfer; that can't be helped. So you'll probably spend two years in Fargo. But you will get two years of experience working on a good mid-size newspaper. You will get a degree from a respectable university. And you will avoid the draft while you're doing this."

"I can't say I'm enthusiastic about North Dakota. But I like the thought of walking out of here with a plan. I mean, ten minutes ago I was so depressed I thought of shooting myself. North Dakota can't be that bad, right?"

"You might even like it. About six hundred thousand people do."

"It's the nation's smallest state, right?"

"No, it's not. It's the least-visited state. But Alaska and Wyoming have fewer people."

"You probably know half the people who live there."

"I know many of them. And here is something I want you to understand. You and I have different names. I think it will be to our mutual benefit if folks in North Dakota don't know of our relationship. You go out there as Chuck Baker and establish yourself. Don't rely on me or my affiliation with the senator. I don't want anyone to find out that the senator's senior aide has a son whose political views differ so much from the typical North Dakota voter."

Pinks chuckles. Then it starts to hit Baker's funny bone, too, and they both laugh. Baker knows what his stepfather is really saying. He doesn't want Baker's screw-ups to embarrass either him or the senator.

"There is another advantage you'll have by moving to Fargo. By moving you into my property there, we can call it your legal residence. That will put you under the authority of the Cass County Draft Board. It already has access to a lot of good, patriotic boys wanting to fight for their country. I think you'll be left alone to finish college even if it takes you two more years."

"I have to admit, that's a real plus. I would sure like to finish college before I have to face my military obligation. Thank you."

"Finish your beer. You've got to get home and start making some plans. Figure on being out of your apartment by this weekend. I'll get you a plane ticket to Fargo. Plan to leave on Sunday. I'll make some calls to Fargo and see about a job on the *Forum*. I know a resident hotel near the newspaper office where you can stay. It will be up to you to figure out how to get back and forth to the campus from downtown. If you have anyone here you want to say goodbye to, do it before Sunday."

"One question, Jerry."

"Sure, what is it?"

"You seemed pissed at me until you read my article. Then you went and made a call. When you came back you were all pleasant and helpful. What gives?"

Pinks stares at the tabletop for a moment. Then he looks at his stepson.

"The congressman you outed? I know him. He has been a royal pain in the ass to the senator and me, no pun intended. He's led the opposition to a project that's of critical importance to North Dakota. It's called the Garrison Diversion. You'll undoubtedly hear about it when you're in North Dakota. We have been trying for over a year to get federal funding for it. Walker has held the program up, saying it's a boondoggle. Well, we won't have Walker around much longer. And that probably means our Garrison Diversion is going to become a reality. I called the senator with the good news. He says to tell you the whole state of North Dakota owes you a debt of gratitude."

Pinks pays for the drinks and watches his stepson leave. He'd lied to Chuck about calling the senator. It was a little lie told by a professional liar who doesn't blanch at the big ones and seldom remembers the little ones. He had called the senator's home, but only talked to his wife Pam. She said the senator was asleep. He said not to wake him; he would talk with the senator in the morning.

Then he'd placed the important call. He knew the number by heart. The phone rang on the desk of Andrew Bachevich, the chairman of the Red River Valley Sugar beet Cooperative, in Moorhead, Minnesota.

When the chairman answered, Pinks simply said: "Andy, this is Jerry. I've got some really good news for you." He told him about the newspaper story he was still holding in his hand.

The sugar beet chairman understood the implications. No explanation needed. "Wow," he chuckled a little. "Fortuitous. Thanks for the heads up, Jerry."

Pinks stands up, leaves the bar and heads toward the 17th Street entrance. He, too, enjoys the beauty of the hotel's magnificent long hallway. But instead of going out the door, he ducks down the stairwell to the basement level and into the men's room. He knows that men's room well. It has a reputation among homosexuals as an excellent place to make contact with one another.

Pinks would deny any homosexual tendencies. He's a married man and enjoys his heterosexual relationships. But something in his makeup keeps bringing him back to the Mayflower's restroom. He can't explain the attraction. He just knows he craves the adventure and enjoys the satisfaction of a successful encounter with a stranger who shares his lust. As he pushes open the bathroom door, he flashes onto Congressman Walker. Pinks wonders how the Alabama congressman would describe his similar compulsion.

Chapter Four

Indian Joe's Rage Turns Deadly

Accepting the fact that the bartender isn't likely to serve them another drink, Sara and Terri move away from the bar and join three regulars at their table. Sam, Mac, and Will are all in their late 40s or early 50s, but they look older. They are disabled World War II veterans who live off government pensions. The monthly checks provide them just enough to live on, as long as the living isn't fancy. They prefer drinking Wild Turkey whiskey and order it when some guilty flag waver who sat out the war buys them a round. When they pay for their own drinks, they order the bar whiskey and consequently have developed a taste for Early Times.

The three veterans have last names. They are printed on their government checks. But folks drinking Front Street liquor in an illegal bar on a Sunday never ask one another for their last names and never feel inclined to offer them.

The garrulous one is Sam, hobbled with crutches and a thirst for whiskey he can't quench. Mac supposedly has a metal plate in his head. At least that's the reason everyone gives for why he doesn't talk much. He does like to drink, though, and seems content to let Sam do most of the talking. Mac doesn't even appear to mind when Sam uses his money to buy the three an occasional round.

But Sam has to be careful around Mac. Earlier in the summer Sam got too generous with Mac's money and started buying rounds without asking first. After having skipped his turn to buy for what was probably the fourth time, Sam found out the hard way that Mac was keeping track. Sam was sitting at the bar next to Mac. Sam leaned over to his friend and began to pull dollar bills out of his billfold, saying, "It's your turn to buy, ol' buddy." That's when Mac hit him.

Others in the Blind Pig that night said it was the damnedest thing. Mac backhanded Sam across the mouth and sent him, his drink, and both crutches through the air into a table full of Mexicans. The table tipped over and sent the four of them and their drinks flying in all directions. There hadn't been that much excitement in the Blind Pig since a drunk farmer from Durbin, North Dakota, snuck a pistol into the place and shot holes into the bar before running out of ammunition.

The Mexicans clamored to their feet and pulled their knives. Their anger was understandable. They had worked a long week hoeing sugar beet and now this drunk had ruined their one afternoon off. Payback was to be expected.

Sam understood payback, but he wasn't sure how he was going to defend himself while lying on his back armed with only the one crutch he could reach. The fight never developed, though, thanks to Bodini's quick thinking. He saw what had happened and before the Mexicans could use their knives, he asked them to set their table back up so he could sit down a tray full of drinks for them, complimentary of the house. Even angry Mexicans will acknowledge that drinking free booze almost always has more appeal than cutting up a crippled drunk.

Sam struggled to his feet and after one of the Mexicans handed him his second crutch, he hobbled back to his bar seat. He sat down next to Mac. Sam smiled as he looked at his friend. Then Sam made a major production out of pulling his billfold from his back pocket. Once he had it on the bar, he stretched it open and pulled out a $5 bill.

He smiled again at Mac. Then he turned to Bodoni and said: "Barkeep, pour my two friends and me some whiskey. This round is on me." Bodini just rolled his eyes, but his two friends seemed to appreciate the hollow gesture.

For weeks the other regulars in the Blind Pig that night talked about what would have happened if Bodini hadn't plopped down those free drinks in front of the Mexicans. Most agreed they would have made short work of Sam. Then they would have gone after Mac and probably Will too.

When Sam is asked his opinion, he just smiles.

"For sure, they probably would have cut a hunk or two out of me. But I figure they would never have touched Mac. Have you ever had Mac give you the evil eye? You don't want to, let me tell you. That boy was an Army Ranger. He's a natural killer. Those Mexicans can sense it. They wouldn't have come at him."

Since the incident, some of the drinkers in the Blind Pig occasionally try to catch Mac's eye. But they don't want to be caught staring. They all agree: You get Mac irritated and he's likely to hurt you bad. Only a damn fool messes with an Army Ranger combat veteran with a metal plate in his skull.

Had they visited his room in the Hotel Donaldson, they would have seen evidence of his violent past. Mac's daughter had pinned his numerous medals of valor onto the American flag that she hung on one of his walls. Mac had been a killing machine trained by the Army and unleashed initially in North Africa. When that campaign ended, Mac was one of the first American soldiers into Italy. And he was on the front lines fighting his way into Germany when the war ended. At that point, the Army had to put him in irons to get his Browning Automatic Rifle (BAR) away from him. Killing was what he did and he insisted he wasn't finished. He spent nearly 10 years in a VA mental institution before he was considered safe to those around him. By then he talked only to himself.

Sam had been a highly decorated combat Marine in the Pacific. He had come to know plenty of killers. But he had been in Mac's room and seen his medals and Ranger patch. That told him all he needed to know. Sam knew that under certain circumstances, Mac would kill again.

Will buys rounds whenever Sam says it's his turn. Will is a thin, pale Army combat veteran of the Battle of the Bulge. He always looks as if someone evil has just turned on the juice to wires attached to his scrotum. His eyes bug out, his nose runs constantly, and he shakes all over. He can't stand noise or bright lights. Car horns torment him. So do headlight beams. And he spends the day in his room and slips out only after dark to drink with veterans he considers friends.

Some of the other regulars have thought about trying to become members of the veterans' drinking club, but are never quite sure how to broach the subject. Sam, for his part, always tells everyone that before sitting down with the group they first have to get Mac's permission. But Sam also says he doubts that Mac will welcome the intrusion. So the veterans' drinking club only consists of its three founders.

The three live in a resident hotel and bond because of their military service and mutual love of whiskey. They look out for each other, too. They help one another get to their appointments at the Veterans Administration Hospital, for example, and they leave no one behind after a night of heavy drinking.

On this pleasant Sunday evening in late August, 1965, they are enjoying the company of the two young women who just joined them. Their glasses are empty, but Bodini has already said the likelihood of them getting another drink is about as good as a snowball's chances of surviving hell. The veterans take some comfort in the fact the closed bar means they have no social obligation to buy the ladies a drink.

The five of them sit around their table enjoying each other's company as drinkers often do after "last call" has sounded. They are all wrapped up in that cozy feeling that bars provide their regulars at closing time. They savor this special time like the last drop or two in a glass, because they all realize that the sheer boredom of the life they had before they entered the Blind Pig will smother them like a wet blanket again as soon as they walk out the door.

Across the room Joe Running Deer sits alone neither thinking about joining any veterans' group or having someone buy him a drink. He's thinking only about fucking the blonde woman sitting with the regulars. He wants to kill her, too. But later; first he wants to have his way with her.

He doesn't think it should be a challenge for a Mandan Indian with a pocket full of money. Joe Running Deer is certain she is a whore; what other reason would a white woman be drinking in an illegal bar on a Sunday afternoon? Besides, somebody already told him she was. Even showed him a picture of her. But she's still ignoring him. Bitch.

He doesn't want to approach her while she's drinking with her friends. But he knows the bartender is about to close the bar. If he is going to have the whore, he has to move fast.

That's when he stumbles to his feet and stands behind Sara. "Let's go do it. I'm ready."

The "ready" comment brings a grin to Bodini's face. He had noticed earlier that the drunk Indian had been standing at the bar rubbing his crotch hard. The bartender now realizes the Indian was simply getting himself "ready."

Mac frowns at the Indian. The veteran doesn't like him and wants him to leave. He threatens to ruin everyone's good time. Soon the bar will close, and Mac will be alone again in his hotel room with his cheap radio with nothing to do but hope it plays for him a Patsy Cline song. Goddamn Indian. Mac starts to think about how best to scare the Indian away.

Sara recognizes the Indian. When she first walked in she noticed him staring at her. She ignored him. She knows men stare at her all the time. But her friend Terri told her to watch herself: "That Indian is looking to get laid."

When Sara doesn't say anything to him, Joe throws down a wadded $20 bill in front of her. She looks at it. She doesn't want sex with this guy. But she is thinking, he's dead drunk; there's no way he's going to be able to screw a light bulb, let alone her. Besides, Bodini is going to throw everyone out in a few minutes. Sara concludes this could be the easiest $20 she'll earn all year.

She tucks the bill away in her purse and hands it to Terri. Sara pushes back her chair, smiling: "I'll be back in five minutes; Terri, watch my purse for me." And she looks at Joe and says, "Come on Chief, let's get this over with."

Chuckles erupt from around the table at the open exchange and Mac relaxes. He doesn't want to hurt the Indian if he is Sara's friend.

Sara walks into the next room and Joe stumbles after her. The back room, which normally serves as an overflow lounge during busy hours, is Sara's bordello tonight.

She looks at Joe with disgust, sighs, and then peels off her panties and bunches them in her right hand. She then bends her face down over a table and flips up her dress, exposing her bottom to Joe. "Come on Tonto, you Indians like it doggie style, right?"

He did. But this isn't right. This isn't what he had imagined when he was standing at the bar rubbing his crotch. He looks at her white fanny. He figures she is bending over the table with her rear in the air just to avoid kissing him. That makes him furious.

Goddamn it, he is paying for the sex. If he wants a kiss, he ought to be able to get one. But with her lying doggie style, he knows that kiss is never going to happen.

Joe's head quickly fills with thoughts of how he can hurt Sara. Normally he welcomes such thoughts. But Joe's head has a limited capacity for complex thinking. So as he fills it with the details of how he is going to hurt Sara, he has to dump all of the hard-earned mental preparation he requires to get himself ready to have sex.

He shakes his head to clear it of the intruding thoughts. He tells himself he really doesn't want to hurt her. He wants to get laid. Sure, that's what he wants. She can lie on her stomach. He can do it that way.

Joe tries to think about his sister and all the funky things they did together when they were kids, but it doesn't help his preparation any. They never had sex doggie style. He drops his pants and pushes down his underwear. Ignoring the stink that rises up to envelope the two of them, he rams himself up against Sara. He shuts his eyes to concentrate better. He reaches forward and grabs Sara by the hips with both hands and begins pumping his thighs and limp organ against her warm rump.

"This isn't working. For Christ's sake, Cochise, you're going to make me all black and blue. Stop it."

After a few minutes of grunting and butt slapping, Joe stops. He is drunk and frustrated and now feeling stupid pressed up against a half-naked lady exhibiting all the passion of a papoose.

"We're done, Tonto."

She stands up, turns around, and drops her dress back into place. Then she hikes her fanny up on the table and lifts both feet up above her waist. Then she kicks him away from her.

Joe stumbles backwards, trips over the clothing knotted at his ankles, and falls on the floor. He isn't hurt. But his sense of honor suffers a terrible bruising. As he struggles to his feet, grabbing at his clothes, he realizes that the whole Mandan Indian Nation needs to be avenged for the way the white whore has insulted one of its warriors.

As he straps his belt around his waist, he feels the knife he always wears at his side. It is a large hunting knife with a handle made out of an antler's horn. Most Indians carry similar knifes. They joke among themselves that warriors have such knives in case an occasion presents itself to scalp a deserving white man. When they are alone, drinking together, they reassure each other they never joke about their knives' purpose.

Joe has a history with knives, all bad. The first time he got caught cutting someone he was in the 5th grade. That landed him in the Mandan Reformatory School. There he had his first opportunity to meet children from Indian reservations other than his own. The second time was when he put his knife into the back of another Fort Berthold Indian. The man was lying on top of a woman Joe thought belonged to him. The Indian lived, and Joe got off with only 10 years in the state pen. That stint gave him the opportunity to get well acquainted with Indians from all of the major North Dakota reservations, including the Chippewa from Turtle Mountain, Dakota from Standing Rock, Spirit Lake, and Lake Traverse, and fellow tribesmen, including his own Mandan tribe, as well as Hidatsa and Arikara, from his home reservation at Fort Berthold.

Sara scoots off the table and uses both hands to hike up her panties. Joe reaches for his knife and punches it, blade side up, deep into her stomach. It slides in easily, which takes Joe by surprise. He closes his eyes and tries to compare it to the sensation he had felt when he had stabbed the Indian. He seems to recall that knife thrust had met with more resistance. Now he isn't sure what to do next. The mind slows down when the body is under stress.

Joe stands there gripping the knife buried in Sara waiting for insight to guide his next move. A movie he had once seen came to mind. A tough guy in a similar position had jerked his knife upward in a sawing motion. This enabled the knife to slice through internal organs, inflicting maximum pain while guaranteeing death. Once Joe's booze-soaked brain has a plan of action, his body obediently executes it.

Sara opened her mouth wide open, but didn't say a word. She probably would not have chosen to share her last thoughts with Joe anyway. She falls against him and Joe feels her warmth gush out onto his Levi jacket and pants. It isn't an unpleasant feeling. But in a minute, he is struck by the smell of the blood as well as the contents of her bowels as they leave her body. He lets go of his knife. It and Sara slide to the floor in front of him. He watches as blood seeps all around her and his shoes. He thinks for a moment about being sick, but fights it off as a strong warrior does.

He wills himself to walk away. But he wants his knife back first. The man who sold it to him had given him a leather sheath with colorful beads sewn on it and long leather strips with silver tips on their ends that move when he does. The sheath attaches to his belt. He can't walk around with an empty sheath. No brave does that. So he yanks his knife from Sara's body and plunges it, with all her dampness clinging to it, back into his decorative sheath. Then he tries to think his way out of the predicament he is in. He can't. Thinking his way out of trouble is not one of Joe Running Deer's strengths. In fact, it has always been his glaring weakness.

Best he can do is to say "shit" over and over again as he moves out of the room and back into the bar.

Sara's companions have been waiting for him. Actually, they expected Sara to show first. They figured the Indian would want to take some time to gather his wits about him before emerging with a story about how he really didn't want to get laid anyway.

They are stunned to silence when they see the Indian come out of the room with his jacket and pants soaked in blood. He stumbles past them through the bar, fumbles with the lock on the door, and then pushes his way out into the back alley behind Front Street.

While everyone sits paralyzed, Bodini slips into the back room to investigate. "Oh my God," he says out loud, and then crosses himself and thinks again about how he has to start going to church more regularly.

He rushes back into the lounge and says to the stragglers: "Listen to me. The Indian gutted Sara. She's hurt, really bad. I'll take care of it. All of you, get out of here. You were never here today, understand? You were never here. You don't want to be involved in this. Now leave."

Everybody in the bar that evening has several good reasons why they don't want to be hauled into the police department for questioning, particularly involving a killing. Sam, Mac and Will struggle out together. They feel terrible about what just happened to that poor girl.

Sam looks at his friends. They clearly are as shook up as he is.

"That was horrible, just horrible," says Will.

"I'm telling you, as soon as things start going right in your life, somebody comes along and screws it up big time," says Sam as he hobbles along on his crutches.

"How soon do you suppose we can go back to the Blind Pig?" asks Will.

"I don't know," says Sam, "I suppose we probably ought to stay away for a couple of weeks just to be on the safe side. Let's remember to get a couple of bottles this week so we have them for next Sunday. We don't want to be caught short."

Mac doesn't say anything, as usual. His buddies don't know if he is worrying about where he is going to get liquor next Sunday or thinking about the pretty girl the Indian has just stabbed.

He isn't thinking about either of those things. He is thinking he wished he had been able to process what was happening quicker. He wished he had jumped to his feet when the Indian came out of the room with blood soaking his clothes. He wished he had stopped him. Then he began to wonder what he could use to kill him.

Terri Squires gets into her car that she had parked down the block on 4th Street. As she drives away, she cries all the way back to the trailer park. Then she sits in her car for an hour before going in because she doesn't want her appearance to upset the kids.

During that hour she wonders what she should do with Sara's purse. She figures Sara would want her to have the $16 and pocket change in it, plus the Indian's crumpled $20 bill. She doesn't want Sara's lipstick because it is the wrong color for her. Outside of a pack of Juicy fruit gum, there isn't anything else of value in the bag. Sara always mooched her cigarettes, and she didn't even carry her own Zippo. On the way into her trailer, Terri dumps the purse into her garbage can, knowing it will be picked up by the trash hauler Monday morning. Terri doesn't know if throwing away the purse is the right thing to do. But she knows she will feel creepy with a dead woman's purse lying around her house.

After his customers clear out, Bodini again locks the door from the inside, packs up all the glasses, cleans the ashtrays, and puts the liquor bottles into a locked cabinet.

When he finishes, the place looks as if it hasn't been used in a week. Except, of course, for Sara Whitlow's bled-out body in the other room. He walks into a tunnel that leads into a small room. He unlocks a door and goes up the stairs where he unlocks another door and enters the Silver Saloon. He locates the payphone in the dark, puts in a dime, and places his call.

When the phone is answered at the other end, Bodini says: "Captain, this is Sam. I'm sorry for bothering you at home. But we had a little problem in the Pig tonight.

Chapter Five

Fargo Isn't an Easy Sell

The pilot of the DC-3 doesn't seem to be in any more of a hurry to reach North Dakota than his passenger in 2A. Twenty thousand feet below lies the Minnesota Lake Country. As the plane passes over, the sun bounces off the surface of the water and throws a bright beam skyward into Chuck Baker's window. He looks down and realizes he is looking at several dozen of Minnesota's famous 10,000 lakes.

Baker stretches in his cramped, single window seat and smiles as he thinks of Paul Bunyan and his blue ox Babe. He hasn't thought about that tall tale since reading it as a child. He chuckles to himself. He recalls that the story of Paul Bunyan had been written by a newspaperman. As he remembers it, a giant logger and his big axe had the job of clearing the forest that engulfed major portions of Minnesota and Wisconsin. As he worked, his boots created crevices in the muddy earth. When they eventually filled with rainwater, lakes resulted.

No, that's not exactly right, Baker decides. The ox had something to do with it. Maybe the lakes were created when Babe went thrashing around as he hauled away the logs Paul had chopped down. Either way, Baker concludes, somebody must have stomped around plenty because the landscape below his plane is laden with a lot of large earthen impressions full of water.

Baker then recalls that someplace up in Northern Minnesota, there is a town with an honest-to-goodness statue of Paul Bunyan and Babe. He tries to remember the town's name, but can't. Then he thinks he's confusing it with a town in Michigan. It too has a statue of Paul Bunyan. This one, Baker remembers, is the "official home" of the giant logger. Well, official because that's what the State of Michigan calls it. Seems the local newspaper in the town carried the first story of Paul back around the turn of the century.

Go to Washington, visit Abe and Tom; go to Minnesota and Michigan, visit Paul and his ugly blue ox.

Geez, he is already losing his mind and he hasn't even arrived in North Dakota yet.

He figures it will take him the rest of the summer to come to grips with the fact he no longer lives and works in Washington, D.C., or attends George Washington University, or has a promising career at the *Washington Star*.

God, North Dakota. On his last night in Washington his fraternity brothers took him to Luigi's for pizza and beer. It's his favorite Italian restaurant in the city and he's been going there since he was a kid. It has a full menu, but he can't remember ever ordering anything but pizza.

When he told his fraternity brothers he was leaving for North Dakota, they thought he was kidding. Most claimed they didn't even know where it was. A lot of them were from New

Jersey, but still, Chuck assumed a few might have an inkling about which states border onto North Dakota. He even gave them a clue. He told them one of the border states had "Dakota" in its name. But that just seemed to add to their geographical confusion.

The best they could do was place North Dakota somewhere near Canada between Ohio and Oregon. Nobody had ever heard of Fargo. Not even Tony, and he is the brightest of his friends.

Being students at a private university, they were completely unimpressed with the fact he's transferring to a state school. And the land-grant designation meant nothing to them.

His fraternity brothers around the tables at Luigi's did think it was cool, though, that Baker had managed to flunk out of college at the end of his fourth year. Nobody could recall anyone ever having done that. There was talk about creating a special "goat" award for him and putting it in the fraternity's trophy case

Burguess, his *Washington Star* city editor, was clearly upset when the GW president's letter about Chuck's failing grades came down from the editor through the managing editor to his desk.

The editor had written on the letter: "Why does this guy still work here?"

Harrison, the managing editor, wrote underneath the editor's comment: "Get rid of him after we wrap up this queer business."

Burguess soon found Baker at his desk. "Come on kid, let's go get a drink."

It wasn't how Baker had expected to get the boot. Nevertheless, he was already enough of a newspaperman to know that bad news would go down easier accompanied by a drink.

Once they got to the nearest bar—a little dive just around the corner—Burguess started out by telling Baker that in his day, reporters didn't need a college degree.

"Hell, I don't think they need one now. I want writers, not scholars. Goddamn it. I hire college graduates all the time and what do they do? They hang around a few years, learn the business, and then go to work for some damn PR. firm. Or they become a flack for some congressman. We train them and then they go off to make the big bucks someplace else shoveling bullshit back at us. Give me college dropouts who want to comfort the afflicted and afflict the comforted. Then I'll give you a Pulitzer Prize winning newspaper every year."

Baker agreed with him and had the presence of mind to order a second round. He noticed the city editor drank expensive single malt scotch on the rocks.

"I'm sorry I've got to let you go kid. You did a hell of a job on that congressman story. The first edition ought to be coming off the presses as we sit here. Your story is on page one. It's a goddamn shame it's the last time you'll ever see your byline in the *Star*. Best of luck to you."

Burguess stood up, grabbed his drink, and tossed it down in one quick swallow, befitting a newspaperman of his experience. Baker was left sitting at the bar with his second beer in front of him. The beer wasn't lonely long. The bartender slapped the bar tab down alongside it.

Baker went back to the newspaper and cleaned out his desk. As he left the building, he picked up a dozen copies of the first edition of *The Star*. His story ran above the fold in the left two columns under the headline, "Homosexual Sting Operation Snares Alabama Congressman." And there was his byline: "By Charles Baker, Washington Star Staff Writer."

They may have fired him, but he figured a front-page, bylined story was one hell of a going-away present.

He was pleased to see there were only a few, minor editorial changes to his story. The newspaper's congressional reporter obviously hadn't gotten anything out of his sources, so Baker was the sole author. With his story in print, the combined weight of the Washington and New York media will force the House leadership to say something about the sordid affair. But that will be somebody else's story, much to Baker's lament.

As his plane nears Fargo, he wonders how the *Forum* played his story. The topic might not be considered big news out in the prairie states. And the *Forum* probably won't want to offend its readers by describing a Republican congressman's homosexual actions. Besides, why would anybody in North Dakota be interested in the problems of an Alabama congressman?

"Attention ladies and gentlemen," booms a confident, masculine voice over the intercom. "This is your pilot speaking. We're approaching Fargo. We should be landing in about fifteen minutes. Please extinguish your cigarettes or other smoking materials, finish your drinks and fasten your seatbelts. Your stewardess will be by to pick up your trash momentarily. Thank you for flying North Central Airlines."

Baker glances out the window again and notices the lakes are gone. So are the trees. A lush, flat prairie under cultivation has replaced them. Large squares of green are interspaced with occasional squares of gold. Every inch of ground seems to be growing something. The plane sinks lower and the propeller motors change pitch. The pilot is about to land the plane. This makes Baker a little nervous. He can see nothing out of the right-hand side of the plane that suggests either an airport or a town.

The plane crosses over a river. Actually, thinks Baker, it's probably called a creek. It is too narrow and sluggish to be a river. Of course, he's in the habit of comparing every river to the Potomac. Now that's a river. This is barely a stream. The ribbon of water below him twists and turns on itself like a sidewinder snake. This creek obviously is struggling to find a downward slope that will enable it to drain what must be the Red River Valley.

Suddenly the plane banks left and dips even lower. He still hasn't spotted a town, but for sure a landing is imminent. It has to be the Fargo airport; the stewardess' demeanor doesn't suggest a crash landing. He spots a cemetery as the plane comes in even lower. Then the plane touches down on a long runway and rolls and rolls. The pilot is determined to use every last inch of it. At the very end, he turns the plane around slowly and taxies back to a turnoff that leads to a terminal.

When the two propeller engines shut down, a relaxing quiet creeps through the plane's interior. At first it seems to Baker that the travelers are relieved to have landed safely. They smile and nod at one another as they gather their belongings. But then Baker realizes it isn't a sense of survival that bonds the passengers. It's a shared feeling of adventure. Each of them has their own reasons for flying to this remote outpost, a place so forlorn that most Americans couldn't explain how to get there. The passengers are not exactly sure what awaits them when that plane door opens. But they are convinced it won't be like where they came from. And that thought makes them all a little giddy.

Baker thinks he knows just how Lewis and Clark must have felt when they first entered the state 163 years before.

He is anxious to get off the plane. It's his third flight of the day. He left in the morning from National Airport in suburban Washington, D.C., on a Northwest flight to Chicago. That was the first time he'd ever ridden in an actual jet, one of the brand new McDonnell-Douglas DC-9s. He liked how it pinned you to the back of your seat when it took off. After a short layover in Chicago, he caught another DC-9 Northwest flight to Minneapolis. Once there, he sat at the airport for three hours and then boarded a smaller, old prop plane—a Convair 440, he's pretty sure—for this North Central flight to Fargo.

He grabs his carry-on out of the open overhead bin, bends back down and glances back out the window. The stairs are just now rolling across the tarmac, toward the plane. Geesh. They're not in a rush up here, are they? He feels the floor rock just a little when the stairs finally push up against the outside of the plane. He looks down the aisle toward the front and sees the stewardess open the door. Sunlight streams in. He glances at his watch. It's 7 p.m., but the sky is still bright, like maybe 4 p.m. back in Washington this time of year, the middle of summer. Definitely closer to the North Pole, he thinks.

As he finally steps outside and starts walking down the stairs, Baker is nearly swept off his feet by the strong breeze blowing across the tarmac. Hector Airfield isn't much, but about what he expects. The terminal is a two-story affair with large windows on the first floor that provide outgoing passengers, and those waiting with them, a chance to watch what is happening out on the airfield. The double doors into the terminal line up with similar double doors across the lobby that open into the parking lot. The waiting room and luggage pick-up are off to the right.

The military presence surprises him. Hangers surrounding the terminal advertise the home of the North Dakota Air National Guard. Baker concludes the Air National Guard must be a big deal locally. Just as he's thinking that, two jet fighters taxi-out in front of the terminal and head onto the runway. That explains why it's so long; it has to accommodate fighter jets. He knows nothing about such aircraft. But to him, these two fighters look modern and lethal.

The two planes have "Happy Hooligans" written on their tails. That means nothing to Baker. But he assumes it must be the group's nickname.

Inside the terminal, as he waits for his luggage, he reads a plaque on the wall.

HAPPY HOOLIGANS

DUANE LARSON WAS THE SQUADRON COMMANDER DURING THE 1950S AND WAS NICKNAMED "PAPPY" BECAUSE HE WAS THE SENIOR FIGHTER PILOT. THERE WAS A CARTOON AT THE TIME CALLED "PAPPY EASTER AND HIS HAPPY HOOLIGANS" AND THE SQUADRON STATED CALLING THEMSELVES "PAPPY LARSON AND HIS HAPPY HOOLIGANS." THE SQUADRON HAS BEEN CALLED THE HAPPY HOOLIGANS EVER SINCE.

NORTH DAKOTA AIR NATIONAL GUARD

Just then he hears the two fighter jets scream into the air, one right after the other. Some of his fellow passengers waiting for their luggage turn to gawk out the large windows at the front of the terminal, enjoying the spectacle. Baker figures the locals must feel pretty damn secure knowing the Happy Hooligans are protecting them from a sudden sneak attack by Canada, just a hundred or so miles to the north.

The luggage eventually arrives and he picks up his two suitcases. With them and his two carry-on pieces he goes trundling out the front door, where he finds a single cab waiting. Unfortunately, he isn't the first person to spot it. A guy carrying a briefcase is just climbing into the back seat. When the driver notices Baker, he pulls up alongside him and says, "You waiting for a cab?"

When Baker nods his head in agreement, the driver asks: "Where you going?"

"Downtown."

"Well, hop in. My fare is going to the north side and I'll drop you off after him. You don't mind, do you mister?"

The guy seems to understand the system. "Not a bit; hop in."

Baker walks around behind the Checker, opens the trunk, and throws in his two bags. He then carefully places his portable typewriter and carry-on bag alongside his suitcases. Then he slides into the back seat. He recognizes the guy next to him as a fellow passenger from his flight.

"Thanks for sharing. I think we were on the same flight in from Minneapolis."

"Yeah, I usually catch that flight this time of day. I don't recognize you. Are you from around here?"

"No, I'm new in town. I'm here to work at the *Forum*. My name's Chuck Baker."

"Glad to meet you. My name's Wayne Gautier. I work for the extension service at the AC. I mean, the SU. I have to get into the habit of calling it by its official name."

"Boy, you've got to help me out here," Baker replies. "I don't know anything about the initials "AC" nor what an extension service does."

"Well, extension service is part of the U.S. Department of Agriculture. We are affiliated with the nation's land grant colleges. We do research and basically help the farmers get better crop yields, raise bigger hogs, make more money, and live happier lives."

Gautier chuckles when he says it.

Baker likes him immediately. But then he generally likes people who don't take themselves or their work too seriously.

"The AC refers to the name of the college. Up until two years ago it was called the North Dakota Agricultural College. Then the voters responded to a lobbying effort by some downtown Fargo interests and changed the name to North Dakota State University. So it's no longer the AC; it's now the SU. Some of us ag guys have just been a little slow to accept the change."

"Thank you. That's helpful. I plan to take some courses at the SU while I'm here."

"What in, if I may ask?"

"Well, not agriculture," Baker smiled, "although my lack of knowledge of the subject would suggest I should. I plan on taking some social science courses."

"At NDSU? I'm afraid we're not noted for our excellence in the arts and sciences.

"What are the university's strengths?"

"Agriculture, of course. But also engineering, chemistry, pharmacy, home economics. I'd say just about everything but social sciences."

"That's just my luck. I'm transferring in from George Washington University and I only need a few credits to complete my degree. I guess I'll look around and see what I can pick up in agriculture."

"You say you're working at the *Forum*? If you're a journalist, then check out the Ag Communication courses. They're primarily for students who want to be extension agents. They ought to be a snap for you. Well, here's my stop. Oh, let me give you a card. Stop by my office when you get settled on campus. You may need a friend. The place can be a little unfriendly to foreigners, which is anyone living more than 50 miles outside of North Dakota."

"Thanks, I appreciate it."

Chuck looks at the simple business card.

> **Wayne Gautier, PhD**
> Department Chair
> Agricultural & Biosystems Department
> NDSU Extension Service
> Merrill Hall, Rm. 123
> (701) 231-8011, ext. 123
> North Dakota State University
> Fargo, North Dakota

Impressive, thinks Baker, even though he has no idea what Gautier does when he goes to work in the morning.

"Where are you going, son?" asks the cab driver.

"Oh, sorry. I'm heading to the Hotel Donaldson."

The cab driver turns around in his seat and looks at his lone passenger. "You sure you got that right? The Donaldson?"

"I'm sure. I'm renting a room there long-term while I work at the *Forum*. I understand it's only a block away."

"That's true enough," says the cab driver, turning back to his steering wheel. "And the Donaldson does rent out rooms long term. You just surprised me when you said that's where you want to go. I don't think I've ever picked up anyone from the airport and taken him to the Donaldson, that's all. It's more of a resident hotel than the kind of place out-of-town visitors stay."

"Is it a decent hotel?"

"I guess that depends on your definition of 'decent.' At one time it was a real popular hotel. But for the last 20 years or so it pretty much just rents rooms to old men living off government pensions. I wouldn't call it a flea trap. But it wouldn't have to lose much of its luster to be one."

That's just great, thinks Baker. I'm moving to this shithole town and now I find I'm going to be living in an ass-wipe hotel. Jerry said it wasn't the Ritz, but he said it was adequate. He said it was probably all I could afford on what the *Forum* was likely to pay me. He also said he owned the place. I guess I figured that meant it was probably a decent hotel. I don't know why I thought anything Jerry Pinks owns would be a class joint.

Baker's attention is drawn to his surroundings as the cab continues driving down Broadway. He notices a mixture of small, insignificant homes and then later, closer to downtown, some large, older homes. Mixed in are some large churches and small businesses. Then he rides through an intersection with a large Lutheran Church on the left and across a square on the right an even larger Catholic Church. Then they cross some railroad tracks, which surprises him. Tracks mean trains run right through the center of town, right across its busiest street. That seems strange. Wouldn't that disrupt traffic?

Along the tracks off to the left stands a large, attractive train station. At the top is a round sign with a red border encasing a white mountain goat and the words "Great Northern Railway." On the right he notices a large neon sign over a bar called the "Bismarck." Strange, he thought, that a bar in Fargo, on the border with Minnesota, would be named after the capital city, located a couple hundred miles to the west, in the middle of the state.

Another block further down into the business district, he sees a reputable looking hotel on his right. He's disappointed when the cab drives by it. Then his eye catches the marquee of a large movie theater: "Fargo." That makes sense. Name your largest bar "Bismarck" and compensate for it by naming your largest movie theater "Fargo."

In the next block he sees what actually looks like a large building. He knows it's tall because it is the first one he has passed where he can't see the top floor while sitting in the cab. He notices the name as he goes by: The Black Building.

Then it hits him. Fargo's Broadway looks like most of the commercial strips in his hometown of Arlington, Va., which means streets of mostly two-story buildings with a few taller ones mixed in to give the town some urban class.

The cab abruptly does a U-turn in the middle of Broadway and stops in front of an old hotel with a sign hanging on the corner that should say "Donaldson" in large neon lights. But the bulbs in the "D" are out, so the sign reads "onaldson." Baker wonders how long it has been like that.

He can see into the lobby from the Broadway side but he can't see any entrance to the hotel. As he pays the cab driver, he asks, "How do I get into the hotel?"

"Oh, the door is over on First Avenue, just around the corner. Need any help with your bags?"

The cab driver's offer of assistance isn't made with any hint that it should be taken seriously. He remains firmly ensconced behind the steering wheel. Baker opens the trunk and takes out his two suitcases. He knows he's going to need more clothes than two suitcases hold and he's counting on his mother to ship him some once he gets settled.

Before he drives off, the cabbie hands Baker his card. "Cab service is pretty slow in this town. Us drivers tend to be pretty independent. We all have our regular clients. That doesn't give us much time to go answering calls from strangers. But you and I are not strangers anymore. I heard you say you're going to be attending classes up at the SU. You don't have a car, best I can tell. Which means you might be needing cab service. That about right?"

"I haven't actually thought about it. I don't know how far away from campus I am. I thought I might walk it."

The cabbie laughs.

"Oh, you might walk it now and then, this time of year. But you won't be walking it come winter. No sir. You'd freeze your fanny for sure walking it then. No, you'll want a cab. Anyway, think it over. You've got my number there. We can probably work out an arrangement about price too."

"Thanks," says Baker. "I'll give it some thought."

Baker knows something about winters in North Dakota. His mother has regaled him more than once with the story about her last trip to the state. But today, at the end of July, North Dakota is hot and humid. A breeze out of the north is the only thing that keeps it from being insufferable. He doubts if the virtues of air conditioning have caught on in this part of the country yet.

He looks at the card. David Behrie. Yellow Cab. The card has two numbers. One for the cab company is in small print. But one for his personal phone is in large print. "Customized Service for our Premier Customers" reads the card.

Baker has been in Fargo less than an hour and has already collected two business cards. He knows, somehow, both will come in handy, eventually.

He lugs his two large suitcases plus his tape recorder and portable typewriter around to the side of the hotel where a large two-door entrance awaits him. He can see that at one time the establishment had indeed been a grand hotel. But not anymore. He wonders to himself how long his stepfather has owned it. Then he wonders why.

Baker pushes his way through the double doors and into a pleasant looking lobby. He immediately picks up the smell of stale tobacco and old furniture. He glances around and sees, appropriately enough, old, stuffed couches, equally ancient leather chairs, and institutional ashtrays full of cigarette and cigar butts. The lobby comes by its odors honestly.

A small, thin man emerges from a room behind the registration desk. He gives his potential new client a look that says: "You'd probably be happier staying somewhere else."

"May I help you?"

"You sure can," replies Baker, trying to sound friendly. "I believe you have a reservation in my name. Charles Baker."

"Oh yes," says the thin man, with a little less chill in his voice. But still a strong German accent. "Charles Baker. We have been expecting you. You are from Washington, D.C., if I recall. Moving back here to work at the *Forum*. Yes, here it is."

He pulls a 3x7 card out of a file folder and shows it momentarily to Baker.

"I see here your first month's rent has already been paid. But I understand you will be handing the account yourself from then on, is that correct?"

"Yes, that's correct."

Well then, the rent is due on the 1st of the month. In your case, that will be September 1. There are no exceptions. If you are late in your payment by more than two days, we will be forced to evict you. If that occurs, we will box up your possessions and place them alongside the garbage cans back in the alley. The garbage is collected twice a week, Monday and Friday."

"Don't worry. I'll be paying on time."

"Good. Then we'll have no problem there."

"We run a decent establishment here. Most of our guests have been with us for some time. If you have any questions about the hotel rules, you can ask any of them. But our rules are quite simple.

"One, no smoking in your room. You are allowed to smoke only in the bar or in the lobby. The bar is closed for renovation."

"Is it expected to open soon?"

"Actually, it has been closed for the past five years. I really don't think the owners have any plans to reopen it anytime soon."

"Oh, I see," says Baker. That's a drag, he thinks silently.

"Two, no cooking in your room. Our wiring isn't sufficient to handle the wattage for hotplates. Their use may cause a fire. If we find you cooking, we will evict you.

"Three, no prostitutes in the rooms. We are not interested in policing the morals of our hotel guests. However, we do not want ladies of the evening parading through our hotel at all hours of the night. If you have a regular lady friend, introduce her to us at the front desk. That way the staff will recognize her and welcome her on the premises. If she comes in and leaves with you, then an infrequent visit now and then is acceptable.

If it appears she has moved in with you, however, we will ask her to leave. This is a resident hotel for men only.

"Four, no fighting. You will be sharing a bathroom down the hallway from your room with five other guests. That sometimes can lead to conflict. We all recognize that sharing bathroom facilities can put a strain on relationships. We expect everyone to act like adults and to be understanding of each other's needs. If on the other hand you resort to fisticuffs, we will have to ask you to leave.

"I think that is enough rules to get started."

Baker had given a lot of thought to the trials and tribulations that probably awaited him in North Dakota. And yet, somehow, the trials and tribulations of sharing a bathroom in a fleabag hotel had never occurred to him. It now is number one on his list.

"What do your guests do about bedding and towels? Is there maid service?"

Even as he asks the questions, he dreads hearing the answer.

"There is no maid service. Each guest is responsible for tidying his own room. Once a week you will get fresh linens and towels. Of course, you will have to turn in your soiled linens and towels to get the fresh ones. We have some guests who prefer to go a month before making the switch. We don't recommend this option, however. After a month's use, you have bought your linens from the hotel and the cost is added to your rent. After six weeks of use, we come in and strip your bed before you foul the mattress."

"Okay, I guess that's all my questions for now. Can I see my room?"

"Certainly. It's room 204. We have an elevator, but most of our guests choose to use the stairs. They are right there in front of you. Here is your key. Why don't you go up? I'll have Mule bring your luggage up in a minute. And oh, by the way, my name is Hans Stutzman. I am the manager here at the Donaldson. Please take a minute to introduce yourself to the other staff when you see a new face behind the desk."

Thank you, Mr. Stuzman. I'll do that."

"We're like family here, Charles. Please call me Hans. I have known your stepfather for a very long time."

"Oh, I didn't know you were aware of our relationship."

"I'm not, officially. He called to tell me you would be checking in and to treat you like any other guest. But that is impossible, of course. You are the owner's son. I will keep that information private. But you will see, you have a very nice room. And if you need anything special, come to me directly. Nobody else on staff knows of your relationship to Mr. Pinks. Do you need anything that you know of?"

"No, but I appreciate you asking, Hans."

Baker goes up the stairs, gets to the landing and looks back down at his luggage. Hans is still standing there, smiling up at him. Baker smiles back and goes up the next set of stairs to the second floor. He turns right and comes immediately to his room. He is pleased to see it is on the street side of the building. He was dreading being housed in a room looking over an alley.

The door swings open to a large room. The bed is a double, with two large pillows, a blanket and a quilt folded at the foot of it. A dresser sits in one corner and a leather reading chair similar to those in the lobby sits in another. Under one window is a small table with two chairs. It will be suitable for eating meals he brings into the hotel and for doing his schoolwork. He checks under the table. The wall behind it has an electrical outlet handy. He can put a lamp on the table and work at his typewriter there. Otherwise, the only light in the room is the one in the ceiling. He mentally tells himself to buy some decent reading lamps.

There is no closet, but against one wall the hotel has installed some closet rods where he can hang his clothes. He's just wondering how far he has to go to reach the bathroom when he hears a thud at the door. Ah, he says, my luggage.

He opens the door to find a short, middle-aged man with one of his bags under each arm.

Baker just stares at him. The bald man can't be five feet tall. And he has to be nearly that wide. He obviously has worked up a sweat hauling the two bags up the stairs. He is wearing dark slacks and a white T-shirt. Pinned to it is a metal name tag that says Donaldson Hotel and, beneath that, his name: John.

"Here, I'll take them," Baker says.

"Tell me where you want 'em, I'll put 'em there."

"Anywhere is fine," Baker responds, as he steps aside so the man can enter the room.

He huffs and puffs his way into the room and drops the bags at the foot of the bed. He takes a deep breath and then turns to leave. By then Baker has a dollar bill in his hand.

"Here," he says. "Thanks for bringing them up."

"You're welcome," the man responds, as he grabs the buck and lumbers out the door.

Wow. He's an interesting guy, thinks Baker, as he wonders why Hans would call a short, wide guy "Mule?" With that thought in mind, Baker opens the door again and heads down the hallway to where he assumes he'll find a bathroom. He is right; two doors down on the left is a bathroom. He tries the door and it opens. It contains two toilets, two sinks, one large mirror, and enough room for two people as long as they are getting along. He goes back out and notices on the door the letter "B." He walks the length of the hall and finds five more bathrooms, "A" through "F". He thinks of his college transcript.

The floor contains 30 rooms. He notices the stairway goes up another floor. Curious, he goes up only to find what looks like a mirror image of the floor he is on. He goes back down to his room, shuts the door, and begins unpacking. For better or for worse, the Donaldson is going to be home for the next two years.

It's finally starting to turn dark outside. He hasn't eaten anything since breakfast and he's hungry. He opens his door and goes back to the B bathroom. The door's locked from the inside. Baker stands there a moment. He isn't sure what the protocol is. He can wait, for sure, or he can walk to another bathroom and see if it's available. He decides to look for an empty one.

As he approaches bathroom "E" he senses a presence behind him. He half turns and is then pushed aside, roughly. He stumbles to regain his balance. By the time he does, an older gentleman has moved by him and entered the bathroom. Backer hears the door lock.

Now Baker is pissed off.

"Hey, what's the big idea?" He yells at the closed door.

He doesn't get any response. He stands there for a minute and then realizes he doesn't have all that much time to waste. He heads back to bathroom B. It is still occupied. He knocks on the door.

"How much longer do you think you will be?" asks Baker.

"None of your goddamn business," comes the reply.

Baker lets out a long sigh. Fuck. He turns and goes down the hall to bathroom A and fortunately finds it empty. He goes in and turns on the light and is just about to lock the door when somebody in the hallway grabs it and tears it open.

"Who are you and what are you doing in this bathroom?"

"None of your goddamn business," says Baker.

With that, he pulls the door shut and throws the lock. He barely makes it to the toilet in time. He ignores the pounding on the door as he sits there. What a fucked-up hotel, he says to himself.

When he finishes his business, he washes up and combs his hair. He isn't in any particular hurry because the knocking on the door has stopped.

He throws back the lock and opens the door. When he does, a party of four men stand waiting for him. He recognizes one of them. He's the red-faced guy who had challenged his right to be in the bathroom. The other two look like tramps. The fourth is a short, pasty looking man with blond hair—what's left of it—wearing a long-sleeved white shirt and a bow tie. He clearly is in charge.

"Excuse me," says bow tie. "We seem to have a problem here."

"Not anymore," says Baker, smiling at bow tie. "Five minutes ago, we almost had a problem. I thought I was going to have to hang my fanny out the window in my room and shit in the street. Then I finally found an open bathroom."

Judging from the looks he's getting, he's the only one who appreciates his sense of humor.

The guy in the bow tie says: "We have strict rules in this hotel and I was led to believe they had been explained to you when you checked in. You're to use the bathroom assigned to your room."

"Nobody said anything to me about an assigned bathroom," replies Baker.

"You mean to tell me Mr. Stutzman didn't tell you that Room 204 uses Bathroom B?"

"Nope. All Hans said is I'm not allowed to get into a fight over my bathroom usage."

"Well, I'll have to talk with Mr. Stutzman about that. But let me make it perfectly clear to you. You are assigned to bathroom B. You are not allowed to use any other bathroom unless directed to by the hotel staff. You understand?"

"What is this, a goddamn reformatory?" asks Baker.

"You might call it that," says an old guy standing on two crutches. "It's not exactly a prison. But it's got prison rules. You got to go along to get along."

"I'm not trying to cause trouble," says Baker. "I was just in a bad way. My bathroom was being used and I had to go, right then. There must be an exception to the rule for cases like that."

Bow tie says, "We would hope you don't wait until you are in that situation. But obviously, we don't want you to be uncomfortable. Had you declared a personal emergency, you could use any of the bathrooms. However, we keep track of the number of emergencies you have and if they are excessive, we may have to ask you to leave."

"I'll keep that in mind," says Baker.

The small crowd starts to break up, sensing all the excitement has gone out of the confrontation.

"Allow me to introduce myself," says bow tie. "I am Tommy Ingstrom, the nightshift supervisor. And you're Charles Baker, I assume."

"That's right. I checked in this afternoon. Room 204."

"Well, welcome to our hotel. I am sorry we had to meet under these circumstances. We really are a very friendly hotel. Ask any of the regular guests."

The guy on the crutches had been moving toward the elevator, but now looks back over his shoulder.

"Yeah. We all love one another. As long as you use your own crapper." He laughs out loud.

"Sam is just being playful," says Ingstrom. "But it is true; our guests are fiercely territorial about their bathrooms. You don't want to use anybody's bathroom but your own."

"I've learned my lesson," Baker says. "Just out of curiosity, which rooms do I share mine with?"

"You share Bathroom B with Rooms 203, 205, 206, 207 and 208. My advice to you is to get up early tomorrow morning and observe the bathroom habits of the five other guests you share it with. You'll find a routine to their morning behavior. There should be a fifteen-to-twenty minute gap during the morning for you to make use of the facilities. I'm not sure when it is. But your room had been occupied up until a week ago. So I know it's in the rotation. Anyway, you might want to do the same thing in the evening. Observe what their going-to-the-bathroom behavior is like. Most of our guests work out a schedule that gives them the same time in the bathroom every night without interference from anyone else."

"Thanks. That's good advice," Baker says, thinking he is going to go fucking crazy living in this boarding home for old men who set their clocks by their bowel movements.

On the other hand, he doesn't want to get thrown out his first week. So he decides to take bowtie's advice. Immediately, in fact. He grabs a chair out of his room along with a mystery novel and one of the small stenographer's notepads he uses for taking notes on the beat, and moves out into the hallway, where he sits until midnight. He watches rooms 203 through 208 and, with the help of his Timex, notes when various occupants visit Bathroom B. Most of the occupants carry a toothbrush and a bath towel with them. But not all of them. The old guy in room 208 just went down and peed, as best as Baker can determine. Baker gives him the benefit of the doubt and figures he could be wearing dentures that he brushes in his room.

While he monitors the bathroom traffic, the users notice him, but say nothing. Baker thinks maybe one of them might just tell him when room 204 has access to the bathroom, but that doesn't happen. He wonders if the difference in age between him and the other guests is a factor. Best as he can tell, he's at least 40 years younger than any of the other bathroom users.

Finally, there is a gap. From 10:15 to about 10:30 nobody uses the bathroom. Obviously, that's the time reserved for room 204. Good to know.

The next morning he wakes up early. He isn't surprised; after all, he is still on East Coast time. It's 6 a.m., Fargo time; 7 a.m., Washington time. He has on shorts and a T-shirt. Flip flops grip his feet. He goes out into the hall, dragging his chair along, and notices the door to Bathroom B is already closed.

When the guy from Room 206 leaves the bathroom at 7:45, no one is waiting. By now, Baker really has to go, so as soon as 206 trundles back to his room, leaving the hallway empty, Baker heads in to relieve himself. He quickly latches the door, hoping he won't hear an angry knock for a minute or two.

Thankfully, he is able to pee in peace.

As he washes his hands, he decides to splash some water on his face, then heads back to his room to grab his toothbrush, tube of Crest and a washcloth, just in case. Coming back into the hallway, he sees the bathroom door still open, room still empty. This would appear to be the time slot allotted to his room. He brushes his teeth and gives himself a quick rubdown with a wet washcloth—he dare not shower, in case some old fart's just running late—and gets out a minute before 8 a.m., just in time to see the guy from 203 totter out of his room with a towel over his shoulder, giving him a grunt as he turns into the bathroom and shuts the door.

He needs a cup of Joe. Bad. He throws on some clothes and heads downstairs, where he's surprised to find a pot of weak-looking coffee and a 40ish guy named Owen Hutchins, who tells him the coffee is "complimentary from six to nine, but you have to bring your own cup."

"Oh, damn, I just got in last night, I don't..."

"You must be Mr. Pink's son," Hutchins says, reaching under the counter and pulling out an old, stained coffee mug. "Here, I'll let you use this. But bring it back clean by tomorrow."

"Thanks, Owen. I owe you." Baker wondered how clean the mug was, but poured some of the barely-brown liquid into it anyway.

"Ah, call me Hutch. Nice to meet you."

"Thanks, Hutch. You, too." Baker slurped a sip. It was definitely hot. But he wasn't sure he could taste anything. He headed back upstairs.

After 8:30, the bathroom remained empty, so he took another chance and quickly shaved. It appears that any time after 8:30 can be his, too. He's pleased that he has the system down pat.

By 9:30 a.m., he is dressed in a blue button-down Oxford shirt under a dark-blue Navy blazer. He has on a dark-blue brushed silk tie and he is wearing khaki slacks. On his feet are tan loafers without socks. His basic go-to-work uniform, in other words. He washes the coffee mug, then stops by the front desk and returns it to Owen "Hutch" Hutchins, thanking him. Baker then asks where the *Forum* is in relationship to the hotel.

"Going to work, are we?" says Hutchins, with a patronizing smile. "You go out the front door and turn left. Go to the end of the block. You'll see the five-story Forum Building straight ahead of you, across 5th Street. It has a large Forum sign on top of it. So, are you excited about your first day at work?"

"I'm not sure this will be my first day. I have to meet with the editor and arrange my hours. I don't know exactly when they want me to start."

"Oh, I see. Well, I'm sure they'll want you to start right away. Good luck to you."

"Thanks," says Baker, walking across the lobby and out the door.

Chapter Six

Cleaning up the Mess

Wayne Thompson, a captain with the Fargo Police Department, hates calls from Sam Bodini. Now a goddamn Indian has killed a whore in the Front Street Blind Pig. Fuck. He tells Bodini to stay put and keep the door locked; he'll be right over. Then he calls Phil Myers, a longtime sergeant on the police force.

"I know you just got off duty," says Thompson when Myers answers the phone. "But we've got a problem on Front Street. I'll fill you in after I pick you up. Can you be ready in ten minutes?"

Sometimes being in charge of the Front Street liquor operation is way more trouble than it's worth, thinks Thompson as he drives to North Fargo to pick up Myers. The 58-year-old former beat cop doesn't like complications in his life. He has enough years on the force to retire and the only reason he doesn't is because overseeing the Front Street operation pays about double his regular salary.

Thompson squeezes his large body—he desperately needs to lose at least 50 pounds—into his unmarked police cruiser and drives across town from his home on Fargo's South Side. On the drive he starts to calm down. An Indian killing a whore is not an insurmountable problem. Nothing he and Myers can't handle. By the time he gets to Myers house, he's feeling in control again.

Thompson tells Myers what Bodini told him: Essentially, a drunken Indian killed a white whore in the Blind Pig about 8:30 p.m. No witnesses to the killing, but a lot of folks had seen the two of them pair off for sex and go into the back room. The Indian came out by himself covered in blood and left. Bodini went in to the check on the woman and found her dead. He then cleared the bar and told the patrons to keep their mouths shut. He said they were all regulars and thought they would.

"Any of our Mexicans involved?" asks Myers.

"No, like I said, it was after they had been loaded up and sent back to their farms. It happened about eight-thirty p.m."

"Well, that's something. It could have been worse, is what you're telling me."

"Yeah, that's for sure. You know, when you think about it, it's amazing that this sort of thing hasn't happened before. I was thinking about it on the way over to your place. I don't recall that a white person, before now, has ever been killed in the Pig."

Myers gives that some thought. Thompson has been on the force maybe five years longer than him. But he too has a sense of Front Street history. Myers lights a Chesterfield. He rolls down the window. He knows Thompson has quit and doesn't like the smell of cigarette smoke. As far as Myers can tell, Thompson also resents the fact his partner weighs just about what he did the day he graduated from the police academy. And yet he eats pretty much whatever he wants. Myers also has a full head of hair and Thompson's losing his. But Thompson has no call for resentment. He still bears a resemblance to

Johnny Weissmuller, while Myers resembles a ferret, and people react to them as such. Thompson gets the better assignments and the faster promotions. Myers learned a long time ago to accept his fate. But that doesn't mean he avoids an opportunity, every now and then, to order French fries with his sandwich and watch Thompson have a silent conniption.

"Every summer a few Mexicans farm laborers get stabbed down in the Pig," Myers thinks aloud, "but then nobody keeps track of those incidents. I know a few of them have died from their wounds, although I have no idea how many. You know as well as I do that when one of the Mexicans dies, the corpse is always claimed by whichever farmer employed him. The farmer then hauls him back to his place and disposes of him."

Heading back to Front Street, Thompson wishes Myers didn't smoke in his car. He is just irritated enough to say something. But it's a city car, not his personal car. Fuck it. It isn't worth getting upset about. Besides, Myers is blowing most of the smoke out the window.

"Our deal with the growers is that we will entertain their workers, but they have to deal with conflicts that erupt among them," says Thompson. "If we started arresting Mexicans who committed crimes against Mexicans, our jails would be full all the time. And then the good citizens of Fargo would start yelling that we should ban the brown people from the city. We would start to see those signs go up again. Remember those, the ones we used to see back in the fifties? 'Dogs and Mexicans Keep Out.' The growers don't want that."

Myers agrees. But then he asks, "Do you ever get bothered by the charade we're engaged in here? I mean, here we are, helping out the sugar beet growers by providing them a place where their workers can unwind for a little R 'n' R on the weekend. This dumps money into the Fargo economy that otherwise would go elsewhere. But to make it work, we have to keep a bar open after regular hours on Saturday night for the Mexicans and then we have to open it up again on Sunday for them, in clear violation of state and local laws. Why do we do this?

"Let me guess what you would say. You would say we do it because the bar is owned by some of our most prominent city fathers, right? And they pay you and me a handsome fee to make sure the bar doesn't come to the attention of the locals. We also make damn sure the Mexicans don't mingle with polite company. That way, everybody in the city can pretend if they want that a couple of thousand Mexicans are not shopping, eating, partying, and sleeping over in their city every weekend for six months of the year."

Thompson is getting pissed with Myers. Maybe it was a mistake bringing him along. It could be Myers is upset that he has to go out again. After all, he worked all day on Front Street herding Mexicans.

"I don't know if I would call it a charade. But I do know it's working. I think most people in town realize the Mexicans are here on the weekend. I think they know the Mexicans have their own movie theater and stores down on Front Street. I don't think the citizens know about the Blind Pig. I think they would be upset to learn that one of the underground bars from Prohibition days had reopened. There would be all kinds of questions about who was profiting from it. The state dicks would get involved, too."

"Why do we let the local drunks use it then? Isn't that risky?

Thompson snorts. "If you recall, we didn't intend to let them use it. But lower Front Street is their turf. As soon as the damn Pig opened, they smelled the booze in the air and were

123

right there at the door. We had to either let them in or shoot them. I made the decision. Ever hear the expression about being better off having the skunk inside the tent pissing out rather than outside pissing in? Well, I guess that's how I felt about the Fargo drunks. If it gets out of hand, I'll just have to line them up against the wall and let you shoot them, okay? Besides, only a small number of the town drunks appear to know about the bar."

Myers stretches in his seat, yawns, and agrees. "Yeah, the growers are pleased. And cooperative. Every Sunday afternoon, as the Mexicans head back to their farms, my boys and I meet for a few minutes with the growers or their foremen to point out the troublemakers among their crews. I don't know what the growers do to workers who get out of line. All I know is that when I identify a troublemaker, we don't have any more problems with that guy. In fact, sometimes we never see him again. And if we do, it might not be for weeks. I sometimes wish we were allowed to use the growers' methods to discipline our scofflaws."

"You can hardly blame the Mexicans for cutting loose on the weekends," says Thompson. "I know the kind of work they do."

"Yeah, so do I. It's where the term 'shit work' comes from," says Myers.

"Remember in 1961 when the sugar growers were going to save money and replace the Mexican workers with local kids? They thought it would be cheaper if they didn't have to transport the Mexicans up here and feed and house them. They had it all figured out: just bus in kids from Fargo and Moorhead for the day."

"I remember that program," laughs Myers. "They called it the 'Youth Beet Program.' It got the city fathers all excited because the growers said it would take the kids off the streets of Fargo during the summer and put them to work. The program was going to solve everybody's problems."

Thompson laughs hard, almost a belly laugh.

"That's right. Somebody even said the kids would be too tired to cruise their cars up and down Broadway at night if they worked all day in the beet fields. That really got the downtown merchants behind the plan."

"Too bad nobody had given much thought to what a short hoe does to a city boy," says Myers.

"Damn straight," chuckles Thompson. "Those kids went out into the fields with those short hoes and discovered what it's like to do stoop labor. Sounds easy, bending over. But after about an hour of it, your back tightens up. A half day of it and you are in agony. A day of it and you can't stand up straight without pain shooting down both legs and across your shoulders. Two days of it and there's no way you can stand, sit, or lie down that doesn't hurt. We didn't have a kid who lasted more than two days. The growers could have tripled their pay and they still wouldn't have come back out."

"Nothing breaks a man down faster than a short hoe," says Myers. "Growers swear by it, though. They say a good man can do a better job getting at the weeds around the plant with it. Workers using a long-handled hoe are more likely to clip the sugar beet plant. That's what the growers claim, anyway."

"All I know," Thompson says, "is I've watched farm workers out in the hot sun hoeing sugar beets with the short hoe. It made me damn glad I wasn't born a Mexican."

"Amen to that. They bust their hump and the growers give them just a day and a half off a week," says Myers. "I don't think they would even do that if their cooperative hadn't told them they needed to ease up on their workers just a bit. After all, other states compete for them. Hell, they could hire out to apple growers or lettuce farmers out west. Unless our sugar beet growers give their workers weekends off, they won't come back next year."

"I can't see where having to spend your time off on Front Street is all that big of a benefit, but I guess you have to compare it to the option of staying on the farms," said Thompson. "Most of these workers are spread among a hundred or so farms, isolated from neighbors and friends. At least when they're trucked into Fargo, they can socialize with a thousand other Mexicans, nobody yells at them, and there's some recreation. It's just too bad all they get to see of Fargo is Front Street."

"Front Street isn't pretty, but that's the arrangement," adds Myers. "We can block off that section of the city and nobody cares. It's not where the action is on Saturday night and Sunday. That enables us to turn Front Street into a large Mexican plaza on the weekends. Sure, our police barriers keep people out; but then, most people think our barriers are designed primarily to keep the Mexicans in. Fargo residents appreciate that, I can assure you."

"Yeah, but at least once a month some local toughs think it's fun to drive down Front Street and hassle the Mexicans," Thompson throws in. "Or some do-gooder group thinks it ought to approach the Mexicans and encourage them to stand up to their oppressive 'slave masters.'

"Two considerations override all others. One, the needs of the sugar beet farmers are the priority. If they think Fargo isn't willing to entertain their Mexican workers, they'll haul them elsewhere on the weekend to spend their money. Two, hosting Mexicans must be done delicately so that the good citizens of Fargo hardly notice they have guests in town."

Satisfying these two objectives every weekend for roughly half the year is Captain Wayne Thompson's responsibility, Myers knows. Essentially, it is his only job. He has two sergeants and eight patrolmen to back him up him during the weekend. If need be, he can have more. If things get out of hand, he can call in every patrolman and reserve officer in the city as well as the Cass County Sheriff's Office and the North Dakota State Patrol—in theory. But any increased police presence on lower Front Street could easily create hysteria among the God-fearing citizens of Fargo. So Thompson knows he can never really call for help.

"We've come a long way in six years, when you think about it," says Myers. "Remember our first summer?"

Thompson remembers. What a disaster. The growers and the city fathers had agreed to bring the workers into Fargo on a Saturday, but nothing had been planned for their recreation other than a cookout in Island Park.

The Mexicans got off their trucks and immediately spread out. The men drifted in small groups all over the business district looking for liquor and something to eat. Women and children went off in search of clothing and shoe stores. Teenagers slipped off into Island Park and began engaging in amorous acts that horrified local residents using the park's tennis courts. That night, Mexicans got into fights with local hotheads in a half-dozen downtown bars. The language barrier prevented the police from getting at the cause, but it was clear that the locals didn't want to drink alongside Mexicans. Other merchants simply didn't want them in their establishments. They were considered "bad for business." That was a polite way of saying that any store frequented by Mexicans soon had few Anglo shoppers.

The local newspaper, the *Forum*, ran an editorial that captured the sentiment of nearly every resident in town: Bringing the Mexicans to Fargo was a bad idea. The editorial said the infamous "Dogs and Mexicans Not Welcome" sign hadn't reappeared yet, but suggested it wouldn't be long.

After the editorial ran, the sign wasn't necessary.

"I'll say one thing for that first summer: It got us hired," says Thompson.

"And it got the Blind Pig opened," adds Myers.

That first summer Thompson was promoted from police lieutenant to captain and given the assignment of policing Front Street. Privately, he was told his job was to work with the sugar beet growers to provide for their workers. At the same time, his job was to make damn sure those workers stayed away from the citizens of Fargo. Then, in a side deal, he entered into a private arrangement with the owners of the Blind Pig—many of whom were the very same city fathers who'd ordered him to work with the sugar beet farmers—to provide security for the illegal bar.

As far as Thompson was concerned, the three assignments were intertwined. He couldn't placate the growers and keep the Mexicans away from the citizens of Fargo without the Blind Pig. It all worked together.

Liquor wasn't sufficient, though, to meet the demands of the thousand or so Mexicans who came to Fargo every weekend from May through October. They also wanted a Spanish-language movie theater. No problem, said Thompson. He told the manager of the Island Park Theater on Front Street that he would now begin showing nothing but Spanish-language movies on summer weekends. When the man protested, Thompson said his choice was to show Spanish-language films all day Saturday and Sunday six months of the year or face closure for a host of code violations. When the manager said he didn't know how he was going to explain this decision to the owners in Minneapolis, Thompson said he could say two things. One, the weekend revenue will be higher than he normally takes in on summer weekends, and two, he won't need to spend any money advertising his weekend movies in the local newspapers.

The Mexican workers also wanted a grocery store where they could buy the kind of food they preferred to eat. There were no grocery stores at all in the Mexican zone on Front Street, so Thompson had a challenge. He drove over to Roberts Street and talked to a Jewish grocer who ran what Thompson thought of as an eclectic store that catered to Jews and ethnic communities. Thompson asked him if he would be interested in stocking and selling Mexican food during the summer months if a storefront on Front Street were provided.

The grocer was interested, but the free storefront wasn't sufficient enticement. He needed Thompson to pull a few strings to get some health permits waived, for both the Front Street property and the Roberts Street store. Shortly thereafter, a Mexican grocery store was in business, run by the grocer's son-in-law. The grocer's brother then opened a shoe and clothing store next door, selling second-hand merchandise that looked a lot like that collected by Fargo churches, but at considerable mark-up from what the churches sold it for.

The Mexican women wanted a place where they and their children would be protected from the elements and safe from the liquored-up men. So Thompson opened up a vacant storefront and designated it a sanctuary for women and children. In addition, he commandeered two abandoned warehouses off Front Street and allowed the Mexicans to occupy them during the weekends. Finally, he allowed families to pitch tents in Island Park and have cooking fires nearby.

Thompson told his officers to look the other way if couples snuck off into the bushes of Island Park for a coupling session, as long as the lady seemed amenable to the arrangement. At the same time, not wanting to offend the sensitivities of Fargo bluebloods, he closed the nearby tennis courts to play during the weekend.

Then he'd opened up the Blind Pig. The underground bar was in the middle of the newly established Mexican zone, halfway between 4th and 5th streets in the alley behind Front Street. Just a short stroll away from Island Park, The Blind Pig became the social center for the Mexicans during their weekend in Fargo. A lot of the money they earned each week ended up there on Saturday night and Sunday afternoon.

The owners of the Blind Pig couldn't believe their good fortune. The place had been in their families for forty years. But when Prohibition was repealed, the dug-out bar had been abandoned, used only as a storeroom by the legal saloon that opened on the first floor above it.

Now, in the mid-60s, the Blind Pig is open again, and somehow even easier and more profitable to run than ever before. When the bar had first opened during Prohibition, the liquor was illegal and so was the bar that served it. The owners had to worry about federal agents, raids from rival rum runners, and double crosses from local cops. It was a lot to worry about. Now 30 years later the owners have none of those worries. The liquor is bought legally from one of the owners who operates a distributorship in town. Another one of the owners has his accountant pay the help and handle the books. And Wayne Thompson, a Fargo police captain, accepts an envelope full of cash every two weeks to provide security. As a consequence, owning the Blind Pig today isn't as exciting for the sons as it had been for the fathers—which is OK by them. And it's at least as profitable.

Thompson turns left from Broadway onto Front Street. Myers is quiet. Thompson is deep in his own thoughts. He is thinking again that there's no denying it: serving Mexicans liquor out of an unlicensed bar on a Sunday violated state and city laws. But as Thompson pulls up in the alley behind the Blind Pig, he has a hard time reconciling the notion that selling liquor on Front Street is an illegal activity. My God, he thinks to himself, there's always been Front Street liquor. It was here before statehood. It was here after North Dakota came into the Union as a dry state. Prohibition made Front Street liquor popular and today it continues to meet the needs of folks who want a drink on Sunday. Front Street liquor is just folks' way of talking back to dumb laws, he concludes. Then he is out of the car ringing the buzzer, demanding admission to the Blind Pig.

Thompson is glad he didn't recognize the dead woman lying on the floor inside. Myers says he doesn't either. Fargo isn't a large city, but at 40,000 people it's too big for a police captain to know everyone.

"Do you know who did it?" asks Thompson.

Bodini looks at him. "Do you really want to know?"

"Yes, goddamn it, I really want to know."

"Some Indian. I don't know his name. I don't think he's been in here before. Ugly bastard. All pockmarked. About five-ten, maybe two-twenty. Mean sonofbitch. Was drinking whiskey, paying for it from a wad of cash he had in his pocket. He had paid the lady here twenty dollars for sex. They left the bar and came into this room together and I don't know what went wrong. He was drunk and I would guess he couldn't get it up. She probably laughed at him or something. I'm just guessing. But he's not the kind of Indian you want to laugh at."

Thompson could tell that by looking at the abused body. "Where did your Indian go?"

"He unlocked the door and left. He shouldn't be hard to spot; an Indian in a Levi jacket soaked in blood. Besides, he was so drunk he could barely walk. I'd be surprised if he made it more than two or three blocks before he keeled over."

Thompson thought about that. Then he said to Myers, "Okay, let's get her out of here. Sam, I need you to clean up this mess."

Thompson and Myers pick Sara up by her ankles and wrists and lower her onto an old door that had been leaning up against the wall in the storeroom. Then they use it to carry her through the bar and out into the dark alley.

"How far are we going to carry her?" asks Myers.

"Down to the end of the alley to 4th Street," says Thompson. "We'll dump her there; make it look as if she were attacked on the street.

So that's what they did.

They took the door back to the Blind Pig and left Bodini to scrub the scene clean. Thompson got in his unmarked car and drove down the alley past Sara's body. He looked at it as he drove slowly by. She was lying face down with her arms at her side. She didn't look like a person who had passed out from too much drink.

"What do you think: Does she look like a mugging victim?" asked Thompson.

She was lying on her stomach, so the wound wasn't visible. But she had bled out pretty bad, and anyone who looked at her closely would see she had blood splatter toward the bottom of her dress, on her legs, and covering her sandals.

Myers said "Anyone finding her is going to guess she had been hurt pretty bad and then tossed into the alley, maybe from a car driving down 4th Street away from Front Street. Prostitutes have been known to work this part of town."

"Not on Sunday nights," said Thompson. "No hooker works lower Front Street when the Mexicans are in town. They can't afford our local girls. Fuck it. Who knows what the first cop on the scene might think about what happened to the victim? Besides, police reports have a habit of getting a little sloppy when they involve matters on Front Street."

Thompson turns his car north on 4th street. He plans to drop Myers off first before heading home himself.

As he drives, he thinks through his next steps. He knows that when the body is found the cops will be called and then they will contact him. They always do, when it's a Front Street matter. He will go down and view it. He will look at the wound and suggest it came from a big knife . . . the kind of weapon Indians carry. He will make a point of saying Mexicans only carry small pocket knives and they could not do this kind of damage. Then he will suggest they round up all the Indians in town and see if any of them have blood on their clothes. Oh, and he will tell them to look to see if any of them are carrying a bloody knife. That's how they'll catch their killer. The cops will listen to him because of his experience working Front Street.

"Hell, the Indian's probably sleeping it off right now down in Island Park," says Myers as the car pulls up in front of his house. "This should be a no-brainer."

Thompson agrees with him.

"Let's just be sure that we're the ones who take his statement. We want to make sure he confesses to killing her in the alley and not in the bar."

"Shouldn't be a problem," says Myers as he opens the door to get out. "Forget it, Captain. It's Front Street. You'll be lead on the case. Getting the confession should be a snap. Damn Indians get so drunk they seldom ever remember anything about what they did the night before. They just got to be told a couple of times what they did; then they'll swear forever afterwards that's exactly what happened."

As Thompson pulls away from the curb, he thinks to himself what a cluster fuck the evening has been. The goddamn Indian was supposed to have killed Sara Whitlow in the alley, after she came out of the Blind Pig. What in the world ever possessed him to have sex with her first and then kill her in front of a dozen witnesses?

Thompson drove on in silence. He goes over the plan again. Joe Running Deer was supposed to kill Sara and then get out of town. On Monday he was supposed to go to Dilworth and hang around the Northern Pacific train station. Thompson would find him and pay Joe more money than he'd ever seen. Then he'd get out of the area for good.

Now, because of the Indian's fuck up, Thompson figures the plan needs to be revised. He will go to Dilworth as planned. But as soon as he sees Joe, he'll handcuff him and throw him in the back of his unmarked cruiser. Then they'll go for a ride. Thompson will just have to administer a little old-fashioned prairie justice and kill Joe with a police department-issued 12-gauge shotgun. Resisting arrest, of course.

Then a small smile crosses his face. He has just had a pleasant thought. He'll be able to keep all the money he had been given to kill Sara Whitlow.

Chapter Seven

The Fargo Forum Isn't the Washington Star

A breeze is blowing, and it's clear and hot in Fargo. As Chuck Baker heads toward 5th Street, he sees few people wandering around. On his side of the street stands a large, stoic Masonic Temple. Devoid of windows, the building reveals nothing about its inner activities as Baker walks alongside it. He thinks it's probably not open. Across the street is an auto parts store. A couple of pickup trucks with their engines running have double-parked out front, so it's apparently open for business.

At the corner ahead, across 5th Street, he sees the Forum Building. It's impressive, given its surroundings. It isn't the Washington Star Building, the architectural grande dame of Pennsylvania Avenue. But that building would look really out of place sitting on the corner of 5th Street and 1st Avenue in Fargo. The Forum Building, on the other hand, seems to belong right where it sits. As Baker looks up, something atop the corner of the five-story building catches his eye: A large, monolithic pillar, about five feet by five feet, reaching another two stories skyward. The capital letters F-O-R-U-M—each letter about five feet tall with what looks like neon tubing inside—run vertically down the two sides of the pillar visible from the street: One set of letters facing 5th Street, the other facing 1st Avenue. Baker decides he must come by at night and see what it looks like all lit up.

He crosses the street and goes in the front door. Circulation and the business office are on the first floor, which makes sense to Baker. Editorial is always upstairs. So, he heads up the stairs. Second floor is classified advertising. Okay. He proceeds on to the third floor. Editorial Department. He goes through the door and into a large, open room containing about 40 desks, each of them loaded with a phone, piles of newspapers, and assorted journalistic flotsam. Open, that is, except for a reception desk with a locked gate to keep the rowdies out, apparently. But Baker suspects its primary purpose is to keep the undertakers away from the news desk, or maybe to give the Women's section a place to greet brides-to-be and their mothers so that all three could be involved in the selection of the "best" picture to run on the social page—that's how it had been back at the *Star*, anyway.

In the newsroom beyond the gate, there's a typewriter on a stand alongside each desk. Five desks sit side by side with an equal number smashed tight up against them to make fat rows of ten. Three of these rows make up the bulk of the newsroom. Reporters are sitting at many of the desks talking on the phones, pounding on their typewriters, jabbering at each other, reading clippings or mail, and smoking. Nearly everybody in the room smokes, it appears, and not just cigarettes. Older reporters and a few of the younger ones can be seen gripping cigars. The room has a high ceiling and at about the 14-foot level, a cloud hangs in the air.

Almost as an afterthought, he notices there's a receptionist's desk just to his left. The receptionist, an attractive brunette in her 20s, is on the phone and smiles at him when he sees her. He should wait for her, he realizes. No sense getting off on a bad foot with the receptionist.

On the left side of the room a handful of desks crammed together constitute the Sports department. It's easy to spot because of all the sports paraphernalia hanging off desks. Posters announcing area high school football schedules are thumb tacked to the walls. The few reporters at their desks are casually dressed, a distinguishing characteristic of sportswriters everywhere.

Next to the Sports department perches the Women's section. All of its staff are prim and proper females, many wearing hats of all sizes and colors. They are the newspaper's authorities on the subjects of baking, weddings, high teas, and social etiquette. Their desks are relatively clean, but their walls are festooned with pictures of beauty queens, cheerleaders, and mothers in their kitchens cooking.

Four old op-ed editors claim space along that same wall. They have aligned their large desks so they sit in two rows facing in opposite directions, allowing the old geezers to turn away from their desks and form a circle, pow-wow style. They remind Baker of the op-ed editors back at the *Star*, looking every inch the same old washed-up newspaper editors with no place to go, sitting at their desks all day going through the newspapers from around the country mailed into the paper each day. They cut out editorials and other feature stories and toss them in a pile for the other old washed up editors to read. Once a week the editors go through the pile and select a reasonable number that will eventually end up on the *Forum's* editorial page.

They also write editorials and read the "letters to the editor." Occasionally one of these letters will comment on a recent editorial one or two of them wrote, and this generates a lot of buzz among the editors. They're not used to getting feedback, and even one letter from a credible author can unnerve them. They spend a lot of time together discussing and then selecting a small, but supposedly representative, set of letters to print on the editorial page.

Baker looks around for the copy desk. They're generally hard to miss, seeing as how they're large and shaped like horseshoes. Around the outside of the horseshoe sit the copyeditors. The top copyeditor, the so-called "guy in the slot," sits "at the top," at a desk in the opening of the horseshoe. Sitting right behind him is the news editor so that copy can be handed back and forth easily between the two. The slot guy operates as a traffic cop. He decides which stories the copyeditors will edit and then accepts or rejects their efforts, including their attempts to write headlines for their stories. He also dictates the size of each headline, its typeface, and the column width he figures the story warrants.

The copyeditors flag the news editor on any story that might get the newspaper into a legal entanglement. The copyeditors also watch to ensure a story, perhaps written by one of the newspapers own reporters, doesn't duplicate a version provided by the AP or even a news release.

Finally, copyeditors torment reporters. Space is always an issue. Reporters assume the newspaper always has plenty of room for their stories. But the copy desk is always looking to shorten stories to ensure space exists for all the news. Consequently, few stories ever get printed in their entirety. Copyeditors slash paragraphs if they don't think they add anything of importance to the overall story.

Then they eliminate unnecessary words, which is a subjective art form. The copyeditors are particularly savage when they think a reporter is trying to turn a straightforward news item into a feature story containing the reporter's attempts to be cute, clever, or insightful. This editing is also a judgment call, and reporters have been known to go ballistic when it happens to one of their prize stories. For this reason, most newspapers don't allow their reporters to hang around the copy desk. Their suffering must take place at a distance.

Reporters, though, have ways to torment copyeditors. The most familiar one is to point out the indignities of working on the copydesk.

"What could be a worse job than being chained to a desk editing someone else's copy?" they ask themselves.

"How about changing sheets in a whore house?"

"No, no. Cleaning toilets in the men's room at the bus terminal."

Copyeditors develop tough skins. But that only provides so much comfort. That's because when the editing chore is complete, they still must write a headline to accompany the article. Writing headlines frequently is the most challenging part of their job and having a tough skin doesn't make it any easier.

Not all headline-writing chores are equally challenging. For example, two- or three-column headlines—two or three columns across—are much easier to write than one-column headlines, which only have space for two small words. Likewise, a double-stacked headline—with one line on top and another below it—has a lot more words to play with than a single-line head. One column, two-line headlines are the bane of any copydesk. They give the writer maybe two words for each line. That's a total of four short words for the headline. A three-line, one column head is a little better: it may give the copyeditor six words to work with.

To add to the copyeditors' woes, the newspaper has headline "rules." For example, each headline has to contain a verb. And it has to appear in either the first or second line of the headline. That's no problem in a two-column headline. But it can be a real challenge for a one-column story.

Experienced headline writers struggle to invent ways to get around the rules. One rule says last names are preferred over nicknames. But what about initials?

It doesn't take long for a copyeditor to realize Vice President Hubert Humphrey's last name doesn't fit into a one-column headline, but his initials, "HHH" do. Same thing with a story about the president. His last name, Johnson, frequently doesn't fit into a one-column headline, so "LBJ" is substituted. On some busy news days, it's not unusual to see the president's initials employed in multiple headlines on the front page.

When copyeditors skirt the headline-writing preferences of their employer, sooner or later management cracks down on the copy desk.

The news editors, who occupy a weird management position just below managing editors, but outside of the normal editorial chain of command, tend to be paranoid anyway. So news editors constantly worry the copyeditors are slipping something by them. It seems they all have read Frank Mallen's *Sauce for the Gander* or heard about it. In his book, about one of the craziest, most colorful newspapers in American history, *The New York Evening Graphic,* Mallen describes a copyeditor who snuck a one-column, two-line headline by his news editor and got it into the newspaper. The story described an inmate at an insane asylum who escaped and raped someone. The headline read: "Nut Bolts and Screws."

News editors are also paranoid because of their low ranking on the organizational chart. They worry about the publisher's frequent cost-cutting initiatives. Publishers and their toadies constantly look for excuses to dismiss news editors. Consequently, they fear they'll be let go at a point in their lives when they can't get another job or survive living off their Social Security checks.

Working under such stress, news editors struggle to demonstrate their importance to the overall efficient operation of their newsroom. So they frequently crack down on the copy desk at any hint of rebellion or sloppiness. One way news editors do this is by restricting the copy desk's use of certain words.

News editors have little personal courage, Baker thinks—they don't have enough power to warrant any confidence, but they have enough to fear losing what they've got—so they try to avoid any direct confrontation with copyeditors. The preferred way for news editors to pass along instructions to them is by taping a copy of their directives to the top of the copy desk next to where the slot man sits.

Baker remembers an infamous news editor's memo that became legendary among the *Washington Star* copyeditors. It read: "From this day forward, the copy desk will no longer use the word 'vie' in a headline. It has been overused. And it is no longer acceptable to use the letters 'OK' for "okay." Spell it out or don't use it. From now on, we will spell out any number under ten. We will make an exception for the Sports page.

"Finally, neither the initials of the president or the vice president will be allowed in a headline. Frankly, they have been overused. We are going to go back to calling these gentlemen by their names, Johnson and Humphrey."

The copyeditors with serious drinking problems or ulcers suffered the most from reading the new rules. But even the relatively healthy and sober copyeditors rock back on their heels and lament the day they decided to become journalists.

Yelling at a copy-paper memo provides the copyeditors little relief and newspaper etiquette and top-down management practices prevent them from directly confronting news editors.

Some copyeditors attempt to throw the news editor a dirty look. But that's risky; such negative behavior can easily backfire. That's because news editors construct the two-week work schedules for copyeditors. Many of them have jobs on the side and they require some regularity in their newspaper hours to manage their personal schedules. The news editors, former copyeditors themselves, know this. Consequently, pliant copyeditors are often rewarded with stable schedules, while rebellious ones are punished by changing their work schedules from one week to the next.

Complacent copyeditors—they might describe themselves as beaten into submission—struggle to get along with management. In recognition of their loyalty, management gives them consistent schedules week in and week out. This enables them to plan ahead for the days they have off.

Rabblerousers, though, seldom know from one two-week period to the next what their schedule is going to look like. They often don't even know what shifts they're going to work any given day. They might be on the early shift one day, the afternoon shift the next, and then face multiple days straight on the evening shift. Such scheduling makes it nearly impossible for complaining copyeditors to lead normal lives. That's why many of them end up mean-spirited, divorced men with drinking problems.

Having a group of unhappy, hostile employees working together around a copy desk is a management challenge. News editors handle this by keeping the copyeditors so busy they don't have time to sabotage the production of the daily newspaper or breed anarchy within the larger staff. The slot man, having distanced himself from the copyeditors by his higher pay and ability to wield authority, generally aligns his personal interests with management. Therefore, he never lets more than one copyeditor at a time leave the desk for a bathroom or lunch break. To further hamper the ability of copyeditors to gather and share complaints, management staggers their start and finish hours. By having them come to work separately, then finish their shifts at different times, management believes it stymies the copyeditors' natural tendency to gather after work at a bar and plot their revenge.

Copyeditors can only take their hostilities out on one person: the slot man. He's a perfect foil. He's the person who determines who around the copydesk gets to write those detested, nearly impossible to compose, one-column headlines. A paranoid copyeditor can easily start to believe he's given more one-column heads to write than anyone else around the copy desk. This leads him to detest the slot man. But it also leads him to dislike his colleagues who he believes "suck up" to the slot man and are rewarded with longer headlines to write. Management doesn't particularly care if copyeditors dislike one another. After all, copy editing is a solitary activity; editing a story and writing a headline does not require a collaborative team effort.

Sometimes individual struggles to write headlines bring the copy desk to a near standstill. Stories begin to back up. Meanwhile, newly arriving stories, some destined for the front page, can't get into the flow because the copyeditors are all busy trying to write one-column heads. This prevents copy from leaving the desk at a steady pace. When the flow of headlines slows or stops, so do the articles accompanying them. Eventually the entire back shop begins to flounder, which in turn threatens the seamless process that produces a daily newspaper. Eventually the shop foreman will storm into the newsroom demanding to know what the hell is holding up the flow of copy? He says if someone doesn't do something about it immediately, the newspaper isn't going to get printed on time. And he will generally add: "You won't have the printers to blame."

At this point the news editor on duty is in a tizzy, which means the fellow in the slot is in trouble. In an effort to get the copy flowing again, the frantic news editor will tell reporters sitting at their desks to write headlines for their own stories. But everyone knows, if the copy desk is having trouble coming up with one-column headlines, it's a safe bet the reporters who wrote the stories won't be any better at it.

Normally when this crisis grips the newsroom, the news editor will push the slot man aside and assume his duties. When that happens, the copyeditors sitting around the horseshoe table all of a sudden come to life. Every copyeditor wants to impress the news editor—he is the guy, after all, who makes out the two-week schedules—and headlines start to appear almost magically. Within a short period of time, snappy headlines and their accompanying copy are heading to the linotype operators.

Once the crisis passes, the news editor leaves the copy desk and retreats triumphantly to his own desk. The slot man moves back into his old position, but without his usual swagger. The copyeditors glance at each other, but don't say anything. They know they are all thinking the same thing: if we were given more two-column headlines to write, we wouldn't find ourselves in this pickle.

Baker gets his head back around to his current situation. He can reminisce about the good ol' days on the *Washington Star*'s copy desk—back during his first summer internship there—on his own time. Now he needs to find work at the *Forum*.

If the Fargo newspaper has a copy desk, Baker sure doesn't see it. The newspaper has a photography staff, though. His eye catches a tall guy wearing a rubber apron coming down a hallway from the left carrying a set of wet pictures.

At this point, the receptionist finishes her phone call and focuses her attention on Baker.

"Sorry," she says, "it's been a zoo around here all morning. May I help you?"

"Hi. I'm here to see Swede Swenson. My name is Charles Baker."

She swivels around in her chair and looks over into the editor's row. Baker thinks he sees her looking at a guy in his mid-50s wearing black, horn-rimmed glasses, smoking a thin cigar. He's talking to an older guy sitting at a desk that runs parallel to his.

"He looks busy right now. Why don't you have a seat and I'll call you as soon as he breaks free." She smiles sweetly and he smiles back.

Baker sits down and sees several days' worth of newspapers lying on a nearby table. Curious, he digs through the stack and finds one for the previous Friday. That was the day his story ran. Then he catches himself. His story wouldn't have run in the *Forum* the same day it ran in the *Star*. He locates Saturday's *Forum*. He looks through it and finds nothing that resembles his story. He is disappointed, but not surprised. The

Saturday paper is generally the smallest paper of the week with the tightest news hole.

Then he picks up Sunday's *Forum*. The front page has two *Forum* staff written articles, but the others are all AP wire stories. That is pretty standard for small daily newspapers. They try to use their own reporters to cover their host city, but rely on the Associated Press (AP) for news of the state, region, nation, and world. The AP is a cooperative owned by its member newspapers. Every member newspaper contributes their stories to the AP and it in turn shares the bulk of these with every other member. In addition, the AP has its own reporting staff. These journalists are housed in bureau offices in every major newspaper across the country and around the world.

He idly starts flipping through the inside of the paper and then he spots it. It's an AP story and it doesn't carry his byline. But it's his story.

> WASHINGTON (AP) Capitol Hill Police revealed Thursday that they had secretly filmed a Member of Congress and a janitor who worked in the Capitol engaging in a sexual act in a Cannon House Office Building bathroom.
>
> The Washington Star said in its Friday editions that the congressman is Jeff Walker, the ranking Republican on the House Interior and Insular Affairs Committee. The janitor's name was not released. However, Capitol Hill police confirm that a male Negro janitor working in the Capitol has been fired for sexual misconduct.

> Capitol Hill Police had sent a notice to all Members of Congress a week earlier announcing that the police would be filming common areas within men's rooms in the three House Office Buildings. The notice said the bathrooms had been used for homosexual activities.
>
> Congressman Walker neither confirms nor denies the allegation.
>
> The Capital Hill Chief of Police, Cory Phelps, said the film has been sent to the House leadership "for whatever action it deems appropriate" against the congressman involved.

Leave it to the AP to give you just the bare facts, ma'am.

Baker takes the page out of the newspaper, folds it up, and puts it under his arm.

Just then, the receptionist says, "Mr. Swenson will see you now."

Baker gets to his feet and approaches the chest-high counter. The receptionist pushes an unseen buzzer and a gate in the counter opens. He guesses the secure gate is the newspaper's way of separating rambunctious or angry readers from the exposed newsroom staff. Now that's probably a good idea, although Baker realizes an angry reader can stand on the other side of the gate and hurl obscenities at the writer of his choice. Better curses than blows, Baker figures.

Just as Baker enters into the press room Swenson moves in front of him with his hand out.

"Good morning, my name is Harold Swenson, but everyone calls me Swede. You must be Chuck Baker."

"Yessir. I'm pleased to meet you."

"Come on in. And welcome to the *Forum*. It must look quite different than the *Washington Star*."

"Actually, sir, I was just thinking about how similar it looks. If I had to point out one major difference, it would be the editors' desks. At my former paper, our editors all sat in individual offices. It looks like *Forum* editors sit out with the folks who do the work."

Swenson laughs. "At the *Forum*, the editors do their share of the work, believe me. The only person here who has an office is the editor in chief, Ben Barnes, and he spends most of his time at his desk out here. I think the only time he uses his private office is when he has to handle a personnel issue."

They walk back to Swenson's desk and a chair is rolled away from an unused desk and given to Chuck to sit on. Leo Stanstead, the city editor, is introduced, and he swings his chair around and joins the conversation.

"I had a call from Senator Christenson's office telling me about a young man coming to Fargo to finish up his schooling. I was told he was a first-rate journalist. I was even told the *Forum* would be lucky to get him on staff. I thanked the senator's office. Normally, we don't pay much attention to a politician suggesting who we hire as a reporter.

"But I was struck by the fact you had worked for the *Washington Star*. That's one of my favorite newspapers. It's an afternoon paper, same as we are. We subscribe to it here at the *Forum* and I read it with professional interest. I think it's the best afternoon daily in the country.

"Anyway, I called the *Star* and talked briefly with a managing editor who said he didn't know you well and suggested I talk to a city editor."

Swenson glanced down at his notes.

"You're talking about Larry Bauguess," says Baker. "He is the city editor. Jim Harrison is the managing editor."

"That's right. Thank you. Larry Bauguess. Nice fellow. We had a pleasant chat about the newspaper business. Come to find out we knew some people in common. I went back to Harvard under a Nieman scholarship and so did he, but in different years. Eventually our conversation got around to you, which after all was the purpose of my call.

"He said you're one hell of a reporter. And he said he wished he had ten more like you at the *Star*. But above everything, he wished he had you back there. He explained that the *Star* has this policy, which he said is stupid, of only hiring college graduates. He said you're a few credits short, so they had to let you go. Is that about the whole story?"

"I might not puff myself up quite as much as Mr. Bauguess did. But yes, I worked at the *Star*, very much enjoyed my time there, and would be there still if I had finished all my schoolwork at George Washington University."

"So what brings you to North Dakota?"

"Two things. My family owns land in North Dakota. Therefore, I'm considered a state resident, which means I can enroll at NDSU and transfer in most of my credits and have them count toward my graduation. Second, I'm hoping to work for the *Forum*. It is an excellent newspaper in a good-size market. I figure I can get a lot more experience doing a wider variety of things here in two years than I could working at the *Star*. In other words, I think two years at the *Forum* will actually be a boost to my career."

"I'm glad to hear you say that," said Swenson. "We think we've got a great newspaper here ourselves. The *Forum* won the Pulitzer Prize a few years back and that isn't easy for a newspaper of our size.

"As far as gaining newspaper experience goes, you couldn't come to a better place. We may not be as big as the *Star*, but we do everything here that it does."

"I am aware of that," said Baker. "In fact, I think you might actually do more. You're a seven-day-a-week newspaper, but in addition to your afternoon editions, you put out a morning paper. The *Star* doesn't do that."

"I'm glad you mentioned the morning paper. Seventy five percent of our readers know the *Forum* as an afternoon newspaper. But our other readers know us as a morning paper.

"I'm going to let that sink in for a minute.

"Most of our readership lives here in Cass County. And most of them live in Fargo. It's the largest city in the state and Cass County is the largest county.

"But we're also the largest newspaper in North Dakota and the largest newspaper between Minneapolis and Spokane. The town across the river, Moorhead, Minnesota, doesn't have a newspaper. It used to have a morning paper called the *Daily News*. We bought it and closed it down. Since then, the *Minneapolis Tribune*, another morning newspaper, has been trying to sneak into our backyard. It's not the only one, either. We get word all the time that other publishers are sniffing around to see if Moorhead is ripe for a newspaper of its own.

"To keep a newspaper out of Moorhead, we publish a morning *Forum*. Its first edition sells almost exclusively in Moorhead. But it also goes to small towns in Minnesota. Our re-plated second edition goes on trains and buses to cities throughout North Dakota. It's the edition that makes us a state-wide newspaper. Finally, our last edition of the morning goes to Cass County subscribers.

"What I'm trying to tell you is, the morning *Forum* is an important newspaper even though it only reaches twenty-five percent of our readership. And I want to offer you a job working on it.

"I got the idea when I realized you intend to go to school too. NDSU doesn't have many night classes. So if you want to finish up your course work, you're going to have to attend classes like a regular student, which means going to school doing the day. If you work on the morning paper, your hours will be from four p.m. to twelve-thirty a.m. That will give you the daylight hours to be a student."

"What exactly will I be doing on the morning newspaper?" asks Chuck.

"You'll essentially have my job on the night side," says Stanstead. "You'll be the nightside city editor. Only thing is, we don't use titles on the nightside. If we did, we'd have to pay you what I earn, and management isn't going to do that."

Both of the editors laugh, and Baker has the good sense to at least smile.

"You'll staff the desk right there," said Stanstead, pointing at a desk not four feet from his. Nobody is sitting at it. Beyond it and to the left is a room full of activity. From where he is sitting, Baker can't see into the room, but he can hear two guys talking and teletypes clicking.

"Sitting here most nights," says Swenson, "will be one of the best editors in the Midwest, Jim Rector. Jim used to be the editor of the *Moorhead Daily News*. We hired him when we bought out his newspaper. I don't think he will ever forgive us for that, but he agreed to come to work for us to put out our morning paper. I think he likes serving the same readers he did when he was editing the *Daily News*. He does one hell of a job for us. You'll learn a lot from him."

There was a pregnant pause.

"That sounds great. When can I start?"

"How about this afternoon?" asks Swenson. Between now and four p.m., you can run by the Personnel Office and get your paperwork done."

"Sounds good to me. I'm anxious to begin working again. Oh, one question: where is your copy desk?"

The two editors laugh.

"Copy desks are for you big-city boys. Us small-town guys have to get by without anything that fancy," says Swenson.

"Here the copyediting and the headline-writing are done by the guys on the news desk. In the evening, for example, the night editor edits the copy for all the national and international news and writes their headlines. The state editor handles all the copy for the state news from North Dakota and Minnesota and writes the headlines for those stories.

"You will handle the local copy. That includes writing a weather story and editing any stories being written that evening by our own reporters. It also includes any obituaries that are called in after our regular obit writer goes home. Any stories you write, you'll show them to Jim. He will tell you what size headline he wants on each and then you'll write them.

"You will also monitor the squawk boxes for city, county, and state police in several jurisdictions. You will do the same for fire departments. Any stories you write will be based on interviews you do over the telephone. You won't be able to get your work done and still chase ambulances. If something big is going on, you call me at home and I'll put a reporter out on the street. Most of the time, though, you can do your own reporting just by picking up the phone. The telephone will become your best friend, believe me."

After handshakes all around, Baker is left on his own. He moves the chair he has been sitting on back to its desk. Then he looks back and sees the two editors have already moved away from their desks to talk to another editor.

Baker walks around the four desks that cluster together to constitute his place of work. All the desks are occupied by the dayside team of editors. They don't acknowledge Baker's presence and he doesn't interrupt their work to introduce himself.

In the middle of the four desks is a contraption that runs from the floor halfway up to the ceiling. Inside it are two large, wide leather belts—maybe 12 inches wide—that cling together until they reach the four desks. The belts are running continuously. There a device separates the two belts as they drop from the contraption. Baker finally figures out what its purpose is. It carries copy from the front room to the printers in the back room. Just then the city editor puts some copy paper in between the two belts and watches it leave. Baker follows the copy as it travels up and then off toward the back shop where it passes through a wall. Nearby is similar sized hole in the wall that allows the belt to circulate back into the newsroom. Baker watches the incoming belts go across the length of the ceiling before they drop down to pick up copy from sports and society editors. Once clear of those two departments, the belts come back toward him and the city desk. Pretty efficient, he has to admit.

Then he studies what will be his desk. The daytime editor who sits at it is already gone for the day. Like the *Star*, the afternoon paper goes to press early in the afternoon. That doesn't leave the dayside editing team much to do once the paper comes out. They could edit copy and save the night shift some work, but generally they just knock off early and allow the copy to pile up. The chair looks worn and so does the typewriter that sits next to it. The desk surface contains little more than a coffee cup full of editing pencils. He realizes then that the *Forum* doesn't use the fancy manufactured copy paper that has the carbon paper built in. If he wants a copy of something, he'll have to put carbon paper and another sheet of paper beneath whatever he's writing on.

He then looks into the room sitting next to his desk. No wonder it looks so active. It is the Associated Press office. Two young men, not much older than him, are in the room pounding away on teletype machines—sending stories from Fargo out to every other paper in the world using the AP. The room is crammed with teletype machines, many of which are rat-a-tat-tatting stories coming in from other AP rooms across the world, onto rolls of white paper unraveling as they fill with text. When one of the teletype machines finishes printing a story, it automatically scrolls a few inches of blank paper forward and stops. As Baker watches, one of the young men gets up and rips several finished stories from machines that have stopped, then pushes each story onto one of the many spikes holding newspaper and radio copy along one of the walls. Baker knows the AP pays well; he also knows the AP staff earn every penny of their pay.

Baker stands just outside the AP office for a few minutes watching the two men work, but they ignore him. That seems to be a trait of AP staffers. The AP, to save money for its members, places its offices inside its member newspapers. That means the AP employees work in a fishbowl environment. They are instructed not to play favorites with their host newspapers by giving them advance notice of stories that will run later on the AP wire. Such an advance notice might well give the host newspaper an advantage over its rivals. To maintain an arms-length relationship with their host newspaper's staff while working alongside them, AP employees learn to block them out.

Baker realizes the AP staff might be the most interesting newsmen in the building. He can live with their cold shoulder. They have a job to do and so does he. It isn't necessary for them to interact. Hell, he doesn't need to know what they're working on. He knows he'll learn that as soon as they file their stories, and the *Forum* receives them on its teletype.

He strolls off to find the personnel office and make himself a permanent staff member. By God, it's a good feeling to have a newspaper job again.

Chapter Eight

Killer Fleeing Fargo Heads to Minnesota

Joe Running Deer is stumbling his way into Minnesota across the Front Street Bridge. He is about halfway across when he bumps into two Indians heading into North Dakota. He doesn't want to stop and talk, but he has no choice: Indians approaching each other in hostile white man's land have to acknowledge one another.

The two Indians had been drinking at an Indian bar in Moorhead and are heading home to Fargo. They are not surprised to see Joseph Running Deer dead drunk. They are just surprised to see him drunk on a Sunday coming out of Fargo and smelling of whiskey. But what really gets their attention is the blood on his clothes. They turn him so his back is facing the traffic and his front is up against the bridge railing.

"Goddamn, Joe, what have you done now? You are covered with blood. It's not yours, is it?"

The Indian asking the question is Henry Whitefish of the Standing Rock Sioux Reservation in South Central North

Dakota. He and Joe had been in the Bismarck Penitentiary together. Consequently, they have a bond, despite the bad blood between the Mandan and the Dakota Indians. The Mandans may have been the first Indians in the state, but the Dakota or Lakota, known by the white man as the Sioux, came in later, from Minnesota, in much greater numbers. The Mandan always thought they might have been able to get the best of the white man had the Sioux not screwed things up by picking a fight with them every time the U.S. Government lied and broke a treaty.

"No, it's not my blood, goddammit. I'm okay. I got into a fight I didn't start."

Joe is already having a hard time remembering exactly what happened. It has been about two hours since he killed Sara Whitlow. He knows for certain, though, that her death isn't his fault.

"White people were insulting Indians," he says angrily. He looks at Henry Whitefish through his bloodshot eyes. "They were insulting the Sioux. I couldn't let them do that. I cut 'em for it."

The explanation satisfies the two Indians. Joe is the kind of drunk who would stand up for Indians when white men insulted them, even though that sort of thing goes on all the time. Most Indians just ignore white men's insults. That's not to suggest Indians are insensitive to what the white man says about them. That's the reason Indians sit around their campfires and tell each other graphic stories of the battle at Little Big Horn. Or they study Edgar Paxson's painting of Custer's Last Stand and discuss how brilliantly the artist captured the pleasure of the Indians engaged in their butchery.

Hanging around Joe Running Deer is making Henry Whitefish anxious. He sure doesn't want to be seen with Joe if a police car drives by. He glances around nervously. They are standing midway between Minnesota and North Dakota, which means city, county, and state cops from two states are equally likely to ask them their business. They need to go either east or west quickly.

"Where are you going, Joe?" asks Whitefish.

I'm going home," says Joe.

Had he identified anywhere else, it might have been plausible. But Whitefish knows from passing the bottle back and forth with Joe that he doesn't have a home. Not unless he is calling the Mandan Reformatory or the Bismarck Penitentiary home. Joe has spent most of his teenage and adult years in and out of those two state institutions.

Whitefish knows that Joe was born on the Fort Berthold Indian Reservation. But now his ancestral home is being buried under Lake Sakakawea, the rapidly growing body of water the Missouri River is creating as it backs up behind the recently completed Garrison Dam. Government agents came onto the reservation when Joe was a boy and gave the Indians pieces of paper. The paper said the Mandans had to move off the land they had lived on for centuries. The Corps of Engineers was going to put their homeland under a lake made out of river water so that white men who lived far away could get cheap electricity and not have to worry about spring floods. The government told the Indians they would be paid a stipend if they lost land they had farmed. But the government said it didn't think the farmland was particularly valuable, so the stipend wouldn't be worth much.

Joe's father had always been a hard-working farmer, but when he moved his family off the reservation to nearby Twin Buttes, he found no work. He did find the new liquor store located just outside Halliday on State Highway 8. His wife and children soon learned he could be violently abusive when he drank, which was soon nearly all the time. Joe left home when it became obvious he took after his father. Whitefish remembers Joe saying he had been banned entirely from the reservation.

The only way Joe's going home, thinks Whitefish, is if a warden holds a cell door open for him.

Joe hadn't even fooled himself when he said where he was going. He didn't know how to answer the question; he had no idea where he was going. He had come out of the Blind Pig, turned left toward the river and started to run. When he got to the banks of the Red River, he was exhausted and sick to his stomach. He heaved his guts out onto the bank, dumped a load into his shorts, and then rolled over into the mess and passed out. When he came too, about 30 minutes later, he was confused and scared and still very drunk. He climbed the riverbank and headed across the bridge toward Minnesota.

He wasn't sure anymore exactly what he was fleeing from, but he had a sixth sense bred into him that said it was time to move on. And when a drunken Indian leaves on foot out of North Dakota, Minnesota is as good a destination as any.

Whitefish reminds him that Moorhead cops don't like to find drunken Indians on the street. "They see you, they'll lock you up for sure," says Whitefish. "Walk straight and tall and head to Dilworth."

Dilworth is a small, wide-open town east of Moorhead that serves as a switching station for the Northern Pacific Railroad. As such, it has railroad crews working 24 hours a day, 7 days a week putting together trains for the trek west across the prairie. Railroad workers are both hungry and thirsty when they finish their shifts and a strip of restaurants and bars line the main drag through Dilworth to meet their needs. They are not allowed—

legally—to serve hard liquor after 1 a.m., or before 8 a.m., but they can sell 3.2 beers—brews with 3.2 percent alcohol—anytime. Consequently, there was always a crowd in Dilworth in the middle of the night: working stiffs, college kids, and party goers order steak and eggs and wash it down with pitchers of beer. An Indian could get lost in such a crowd, Whitefish is thinking.

Joe knows about Dilworth's all-night drinking. That's about all he knows about Dilworth. Then his mind suddenly flashes an image of that big guy in the car saying something about meeting him in Dilworth to get some money just before he pushed him out into the alley with all the Mexicans waiting for that stupid bar to open. But then Whitefish's companion, Jerome Flying Eagle, makes a keen observation. "Cops might ask you about your bloody knife."

Whitefish agrees. "You might want to dump it into the river. Otherwise the cops will say you used it in a fight. You probably should toss your coat too."

Joe now realizes why he wished he hadn't run into these two Sioux. They were going to talk him out of his knife. But he knew they were right. An Indian has a few drinks and his bloody knife immediately makes every cop think he's cut someone. It's just one of those things urban Indians have to cope with.

"Okay," says Joe, and he unbuckles his belt and slides the knife sheath off. He has already figured that it has to go if the knife is missing. He isn't going to walk around with an empty sheath. No brave would. Holding the leather sheath between his knees, he buckles his belt and looks down at the river. He can't see it.

But then it isn't much of a river. It's only key to fame is that it flows north rather than south, making it one of only two rivers on the North American continent that can claim that distinction. There never is much water in it. Most months of the year a grown man can find a place to wade across it. Fargo residents like to say that if they didn't flush their toilets before going to bed, folks in Grand Forks downriver wouldn't have enough water to brush their teeth in the morning. That joke never gets much of a laugh in Grand Forks, but a variation of it always gets a chuckle when told in Wahpeton, located upriver from Fargo.

With the assistance of Whitefish and Flying Eagle, both relatively sober because they have only been drinking 3.2 beer, Joe finally spots the Red River beneath the bridge. He drops his knife and sheath into it, but he keeps his jacket because he knows how cold nights can get on the Northern Prairie, even in the summer. Besides, it's a Levi jacket and he knows if he grinds a little dirt into it the blood will darken and perhaps not be readily noticed.

Joe now asks if he can accompany the two Indians, but they sense trouble will follow wherever he goes. They urge him to head to Dilworth, away from North Dakota.

"You might wake up tomorrow and want to be far away," says Whitefish. "If you do, you can hop a freight in Dilworth. And if you decide to stay in Dilworth for a while, there are several hobo parks around the railroad yards. Just watch out for the bulls. They don't like Indians."

"Huh, who does?" responds Joe.

"We do," says Whitefish, reaching out to grip Joe's right arm for a moment. With that, he and Flying Eagle move away from Joe and begin walking toward the lights of Fargo.

Joe turns the other direction and heads into Moorhead. He feels as if he has more spring in his walk now that the knife and its sheaf are off his belt. He is glad he kept the jacket. It is after midnight and it's going to get chilly before sunrise. Dilworth is seven miles away and at the rate he's walking he'll be lucky to get there by noon.

In the back of his mind, it seems to him he has a reason to go to Dilworth, but he can't put his finger on it. He hardly ever goes to Dilworth. He doesn't fret about it; he figures by morning it will come to him why he's heading east.

As it works out, he doesn't have to worry about it. About two hours after the incident on the bridge he is strolling through Moorhead with all the good intentions he can muster when a city patrol car stops him. Two young cops get out and shine flashlights on him. They move up close and personal and get a whiff of him. Joe recognizes the look on their face: They are repulsed.

The cops size up the situation quickly. They have a drunken Indian on their hands. He has obviously vomited, rolled in it, and shit himself. Probably more than once.

The two cops are not exactly rookies, but what they learned about being peace officers they gleaned from reading *Police Gazette*. Patrolman Tom Wright has been on the force two years and Patrolman John Self less than one. It never occurs to them to think of Joe Running Deer as anything but a drunken Indian, even though his clothes are covered with blood.

Wright and Self don't notice the blood. It has already darkened enough so that it is indistinguishable from the vomit, urine, and feces that cover his jacket and pants. When they ask him a few particulars, they learn he has wandered into their city from across the river. In fact, it doesn't appear he's done any drinking that night in their jurisdiction. Best they can tell, he actually hasn't violated any crimes in Moorhead, although they can probably lock him up for public intoxication and/or vagrancy. Both charges are frequently used when cops need a reason to arrest vagrants.

Patrolman Self assumes his senior partner is planning to take the Indian to jail. But the more experienced Wright knows that if they do that, he will have to put up with the desk sergeant's rancor. Desk sergeants hate to house a drunken Indian in one of their nice clean cells. Most Saturday nights they wouldn't care because the jails would be full of Indians in dirty cells. But come Sunday the jails empty out and the trustees clean the cells. Bringing in a drunken Indian on a Sunday night is one sure way for a patrolman to get on the wrong side of a desk sergeant. Because he is the senior officer, Wright also realizes he would have to fill out all the paperwork.

Wright motions for Self to join him at the back of the patrol car. Meanwhile, Joe Running Deer sits on the pavement in front of the car with his hands handcuffed behind his back.

"Here's what I'm thinking," says the more experienced cop. "I am thinking we should just run him over to Fargo and let him out there. When you think about it, he really is Fargo's problem. He just drifted over into Moorhead by mistake. Probably got confused about where he was going. We would be doing everyone a favor if he ended up back where he started. We just need to drop him off really quick, you know, just in case anyone raises a question about what we're doing."

His partner senses this is a learning moment.

"You know, by golly, you are right. The Indian did his drinking in Fargo; he ought to be arrested for it in Fargo."

So Joe ends up back on Front Street. He is let out of the Moorhead squad car at the corner of Front Street and 4th Street at about 12:30 a.m. The Moorhead cops pull a U-turn and speed back to Minnesota. He stands there rubbing his wrists, wondering why in the hell he's back in Fargo.

He turns south to walk down 4th Street toward Island Park, thinking he can sleep there until dawn and then find someplace to get coffee and maybe breakfast, if he feels like eating by then. But as he's turning, he notices four police cars and an ambulance halfway down the block, all with their lights flashing. A bunch of cops are shining lights on something in the alley. He is about to wander down there to see what is going on, but then thinks better of it. He doesn't want another run-in with cops. So instead, he stumbles west along Front Street, crosses 4th Street and heads toward Broadway. He gets about a block before a Fargo police car pulls up alongside of him and switches on its flashing lights, bathing him in red. Two policemen get out with their guns pulled.

"Stop right there and get down on the pavement," the bigger of the two cops yells at Joe.

"What?"

Steve Packer grabs Joe by his jacket, spins him around, and then kicks his feet out from under him. Joe falls to the ground, face forward. "I said get on the ground." Packer puts his knee into Joe's back and grabs his right arm and slaps a handcuff on his wrist. Then he puts one on the left wrist too.

"Christ, this guy stinks," says Packer as he gets up off Joe. His partner, Ryan Baum, has a large flashlight shining on the suspect.

"Is that blood on his clothes?" Baum asks.

"Sure looks like blood to me. See if you can find a knife. But be careful where you stick your hand."

Baum doesn't much like the thought of searching Joe's clothing, but he does it anyway. He checks Joe's two back pockets first and comes up empty. Then he rolls him over and from the two front pockets of his pants he pulls out a wad of bills, some small change, two books of matches, and a smooth river stone. He finds a pack of Lucky Strikes in a shirt pocket and nothing in the jacket pockets.

"No billfold or any identification," says Baum.

"What's your name," asks Packer.

"Joe Running Deer."

"Why did you kill the lady? Did she say something to you that pissed you off?"

"What lady?" asks Joe.

"Did you find a knife on him?" asks Packer.

"No, but he could have tossed it somewhere," says his partner.

"Where is your knife?" says the larger of the two cops.

"I don't have a knife," says Joe.

"Every fucking buck has a goddamn knife," says Packer. "What did you do with yours?"

Joe thinks hard for a minute. "I lost it in a card game. Three weeks ago. Over in Moorhead. I haven't bought a new one."

"How about the blood on your clothes? Where did that come from?" asks Packer.

Joe is waiting for that question. "I helped some Mexicans this afternoon. I butchered a deer. They caught the deer, but didn't know how to butcher it. I showed them how, for some money. You are holding it now. They got the meat. They took it with them when they got back on the trucks."

The two cops look at each other. Packer says: "Let's take him in. The detectives can sort this out. I think he's guilty of something."

Meanwhile, back in the alley, Detective John St. Claire has finally arrived on the scene. He is Fargo's best homicide detective. He is also the only one of the two homicide detectives on the Fargo police force available that night. He had thought of himself as unavailable. He had been off duty at the lake cottage of his in-laws near Perham, Minnesota, and did not want to have to drive into Fargo to catch this call. But the other detective was out of town at some federal conference in San Francisco learning how to do his job better, or so he'd been able to snow the chief.

So St. Claire is on Front Street at 3 a.m., and he isn't happy about it. When the call had come into the lake cottage saying it appears a whore had been knifed on Front Street, he had responded: "Leave her be and we'll find her Monday afternoon." Then he has to tell the dispatcher he was just kidding; of course, he'll get out of bed and drive 60 miles to view the body.

He pulls a pack of Winston's from his short-sleeve summer shirt. He'd put on a pair of slacks when he decided to respond to the call, but left on his summer-going-to-the-lakes shirt. He lights the cigarette and stares at the body. She is still lying on her stomach when he arrives, but now that he is onsite, the officers on the scene turn her over. He wants to see the wound. But what catches his eye first is the victim herself. By God, he knows her.

He gasps. He can't remember the last time he did that at a murder scene. Years.

He once knew her really well. They had gone to Fargo Central together. She was a grade ahead of him. They had even dated once.

Well, it wasn't really a date, not in the traditional sense. He hadn't gone to her house and picked her up and then taken her home or anything like that. He had met her at a house party, and they had gone out to her car together. That had been her idea. But he was all for it. She was beautiful and exotic and a year older than him. He was hoping on the way out the door his buddies had taken notice of who he was leaving with.

After some introductory kisses, she had encouraged him to take off her sweater and then her bra and then her panties. She kept her skirt on because it was chilly and she said it wouldn't get in the way of anything.

He still had all his clothes on when she asked him what it was worth to him to go all the way.

He was a high school junior. He had never paid for sex. Hell, he had never gone all the way. At that moment, though, money wasn't an issue: he would pay whatever she was asking. Trouble was, he only had seven dollars on him. He told her what he had in his billfold, but promised her he could get more money later. She smiled and said he had enough.

They were sitting in the back seat of her parent's car. He didn't remember what it was, but it was big and comfortable. She told him to slip his pants and underwear down; he did, beyond his knees. She then handed him a Trojan in a lubricated package. When it was obvious he didn't know what to do with it, she took it back from him, opened it, and put it on for him. She didn't seem upset by his inexperience. She kissed him, passionately, and then climbed into his lap and took charge of their lovemaking.

He had always believed it to be the best expenditure of seven dollars he'd ever made.

He had never hooked up with her again. He had tried, but she was always too busy. He finally figured out that his one-night stand must have been made possible because somebody else hadn't shown up at the party that night.

Sara Christenson. That was her name.

"Did anybody find any identification on her?"

A sergeant standing over her said she had no purse or pocketbook on her and they found no other forms of identification in her clothing.

"I don't know her married name," said St. Claire, glancing at the wedding ring on her left hand, "but her maiden name was

Sara Christenson." He looked around at the group of men surrounding the body. The name meant nothing to any of them.

"Sara Christenson," he repeated, his voice now rising. "For fuck's sake. Her father is the senior senator from North Dakota."

Just as the significance of that sunk in, a squad car with its red lights flashing drives up and Patrolman Steve Packer yells through his open window to St. Claire: "We got your killer for you. He's soaked in blood. But you're going to have to find the murder weapon."

St. Claire looks into the backseat at Joe Running Deer. Then he looks back at Sara. He says to himself a murder like this doesn't get solved that easily. There's got to be a complication.

He turns back and stands, looking down at Sara. Thinking back on it, he tries to recall if he had ever gotten anything else close to the bargain Sara had given him in the back seat of her father's big car. He shakes his head. He can't think of what it would have been.

The middle section of her dress is covered with blood. He notices, however, very little blood lying on the ground. He finds that strange. If the Indian had killed her there, judging from the amount of blood on him, the ground should be covered with it too. But the only blood he can see is a small spot directly under Sara and it appears to be offset from her dress, not blood from her wound.

He looks at the sergeant. "Call Captain Wayne Thompson. Get him down here. Tell him we've got a Front Street murder. Tell him it's going to be a complicated case. Oh, yeah, you might mention to him the victim is the daughter of our senior senator. And we got an Indian in custody. That ought to please him.

Chapter Nine

The Forum Is on the Story

Chuck Baker strolls back into the *Forum* newsroom 15 minutes before his shift begins. He's eager to go to work.

He sits down at the desk assigned to him and notices the one directly across from him is empty. He has beaten the night editor to work. That is probably a good thing. The managing editor had seen him come in, then glanced up at the clock on the wall before smiling at him.

As he sits there, a cute, young thing walks up to his desk and says, "Hi, you're new here, aren't you?"

Barker runs his eyes from the top of her head to her ankles and back in a flash. She is the perfect package. About five foot six, one hundred ten pounds, blond hair, great figure, movie star looks, and friendly to boot. She might be 17 years old. Tops.

"Hi yourself, yes, this is my first day."

"Welcome then, my name is Maggie. I'm the copy girl." She throws him a smile that melts his heart.

She's standing so close to his chair he can smell her perfume. He doesn't know anything about perfume. But he likes hers.

"What does a copy girl do at the *Forum*?" is the best he can do under the circumstances.

"Why, we bring you copy paper, silly," and she bends over to pull out his desk drawer to show him a ream of copy paper. He isn't looking at the copy paper. He is staring down the front of her blouse and quickly determines that she fills out her bra without necessity of padding.

Still leaning over, she moves across him so that their bodies touch in several places, not all of them inappropriate, to grab a paper cup off his desk.

Once she has it in her hand, she stands back up.

"I also fill your cup," she says in a voice that encourages Baker to fantasize about how she might go about doing that.

She points the cup at him so he can see into it.

My God, he thinks, that can't be what it looks like. He grabs the cup out of her hand and looks carefully at the white, chalky, pasty stuff coating the bottom of the cup.

"What is it?" he finally asks.

"Glue, silly. What did you think it was?"

"I don't know," he replies, as he hands the cup back to Maggie. "What do I do with a cup of glue, Maggie?"

"I can see we have much to teach you, don't we?"

Maggie reaches back into the drawer and grabs two pieces of copy paper.

She hands him one.

"Put this in your typewriter."

He complies.

"Okay. Now pretend you're typing a story.

He complies.

"That's right. Just pound away. Now skip to the bottom of the page. What do you do at this point when you have more to write?"

"I guess I pull the paper out of the typewriter and put another sheet in and continue typing."

"That is exactly what you do." She smiles at him and adds, "So do it."

Baker puts the second piece of paper in his typewriter and does as he's told. He feels a little silly, but he's enjoying the young woman's attention.

"Okay, enough typing. Your story is done. Pull the paper out of the typewriter. Now you have to send it into the back room to the typesetters. Here is where your glue comes into play. You spread the glue on the top of your second page. Now grab your first page. Lay the bottom of it over that portion of the second page that contains the glue. Squeeze the bottom of the first page onto the top of the second page. See how they stick together? You're done. Now you can send it to the backroom knowing the printers won't lose any of your pages."

"Wouldn't it be just as easy if I numbered my pages?"

Maggie sighs.

"Think of how many page twos there are likely to be floating around the back room at the same time. How are the printers to know which page two goes with your page one?"

He has to admit she has a point. But the *Washington Star* wouldn't do it that way. It would have "Baker 1" written on the first page and "Baker 2" on the second page. Then the two pages would be stapled together before going to the composing room.

But, concludes Baker, when in Fargo, do as the Fargoneans do.

"I'll go get you some glue. And a new glue pot." And with a quick smile, Maggie turns on her heels and sashays off while he watches her every step.

"Look all you want, just don't touch," says a large man with a crew cut sitting at the desk kitty-corner from his.

Baker looks up, embarrassed at having been caught eyeballing the young copy girl. He hadn't noticed the man when he sat down at what he had been told earlier was the state desk.

"Hi, I'm Harold Morrison. Call me Harry. You must be the new guy I've heard about. From back East, I'm told."

"That's right. My name is Chuck Baker. I'm from Washington, D.C."

"Welcome to the *Forum*. You have a lot to learn in your new job and almost no time in which to learn it. I don't know if anybody has told you this, but you've been given a tough assignment. Nearly everything you do can result in a screw-up. Screw-ups are what gets you fired around here. In the military, which is my background, we give people who have jobs with the potential for screw-ups a lot of training so the likelihood of screw-ups is reduced. At the *Forum*, we don't give people in your position any training at all. That doesn't make any sense. But that's the way it is. Welcome to the *Forum*.

"Did you start out in this job?"

"No way. I was working for the Grand Forks *Herald*. I came down here to be the state editor. I don't think there are more than one or two people working here who started out in your job. It's a killer."

"Thanks for the encouragement."

"Look, I don't want to discourage you. I'm here to be helpful. I mean that. Your editor, Jim Rector, doesn't want you to fail either. He has a newspaper to get out. You screw up and it makes his job tougher. So we're going to be pulling for you. You work at it and we'll do our best to see you succeed."

"I appreciate that."

"One piece of advice to start out?"

"What's that?"

"Stay away from Maggie."

"The copy girl?"

"Yeah, the copy girl. She's a little slow mentally, but she's fast other ways, if you know what I mean. She'll come on to you all the time. It's going to be tempting, I know. Ask every guy in this place. But keep your hands off her. If you don't, you'll be out the door in a minute."

"For dating the copy girl?"

"No, for messing around with the publisher's granddaughter."

"Oh, I get it."

"You looked like a clever boy."

Just then a tall, fashionably dressed gentleman approaches the desk across from Baker's. He is wearing a tailored summer suit and a cream-colored fedora. He takes three large, green-colored cigars out of his suit pocket and lays them on his desk, then he walks away to hang his suit coat on a rack by the front door. He puts his hat on the shelf above his coat. Chuck notices he walks with a limp. His hair is elegantly long and all white. As he walks back toward the desk across from Baker's, he rolls up his sleeves past his elbows. All serious newspapermen do that. It keeps the newspaper ink from ruining their shirt sleeves. Then he looks over at the news editor's desk and nods, but doesn't say anything. Then he pulls out the editor's chair and sits down.

Harry stands up from his desk and walks the few steps to Rector's desk.

"Jim, let me introduce the new man to you."

Rector looks up at Baker with benign interest. It was obvious he'd seen a lot of young men come and go in his years in the business.

"His name is Chuck Baker. This is his first day. I'll let him give you some of his background."

Baker sits staring at the editor. He suspects this isn't going to be easy.

"Hello. As Harry said, my name is Chuck Baker. I'm from Washington, D.C. I worked there on the *Washington Star*. It's a real pleasure to be here at the *Forum*. I'm looking forward to working with you. Mr. Swenson sang your praises earlier today and I think I can learn a lot from you."

The night editor stares at him with a frown on his face.

"First of all, this isn't any goddamn classroom. And I'm no teacher. If you don't know what you're doing, you shouldn't be sitting in that chair. I am sick and tired of Swenson sticking me with people who don't know their job. I suppose you're going to tell me that when you worked at the *Star* you were a reporter, right?"

"Yes, sir. I was a general assignment reporter."

"That's just great. That means you don't know a damn thing about being a desk editor."

Baker is tempted to argue the point, but thinks better of it. Besides, Rector has already deserted his chair and is heading toward the back shop.

"I guess that didn't go all that well," he says to Morrison.

"I said you're going to have to prove yourself," he replies. "Jim Rector is one of the best editors in the business. You can learn from him. You just can't expect him to teach you. Learn by watching what he does.

"For example, you'll notice he groups three or four stories together on the corner of his desk during the course of the evening. He'll keep looking at them all night long. Then he's likely to add still other stories to his pile. When he comes back from dinner, around nine p.m., he'll pick one story from his pile and designate it as his lead story. It will go on the front page under a banner headline. The others will probably end up on the front page too, but with smaller headlines. Ask yourself, why did he select the one that got top billing? What did it have that the other stories in his pile didn't?

"Then he still has to fill up the entire front page. How does he decide what else to put on it? Does the presence or absence of an accompanying photograph influence his decision about his top story? Each story has a headline. How big will he make them? How many columns wide will they run? Will they all be in the same typeface?

"All during the night the AP will be sending us pictures to accompany the stories it's also sending us. Jim will select some to go into the newspaper. One or more of them will end up on the front page. He also has to decide how big to make the pictures. How does he decide that?

"Finally, he can start a story on page one and continue it someplace else in the paper. How does he decide how much of the story to run on the front page and how much to continue on another page?

Baker thinks he knows the answers to all these questions. He had been the editor of a daily newspaper in college where he made these same decisions himself five days a week for a year. But he doesn't know if Rector has different criteria he uses to make these editorial decisions. He is curious to find out.

"I'll be anxious to learn from him," he assures Morrison.

"I know I learned a lot from him. And that's after having worked years on a daily newspaper, including a stint as a desk editor."

That first night, Baker finds out that the local weather story he's to write will end up on page one. Before he begins, Baker spends a few minutes looking at the previous three days' worth of newspapers to see how it's done. He quickly figures out that each story follows a similar format. That's to say, they're bland and right to the point. They don't appear to include humor or the author's personal observations. Just the facts, straight from the weatherman, Baker concludes. He can do that.

He calls the U.S. Weather Bureau and gets the official forecast. Then he pretty much writes up the information just as he heard it from the weatherman. His story seems unexciting, but that seems to be the *Forum's* style. He guesses that the weather is always big news in the Upper Midwest. And he can't believe anyone concerned about weather relies on a newspaper for the forecast or current conditions. By the time the newspaper prints a weather story, it's old news to anyone with access to a radio. Baker figures all the *Forum* is doing is printing an official weather story that can be pasted in a family scrapbook alongside the picture of their dog to explain what was going on outside when it died.

He also finds out he's expected to write obituaries called in from area undertakers. Harry says they prefer to be called "funeral home directors," but everyone on the night desk calls them undertakers. He also says they're notoriously sloppy with their facts. Harry recommends Baker keep good notes of his conversations with undertakers. That way, he can defend himself when the funeral home insists that any mistake in the obituary was made by a *Forum* writer.

Over the next couple of weeks, Baker finds his job primarily involves editing copy that comes in from reporters covering public meetings in the early evening, like school board or city council meetings, as well as public events. A regular contributor he discovers is a retired music professor from NDSU. He regularly files stories about concerts and plays performed by area colleges and high schools. He always writes positive reviews of these, but doesn't hesitate to heap scorn and criticism on visiting musicians and thespians who perform for pay.

Sitting as his desk, Baker monitors the police and fire squawk boxes. These are usually pretty quiet, and most of what he hears seems pretty routine; a fire run to investigate smoke pouring out of somebody's garbage can, a police car being directed to a city park to break up a gathering of teenagers. Highway fatalities are front-page news in the morning newspaper, so Baker keeps an ear open for reports of serious accidents.

When an accident includes a death, Baker calls the Highway Patrol and asks to speak to the officer on the scene. He can also call the hospital for information. He seldom gets the full story from anyone, but at least the morning newspaper can tell its readers about the accident and where it occurred. In the morning, a reporter on the afternoon *Forum* can then gather up all the facts and write the full story. Then the morning newspaper can reprint it the next day.

The night editor never compliments Baker on his work. On the other hand, Rector doesn't rewrite many of his headlines or heavily edit his written copy. Baker is bothered at first that Rector seldom speaks to him, but he notices he doesn't have all that much to say to Morrison, either. The man comes in, does his job, and goes home. Can't fault him for that.

Rector works Monday through Friday. On Saturday and Sunday other old-timers sit in as night editor, in place of Rector. The workload is always lighter on the weekend. Sunday's paper is gigantic, but most of its contents have been edited and the pages printed during the week. All that remains to be put together on Saturday night are a few pages to capture late-breaking news. Only the sports desk and general assignment reporters covering special events work Sunday, so Monday morning's paper has to rely on copy from the wire services to fill its pages. This means the newsroom is usually quiet Sunday nights, sometimes eerily so.

This August night has been one of those. Nothing happening, the newsroom quiet enough that Baker can hear a little echo off the walls when he accidentally knocks a pen off his desk and it hits the floor. He doesn't like Sunday nights. He's looking forward to hitting the sack in his room at The Donaldson in a few hours.

Suddenly, just after 9:30 a.m., the Fargo Police squawk box starts making a lot of noise. Baker focuses in on the chatter. Something about a body in the alley at Front Street and 4th Street. He takes his map of Fargo out of his desk and looks for the intersection. It is only about three blocks from the *Forum*.

Morrison is sitting in as the night editor. They have an hour before the last edition has to be locked up; plenty of time, in other words, to get a local story onto the front page.

"Harry, I think I'll run down and check out this murder scene. I might be able to get enough from the police for a short story. Got any objections to that?"

"Go ahead. If you can get anything we can use, I'll put it up front. But get moving."

Baker pushes out the side door of the *Forum* onto 5th Avenue and turns left. He goes down to 4th Street, turns right and heads for Front Street. He jogs most of the way. It feels good to be out of the office. Nobody is on the streets. A typical Sunday night in Fargo.

He crosses over the Northern Pacific Railroad tracks just before a lengthy, slow-moving freight train comes through town, heading east, blocking the intersection for nearly ten minutes. Baker glances over his shoulder at the train and sees it's hauling car after car full of lignite coal.

At the intersection of Front Street and 4th he sees the flashing lights of the emergency vehicles. He stops jogging—no need to call undue law enforcement attention to himself—and heads down 4th Street toward the scene. As he gets closer, he can see men milling around something lying on the ground covered with a sheet at the end of a well-lit alley. That's the body, Baker knows.

Baker approaches the group slowly, coming in just close enough, maybe within fifty feet, to hear two men talking to each other. They don't appear to be friends, and they don't notice him. They're not wearing police uniforms, so they're probably detectives. He stops and listens.

"Listen to me, St. Claire, I don't need you telling me my business," says the larger of the two men.

"Hey, lighten up. I'm sorry I had to get you down here. I realize it's late. It's your case. Handle it anyway you want. I'm just telling you this lady wasn't murdered at this spot. If she had been gutted here, the ground would be soaked with blood."

"Thank you for your splendid analysis, Mr. Homicide Detective. Now the Front Street Detective is on the scene and you can go home."

Baker moves back slowly, deciding not to be seen yet if he can help it. It would be awkward to be caught eavesdropping, and he doesn't need to get off on the wrong foot with either of these men. He'll probably be getting to know them pretty well covering crime scenes over the next couple of years.

He notices the streetlight above him is out, possibly explaining why he wasn't seen. He heads back toward Front Street. Turning the corner, he jogs down to 5th Street and heads down to the same alley where he saw the body, but now he's a block away. He turns into the alley and heads back toward the crime scene. The alley is well lit and they'll probably see him coming from half a block away.

As he approaches mid-block, he finds himself standing under a dim light in front of a heavy brown door. He glances down and sees what looks like drops of blood. He bends down and puts his finger into a dark puddle and pulls it back and looks at it. For God's sake, it's blood all right. He steps away from the door and looks for some more. There's a lot of blood trails by the door and they all lead into the alley to where the victim is lying.

He looks again at the door. "For Deliveries Only" says the old sign attached to it. Then he notices the buzzer next to the door. He wouldn't have been able to explain why, but he rings it. Then he stands back. And he jumps when the old door opens.

Sam Bodini heard the bell and assumes Detective Captain Thompson has come back for something. As soon as he sees the kid, he realizes he shouldn't have opened the door.

"What the fuck do you want?"

"I'm with the *Forum* and I want to know whose blood is on your doorstep."

"None of your goddamn business," responds Bodini, as he slams the door shut and turns the lock. Why is a *Forum* reporter snooping around the Blind Pig? He shrugs his shoulders and decides he better call Thompson.

Baker doesn't know what to make of the exchange at the door. He hadn't expected it to open and was shocked when it did. He had tried to see around Bodini, but the man had appeared to be standing in some kind of coal-black vestibule.

Going back to his original intentions, he walks further down the alley toward a small knot of policeman, most in uniform. He doesn't get far before he draws their attention. At that point, they yell at him to put his hands in the air and to walk toward them slowly.

When he identifies himself, flashing his press card, they all relax, but remain hostile. The guy he heard earlier telling the homicide detective he was the Front Street detective says: "What are you doing here?"

"Investigating a murder. What can you tell me about it?"

"Not a goddamn thing."

"Sir, I know there's a dead woman under that sheet—"

"I told you I'm not going to tell you a damn thing. Now get lost."

"Okay, I'm leaving. But can you do one thing for me. Can you identify the body?"

"There's no identification on the body. Now get out of here."

Baker turns to leave and then thinks he ought to make one more try.

"Oh, by the way, just in case you're curious. Blood trails lead from a doorway about halfway up the block. See that pale light down the alley? It's over a heavy, brown door. Anyway, out in front of that door is a lot of spilled blood. Next to the door is a buzzer. When you ring it, a very unfriendly fellow appears and tells you to get lost. He might be worth talking to. Just thought you ought to know."

Baker can tell by the look on the detective's face that he's unlikely to follow up on the tip.

Back at the *Forum*, Morrison hands him a few notes about what he's heard coming off the chatter from the squawk box. Baker sits down and writes a one-column headline and a story to go with it.

```
Fargo Police Find Woman Dead in Alley
```

Fargo police Sunday night found a woman lying dead in an alley behind Front Street near the intersection of 4th Street. Police believe she was murdered, but probably not at the location where she was found.

Police said the woman carried no identification. Police were unable to release her identity as of Sunday night.

Blood trails leading to the dead woman appeared to originate from a doorway below the Silver Saloon Tavern, about a half-block away from where the body was found. The doorway opens to an apparent basement storeroom beneath the Tavern. An unidentified man opened the door from the inside late Sunday night, but refused to answer media questions about the blood on the doorstep.

Captain Wayne Thompson of the Fargo Police is in charge of the investigation.

While Baker was composing his story, the ambulance was loading up Sara's body for transport to Nestvold Funeral Home. The police were finishing up their work and Thompson was waiting for his colleagues to leave so he could go talk to Bodini and find out about the exchange between him and the young reporter.

That's when St. Claire drove up in his unmarked police car.

"I'm out of here. This case is all yours. By the way, anybody tell you her name yet?"

"I thought you said she had no identification on her."

"That explains why you're remaining so calm. I told dispatch to tell you her name when you were called out here to examine the body. How come nobody ever wants to deliver the bad news? Well, here it is, ol' buddy. You have got your hands full. Your vic is the only daughter of the senior senator from North Dakota."

"What? You've got to be kidding. This woman is a goddamn whore. I mean, she turns tricks for drinks. She's no senator's daughter."

"She may not be the daughter Mr. and Mrs. Thomas Christenson would have preferred, but she's the only one they have. And now she's dead in your alley. They probably would appreciate a phone call before they hear about it on the news.

And with that, St. Claire drove his unmarked police car through the alley and lit up another Winston. He was thinking he had just made Thompson's job tougher, and he didn't give a damn.

At 1:30 a.m. Monday, St. Claire is climbing into his bed, Thompson is huddled over the bar in the Blind Pig with Bodini, and Baker is walking out of the *Forum* with the morning newspaper under his arm containing his front-page story of the murder. Joe Running Deer is sitting naked in the county jail and Sara is lying dead in the city morgue. Senator and Mrs. Christenson are asleep in their respective beds back in Arlington, VA., hours away from learning their only daughter is dead.

Out in Western North Dakota, near Dickenson, a long-haul truck driver is having a pleasant dream about his lovely wife. He won't know until morning he is a widower.

Chapter Ten

Wife Weeps for Slain Daughter

The receptionist in Senator Christenson's office picks up the phone on the second ring, well within the office's policy of no more than three rings, and says: "Good morning, Senator Christenson's Office, how may I help you?"

Wayne Thompson does not want to make this call. He has waited until morning to do it. He doesn't personally know the senator. But he has been obligated to tell other fathers that their daughters are dead and he never relishes the task.

"This is Detective Wayne Thompson of the Fargo Police Department. May I please speak with Senator Christensen?"

"I'm sorry, the senator isn't in his office this morning," says the receptionist. "Would you like to talk with his chief of staff, Mr. Larry Mowrey?"

"Sure. Put me through."

"Please hold."

"This is Larry Mowrey."

"This is Detective Wayne Thompson of the Fargo Police Department. I understand the senator is out. However, I have a personal message for him. Can you tell me how to reach him?"

"I can deliver that message to him, if you would like."

"I would prefer to do it myself, if that's okay with you."

"I am the senator's chief of staff, detective. You can convey any message to the senator through me. I will assure you it will reach the senator."

"Okay, big shot. You can play messenger boy. Got a pencil and paper handy? I don't want to say this twice."

"Go ahead."

"Last night, at about ten p.m., Fargo time, Sara Whitlow, the only daughter of Senator and Mrs. Thomas Christenson, was found murdered in an alley behind Front Street near the Fourth Street intersection in downtown Fargo."

Mowrey interrupts Thompson at that point.

"Slow down, please, I'm trying to write down the message exactly as you say it."

Thompson continues, but he speaks a little slower and just a little louder.

"The Fargo police have arrested an Indian, originally from Fort Berthold, and now of no fixed address, and are holding him on suspicion of murder. He was intoxicated at the time of his arrest. He has not made a statement concerning the events of last evening.

"Sara Whitlow's body was taken to the city morgue for an autopsy. Later today it will be transferred to whatever funeral home the family chooses.

"Did you get all that?"

"I think so. The senator's daughter, Sara, was murdered by a drunken Indian in an alley off Front Street in Fargo last night. We need to designate a funeral home. Can you tell us what she was doing in that alley?"

"No. We looked around the area for her car and didn't find it. There was no identification on her. We looked for a purse or a pocketbook and didn't find one. That would suggest a theft. But the Indian had nothing on him to indicate he took anything from her. Of course, someone could have come along after the murder and lifted the purse."

"How can you be sure it was Sara Whitlow?"

"She was identified by one of our detectives who knew her from high school. When we went to her home—she lives in a trailer park off Fifth Avenue on the South Side—a car registered to a Bruce Whitlow was parked in her space. A light was on in the trailer, but nobody answered the door. She had on a wedding ring, so we assume she is she married to this Bruce Whitlow. Do you know anything about her husband?

"No I don't. But I'll find out and let you know. Can you leave me your name and phone number?"

Thompson does and then hangs up, glad that call is over. He isn't at all disappointed he doesn't have to talk directly to the senator.

Mowrey isn't any more eager to pass on the news to the senator than Thompson had been. He picks up the phone and calls Jerry Pinks.

"Jerry? This is Larry Mowrey. Can you come over to the senator's office right away? It's terribly important. Thanks."

Mowrey realizes that nobody is closer to the senator than Pinks. He should be the one to convey the bad news.

Fifteen minutes later, Pinks walks into Senator Christenson's suite of offices, nods to the receptionist as he breezes past her desk and heads straight back to Mowrey's office, which is just outside the senator's. He pokes his head in. Mowrey looks up and Pinks motions his head toward his own office, also outside the senator's, directly across the hallway. He flips on the light and walks around his desk. By the time he sits down, Mowry has closed the door behind them and is sitting down across from him.

Pinks tells Mowrey he has made the right decision, even though Pinks knows he has done so because he's basically a chickenshit. Pinks had the senator hire Mowrey to be his chief of staff only because his father was the former governor of North Dakota and still had a lot of friends in the state, particularly in West River, where the senator needs all the votes he can get on election day.

Pinks asks Mowrey if he has the phone number for the Fargo detective who told him of Sara's murder.

"Yeah,"

"Well, call him back and tell him that Sara's husband is named Bruce. He drives a truck for a construction company building the interstate across North Dakota. The Fargo police ought to be able to find him with that information. Suggest to the cops that they talk to Sara's neighbors in the trailer park too. Somebody ought to know the company's name because it's a sure bet some of the neighbors work for the same outfit."

"Okay," says Mowrey, immediately heading back across the hall to his office.

Finished with Mowrey, Pinks picks up the phone and calls the senator's home number. A maid answers. Pinks asks for Mrs. Christenson. When she gets on the phone, he asks her if she and the senator will be home for the next hour. She says they will. Then he says he will be right out to talk to them both. In response to her question, he says he has some news that concerns the two of them. Then he says he prefers to deliver it in person rather than over the phone.

Pinks leaves the senator's office and descends into the lower reaches of the Hart Senate Office Building to get his car. He drives onto the 395 Freeway and across the 14th Street Bridge where he picks up the George Washington Parkway. Normally he enjoys this drive because of its beautiful views of the Potomac River and urban forests on both sides of the highway. Today all he sees is the highway.

The senator has never said much about his daughter and rarely ever mentions her when campaigning in North Dakota. But Pinks knows the senator's wife has a strong mother-daughter relationship with her only child. Even in recent years, after the senator banished Sara from the family for her many screw-ups, Pam has stayed in touch with her. Whenever Pinks accompanies the senator back to Fargo on business, Pam always finds a moment away from the senator to ask him to find Sara and see how she is doing. He had a routine when it came to the senator's daughter. He would find her, meet for lunch or dinner, and provide her with some of her mother's money. Then when he got back to Washington, he scheduled a meeting with the senator's wife to give her a detailed description of Sara's appearance and share what he had gleaned about her daily routine.

Pinks thought Sara was a loser. Attractive, spunky, and full of life, to be sure. But no common sense and a penchant for making bad decisions. Every time he visited with her he felt pity for her mother. He believed the senator made the right decision to push her away. But he never shared this sentiment with Pam.

There was something else about Sara he hadn't shared with Pam. He had also given Sara money. The money was in payment for services rendered. Pinks couldn't get over how much the daughter resembled her mother. Having sex with Sara always enabled him to fantasize about making love to Pam again. When Sarah had an orgasm, she would call out his name, loud, over and over again, just as her mother used to do. It was the thing he liked most about Sara.

He got off the Parkway at Spout Run and drove up to Nellie Custis Drive where he turned right and then straight ahead until the street crossed Lee Highway. He turned onto Lee and went to the intersection of Lee and Glebe where he turned right. He drove past the country club and nearby stately homes until he came to Chesterbrook Road. He turned left and then took an immediate left again into the long driveway that led to the mansion where the senator lived.

When he rings the bell, Pam opens the door, looking apprehensive, but beautiful, as usual. She is in her early fifties, about 5'6" and 130 pounds. She has a personal trainer and it shows. She is a natural blonde, which makes her blue eyes that much more attractive. Jerry was smitten by her the first time they met, and every time since. She smiles at him, knowing the effect she has on the senator's aide.

"Jerry, it's good to see you," she whispers as she gives him a light kiss on the lips and a hug that is more than friendly. "But I have to admit, you have me a little anxious when you say you have to tell us something you can't share over the phone."

It occurs to Pinks that he didn't often come to the senator's home with bad news.

"I'm sorry, Pam. Is the senator up and around?"

"You really are serious, aren't you? Yes, he's in the sunroom reading newspapers. Why don't we go in there? Would you like some coffee?"

"No thanks. I'm fine."

Pinks walks with the senator's wife through the house and into the sunroom. The senator is sitting in his favorite chair dressed for work except for his suit jacket. He seldom comes into the office before noon unless he has a key committee hearing to attend or an important floor vote to cast. With the Democrats in charge of the Congress and the White House, he figures the best way for a ranking Republican senator to demonstrate his disdain for the whole bunch is to boycott their smarmy efforts to legislate his country into a socialist state.

"Jerry, how are you? Have a seat."

The senator isn't well, and it shows. He was elected to one of the two North Dakota House of Representative seats back in the early 50s and then moved into the U.S. Senate when the state's senior senator died in office. Senator Christenson has been re-elected twice. He is now in his late seventies and suffering from the effects of two minor strokes, high blood pressure, diabetes, bladder cancer, and several less-serious ailments. None of this is shared with his constituents, of course, and only a handful of his staff know the truth about his declining health.

Being a politician has made the senator a rich man. He entered office a dirt-poor farmer who caught a lot of breaks, most of them from people who knew how one hand could wash the other. He serves on the Senate Appropriations Committee as well as the Senate Agriculture Committee. This means he is positioned to promote farm legislation beneficial to folks back home and then see to it that federal funds are appropriated to pay for it. Sometimes these programs benefit just a small number of wealthy individuals. But these same individuals, grateful for all the hard work the senator does on their behalf, seem pleased to give him tips about prime farm property when it becomes available, along with a recommended buying price. Of course, they know the senator has a modest income as a public servant, so his friends steer him to their banks where loans to select clients can be obtained at extremely favorable rates.

And the favors just keep coming. These same friends also recommended several years ago that the senator mortgage some of his newly acquired land to purchase even more Red River Valley farms.

Finally, these friends—now his business colleagues—keep suggesting he grow sugar beets on his Red River Valley land. He doesn't know anything about growing sugar beets; he's a former grain farmer. But not to worry. His friends, many of whom serve on the board of the American Sugar beet Cooperative, know people willing to manage the senator's operations for him.

With this assurance, his friends agree with him that he can spend most of his time in Washington. Besides, this arrangement ensures he has the time to carry out the bidding of the American Sugar Beet Cooperative, which benefits the state's sugar beet growers. And himself.

Pinks, the senator's trusted aide, also receives guidance from the Cooperative about how he might wisely invest his nest egg in the production of North Dakota sugar beets. And he has done so, for many years. After all, he knows he's not going to remain a senior staff member on the Senate Appropriations Committee forever. Someday he'll have to get a real job. Or simply live off his sugar beet earnings.

Outside of his financial holdings, Senator Christenson considers his trophy wife Pam to be his most valuable possession. She is nearly 30 years his junior. From all indications, she adores her husband. He had been married once before, a long time ago, but divorced the woman after she grew bored with the challenges of being a congressman's wife.

Not long after the divorce, Christenson met Pam, a Congressional staff member from his home state who worked on the House Agriculture Committee. At first the relationship was platonic. But he started bringing her to some of the social functions he was constantly being asked to attend. The relationship eventually grew serious, and then intimate, but the difference in age was too much for her to agree to anything permanent. That is, until she got pregnant. She then consented to marry him. He was thrilled. He loved her, for sure, but he also knew having a child with a North Dakota beauty would please a lot of voters back home.

He wanted a big wedding in Fargo during a congressional recess, but she insisted on an immediate, small ceremony in Washington, D.C. She reminded him that his constituents could count to nine and the quicker they got married the less likely the voters would be to think he had to. He agreed, but insisted they have a follow-up party among their friends back home. As soon as she said yes, he arranged for large wedding receptions in Fargo and Grand Forks. He knew before asking that the American Sugar beet Cooperative would be pleased to host both.

Pam always reminds Jerry Pinks she couldn't have made it through those early months of marriage and childbirth if it hadn't been for his friendship and support.

The two of them were friends before she married his boss. They maintained their friendship after she became the congressman's companion. They found themselves together doing congressional work and at social functions that occupy much of the free time of congressional aides. The two even occasionally pondered how things might have turned out different had he shown more interest in her early on in their relationship.

All that was shoved into the background when Pam announced she was pregnant. Jerry decided his romantic interest in Pam was over. Pam agreed with him, but couldn't bring herself to say it. And until she said it, she knew she would never be sure their special friendship had spun to a stop.

"What brings you across the river this morning?" the senator asks, bringing his senior aide and his wife back into the moment. "What couldn't wait until I got into the office this afternoon?"

"I'm afraid I have some very bad news," Pinks says as he sits in the chair opposite the senator. Pam sits on a love seat across the room.

"A Fargo detective called the office this morning. Last night your daughter Sara was found dead. It appears she was murdered. I am so sorry."

Pinks waited for them to absorb what he has just said.

The senator stared first at the floor and then at his wife. Pam stared only at Jerry. Then her eyes welled with tears and her hands flew to her mouth.

"Oh my God, Jerry."

Pinks looks around for some tissues. He sees a box next to the senator and gets up out of his chair, grabs it, and hands it to Pam.

By now sobs have gripped Pam. Jerry wants badly to hold her. Then he wishes the senator would go over and comfort her. But the old man just sits in his chair still staring at the floor.

Pinks isn't surprised at the senator's reaction. He probably isn't unhappy to learn that his daughter is now out of his life permanently. He has told Pinks many times that he worried his daughter would spread stories around about how he's legislating for his own personal interests.

But that isn't why the senator is sitting silently. He is trying to figure out why his staff member is behaving as if the news he just delivered is all that tragic. He supposes it's for Pam's benefit. But the senator knows Jerry shares his concern that Sara's big mouth could have exposed the senator's vulnerabilities, and his aide's, too.

Then the senator relaxes a little; he realizes that Jerry is just being conscientious and doing what he can to help them cope with their grief.

"Where was she when she was murdered?" the senator asks. His voice betrays no emotion. He could just as well have been talking about the price of pork belly futures.

"The police say her body was found last night in an alley behind Front Street. They've picked up an Indian and are holding him. He hasn't said anything about the killing. I would guess they don't know if he did it or not. Sara's purse was missing, but the Indian didn't have anything on him that could link him to Sara."

"Are they sure it's Sara?" sobs Pam.

"The detective said one of the policemen identified her. Apparently, they went to high school together."

"What in the hell was she doing in an alley behind Front Street on a Sunday night?" asks Pam.

"I have no idea. There is nothing open in that part of town on a Sunday night. The police say they don't know either."

"I can't believe Sara got herself tangled up with a goddamn Indian," says the senator, finally with some emotion. "Even Sara wouldn't stoop that low."

"Thomas, don't you dare start trashing my daughter. I don't ever want to hear you trashing Sara again. I promise you, if I do, I'll walk out on you. You hear me. You hear me." Pam is now screaming and on her feet, eyes brimming with tears, her nose running, and her face turning red.

The senator slowly gets to his feet and goes to her.

"I'm so sorry my sweet. I didn't mean to say that. I'm as upset as you are and I am not thinking straight. Please forgive me. This clearly isn't Sara's fault. My God, the dear girl was murdered. We need to find out what happened. Trust me, I will never say anything bad again about our daughter."

The old man tries to hug the younger woman, but she isn't accepting either his apology or his affection.

The senator releases his wife and turns to his aide.

"Jerry, has anyone notified Sara's husband?"

"I don't know. The police apparently had no knowledge of Bruce. I had the office call the lead detective with information about how to locate him. So I would guess by now they have. I can check on it, though.

Taking a step back to look squarely at both the senator and Pam, Pinks continues: "You two need to decide, by the way, on a funeral home for Sara. Right now her body is at the city morgue. But it can go to a funeral home as soon as one is selected."

"Hanson-Runsvold, I guess," says the senator. "That okay with you, darling? Christenson's have been using that funeral home for decades."

"Sure, that's fine. I don't care." Pam is shaking her head and looking at the floor. She covers her face with her hand.

"I'll give them a call," says Pinks. "Anything else you would like me to do before I return to the office?"

"Don't go, please," says Pam. "I need you here. Tom, you ought to go to the office. The media are going to be calling and you'll need to get with your folks to get a press statement ready.

I want Jerry to help me work out the arrangements for the funeral. Is that okay?"

"You're right, as always, my dear. The media are going to be all over this story. I would guess the *Forum* and the Associated Press have already called the office. I had better get in there and get something ready for them.

"Jerry, is your day such that you can spend a little time here helping Pam?"

"Sure, senator. I'll call the office and tell them where I'll be for a couple of hours. It won't be a problem."

"Okay, call me, dearest, if you need anything." And with that, the senator has his cane in hand and goes shuffling out of the sun- room to find his suit coat and call his Senate-provided driver.

"Thank you for staying," says Pam, still standing in the middle of the sunroom. "I'm so angry. I just can't believe my daughter is dead. My lovely Sara. Jerry, she was so beautiful. You saw her last. Didn't she look beautiful?"

Jerry thought back to his last visit with Sara. Yes, she was certainly beautiful. And naked, too.

"She was beautiful," said Jerry. "Radiant, I guess, would be the word I would use to describe her."

He figures it doesn't hurt to gild the lily when discussing your boss' wife's dead daughter.

"Oh Jerry, I wish you could have gotten to know her better," Pam says as she moves into his arms and buries her face into his shoulder. He has no choice but to put his arms around her.

"There were so many times I wanted to get the three of us together, but I could never find the right circumstances," Pam says, between sobs against Jerry's coat. "I loved her so much. I don't think Tom ever felt close to her. Not ever. He was always too busy being a politician. I raised her by myself. Then he drove her away. You became my only link to her. I appreciate that so much."

Having said that, Pam leans back from Jerry just enough to look up at him and when she does she moves forward and kisses him with the passion she always has to struggle to keep under control.

When they finally break from the kiss, they stand together holding each other, mindful that maids and cooks also occupy the house. Although the help is discrete, they probably can't be trusted to keep to themselves the matter of the mistress of the house and the senator's top aide bussing in the sunroom.

Pam pulls away from Jerry, a sad smile on her face.

"I really do need your help. Would you be kind enough to assist me?"

"I don't think there's anything I would deny you," says Jerry, and Pam looks deep into his eyes and sees that he is telling her the truth.

Pam goes off to get the two of them some coffee. Jerry sits in the sunroom thinking of Sara and their last visit. She was beautiful and she was radiant. That's all true. But damn, she was a walking time bomb.

He remembers Sara sitting naked in the bed telling him how furious she is at her father for not giving her money. She was going to turn 30 and she and Bruce couldn't afford their preferred lifestyle. She had called her father asking for an advance on her inheritance and he had turned her down.

"I told that old man he had better give me some money or I'll get it from him another way," she had told Jerry.

"What do you mean?" he had asked.

"I've listened to you describe what you do for daddy dearest, him and those sugar beet buddies of his. I know they're trying to get that Garrison Diversion project funded so the Missouri River will back up behind a gigantic damn and create a huge reservoir. But then, and nobody talks about this, they intend to draw down the reservoir to divert water into the Red River. You told me growing sugar beets requires a lot of water and the Red River can't provide enough to satisfy the greedy growers, which includes my father. Now they intend to get their precious water from the Missouri River by diverting it into the Red River. Does anyone in North Dakota even know what they intend to do? The Garrison Diversion project has been sold to the voters as a way to reduce spring flooding on the Missouri River. Plus it will create a recreational area around the reservoir. Did I forget anything? Oh yeah, the lake will be stocked with bass and trout for the enjoyment of North Dakota fishermen. How would your colleagues back in the Senate react if they knew my father was sponsoring a billion-dollar federal boondoggle primarily to benefit sugar beet growers?" And haven't you told me there's a glut in sugar on the world market? Do we even need to grow sugar beets?"

"Whoa, Sarah. That's enough. I was only talking about my work. I thought you were interested in what I do for a living. I didn't think you were trying to collect dirt on your father."

"I wasn't. I was really interested in what you do. But I hate that old man. He treats me like trailer park trash while he lives like a king. I know he came from poverty. Now he's rich. How did he do it? Not on his government salary. So why doesn't he share some of his ill-gotten gains with his only daughter? Is that too much to ask?"

"Listen, Sara, I know you're really upset. But don't do anything stupid, okay? I promise I'll talk to your father. I will see what I can do for you. I'll tell him I talked to you. I will say you appear to have grown up a lot. Anyway, I'll find a way to get you some money is what I'm saying. Don't do anything rash. Will you promise me that?"

"I'm not promising anything. I want the money, sure. But I would really like to see that bastard suffer too. I want him to experience a little of what I've gone through these past few years. I would like him to have to live in a goddamn trailer park like I do.

"Seriously, though, I'm really just interested in getting some money. It doesn't do me any good to ruin him, even though I know I could. I just need to get on with my life and to do that I need some money. Now, can you help me or not?"

"Sure, I can get you some money. It will be enough to get you out of the trailer park and on with your life. Would that make you happy?"

She had smiled then, turning and laying her naked body against his, where he lay in the bed. She moved her right leg over his and slid her hand down below his stomach. "You've just made me very happy, Jerry. Now let's see if I can return the favor."

When Pinks had gotten back to Washington, he'd met with Senator Christenson and told him about his conversation with Sara. He mentioned the harm she could do if she didn't start receiving money from him. The senator had been livid. Jerry suggested the senator just give her some money; after all, she didn't want much. The senator disagreed. He'd said, "Any money Sara gets won't be enough. She'll always want more. The threat of exposure will always hang over my head. Who knows what she'll do, who she'll call in the middle of the night when she's too drunk not to kill the golden goose? I won't live that way. Goddamn ungrateful spoiled brat!"

The senator had ended his meeting with Jerry when he left to go to the floor for a vote. They didn't come to any resolution about Sara, but both knew something had to be done, and sooner rather than later.

Late that evening, Andrew Bachevich of the sugar beet growers cooperative got a call on his private line in his study at home. Not many people knew that number, and it didn't ring often. He picked it up: "Hello, Bachevich here." When he recognized the voice at the other end, he relaxed. "Hello, my old friend. What can I do for you?"

Bachevich listened intently. He jotted down some notes. He was a good listener and a very good problem-solver.

"Don't worry about a thing. I'll take care of it. I've got a person in Fargo who can help Sara realize that spreading stories about her father is not in her best interests. He's persuasive, I assure you. She'll catch on really quick as to her best course of action. I don't think you'll have to worry about her spreading damaging stories."

Sara's father told the powerful sugar beet executive that if there was ever anything the senior senator from North Dakota could do for him, he shouldn't hesitate to ask. Then he ended the call, pleased that the problem caused by his daughter was going to be addressed.

The executive hung up the phone and turned to his rolodex. He didn't enjoy doing business with this fellow he knew in Fargo. The two were not friends and interacted as little as possible. As he picked up the phone again, Bachevich sighed. At least he'd never run into the son-of-a-bitch at his country club or a Rotary luncheon.

Chapter Eleven

An Indian Killed My Wife?

Fargo Detective Wayne Thompson is surprised when he's told he has a call from Senator Christenson's Capitol Hill office holding on line two.

He picks up the phone tentatively. "This is Detective Wayne Thompson."

"Hello detective. This is Larry Mowrey, chief of staff to Senator Tom Christenson."

"What can I do for the senior senator from North Dakota?" Thompson asks.

"Well, I'm just calling as I said I would when I got some information about Sara Winslow's husband."

"Oh, yeah," Thompson remembers, feeling himself relax. "What did you learn?"

"She has a husband named Bruce. He works as a truck driver for a company building the interstate highway across North Dakota. We don't know the name of the company. But we believe many of its employees also live in the same trailer park where he and Sara live, uhh, or uhh, lived. So, you might go back there and ask some of her neighbors how to reach him."

"Thanks. That's a good tip. When you get tired of politicians, you might try being a detective. You're a natural"

"You really think so? I once thought about applying for a job at the FBI. When I got out of the service, I was going to…"

Thompson hangs up.

The dumb fuck. A good detective needs a bullshit detector working at all times. *I guess his is turned off,* Thompson thinks to himself.

Thompson pushes away from his desk and walks out of his office. He has to admit, he hadn't thought about talking to Sara's neighbors. They probably would know how to get ahold of her husband. He dreads that call, too, but he has to get it done. He walks over to the desk Sergeant Myers occupies.

"I need you to do me a favor," says the captain. "I need you to run out to the Slough and check with the neighbors of that dead woman we found near the Pig to see if you can get a lead on where we can find her husband."

"Got it," said Myers, happy for the chance to get out of the office.

The police sergeant pulls into the beat-up looking trailer court and drives slowly down the first row of mobile homes until he comes to one that has a mailbox with Whitlow's name on it. A 1960 Ford is parked outside. He checks his sheet. The license plate and car are registered to Bruce Whitlow. He puts the unmarked squad car into park and sits with the windows down listening to the chatter on the police radio. He figures it won't take long before somebody will come to him. Experience teaches him that in trailer parks an idling police car always attracts attention.

Sure enough, after about five minutes, a housewife from two trailers down appears and begins sweeping her driveway. While she sweeps, she keeps glancing over at Myers' car. He gives her five minutes. Two minutes later she is at his window.

"You looking for Sara?"

"Nope. I'm trying to locate her husband. Would you know how I go about doing that?"

"I think he works for Great Northern Construction Company. They have an office here in Fargo. But Bruce is working out in West River someplace. He drives a gravel truck, I know that. He's helping to build the interstate highway across the state. I don't think you can reach him directly. But the company probably knows how to get ahold of him."

"Thanks, that's helpful. And what did you say your name was?"

"Oh. I'm Terri. Terri Squires. I live just two trailers down. I'm a good friend of Sara Whitlow, Bruce's wife. You are parked in front of their place. I haven't seen Sara all day. So when I saw you drive up, I thought maybe you are a friend of hers and might know where she is."

Myers looks at Terri Squires. He has nearly 30 years of experience looking at people who, for a variety of reasons, chose not to tell him the truth. He decides Terri Squires is one of those.

"When was the last time you saw Sara?"

"Oh, geez. When would that have been? This is Monday. I guess I saw her Saturday afternoon. That's right. Saturday afternoon. She said she was going to go shopping."

"Without her car?"

Terri looks at Sara's car. She starts to bite at her lower lip. She pulls her sweatshirt down sharply with her left hand while her right hand starts to scratch an itch on her neck.

"It is strange she didn't take her car to go shopping, now that you mention it. I guess she wasn't going to go far. I mean, you can walk from here to downtown easy enough. Not all the time, for sure. But it was nice and warm Saturday. Yeah, she must have decided to walk downtown."

"She do that a lot . . . walk places rather than take her car?"

"Um, no, I don't believe so. Sara normally drives places. Or people pick her up. Hey, maybe somebody did just that. I bet that's it. Somebody came and got her on Saturday and took her shopping."

"Did you see anybody come and get her?"

"No."

"Wouldn't you have seen somebody drive in here to get her? They would have to drive right by your trailer."

"Normally I would have. But I may have been changing the baby or sitting on the toilet or something. I don't see everything that goes on in the trailer park, that's for sure."

Terri looks as if she has a stomach cramp. She has both arms wrapped around herself and she is half bent over with a pained expression on her face. Not only is she an ineffective liar, concludes Myers, but she makes herself miserable doing it.

"Okay, thanks for your help."

Myers starts up his car and puts it in reverse.

"Is Sara okay? Do you know where she is?"

"Yeah. She's lying on a slab in the city morgue. She's dead."

As Myers pulls away, he knows he's broken a basic police rule: No one is to be notified of a person's death before next of kin. But he wanted to see Terri's reaction to the news. He glances in his rear-view mirror and sees Terri standing in the driveway, with both hands covering her mouth, choking down large sobs.

He decides Terri hadn't known Sara was dead before he told her. There is always a certain amount of grieving that goes along with learning that a friend has died. But having someone pass along that information as they drive away is a whole different kick in the stomach.

Myers is philosophical about trailer-park residents. He believes trailer parks attract young married couples with kids and no money, old folks with debts and no money, and middle-aged drunks, deadbeats, and welfare cheats, all with no money. Besides that, he knows trailer parks attract tornados.

Earlier in his career he felt sorry for the Saras and the Terris of the world. But he is a cop, not a goddamn social worker. They ought to know better than to live in a trailer park. Or go drinking in an illegal bar. And what in the hell compels a daughter of a U.S. senator to get involved with a drunken Indian? Her poor folks. Now he has to call her husband and tell him his wife is dead. They pay him to arrest bad guys, not go around sucker punching folks with bad news. He doesn't need this shit.

Tracking down Bruce Whitlow isn't easy. The Fargo office of Great Northern Construction Company says he's an employee. But some dipshit clerk says he has no way of reaching him. Instead, she tells Myers he would have to call the company's Dickenson office to see if anyone there can get a message to Whitlow. She says nobody's likely to reach him while he's working because he's in a gravel truck somewhere along an 80-mile stretch of freeway being built out near Belfield. Myers adopts his police voice and tells the clerk she can call Dickenson. Someone has to tell Whitlow that he needs to call the Fargo police immediately. Then he leaves her with Thompson's number and hangs up.

Six hours later Bruce Whitlow calls Thompson's number.

"Hello. My name is Whitlow. I was told to call you. Is there a problem? Is Sara okay?"

"Thanks for calling. I am Detective Wayne Thompson. I am with the Fargo Police Department. I am sorry; I have some bad news for you. Your wife, Sara, was found dead last night in downtown Fargo."

"What do you mean, she was found dead. Sara is dead? How can that be? Was she in an accident?"

"No, we think she was murdered. We have arrested an Indian who we think may have killed her. She died as a result of wounds to the abdomen inflicted by a large knife."

"God. You mean a fucking Indian killed my wife? How did that happen?"

"We are not sure. We found the body in the alley behind Front Street at about nine p.m. Sunday. We don't know if she was killed there or someplace else and then dumped in the alley. No purse or pocketbook was found at the scene, so we are assuming the motive for the murder was robbery. The coroner said there had been no sexual assault. She was still wearing her diamond ring, so the robber, if that is what he was, must have just been interested in the contents of her purse or pocketbook."

"I hope you killed the son of a bitch. I mean, you guys shot him on the spot, right? No Indian gets away with killing a white woman in North Dakota, isn't that right?"

"Sir, nobody gets away with killing anyone in North Dakota. But no, we didn't shoot the Indian. We have him locked up in jail. He will face charges for the crime he committed."

"Leave me alone with him for five minutes, and I'll take care of the bastard. I grew up with Indians. I know how you have to deal with the bad ones."

"Would you like to know where your wife is now?"

"Have you got ahold of her folks?"

"Yes, the senator and his wife have been contacted. And at their request, the body has been moved to Hanson-Runsvold Funeral Home."

"I figure they'll take over at this point. Nobody is going to care what I want. They didn't give a shit about her when she was alive. Now they'll bury her and act like she was their wonderful little angel. Well, that's just fine."

"You have my number. If I can answer any more of your questions when you get back to Fargo, give me a call."

"Sure. Thanks. Sorry I'm so pissed. I just hate Indians. And now one of them has killed my wife. That's just perfect. Just fucking perfect."

Thompson hangs up the phone and sits at his desk shaking his head. *What a guy.*

*   *   *

Monday afternoon, Baker shows up at the paper early and sits at his desk reviewing the afternoon edition of the *Forum*. He assumes the Front Street murder story will be on the front page. It isn't. He flips through the paper. He finds it finally among a string of local news stories, most of them with one-column headlines.

"Fargo Woman Found Dead in City Alley," reads the three deck, one-column head. Wow, he says to himself, that's a strange way to play the story. She was murdered, for Christ's sake, not just found dead.

He reads the article and is shocked to learn that the woman has been identified as Sara Whitlow, "the only daughter of U.S. Senator and Mrs. Thomas Christenson of Fargo and Arlington, Virginia."

My God, the woman is a senator's daughter and the *Forum* buries the story on the inside of the paper? What the hell is going on?

The story says her body was found near the intersection of 4th Street and Front Street.

That's not correct, Baker says to himself. It was found in the alley behind Front Street. And it had been dragged there from that room under the saloon, the one where the guy yelled at me when I rang the buzzer.

He reads on. The story says Sara had been stabbed. At least that's correct. And the article says an Indian by the name of Joe Running Deer is being held in the County Jail for questioning related to the incident. The article goes on to say that his clothing was covered with blood.

The article ends by saying funeral services are pending and that the arrangements are being made through the Hanson-Runsvold Funeral Home.

Baker jumps out of his chair with the newspaper in his hand and marches over to the city desk where he confronts the city editor, Leo Stanstead.

"What is this bullshit?" says Baker. "You've got the daughter of one of your U.S. senators murdered in an alley in his hometown and you bury the story on the inside of the paper? The story doesn't even correctly identify the place where her body was found. What the fuck am I missing?"

Stanstead looks up at his angry, new hire.

"Calm down, young man. I'm not used to being addressed in that tone of voice. Now, would you like to start over again?"

Baker takes a deep breath and rocks back and forth on his heels twice. He is aware that he has caught the attention of more than a few reporters in the newsroom.

"I apologize. I guess I am just upset by this story about the murder of Sara Whitlow. I was on that murder scene last night. I wrote an article about it for the morning paper. I said something about blood trails leading from a room underneath a Front Street bar. Why didn't anything about that get into the afternoon story? Then I really can't understand why it isn't a front-page story when a senator's daughter is murdered in his home state."

"Those are two reasonable questions. Let us take them one at a time.

"First, the police maintain they didn't find blood trails leading from the doorway. This morning when our police reporter went down to the scene he didn't see any either. We had no choice but to accept what the police told us. We were wondering how it is you saw blood trails when nobody else did.

"Second, we played down the story intentionally. It's not news around here that the senator and his wife have been estranged from their daughter for years. She was, how can I say this, a woman of loose morals. I would guess she was down in that part of town working as a prostitute. We are not publishing a tabloid. So we didn't put that in the newspaper. It would have just caused the senator and his wife even more shame. For the same reason, we decided to just downplay the whole tragedy. The police have her killer, and that pretty much wraps up the story.

Baker stands there and stares in disbelief at the city editor. He realizes he isn't working at the *Washington Star* anymore.

"I saw the blood trails. I also saw a pool of blood outside the door of the storeroom under the Silver Saloon. When I pushed the buzzer, an irate guy came to the door and then slammed it in my face when I told him I was from the *Forum*. Don't you think it was odd a guy would be in the place at ten p.m., on a Sunday night? I mean, the saloon is closed on Sunday."

"I don't know what you saw on the ground. I wasn't there. The police were. And they say it wasn't blood. The guy in the storeroom was probably a stock boy working a late shift. That doesn't seem unusual to me. And the fact he didn't want to talk to you makes perfectly good sense to me. Now, is there anything else I can do for you before I go back to work?"

Baker knows he has been dismissed, and he has the good sense to realize anything else he says is only going to make matters worse with the city editor.

"No. Thanks for hearing me out."

As he walks back to his desk, he glances at the reporters sitting across from the city editor. He hasn't been introduced to any of them and yet they all seem to enjoy the fact the new kid from Washington, D.C., has just had his ass handed to him. Fuck them, he says to himself. He knows what he saw, and it isn't what the *Forum* printed.

*   *   *

Thompson is just about ready to leave the police station for the day when his phone rings. It is one of the city fathers, Harold "Buck" Callahan, president of Dakota Manufacturing, Inc., and a part owner of the Blind Pig.

"Wayne, glad I caught you. Got a minute?"

"Sure, Buck, what's on your mind?" as if Thompson doesn't know. He has been expecting a call all day from the city fathers. They don't like Front Street news hitting the newspaper.

"I hear we had a little ruckus down on Front Street last night, that right?"

"Yes sir, we had a senator's daughter murdered. We think an Indian stabbed her and then left her to die in the alley behind Front Street near 4th Street."

"That's pretty damn close to our Blind Pig, isn't it?"

"Not far, that's for sure. About half a block, I'd guess."

"Any chance the two of them were drinking in the Blind Pig before this whole thing took place in the alley?"

"Why do you ask that?"

"As you know, it could prove embarrassing to us if the Blind Pig gets dragged into a murder story. These kinds of things ought to happen out in the park or on the riverbank someplace. Folks don't like to think vicious crimes happen in downtown Fargo, even if it's on Front Street. And they would be downright furious if they learned it happened in an illegal drinking establishment. I'll remind you the city fathers pay you so that such a thing never happens. I'm calling you to ask if we made a mistake putting our trust in you? What do I tell the other city fathers, Wayne? You know they're concerned."

"You didn't make a mistake. This was a fluke. The Indian was drunk. We figure he grabbed her after she left the Pig. Why he didn't wait until she got further away we don't know."

"But can you explain to me why he hung around and got himself caught?"

"As I said, he was dead drunk."

"Wayne, do you read the morning newspaper?"

"You mean the *Minneapolis Tribune*?"

"No, Wayne, the morning edition of the *Forum*."

"No, I read the afternoon paper that's delivered to my home."

"I do the same. But my office subscribes to the morning edition of the *Forum*. This morning's paper had an interesting article in it. At least one reporter believes the senator's daughter was killed in the Blind Pig. He thinks she was then dragged from there out into the alley. Do you suppose he has got the facts right?"

Thompson is stunned. He'd not caught wind of the article published in the morning paper, and is surprised at the revelations it contains. He covers using his best police voice: "I'm pretty sure the Pig was closed at the time of the murder. Normally Bodini closes it down early on Sunday night. The Mexicans all clear out by 5 p.m., and he lets his help go at the same time. He generally stays around an hour or two to clean up and then shuts the place down. No, the morning *Forum* has it wrong."

Thompson was glad Bacevich couldn't see him sweating.

"Well, we may have a rogue reporter you need to keep an eye on. By the way, has the Indian said anything to anyone about the murder?"

"No, he is under wraps in the County jail. And when he does start to talk, I'll be the one doing the listening. He may need some help with his story. As I said, he was dead drunk at the time."

"You have some loose ends to tie together, my friend. And you know what they say about there only being one kind of good Indian."

"Yeah, a dead one." Thompson feels a bit of relief when he hears Buck give off a little chuckle.

"You have a good night, now," Buck says. "We'll be talking."

Thompson hangs up his phone. He wishes he had never signed on with Bacevich to do his dirty work. Then he gets up and heads for the door. He is officially off duty. On his way out he recalls the large cash payment Bacevich gave him to kill the senator's daughter. He concludes that the only mistake he made was the spur-of-the moment inspiration to avoid the dirty work himself by making that goddamn Indian do it.

*   *   *

Senator and Mrs. Thomas Christenson arrive in Fargo on Wednesday afternoon to attend their daughter's funeral, scheduled for Thursday. Jerry Pinks, with a lot of input from Pam Christenson, has made all the arrangements. Nobody even thought of asking Sara's husband, Bruce, for his opinion.

The closed-coffin service is going to be held at St. Anthony's Catholic Church on South 10th Street. Sara had attended the church's school next door through the 8th grade. Then she switched over to Agassiz Junior High School and went on to Fargo Central High. She was born a Catholic, but quit going to church after her father and mother went to Washington and left her home with caretakers. Nevertheless, the parents elected to hold her funeral in a Catholic church. Relatives always want to assume the dear departed, in their final moments of life, atoned for their sins and made a sincere act of contrition. Having done so, the Catholic priest presiding at the funeral can assure her relatives that their loved one resides with Jesus.

Pinks and the senator's press person, Ashley Briggs, are on the same flight as the senator and his wife. The senator wants Ashley along to handle the media. Ashley is tall, slim, attractive, and smooth as silk. She can tell you to go fuck yourself and make you think it's a reasonable idea that you wish you had thought up on your own. She is the aging senator's perfect front person.

Pinks comes along to handle business. Whenever the senator is back in the Red River Valley, constituents figure he ought to address their needs. On this trip home, Pinks' job is to meet with individuals, small groups, and large assemblies to explain that the senator would have been there himself, but was tending to important family matters. Then he adds, "What can the senator's office do for you today?" He isn't called North Dakota's third senator for nothing.

*   *   *

James Foster has just received a call from the courthouse. He hasn't worked much lately, and he's pleased to learn he's been appointed to represent a man in jail for supposedly robbing and killing a woman. A murder trial means a lot of billable days of work, and he can use them. He just has to stay sober.

Actually, his selection surprised him. His reputation as a drunk is well known around the courthouse. Although he makes his living picking up clients forced to go with a court-appointed attorney, he isn't the only bottom feeder in the business. He's just the least reliable.

Now he's given a murder trial to prepare for and he realizes he's more than surprised. He's suspicious. Does someone want the poor bastard convicted?

The guy's name is Joe Running Deer. As Foster heads over to the Cass County Courthouse and jail, he figures a name like that means his client is an Indian. Probably a Sioux, although it's hard to tell. He could be an Indian from any dozen different tribes in the Dakota-Minnesota region.

Foster has only had one drink that morning, to settle his nerves, so he's feeling sharper than usual. His clothes look like he slept in them, but that's because he does his own laundry, and he does it poorly. His white shirt is yellow from age and frayed at the collar and cuffs. His tie is properly tied, but it's old, stained, and out of style. The same can be said for his suit.

He doesn't look completely like a bum, though. Foster has a fresh haircut, a clean shave, and his shoes are shined. That's because his brother Henry owns a successful barbershop on Northern Pacific Avenue. James stops by every time he has a new client to assure his older brother he's still in business. In gratitude, Henry gives him a shave, trims his curly locks, and has one of the boys shine his shoes. Henry also lectures his brother on the evils of too much drink, which Foster acknowledges by saying he has already started cutting back.

* * *

Joe Running Deer hears the clang of keys in his cell door and opens his eyes.

"C'mon, Indian," the guard now standing in the open doorway says. You got a lawyer comin'."

Joe Running Deer hates lawyers. They're just white men protecting white men pretending to protect justice. *They protect only lies.*

He gets out of his bunk. His head hurts. The guard takes him to a holding cell where he sits and waits.

Again, he hears the clang of keys in a cell door and opens his eyes. A man in a suit carrying a briefcase steps into the cell where Joe is sitting.

Foster sees his new client for the first time. He looks about what Foster expected: big, dumb, and guilty as hell.

"Good morning, my name is James Foster, I am your court-ordered attorney. I will be representing you at your court appearance tomorrow afternoon to determine whether you go to trial on the charges against you."

Foster doesn't offer to shake hands, but instead takes a chair opposite Joe and sits down.

Joe looks at the attorney and recognizes him for what he is: a drunk with a clean shave and a good haircut.

"Don't I get to choose my own attorney?"

"You sure do. Can I assume you have the money to hire your own attorney? I was led to believe you asked for a court-appointed attorney. If that is the case, I am your attorney."

Joe sighed. Why would he think he would catch a break at this point?

"Let's begin with you telling me why you think the police arrested you."

"They said I killed a woman."

"Did you?"

"I don't remember."

"What do you remember?"

"I remember being drunk, sick, and then arrested and thrown in jail. I remember being in Moorhead. I was arrested in Moorhead, I'm pretty sure. But the cops didn't take me to jail. They took me to Fargo and dropped me off. Then I was arrested in Fargo and taken to jail."

That story didn't make any sense to Foster. If the Moorhead police had arrested the Indian, he would have ended up in their jail.

"It was a Sunday. Where were you drinking?"

"At the Blind Pig."

"Where?"

"The Blind Pig. The place where all the Mexicans drink on Sunday."

"I guess I don't know the place. Where exactly is it?"

Joe told him that it was in the alley between 4th Street and Broadway behind Front Street. He told Foster that the place had a dirty brown door with a sign on it that said, "Deliveries Only" and a buzzer that you push if you want to go in. Then, when you push the button, explains the Indian, you shout: "I'm here to see the blind pig" and a fat guy lets you in.

"Really?" said Foster. A blind pig. He was familiar with the term. But he thought those illegal bars had all closed after prohibition. He finds it highly unlikely that one remains open in Fargo in the mid-60s.

"So. you were drinking in this blind pig. This woman the police say was murdered; did you see her there?"

"She was a goddamn whore. She kept toying with me. I asked her how much she charged and she made fun of me. I don't remember what she said, but she made a joke about it. People in the bar laughed at me. I was really mad at her. But I still wanted to fuck her."

"Did you?"

"No, I don't fuck too good when I'm drinking."

Foster knows exactly what his client is talking about.

"So, you were drinking and this woman, this whore, was in the bar with you. Did you leave before she did? Or did you notice that she left before you did?"

"I think I left before she did. I know the bar was closing. I couldn't get another drink. So I left. But there were still people in the Pig. I remember that. I don't remember if she was there or not. She could have been."

"Okay, this is going very well. Tell me, did you hurt her in any way?"

Joe sat still and starred at the floor.

"I know I wanted to hurt her. I remember that. I wanted to fuck her and I wanted to hurt her. I didn't fuck her. I know that. I'm not sure if I hurt her. I don't remember. I know I had blood on my clothes when I was arrested. But I didn't have my knife. I always have my knife. But I didn't have it when I was arrested. I don't know what happened to it."

"The arresting officers say you told them you had butchered a deer. Did you?"

"I told them that, I remember. But I didn't butcher a deer. I just told them that. I couldn't have anyway. I didn't have my knife."

"Where are your clothes now?"

"They made me take them off when I got to the jail. Then they took them from me. After that they took a fire hose to me. They said I stunk. I had to sleep naked the first night. The next morning, they gave me these clothes I'm wearing now. They didn't give me any underwear though. I just have this shirt and these pants, which are too big. They are always falling down because they won't give me anything to tie them up with."

Foster was taking notes fast and furious. And he was grinning.

"I think we are ready for your court appearance. Here's what I want you to do. When we get into court, the judge is going to ask you how you plead to the charge of 2nd degree murder. I want you to say 'not guilty.' Do you understand? Say 'not guilty.'"

On the way out of the jail, Foster asks to see the head jailer. The beefy sergeant makes it obvious he doesn't like court-appointed attorneys, even if they do have their shoes polished.

"What can I do you for, counselor?"

"I have one question: What happened to the clothes my client was wearing when he was arrested?"

"The Indian's clothes? We burned the goddamn things. Shit. He had blood and vomit and snot and who knows what else on his shirt and jacket. And he had shit and pissed in his pants. I had just had some inmates clean the goddamn jail from top to bottom earlier in the day. No way I was going to allow that dirty Indian to stink up my clean jail. So I had his clothes burned. Then I had him scrubbed up really good before I stuck him into a cell. Anything else you want to know, counselor?"

"No," smiles Foster, "you have been most helpful."

Foster limits himself to a double Beefeaters that night, far below his usual quota. He is riding a professional high few lawyers ever experience.

*   *   *

The 10 a.m. funeral attracts a large crowd of the senator's friends and supporters. The only two people from the trailer park are Sara's husband and her best friend, Terri Squires. Bruce and Terri have become almost inseparable since he arrived in town from Dickinson. Terri has discovered she has a natural ability to comfort a grieving spouse.

The family all sits together in the first two rows. The senator ignores Bruce when the younger man attempts to shake his hand. But Pam takes it and then pulls him in toward her for a motherly embrace. She never cared for Bruce, having thought Sara could have done so much better. But she feels sorry for him, knowing that her loss is also his. Bruce has Terri alongside of him in the family pew. Nobody knows who she is and Bruce doesn't introduce her to anyone.

Pinks shakes Bruce's hand and expresses his condolences for the loss of his wife. Pinks then wonders what Bruce would do to him if he knew about all the intimate pleasure Sara had provided him over the years.

Pinks notices the woman with Bruce. He wonders who she is, but not enough to ask Bruce. The women in the church notice her too. They have her pegged as white trash. Who else would wear an ill-fitting, cheap, pink cocktail dress to a funeral? Terri's irreverence, demonstrated by the fact she wears nothing on her head, isn't lost on the Catholics either.

During the service, the priest asks the congregation if anyone wishes to say anything about Sara. Earlier the senator and his wife had told the priest that they did not intend to speak, fearing that their emotions would not enable them to finish. Frankly, the senator didn't have anything to say and Pam was seriously worried that she would go to pieces if she started to talk about her daughter.

When the priest repeats his request, Bruce stands up.

"I would like to talk about my wife," he says.

"Please come forward, my son."

A murmur runs through the audience. Few of the people in the crowd know Sara's husband. Of course, few knew Sara either. They are friends of the senator and are present at his daughter's funeral in hopes he will notice them and remember their act of kindness.

Bruce walks to the front of the gathering and stands next to the casket. He is a rugged, good-looking guy. The Western sun has turned him brown as a chestnut. He wears his black hair long, and it hangs down over his ears and flows down his neck. He has bushy eyebrows and a thick neck to go with his wrestler's body. He wears an ill-fitting corduroy coat over a pair of Levi jeans and a western shirt with a bolo tie. He looks uncomfortable. Most people in attendance figure he probably feels out of place in a church. The more charitable think he just might be nervous because he's attending his murdered wife's funeral.

"Sara was a good woman. She had a tough time of it. Living with me wasn't easy. I was gone a lot. I drive a gravel truck out in the Badlands and I'm away from home for a month at a time. It was hard on her. Then too, we couldn't afford the things she liked to have. I know that really bothered her. It bothered me too. But I worked as hard as I could, and I couldn't do any more. There are only so many hours in the day.

"In the winter, we were together a lot because I was laid off then. They don't build highways in this part of the country in the winter. So everyone gets laid off. Sara and I would hang out and play pool and watch television and go to movies and eat pizza. And dream. Boy, would we dream.

"We were going to go to Arizona to live. Sara said someday she was going to get an inheritance. She didn't know how much. But enough, she said, to move us to Arizona. No more snow boots or head bolt heaters, she used to say. She hated head bolt heaters."

That elicits a chuckle from the church audience.

"We were going to go to Arizona so I could work year around. Then maybe have some kids.

"That's what we dreamed about all the time.

"I loved my Sara. She was the best thing that ever happened to me. For the first year of our marriage I kept pinching myself to make sure I wasn't just dreaming."

His face suddenly turns dour. "Now she's **gone**," he says, his voice rising in anger. "All because of some Indian. I'm here to tell you, I will have my revenge." He's now yelling. "I will get even! An eye for an eye! Just as the Bible says."

At this point the priest is back on his feet frantically signaling to the organ player to play a hymn, any hymn. He hustles over to Bruce and escorts him back to his seat in the family pew.

The church audience is simply amazed by the hostility Bruce displayed. In a church, no less. Many of the women sit with their hands over their mouths. The men fidget in the presence of such masculinity. To a man, they are glad Bruce isn't mad at them.

Pam Christenson sat through her son-in-law's presentation in awe. She realizes she really doesn't know him. Now, for the first time, she wants to get better acquainted. She looks over at him and smiles. She mouths, "Come see me after the service."

He smiles back. What the fuck do you suppose that's all about, he wonders.

When the service ends, the funeral procession goes from the church over to University Drive, then turns straight north under both the Northern Pacific and Great Northern underpasses. No undertaker ever wants a hearse's final trip to be delayed by a passing train. For that same reason, off-duty Fargo policemen on large motorcycles lead and stop traffic along the route. The hearse passes North Dakota State University, the beneficiary of so much of the senator's efforts. The procession speeds up as it heads out of the city limits alongside Hector Airport before turning left on a dead-end county road. At its end sits the awaiting cemetery, directly east of the airport control tower; only two runways separate the dearly departed from the air traffic controllers overseeing Fargo's more prosaic departures.

Sara is buried in the Christenson family plot among Catholics.

Afterwards, a select group of people are invited up to Senator and Mrs. Christensen's top-floor apartment located in one of Fargo's newest high-rise buildings overlooking Island Park. Although the three-bedroom apartment is rarely occupied, a cook who doubles as a maid lives in it full time so that it's always ready for the senator when he comes back to the state.

Finger foods and drinks fill tables in the dining room where the women gather; the men, on the other hand, retire to the senator's study for cigars and suitably aged scotch whisky. Condolences are offered and accepted and then the conversation switches to a more comfortable topic. The Republicans in the crowd, and they are all Republicans, wonder what Lyndon Johnson is trying to do to the country and why don't Congress and the courts stop him?

Bruce tells Terri that he thinks they should go to the senator's gathering, but she decides to take a pass.

"I know where I'm not wanted," she says to Bruce as they drive away from the cemetery. "Did you see how the family all looked at me? Fuck them. I was their daughter's best friend, and nobody even asks me how I feel about her death. I'm going home. You can drop me off and go over there by yourself."

"Okay, that's what I'll do. I'm curious about what Sara's mother wants to talk to me about. I'll drop by later. Maybe we can go out for a drink or something."

She smiles at him. "I would like that, Bruce."

She leans into him, playfully. But not too playfully. After all, the guy has just watched the undertaker bury his wife.

When Bruce gets off the elevator on the top floor of the Christenson's apartment house, he spots a man in a black suit standing at the senator's door screening guests. He frowns when he sees Bruce approach.

"I'm the senator's son-in-law. It was my wife we just buried."

The guy in the suit jerks to attention and says, "Of course, sir. I'm sorry for your loss. Please, go right in. The family is expecting you."

When Bruce walks in it appears a party is underway. If any guests are mourning the loss of his wife, he doesn't spot them. The ladies in the dining room are laughing and drinking and enjoying themselves. He can see the senator in his study with a distinguished group of gentlemen and decides to steer clear of that room. He doesn't spot the senator's wife, so he heads to the kitchen.

He sees her just as she spots him.

"Bruce, I'm so glad you could make it over. Come with me. I want to talk to you."

She grabs him by the arm and leads him into the master bedroom. She closes the door and directs him to a chair next to the bed. She then sits on the bed facing him.

"Bruce, I was really moved by what you said about Sara this morning. I had no idea that you two were so much in love. I guess you know that Sara and I were not close. That was my fault, and I will take that mistake to my grave. I can't believe how stupid I was to allow her father to break up our family. She has only been gone a few days and yet I feel such a tremendous loss."

"I know what you mean. I feel as if something has been ripped from my insides."

"Bruce, you mentioned that you and Sara had this dream about going to Arizona. What kept you from doing that, just money?"

"Yes, Mrs. Christenson."

"Please, call me Pam."

"Okay, Pam. The senator had told Sara that if she kept her skirt clean he would leave her an inheritance. I don't know if you knew that. Sara talked about it all the time. She had high hopes for that money. She figured it would break us out of our doldrums. It would be the money that would get us out of North Dakota and into a better life. I never really ever counted on it, though."

"I didn't know about that promise. But it sounds like something Thomas would say. Why didn't you count on it?"

"Well, for two reasons. One, I guess I don't trust people who make those kinds of promises. You know, the kind that says, 'you do something for me now and I'll reward you down the road.' Second, I guess I was never convinced that Sara could stay out of trouble. I figured she would do something that would piss off her father and that would be the end of the promise."

"Bruce, I am not going to ask you to trust me, because that would be foolish, and you have already demonstrated to me you're too smart for that. But here's what I'm going to do. I am going to work on Sara's father. I am going to see what kind of inheritance he had planned for Sara. Then I'm going to do what I can to see to it that you receive that money.

"Don't hold your breath any more than you have already. It might take me some time to pull it off. But I think that's what Sara would have wanted. And now, that's what I want. I do have some influence with the senator. So let's just see what I can do for you. I'd like to think you could spend the rest of your life in the warmth of Arizona rather than the cold of North Dakota."

"That would be wonderful, Mrs. Christenson. I won't hold my breath, as you say. But I'll tell you one thing. It will give me something to dream about. That and my memories of Sara."

"You know, Bruce. You and I are both products of West River. I grew up in Williston. And if I recall correctly, you grew up near Mott, right? Folks on the West side of the Missouri are a different breed than those raised on the East side of the state. We need to stick together. Now give your mother-in-law a proper hug and let me go back to my guests before they start talking about us spending too much time together in a bedroom."

Bruce did as he was instructed and found that he enjoyed it nearly as much as he did when he hugged his former wife.

Just as he turns to leave, Pam asks him a question.

"Bruce. Your comment about killing that Indian. You didn't mean any of that, did you?"

He looks straight at her and doesn't say a word. Finally, she smiles.

"I'm glad we had this chat, Bruce."

She escorts him to the door, and he leaves without saying another word. He figures he might head to Terri's trailer. He knows he can find a cold beer there. And he might just be able to have a conversation about Sara with someone who really knew her.

Chapter Twelve

A Killer Needs a Good Lawyer

Immediately after Sara Winslow's funeral, Jerry Pinks calls his stepson Chuck and asks him to lunch. He accepts the invitation, but says he has to report to work at the *Forum* by 4 p.m.

Once seated at the Powers Hotel, just across the street from the Federal Building where Senator Christenson has his main in-state office, the two men are noticeably uneasy with one another. They're off their normal turf. Fargo is a world away from Washington, D.C.

Baker knows his stepfather had accompanied the senator to his daughter's funeral. The young reporter finds it hard to believe the dead woman he saw lying in the alley behind Front Street was a U.S. senator's daughter.

Her obituary ran in the *Forum* that morning. Baker read it and figured her parents had heavily influenced the slant taken by the *Forum's* obit writer. That is, it contained the minor highlights of a young woman who went through life without leaving much of an impression. Outside of being the daughter of a U.S. Senator, a fact she seldom shared with anyone, Sara graduated from Fargo Central High School and then married Bruce Whitlow and had no children.

Baker had read through her clipping file at the *Forum* and knew there was more to Sara Winslow that what the family chose to share. The obit said nothing about her sexual appetite, her year in jail, and her life living with a man she seldom saw in a trailer park out by the slough. Sara was unsuccessful, unsatisfied, and unhappy. Her death was tragic, but not surprising. Baker recognizes that the *Forum* wiped her obituary as clean as it did his earlier story of her murder. For sure, the *Forum* is no tabloid.

Baker doesn't think the Sara Whitlow story should end with her obituary. Questions still linger about where the murder actually occurred. And that room under the Silver Saloon—why was Sara Whitlow's body taken from that room and dumped in the alley?

Baker is also curious about the storeroom: Is it just a front for an off-hours bar? Back in Washington, D.C., Baker knows off-hour bars exist. They open up after the regular bars close and then stay open most of the night. They cater to men and women who work the late shifts and want to unwind a little before heading home to bed. These include cops, firemen, newspapermen, and waiters from upscale restaurants with pockets full of money earned from the day's tips. Then too, the after-hours bars attract drunks and misfits, many of whom stay inside during daylight hours and only come out at dark.

"It seems strange, doesn't it, meeting together in Fargo?" asks Baker. "I mean, the last time we had lunch was in the Mayflower in Washington. This place is no Mayflower Hotel."

Pinks looks around and smiles.

"You are right about that. But I bet the prices are a lot more attractive. I notice the Cobb salad is about half what I pay for it at the Mayflower. And keep in mind, this is the hotel where Peggy Lee started her singing career."

"I'll grant you, the prices are lower, but then so is the sophistication of the clientele," says Baker.

"So, how is life out West treating you?" asks Pinks. "Things at the *Forum* going okay? I suspect you are finding provisions at the Hotel Donaldson a little rustic for your tastes. I don't have any problem with you moving out of the place if you can find somewhere else you can afford on your salary."

"No, it's okay. I have a decent room and now that I figured out the routine for sharing the bathroom with my fellow inmates, I think I'm going to get along fine."

Pinks gives him a puzzled look, but decides not to pursue that line of inquiry.

"So how is the newspaper business?"

"Well, it's no *Washington Star*, that's for sure. But it is a good midsized newspaper. I like my night editor. The paper is fairly conservative, but he is an old-fashioned yellow journalist who likes big headlines and flashy leads. I get the sense he has few opportunities to show his stuff. I think we'll get along fine, but I'm not sure how much flexibility the newspaper brass will give either of us."

"The *Forum* is conservative. But then so is the state. The two sort of go together."

"I'm not really talking about conservative in the political sense. I'm talking about the kind that keeps the paper from writing the truth about crime for fear it might offend its readers."

"I didn't realize it does that."

"Take the story about the senator's daughter. We completely whitewashed that story."

"What do you mean?"

"Let me ask you. What do you think happened to her?"

"She was murdered in the alley behind Front Street, probably by an Indian now in police custody. We don't know why she was in that part of town on a Sunday. I guess that about captures it."

"That's about all that was in the paper, too. But I was there, on the murder scene. I can tell you she wasn't murdered where she was found. I discovered blood trails that came from a doorway further down the alley. I discovered fresh pools of blood at the basement door of a Front Street saloon. I rang a buzzer next to the door and it was opened by a guy inside. He was surprised to see me. I think he was expecting someone else. I asked him about the blood outside the door and he said, 'none of your business.' Then he slammed the door.

"I followed the blood trails into the alley. They appeared to lead right up to a body that lay under a sheet. I couldn't tell for sure because the alley is dimly lit. But when I walked up to the body, I heard two detectives arguing. One of them insisted there was no way the body could have been murdered where it was found because there was insufficient blood on the ground."

"Did you tell any of this to the police?"

"I tried to. I really did. But they were not the least bit interested in anything I had to say. They told me to get lost. I wrote some of what I had into a story that ran in Monday morning's paper. But that afternoon all my stuff was dropped, and the so-called 'official' version ran in the afternoon editions. It said the police insisted the murder took place where the body was found."

"That's very strange."

"What's even stranger is that the Indian they caught didn't have any weapons on him nor anything that linked him to the murder. I mean, the police are saying it was a robbery. But they caught this Indian less than a block from the scene without a weapon on him or anything in his possession that suggested he had robbed Sara Whitlow. And she was still wearing her diamond ring. Wouldn't you think a thief would have taken her ring?"

"So what do you think happened?"

"I think she was murdered inside what I assume is a storeroom underneath a Front Street bar and then the body was moved outside to the alley. I honestly believe the Fargo police are involved in the cover-up. I don't know why, but I would like to find out. I'm not even sure who murdered her. The drunk Indian was covered with blood. I saw it. He may be involved. But if he killed her, it wasn't for her money."

"I don't want to tell you your business, but I think you are overreaching here. I think the Indian got drunk, spotted an attractive white woman on the street, made a pass, got rejected, and killed her. Isn't that plausible?"

"What about her purse or pocketbook?"

"Somebody could have walked by and grabbed it. The Indian obviously didn't take it."

"Where is his weapon?

"He may have been drunk, but that doesn't mean he's stupid. I would guess he ditched it someplace, probably down a storm drain. He had plenty of time and opportunity. No, if I were you, I'd leave well enough alone. Don't you have to get registered for school?"

"Yes, sometime in the next two weeks."

"Well, that's what you should be focusing on. Leave the cops and Indians story to someone else. Trust me, these kinds of things go on all the time out here."

"It certainly is obvious nobody takes them seriously. I can't believe the story of the senator's daughter getting murdered didn't make the front page."

"I'll have to admit, that surprises me too. But I guess that's out of respect for the family. In many ways, Fargo is still a small town. People here still respect the privacy of a grieving family."

"That's all well and good. But there's more to this story than the *Forum* has reported. I'm certainly going to keep my eyes and ears open. I don't' know what I can learn sitting on the desk. But I probably will learn as much as anyone on the *Forum*. At least I'm paying attention."

"Promise me this. If you learn anything involving Sara Whitlow, call me first before you go flying off the handle, would you please? No more surprises for the senator and his wife. That's all I ask. Can you promise me that?"

"Sure. You are paying for this lunch, right?

* * *

James Foster appears in county court looking almost dapper with a fresh shave, shined shoes, and new haircut. He has on his best tie and newest old suit. Above all, his eyes are clear and his breath clean.

The jailer brings in Joe Running Deer and stands him alongside Foster. Joe is bound in handcuffs and has chains around his ankles. His pants are taped around his middle, so they don't slide down his legs.

The judge is Robert Williams, a respected jurist who had been a law school chum of Foster's at the University of Minnesota. They haven't been close socially since Foster's wife died a decade ago. But Williams has always admired his classmate's legal mind.

Prosecuting Joe Running Deer is Mary Peterson, an aggressive Cass County state's attorney.

Judge Williams asks what the charge is. Peterson says murder in the second degree. Williams asks how the client pleads and he looks at his lawyer before responding, "Not guilty."

At that point, Foster asks the court to dismiss the charge against his client because Cass County has no evidence to link his client to the alleged crime.

Peterson is on her feet with fire coming out of both nostrils. She says police had arrested Joe Running Deer within two blocks of the murder scene and that his clothes were soaked in blood.

Foster glances over at her like a hungry snake looks at a cornered mouse. Then he turns back to the judge.

"I ask the Court to request the prosecutor to produce those clothes. I also request that the Court ask the prosecutor to produce a weapon used in the alleged crime and to identify any eye witnesses to it. Your honor, I don't believe the prosecutor has any evidence at all that would tie my client to the victim of this alleged crime."

Judge Foster looks directly at Peterson.

"I assume you have a different point of view."

"Your honor, I can produce witnesses that will testify that on the night of the murder Joe Running Deer was wearing clothes soaked in blood. I can produce witnesses who will testify that he was within two blocks of the murder scene. I have lab reports that will show both he and the victim had been drinking, suggesting they were probably doing it together."

Foster scrunches up his face.

"What I don't hear you saying is, one, you have the bloody clothes worn by the accused; two, you have a murder weapon; three, you have evidence that puts the accused at the crime scene; and four, you have eyewitnesses coming forth who will place the victim and the accused together during the day the crime was committed. What I do hear you saying is that the police arrested an intoxicated Indian two blocks from the crime scene with no weapon on him nor anything else that would tie him to the victim. While the Indian might have been covered in blood, as the police allege, his clothes were burned while he was in jail. No analysis was done to see if the blood was even human, much less came from the victim. Does that about sum up your case?

"That would be putting the worst face on it, your honor."

"Yes, I believe that is a fair assessment. And here now is my assessment, equally fair. The motion to dismiss due to a lack of evidence is accepted. Mr. Running Deer, you are free to go."

Foster turns to a stunned Joe Running Deer still sitting at the defendant's table and shakes his hand. Foster whispers to the Indian, "I think we deserve a drink. Maybe two." As soon as the cuffs and chains are removed from his client, Foster walks him out of the courtroom and down the street into a nearby bar.

The outcome doesn't surprise Detective Wayne Thompson, sitting in the courtroom. He had expected it. His years of experience gave him the clue to call the County jail as soon as he heard that Joe Running Deer had been picked up last Sunday night. He got the duty sergeant on the phone and asked about Joe. As expected, he was told Joe was drunk. He was also a mess, covered with blood, urine, vomit and feces.

The police captain suggested the head jailer not allow the drunken Indian to foul up his clean jail.

"Strip off his clothes and put him under the hose," Johnson suggested. "Do it until he's good and clean. And his stinking clothes? Pick them up with a broom handle, take them out back, and burn them."

And by God, that's exactly what the jailer had done.

Without the clothes, weapon, or witnesses, Thompson knew Joe Running Deer was never going to court where he might have to testify about being in the Blind Pig with Sara Whitlow or killing her in the alley behind it. More importantly, the Indian wouldn't have the opportunity to tell the court that he was hired by Detective Captain Thompson to kill the young woman.

Thompson just has one last detail to take care of before he can put this saga behind him.

He leaves the courtroom and drives straight out to the trailer park on 5th Avenue. He pulls up to the Whitlow's trailer and gets out. He knocks on the trailer door and gets no response. He knocks again and still nothing. He is walking back to the car when he sees Bruce coming out of Terri's trailer, tucking his shirt into his Levis.

"You looking for me?"

"Yes, got a minute?"

"Sure. What's up?"

"I just left the courthouse. I thought you might be there. The Indian who killed your wife, Joe Running Deer, had his preliminary hearing this afternoon to see if he was going to stand trial for second degree murder."

"Yeah, I knew it was scheduled. I figured that was just a formality. I thought I would wait for the real trial."

"There isn't going to be one. The judge threw the case out. Said there wasn't enough evidence."

"What? He threw the case out? The fucking Indian killed my wife and the judge says he's innocent? What's going on?"

"The judge didn't say he was innocent. He just said the prosecutor hadn't assembled enough evidence to go to trial. I think the big problem is the fact the jailer burned the Indian's clothes the night he was caught. Without the bloody clothes, nobody can link him to Sara's murder. And there never was any murder weapon or eyewitnesses."

"I can't fucking believe this. So he just walks away?"

"I'm afraid so. He and his attorney went out for a drink as soon as the trial was over."

"God, I am so pissed. The guy is guilty as hell. Isn't he guilty? I mean, you were there. Isn't he guilty?"

"I'm no judge and jury. I'm only a cop. But I'm not going to play cute with you. Yes, the bastard is guilty. He killed your wife. I know he did. I just can't prove it. He deserves to hang and I'm not sorry to say so."

"So that fucker is walking the streets of Fargo. There isn't going to be any other white woman safe as long as he is out. Goddam. Somebody has to do something. I can tell you this. I know what needs to be done. But I better quit talking about it in front of you."

"I don't want to hear it either. You have to do what a man has to do. Just don't tell me."

Thompson turns as if he is about to leave. Then he turns back to face Bruce.

"I will say this," Thompson says in a stage whisper while looking around. He grabs Bruce by his shirt front and pulls him close.

"I will deny having ever said this, you understand? Every cop in Fargo will applaud if something bad happens to Joe Running Deer. Every cop in Fargo is going to look the other way if somebody puts a bullet through the heart of Joe Running Deer. Now, I never said that. You never heard me say that, right?"

"Loud and clear, detective. Loud and clear."

Thompson gets in his unmarked car and drives out of the trailer park. He wonders to himself what kind of gun Bruce will use.

*   *   *

Sam comes out of the bathroom on the second floor of the Hotel Donaldson and thumps down the hallway on his crutches. He needs the crutches because of his bum left leg. He might be able to get by with a cane rather than crutches if he does plenty of physical therapy. But the doctors at the Veterans Administration Hospital didn't want to fuss with him, so when he said his leg was shot, they agreed. The analysis earned him full disability pay and the opportunity to never work again. He isn't about to screw that up by making the case his leg might be stronger than he initially suggested. So he thumps around town on crutches. And when he goes to the VA for his checkups, he moans and groans about how much the damn leg bothers him. He even agrees to take pain shots in the leg while he is there. "Whatever you think will help, Doc," is his normal response to offers of treatment.

When he gets to Mac's room, Sam knocks quietly on the door. He never knows what to expect when he does so. Mac has the personality of a rhino: calm and charming one minute and then fierce and attacking the next.

The door swings open and Mac stands there staring at his comrade in arms. Sam smiles and Mac smiles back. Sam relaxes; Mac is calm.

"Mac, have you seen The *Forum* this morning? No, of course you haven't. You don't subscribe to the newspaper. Let me fill you in on the news. Remember that incident at the Blind Pig last Sunday, where that fucking Indian stuck our girl Sara? Well, her obituary is in the paper this morning. Kind of interesting."

Sam moves into the room and sits in the one chair present and puts his two crutches against the dresser. Mac sits on the bed across from him.

"The paper says that Sara's father is a United States senator from North Dakota, a guy named Thomas Christenson. I think we've met him. Do you remember the guy? Old fart. I think he pinned some of our medals on us at the VA Hospital a couple of years ago. Anyway, Sara was his daughter.

"Sara had a husband. Guy named Bruce. He works driving truck for some construction company building the interstate highway project. That probably explains why Sara came into the Blind Pig alone all the time. Her hubby must have been gone a lot.

"Anyway, they buried her this morning out at the Catholic cemetery. She was sure a pretty girl. And I think she liked us old boys. Not that she was going to give anything away for free, mind you. But she was just fun to be around. Don't you agree?"

Mac looks at his friend. He nods his head. Mac isn't capable of loving anyone. But if he did, Sara would have been high on his affection list.

The two men sit in silence. They do that a lot and are comfortable with it. Time spent in frontline foxholes produces an acceptance of that behavior. Of course, Mac hardly ever says anything and that sort of requires even someone as talkative as Sam to get used to long periods of silence when he is with his buddy.

The radio is on and some new guy named Waylon Jennings is singing "That's the Chance I'll Have to Take" when the door, which hadn't been closed shut, bursts open. In walks loony Will.

"Hey, did you hear the radio?"

"Hear what, Will?" asks Sam.

"The Indian was set free."

"What are you talking about?"

"Turn over to WDAY. It's on the news. That Indian. The one that killed Sara. They let him go."

Mac gets up and changes the radio dial to WDAY.

The three men listen to the WDAY broadcaster repeat the news from earlier in the day: County Court Judge Robert Williams had released Joe Running Deer from jail because there's insufficient evidence to hold him for trail in the murder of Sara Whitlow.

The three veterans sit stunned. Two of them are immediately angry. The third initially is angry. But then his Ranger training takes over. The anger is replaced by determination. Then he slips into action mode. He knows what he has to do.

He has to avenge Sara.

Chapter Thirteen

The Daily Newspaper is a Minor Miracle

Steve Klundt wants to make sure word of Joe Running Deer's release from jail sweeps through the *Forum* as soon as he gets back from the courtroom. Klundt walks into the newsroom and shouts, "The murdering Indian is out of jail. Can you believe that? The judge let him go."

A dozen reporters decide the stories they are working on can wait as they bolt from their desks to hear Klunt deliver his scoop. Klunt already has his sport coat off. He perches on his desk, rolls up his shirt sleeves, and loosens his tie. He slowly lights up a Chesterfield. He has a story to tell and he knows his news-hungry audience isn't going to go anywhere until they hear it. He stalls an extra minute when he notices Swede Swenson drifting over to listen.

Klunt at one time thought about being a cop. A former military policeman, he discovered he liked carrying a gun and police baton. But when he got out of the army, he went back to school and got a degree. He found he could work as a newspaperman, write for the *Police Gazette* on the side, and still carry a gun as a volunteer for the Police Auxiliary. In other words, he figures he has the best of all worlds. He is tight with the local police and considers several cops to be close friends. When it comes to police matters, he long ago lost his objectivity, but that doesn't seem to be a problem at the *Forum*, which backs the police wholeheartedly.

At this point Chuck Baker comes into the newsroom after having a late lunch with his stepfather. He is all set to go to work on the night shift. But when he sees the group gathering around Klunt, he stops to listen.

"Here's the scene in the courthouse," says Klunt, setting the stage for his story. "The Indian is represented by this drunk," and then he stops to check his notes. "A guy named Foster."

"Jim Foster?" asks the executive editor.

"Yeah, Jim Foster, that's the guy."

"He used to be a pretty sharp attorney. But then he began hitting the bottle hard. I didn't know he was still practicing law."

"He was doing a hell of a job of it in court today, believe me.

"Anyway, the prosecutor from the Cass County State's Attorney's Office makes the case that the judge ought to put Indian Joe away for second degree murder. I guess the county figured he was too damn drunk when he gutted the senator's daughter to pin a first degree murder rap on him. That would require proving he intended to kill her. I don't think anyone believes that to be the case. Everybody assumes the two of them just bumped into each other on the street. She probably just said something to him that really pissed him off."

"Yeah, like "How," said one of the reporters, holding up his right hand in a movie-style Indian greeting. That got a laugh out of the reporters.

"Let me finish," said Klunt. "Then as soon as the prosecutor wraps up her opening, Foster is on his feet. Let me tell you something. He may be a drunk. But he looked sharp. He had a fresh haircut, a clean shave, and the shiniest shoes in the room. His suit looked worn, I'll grant you that, but it had been an expensive brand when bought new. I mean, the guy looked like he belonged in the courtroom. And did he ever do a number on the prosecution.

"Foster gave the prosecutor the evil eye. Then he asks the million-dollar question. Can anyone guess what it was?"

Klunt takes a long drag on his Chesterfield.

The reporters exchange puzzled looks. Swenson frowns. He's beginning to realize no work is getting done while Klunt holds court.

"Get on with your story, Steve. Some of us have a newspaper to get out."

Everybody in the crowd except Baker works on the afternoon paper. Its next edition won't go to press until the following afternoon. But the boss had made his point.

"He asks her if the prosecution has the Indian's blood-soaked clothes."

The reporters seem confused. The significance of the Indian's clothes is lost on them.

"Hey, the clothes are the key to the whole murder. There are no witnesses, okay? The police find no murder weapon, right? They pick up an Indian a couple of blocks from the murder scene. But he has nothing on him that ties him back to the victim. So far the police have a pretty weak case against Indian Joe.

"But wait a minute."

Klunt has the entire group of seasoned reporters and Baker spellbound.

"The Indian was covered in blood when he was arrested. No brainer: if the blood on his clothes matches the victim's blood, no jury in the state would deny the hangman his daily rate to stretch the Indian's neck. See why it's so important for the prosecutor to have the Indian's clothes?"

One of the reporters asks: "What happened to his clothes?"

Klunt laughs out loud.

"It didn't come out in court. But I asked the prosecutor that question after the session ended. She was so upset she could barely talk."

Klunt picked up his notes again and then went on talking.

"She said to me, and I am now quoting her exact words: 'Go talk to the county jailer. The jerk burned the Indian's clothes. Can you believe that? He said he did it because he didn't want them to stink up his nice clean jail.'

"So I went and talked to the jailer and that in fact is exactly what he did. He said the Indian came into his clean jail in the very early hours of Monday morning wearing filthy, disgusting clothes. The jailer made him take them off. Then the jailer hosed down the Indian and took his clothes out back and burned them. Goodbye evidence."

Another reporter asked: "Shouldn't the jailer have known better?"

"Good question. I asked him that. He said the arresting officers and Captain Thompson of the Front Street squad told him they knew the Indian had committed the murder. The jailer assumed there had to be tons of evidence for everybody to be so confident of the Indian's guilt. The jailer didn't know everything depended on the bloody clothes. Nobody told him to save them. In fact, he remembers somebody even suggesting they be burned."

"Who suggested they be burned?"

The reporters all turned their heads to see who behind them had asked that question. They recognize the new guy, but don't know his name.

Klunt didn't know his name either. "He didn't say."

The way Klunt responded made it clear to Baker that a follow-up question wouldn't be appreciated.

"Anyway, the Indian and Foster left the courthouse together looking for a bar. I've never seen two happier guys."

"Good story," says Swenson. "I trust you can retell it on paper so the readers who pay your salary have the benefit of your insight. We'll run it tomorrow morning, maybe on the front page. It will make a good feature story."

Klunt smiles and slides off his desk and into his chair. Like most crime reporters, feature writing is one of his strengths.

The other reporters drift back to their desks, many of them wishing they had a beat that gave them the opportunity to write front page feature stories.

Baker moves over to his corner desk by the AP Office. He still wonders who told the jailer it was okay to burn the Indian's clothes. Then he has another thought.

What if a black man had murdered the senator's daughter in Washington, D.C., and then was set free because of a jailer's screw-up? Would the police allow the guilty guy to walk the streets a free man? No way, concludes Baker. The Negro would be dead within a week. And his killers would never be identified.

Baker opens his desk drawer and pulls out the phone book. He looks up the telephone number for James Foster, attorney at law. He glances at the clock. It was already after 5 p.m. He dials the number. He can only hope the attorney went back to his office after he and his client had gone to the bar.

"James Foster, attorney at law."

Baker is surprised to get an answer.

"Hello, my name is Chuck Baker. I'm a reporter at the *Forum*. Congratulations, by the way, on your court victory today. Everyone here was amazed that your client walked away a free man,"

"Thank you. I guess I wasn't expecting a congratulatory call from the media."

"Actually, I was calling to ask you if you know how I can reach your client, Joe Running Deer."

"Why do you want to contact him?"

"I would like to do an interview with him following his court appearance today."

"I will advise my client against it. I don't want him to say anything that could be used against him in court later."

"Oh, that's not the purpose of my interview. Let me explain. I've had some experience working on an East Coast newspaper. That experience tells me that your client might be in some jeopardy having escaped from the clutches of the law. In other words, the cops might be really upset that he was released when they think he's guilty of murder. So I wanted to ask your client if he is worried about walking around town with a bull's-eye on his back."

"I see. My client is sitting right here. In fact, he's going to spend the night here for the very reason you articulate. I will let you talk to him. But I'm going to remain in the room. And if I hear him say anything to you about the crime in question, I will terminate the call. Do you understand?"

"Yes, I'm comfortable with that arrangement."

"Okay, here's Joe."

Baker can hardly believe his luck. He threads some copy paper into his Royal typewriter and braces the phone to his ear with his shoulder and cheek. Both hands are on the keyboard.

"Hello. This is Joe. Who's this?"

"Hi. My name is Chuck. Chuck Baker. I'm a reporter with the *Forum*. Can I ask you a few questions?"

"Okay. Mr. Foster said I could talk to you. Just don't ask anything about what I'm not allowed to talk about."

For the next fifteen minutes, Baker conducts his interview.

While Baker is on the phone, night editor Jim Rector comes in, lays his three large cigars on his desk, and looks over at his young city desk editor. He wonders who Baker is interviewing so feverously. Rector admires initiative in young journalists. He knows any interview Baker is conducting concerns a story he's dug up on his own. That puts a smile on Rector's face.

When he finishes interviewing Joe Running Deer, Baker hangs up the phone and smiles. He turns to Rector to tell him what he has, but the night editor is in a discussion with Swenson, the managing editor. So Chuck starts to write his story, leaving the headline writing to the night editor:

```
By Charles Baker Forum Staff Writer

Joe Running Deer stood accused of
second degree murder Thursday
afternoon, but that night he slept in
his attorney's office a free man,
released from jail because the Cass
County State's Attorney Office lacked
the evidence to hold him. But he
slept lightly, worried that local
police may not want to see him escape
punishment.
```

The Mandan Indian was accused of killing Sara Whitlow, daughter of Senator Thomas Christenson and Pam Christenson of Fargo and Arlington, VA. The murder took place last Sunday in or near the intersection of 4th Street and the alley that runs behind Front Street. She was found at that location stabbed to death.

At his hearing Thursday afternoon, the Indian was set free because the prosecution was unable to produce any evidence to tie him to the crime. When he was arrested near the crime scene, Joe Running Deer was covered with blood. He told arresting officers it was deer blood from a carcass he had butchered. Police believed it was Sara Whitlow's blood.

A simple laboratory test would have confirmed the origins of the blood and potentially the Indian's guilt or innocence.

But the bloody clothes were taken off the Indian when he went to the Cass County Jail. That same night the jailer burned them. He told court officials he didn't want the Indian's clothes to stink up his clean jail. As a result, there was no evidence on which to hold the Indian.

After the judge released Joe Running Deer for lack of evidence, he and his attorney, John Foster, discussed the Indian's options. They were limited. They fear that an

Indian who stands accused of killing a prominent white woman and then gets off free because of a jailer's error is a marked man. When that error ends up embarrassing the local police force in the city where the victim lives, an obvious option is for the accused to relocate, quickly.

"I'm going to move out of Fargo as soon as I can," said Joe Running Deer Thursday night. "I don't feel safe here anymore. I think the Fargo cops are gunning for me."

Thursday night he slept on the sofa in Foster's office. They agreed it was safer than a hotel room and possibly even Foster's apartment.

"In the morning, I'm leaving. Mr. Foster is going to give me some money. I don't know how much. But I'm going to catch a Greyhound. He told me not to say which way I'm heading. But it will be out of state, I can say that. I don't plan to come back."

Joe Running Deer said he wasn't going to drink any liquor before he leaves town.

"Mr. Foster said I should stay sober until I get to where I'm going. He said I need to stay alert. I think that is good advice."

Baker reads the story over and decides it's good enough for the *Forum*. He hands it to Rector who throws it on a pile, then gets up to do his walkthrough of the back room.

After 10:30 p.m., Rector spends most of his time in the back room with the printers, guiding their assembly of the newspaper pages, making sure the stories, headlines, cutlines, pictures, and carryover stories go where he wants them. He then makes decisions about what to do when a story is too long or too short for the space he has intended for it. He also decides what to do when his layout results in headlines "bumping" into one another across multiple columns. When this happens, readers can be misled into reading two separate headlines as one, with very confusing results.

After Rector walks through the vast back room checking the lay of the land, as he describes it, he pushes back through the swinging door into the newsroom.

He heads back to his desk and looks over at Baker. He remembers the telephone interview the young city editor was so engrossed in.

"What were you working on earlier?"

"I did an interview with that Indian that they freed from jail this afternoon. The story is lying on your desk."

"You know that the city desk already has a story about his release from jail, don't you?"

"Yes, Klunt's story. I haven't read it. But I think mine's probably a little different. I figure mine can run as a sidebar to his. You decide."

Rector fishes through the copy on his desk and locates both Klunt's and Baker's stories. He reads Klunt's first and then Baker's.

"You're right. They work well together. Do we have any art?"

"Good question. I don't know. I'll go find out."

Baker gets out of his chair and walks past the city editor's desk, now deserted, and back to where the Women and Sports staffs reside. The women have all left and the sports desk only has a skeleton crew. He turns the corner in front of the Sports section and goes back to the photo lab.

"Anybody in here?" he yells at the closed curtain hanging over the entrance to the darkroom. He doesn't get an answer. On the counter he sees a wire basket. In it are several photographs of two men in what appears to be a courthouse. They're standing in a hallway with their arms around each other and wearing huge grins on their faces.

A typed caption is paper-clipped to the photo. "CELEBRATING FREEDOM—Fargo attorney James Foster (left) and his client, Joe Running Deer, celebrate the latter's release from jail Thursday after County Court Judge Robert Williams ruled the county had insufficient evidence to hold the man on murder charges stemming from the death of Sara Whitlow, daughter of Senator and Mrs. Thomas Christenson."

He looks through the photographs and selects what he considers to be the best one.

"We've got a great picture," says Baker as he drops it on Rector's desk.

Rector looks at it. Then he flips it back to Baker.

"Crop it for a three-column shot and get it down to Engraving. We'll go with the photographer's cutline. Mark it for three columns as well. I'm going with both stories and the picture on page one."

Baker says okay, but he has no idea where Engraving is. When Rector gets up to go to the bathroom, he looks over at Morrison.

"Harry, how do you send prints down to Engraving?"

"Nobody has shown you? They're right below us in the basement. Follow me."

Morrison leads Baker back to the photo lab where they come across a chute containing a hoist and basket.

"Put your print in there with instructions on the back for how big or small you want it to be. Then push the button and it will end up downstairs in Engraving. Engraving will send the finished piece back upstairs later. Simple as that."

The rest of the night goes smoothly. When the newspapers come off the press Baker thinks the front page looks super. Rector has run the two stories and photo below the fold, and they take up most of the bottom half of the page. His story plays second fiddle to Klunt's story, as it should. Klunt's story is straightforward and factual. The young author personally thinks his story is better written. But he concedes that Klundt will probably think otherwise.

No matter, shrugs Baker. Both articles carry bylines; the readers can decide which reporter wrote the more interesting story.

Chapter Fourteen

An Eye for an Eye

Chuck Baker grabs several extra copies of the Morning edition of the *Forum* when he leaves work just after midnight and takes them with him to the Donaldson.

When he gets to his room, he wonders why he grabbed extra copies of the paper. He only needs one for himself. Not wanting to waste two perfectly good, brand-new newspapers, particularly with his byline on the front page, he decides to drop them off in a couple of the bathrooms. He's sure some of the hotel's other guests will enjoy reading the paper; hell, they might even notice a front-page story carries the name of one of their neighbors.

Sam hears Baker come in at his usual time. Sam isn't a heavy sleeper and he knows he's going to have to get used to having this kid wake him up around 12:30 a.m. Normally the floor is quiet at this time of night. Not anymore.

He lays there in bed fighting the urge to take a piss. He sighs deeply realizing he isn't going to be able to postpone it for long. Either piss now or lie in growing agony and piss in 10 minutes. He grabs his crutches and gets up. He finds his robe, puts it on, and scampers as best he can out of the door and down the hallway to the bathroom.

Once he finishes his business, he notices the *Forum* lying on the sink. That's strange, he thinks. He doesn't remember anyone ever leaving the morning newspaper on the sink before.

He flushes the toilet but leaves the seat up. One of the joys of living with men is knowing nobody cares if the toilet seat is left up. He picks up the newspaper and notices Friday's date on it. That means the kid must have left it. Sam can't for the life of him figure out why. This isn't even his bathroom.

Sam tucks the *Forum* under his arm and leaves. When he gets back to his room, he sits on his bed with the light on and glances at the front page. McNamara was saying things were not going all that well in Vietnam. What a surprise. He should have talked to the French before he went charging into Indochina. Sam sighs loudly and flips the paper to see if the bottom half of the front page contains anything worth reading.

Ah, he says to himself. Stories about the Indian who killed Sara. Sam reads both stories with interest. The son of bitch is still in town, staying at his attorney's office, Sam learns. I'll be damned, he says to himself, gets up and grabs his crutches. He tucks the newspaper under his arm and barrels out the door.

He raps on Mac's door softly. "Mac, it's me, Sam. I've got to talk to you. Open up, okay? I've got something important for you to see."

Sam looks up and down the hallway. Then he knocks again. Now he has to worry about waking up others on the floor.

"Mac, for God's sake, open the door; it's me, Sam." And he knocks again, a little louder.

The door finally opens to reveal Mac standing there in nothing but his shorts. His bare chest is massive. It also is heavily scarred from the operations he has endured to remove shrapnel and patch up bullet wounds. Sam has never seen him with his shirt off.

"I'm sorry to bother you buddy, but I knew you would want to see this." He hands the newspaper to Mac.

Mac looks at the bottom half of the paper handed to him. He reads both stories standing in his doorway. For three full minutes, he makes no move to allow Sam into the room.

Sam believes he can tell when Mac gets to the part in the second story where it reports that the Indian is staying the night at his attorney's office. Mac moves back into his room. Sam takes that as a sign it's okay for him to enter.

But Mac puts his hand on Sam's chest and stops him. The look on his face makes it clear to Sam that he isn't invited in.

"Well, I'm going back to bed. I just thought you would like to see these articles, that's all," says Sam, as he backs into the hallway. "I'll get together with you in the morning."

Mac closes the door quietly behind Sam. Then he reaches for the telephone book he keeps in his room. He needs the address of James Foster's office.

A few blocks to the north, Bruce Whitlow is leaving the Bismarck Lounge after last call has emptied the place. He isn't drunk. He went to the bar to get shitfaced, but he failed to get it done. He's never been much of a drinker. He likes beer okay, but only in small quantities. Sara used to make fun of him. She would tell him she wished he made love as slowly as he drank a beer. Then she would laugh and say she was just kidding. After all, the less he drank, the more drinks he could afford to buy her.

He heads out of the bar and thinks about getting something to eat. He knows he has nothing back in his house trailer. He thinks he might be able to get a cup of coffee and a piece of pie at the coffee shop in the Fargo Hotel across the street. He heads straight over—there's not that much traffic in Fargo after midnight, even on a Friday—and walks into the empty lobby, only to find the coffee shop closed. But in a corner of the lobby, he sees a bundle of *Forums* lying on the floor wrapped with a string waiting for someone to put them into the newsstand. He's not much of a newspaper reader, but he can't help but wonder if there's news about Sara's killer. He grabs the paper at the top of the bundle, pulls it free and looks at it. He turns it over and sees the picture and two stories about the man who killed his wife filling the bottom of the front page.

Whitlow takes the newspaper with him into the lobby phone booth where he finds what he's looking for. When he comes out, he no longer has the newspaper. But he does have a page out of the telephone book that contains James Foster's office address. He's no longer thinking about coffee and pie. He is thinking about the revolver under his truck seat and the bullets in the glove compartment.

After a short drive, he finds the office. It's in an old house that has a screened-in porch wrapped around it. He parks on the street, one house down. Whitlow locates his gun, loads it, makes sure the safety is on and tucks it into his pants at the waist. Then he slips out of the truck and makes his way up the sidewalk to the front porch, gun in hand. Just as his foot hits the front steps, an overhead light snaps on. And he hears a booming voice: "Don't take another step."

Whitlow freezes in place. Then he notices a large man lift himself up off a rocker on the porch. He's holding a shotgun and it's pointing directly at him.

"Who are you and what do you want? says the voice behind the screen.

I'm Sara Whitlow's husband. I want to talk to that goddamn Indian who killed her."

"Sorry for your loss," says the voice. "But there's no Indian here. I loaded him into a boxcar heading out of town just about an hour ago. You might be able to catch the train, if you knew which way it was heading."

"It's just not fair. He's alive and okay and my sweet Sara is dead and gone. Where's the justice?"

"Well, you won't find any justice here. Why don't you just put your gun away and go home. Things always look brighter first thing in the morning."

Bruce knows he won't feel any better in the morning, but he's no match for a man holding a shotgun on him.

"Okay, I'm leaving. But if you ever talk to that sonofabitch, tell him Sara's husband is on his trail. Tell him I'm aiming to kill me an Indian."

Whitlow leaves and returns to his truck. He's disappointed he didn't find his Indian. But he's relieved he didn't get shot trying. He decides he might just as well go back to the trailer park.

As he drives away, he recalls his promise . . . call it his threat. He said he was going to punish an Indian for what happened to his wife. And just like that, Whitlow is mad all over again. He turns the corner and decides to head to Front Street. If there's an Indian anywhere in Fargo, that's where he's likely to be.

Whitlow calls it right. As he drives slowly down Front Street he sees a variety of Indians, but always in pairs or better. He turns the corner and enters the alley behind the Front Street bars. And he finds what he's looking for. A drunk Indian is leaning against a telephone pole puking. Whitlow shuts off his truck lights and drives up to him slowly with his driver's side window down.

"Hey, do you know Joe Running Deer?"

Although the Indian seems intent on finishing throwing up, Whitlow appears to believe he has the answer he wants. He points his revolver out the window and shoots the Indian three times. Whitlow is pretty confident he's dead before he even hits the ground.

Whitlow drives away. He's still sorry he didn't get the Indian who killed his wife, but figures he got the next best thing, the killer's Indian friend. Satisfied, he heads to his trailer park. On the way he decides he's going to pack up his truck and head to Arizona. He can contact Sara's mother from there about the money she promised to give him. Hell, he can even call Sara's friend Terri and see if she would like to take a trip with him.

*   *   *

Back at attorney Foster's office, things have quieted down. Foster had a sixth sense that something would happen, so he'd stood watch on the porch while his client slept on the sofa in the waiting area. But not long after Whitlow leaves, Foster goes inside and switches on the desk lamp in his office. He pulls the bottom drawer of a filing cabinet all the way out and grabs the bottle of Scotch he keeps at the back, behind the files. He pours himself a drink to settle his nerves from the encounter with the angry widower, then switches the desk lamp back off. He walks in the dark over to his favorite leather couch, along the back wall of his office, where he's slept many nights before.

As soon as the office has been quiet for a good 30 minutes, a professional killer begins his approach. The screen door isn't locked and surprisingly, neither is the front door. From the racket he hears, he knows more than one person is snoring inside. He goes into the waiting area off the entryway and sees Joe Running Deer lying on his back, sound asleep. The killer recognizes him from the night in the Blind Pig, the night he gutted Sara, the senator's daughter.

The killer isn't sure what might be the best way to kill Joe Running Deer. He has a gun, which he can use, but now he wonders if that's his best choice. The gun will wake up the other fellow in the house and then he will have to be killed, too. That would require at least one more shot. With each shot fired, the killer knows he is increasing the likelihood someone will hear the noise and call the police.

He puts his revolver away and reaches for his knife.

He's comfortable killing with it. The knife, a V-42 Stiletto, has been his for nearly 25 years. It was developed initially for the "Devil's Brigade," an elite force of allied troops fighting in French-held Algeria during World War II. At one point the Brigade joined forces with a special unit of American Army Rangers to attack a heavily fortified German position. After the battle, the commander of the Devil's Brigade gave a V-42 Stiletto to a large, BAR-carrying ranger who had fought gallantly in the battle. That ranger from then on carried the blued stiletto—with its jagged knife point—in a sheath he wore on his thigh. It saw use during savage fighting in Italy and Germany. The knife could kill several ways, depending on the preference of its user. A useful feature was its small, jagged point on the pummel that soldiers called a "skull crusher." At war's end, he carried the knife home with him to Fargo.

That night, the skull crusher avenged Sara Whitlow.

*   *   *

Just after 10 a.m., Senator and Mrs. Thomas Christenson and their two aides board Northwest Orient Airlines Flight 207 from Fargo to Minneapolis, where it will then continue on to Washington National Airport in Arlington, Virginia, just across the Potomac River from the nation's capital.

It's been less than 24 hours since the funeral, and everyone is still solemn, if only for purposes of decorum. Pam is the only person truly mourning the loss of her daughter. She and her husband board first, sitting in the front of first class.

Jerry Pinks and Ashley Briggs head toward the back of the Boeing 707, sitting in the coach section. They don't sit together. Personal staff and committee staff seldom mingle away from the office. Although both work for the senator, technically only Briggs is employed on the senator's personal staff. The Senate Appropriations Committee pays Pinks' salary. Staff members who work in a senator's office tend to think they have higher status than the senator's committee staff. Some do; most don't. One indication of importance is determined by an individual's compensation. And the personal staffs' modest paychecks don't compare to the more substantial ones earned by the committee staff.

Pam looks at her husband's profile, then out the window at the tarmac and the high Fargo skies. She is glad they are together. But she knows she is alone in her grief.

The funeral took a lot out of her. She's just now beginning to realize how much she's going to miss her only daughter. She's sad and angry at the same time. Sad that Sara is gone. Angry that her husband seems completely indifferent to the situation. She even suspects he is relieved that he doesn't have to worry anymore about what Sara might do to damage his precious reputation.

Then too, she is also disappointed in Jerry. She wants him to grieve more for Sara. After all, he knew her, having visited with her at Pam's insistence at least a dozen times. He knew her as an infant, a child, a young lady, and then as a woman. And yet he doesn't seem all that despondent about her death. Pam wants to believe Jerry cares about her daughter just as she does, but obviously that isn't the case.

The senator's wife has been tempted many times to tell Pinks the truth about Sara. Had he expressed any feelings toward her daughter, she would have. She doesn't understand why it has never occurred to him that he just might be Sara's father. She thought about telling him many times, but didn't because she could see that information would be of no benefit to anyone. Sara was better off thinking the senator was her father. The senator sure didn't want to learn that his daughter was fathered by one of his senior staff members. And Jerry could do nothing with the information but keep it to himself.

But that meant the only one who seems to have loved Sara as much as her mother did was her husband Bruce.

Bruce's reaction to Sara's death had surprised Pam. During the funeral, his eulogy was not only elegant, it was scary in its boldness. He left no doubt that he was going to get revenge for Sara's murder. Nobody else had talked about revenge. Nobody had asked her what she wanted, like Bruce had. But Bruce had articulated it in church. He said it forcefully in front of the senator and all his stuffy friends. And he said it in front of God. Bruce wanted revenge. Pam hopes he gets it, for both of them.

Revenge is all she has thought about since this morning. There it was, atop the morning paper: Sara's killer was set free. All because a jailer burned the Indian's clothes. Everyone says he's guilty and should go to prison for life for what he did to

Sara. That wouldn't be enough, she'd thought. Locking up the Indian had seemed insufficient punishment for his crime. And now he's free.

Godspeed, Bruce, she thinks to herself, as she rises into the high skies over Fargo.

*   *   *

When Baker arrives at work around noon, Klunt, whose desk is close to the door, asks him if he has seen the afternoon paper yet. When Chuck says no, Klunt tosses him one.

The main headline reads: "Released Indian Murdered in Lawyer's Office." The byline carries Klunt's name.

Baker reads standing up. Somebody broke into the office overnight and killed Joe Running Deer with a blunt object, presumably while he was sleeping on John Foster's couch. The lawyer says he found his client in the morning. The story said the police are investigating, but so far have no clues as to who might have killed him. The police also say that the attorney maintains his residence in the same building as his office, but don't consider him a suspect.

When Baker finishes, he looks up to see Klunt grinning at him.

"Is this your first kill?" Klunt asks.

"What are you talking about?" says Baker.

"I was just curious. Your cutesy story in this morning's paper obviously tipped the killer off to the Indian's location. Otherwise nobody would have known where he was. I figure you deserve part of the credit for killing him. So I was asking, is this your first killing? And how does it make you feel?"

By now most of the reporters sitting near Klunt are staring at Baker.

"Fuck you, Klunt," says Baker, as he turns and walks toward his desk.

"I think you better stick to weather stories and obits, preppie."

Baker hears the chuckles behind him as he walks away. He wants to turn around and say something clever. But nothing clever comes to mind.

What really bothers Baker is knowing the reporters feel superior to any new guy sitting on the nightside city desk. They are, after all, reporters. He's nothing more than a glorified rewrite man. He wants to be sitting among them. Instead, he is chained to a goddamn desk playing second fiddle to an old man who really doesn't need any help except to have somebody answer the phone and write the fucking weather story. He has to hope a hard news story falls into his lap, and then when one does, like the Indian sleeping in his lawyer's office, it turns into a damn tragedy. Worse yet, he says to himself, someone else gets to write up the aftermath.

The preppy comment also upsets Baker. He thinks he dresses better than everyone else in the newsroom, but he hardly thinks of himself as a preppie. He's just three years ahead of the fashions worn by the average North Dakota male; make that five years ahead if men in the newsroom are included in the equation. Ten years ahead if you take into consideration the dress code adopted by the sports staff.

He plops down into his chair and looks over at Rector who is laying out his cigars.

"Notice the weather when you came in?" Rector asks.

Baker shakes his head. He's steamed about Klunt.

"We're in for a big storm. You haven't been through one of these yet. It's going to be a busy night for us. Get ready for it."

As soon as Rector walks out into the back room, Baker leans over and askes Morrison what the hell does Rector mean, "get ready for the big storm?"

*   *   *

Pam is just about to doze off in her "TV chair" when the phone rings. She and the senator arrived home from the airport a couple of hours ago, just in time for a quick bite of supper. He's already headed off to bed. She was watching a little Friday night *Rawhide*, to see if she could catch a glimpse of that handsome young actor who played Rowdy Yates. Clint somebody.

She heads across the room to the Victorian Eastlake parlor table that the living room phone sits atop. She grabs the receiver at the end of the second ring.

"Hello, this is Mrs. Christenson."

"Hi, Pam." It's Jerry Pinks, sounding like he's still trying to console her. It already feels like that's the only tone of voice she has ever heard anyone use when speaking to her.

"Hello Jerry. Has something happened?" She asks, sitting down in the small vanity chair alongside the phone table.

"Yes. You can relax now; the Indian who killed Sara is dead."

"Oh." It's good news, but it still comes as a bit of a shock. So soon, at least. She's glad she's sitting down. Then she thinks of Bruce and his promise. "What happened?"

"Remember the judge released the Indian from jail for lack of evidence?"

"How could I forget?"

"Well, his lawyer took him to his office to sleep in the waiting room. The lawyer even stayed with him overnight, sleeping on the couch in his office, according to the *Forum*. But when he woke up, he found the Indian in his waiting room with his head bashed in.

"Who did it, Jerry?"

"They don't know, Pam. I already called and asked the Fargo detective in charge of the case that question myself. He said off the record they suspect Sara's husband, Bruce. He certainly had a motive; having said at the funeral he was going to get revenge. But they don't know for sure. The police have staked out his trailer, but nobody has been in it. Just between you and me, I don't think the police are looking all that hard for Bruce. I think they're glad the Indian is dead too."

"Well, I don't mind saying that I will rest a little easier knowing Sara's killer is dead. And if Bruce killed him, I say, 'good for him.'"

"I don't imagine we'll ever know, Pam. I suspect we have heard the last from Bruce."

"Jerry, do you remember that young woman who was at the church with Bruce, the one who was a friend of Sara's?"

"The one with the poor taste in funeral attire? Yes, I remember her. What about her?"

"Do you have her name by chance?"

"Not off the top of my head. I think the press office still has the book that everyone signed who came to the funeral. I could check and see if I can pull out a name and attach it to a face. Why do you ask?"

"Oh, I would just like to tell her that she should feel free to drop by Sara's trailer and help herself to anything she wants. I think most of Sara's clothes would fit her, and as you saw, she could use a new wardrobe. Sara's friend ought to have first choice of stuff."

"I'll see what I can do and I'll get back to you."

"You're a sweetheart, Jerry. Thanks."

Pam hangs up the phone and starts to think. She doesn't care what happens to the junk in Sara's trailer. But she saw the way that hussy hung onto Bruce at the funeral. If anybody knows how to get a hold of him, she does. All it will take to get her talking, Pam figures, is money. And Pam has plenty of that.

*   *   *

"A big storm out here can be a mean son-of-a-bitch," Morrison says. "It will have high winds, big hail, heavy rains, and then when you think it's over, a tornado will touch down. The storm will pull roofs off of barns, flip over trucks on the highway, and kill people, particularly if they're unlucky enough to live in trailer parks. Lightning will hit a few barns and start fires. People will get hurt trying to rescue their livestock. All hell will break loose, in other words, and your police and fire radios will all be chattering at the same time. You're going to be busier than a one-armed paper hanger."

"What do I do?" Asks Baker.

"First thing you do is go to the bathroom. You may not get another chance. Then go out and buy yourself a sandwich and a couple of Cokes. You won't get a dinner break later. You don't smoke, or I'd tell you to lay in a couple of packs of cigarettes.

"When you have your provisions all set, call the Weather Bureau. Find out who's working the shift tonight. Introduce yourself. Tell them you're in this with them through the night. Make sure they think it's okay that you keep calling back for updates. You're going to be doing that about every half hour throughout your shift.

"You will need to have a sense of where the storm is and where it is heading. In your desk you'll find a laminated map of the Red River Valley. Keep it on your desk. Get some colored grease pencils and plot the storm. There are probably some in your desk somewhere. Then when you hear the county police squawk boxes, you'll know the towns they are talking about. If you hear anybody talking about a tornado, let Jim or me know. Tornados are big news around here. We may want to get a photographer and reporter on the scene if there's sufficient damage or injuries."

"Alright, I think I've got it."

"The tough part is sorting out what's important and what's just noise. These country police and volunteer fire departments can get really excited about big storms. So they're likely to say the sky is falling the first time a hailstone falls. Your job is to sort out where the real action is. And you may not learn about it from the guy who yells the loudest."

Baker rifles through his desk and finds a handful of colored grease pencils.

"So what exactly do I do with all of these?" He asks Morrison.

"Develop yourself a coding system. Red dots for barn fires, let's say. Green for hail. Blue for tornado sightings. Black for injuries. Black circles for fatalities. And so on and so forth. Then when the squawk boxes report on anything occurring in a community, you can mark up your map accordingly. This will help you keep track of where the storm is likely heading and where any damage behind the storm can be located. You'll need to know this to make your calls and have some notion about what to ask. Your color-coded map will give you a pretty good overview of the storm's impact across the region. This will help you when you start to write your wrap-up story.

"My final piece of advice: start writing the story early. You can always revise. Don't wait until you think you have all the facts identified and confirmed. If it's a bad storm, you're going to have many subplots, with mini-stories about what is going on in a variety of different locations. So write up each event or occurrence as you get information on it. Then update these as you get better information. As we get closer to deadline, pull them all together under a tight lead and let it go. You can update the entire story for the last edition. All the dayside team should have left to do in the morning is to bury the bodies and round up the strays."

Morrison is grinning. But Baker isn't sure if he's kidding.

"Look Baker," Morrison says, detecting his doubt. "A Midwestern storm kills people, tears down their barns, destroys their homes, and sends their surviving livestock wondering around in a daze. Complicating matters, county and local police departments are so overwhelmed they treat the inquiring news media with absolute and utter disdain. They don't take calls from reporters. Nor do they return calls. And if reached, they don't share a single damn thing except to say a big storm apparently has done a lot of damage to the region."

Baker got the message. He'd never worked the phones harder than he did that night. He quit on the police almost immediately. He found the fire chiefs much more helpful. For one thing, a lot of them are volunteers. They haven't yet developed a complete distrust of the working press. And they have a title—fire chief—and the big picture of what is occurring in their communities. The police be damned, thinks Baker. Other emergency officials can provide him the facts for his story.

His resulting story plays on page one across the top under an eight-column headline. It's the first banner story of his career. Rector even gives him a byline. Eight dead in the first six hours of the storm; barns hit by lightning and tornados; trailer parks wiped out; dozens of area residents without homes; and emergency crews working overtime. Baker's story heaps praise on the volunteer fire departments and quotes their fire chiefs extensively.

The second edition comes up from the press room and for some reason that triggers a thought for Baker: While he had been working, Joe Running Dear is lying in the city morgue. Then he starts wondering again about the comment Klunt made.

Which cop told the jailer to burn Joe's clothes? The jailer is only likely to listen to someone senior to him. Klunt mentioned a police captain. His story referenced a Captain Wayne Thompson. Baker wonders if he was one of the two detectives he saw arguing over Sara Whitlow's body the night she was killed. He decides to investigate.

But then he thinks about all the other things he has to do. For example, he has to get registered for school. He has to take a driver's test and get a North Dakota license. And then he has this invitation to a Sunday brunch he has to fulfill. Seems a sugar beet association over in Moorhead heard he is in town and its president wants to welcome him to the Valley. Baker figures his stepfather probably set it up. Strange, though, because Pinks had said Baker should strike out on his own. Oh well, he accepted when the young woman called and asked him to meet with members of the board of directors for a Sunday brunch at the Fargo County Club. A free meal in a classy joint appealed to him. Besides, after a couple of weeks at the Donaldson, he's curious about how Fargo's better half lives.

Baker takes two copies of the newspaper with him as he leaves the *Forum* to walk the block to his hotel. The streets are wet from the storm passing through Fargo while he had been inside capturing its devastation on newsprint. He was bone tired and ready for the sack.

He didn't pay any attention to the late model Ford parked ahead of him with two men in it as he crossed 5th Street by the Shriners' Temple. They both quickly got out of the car as he passed by. They were wearing sport coats and ties, Baker noticed, which seemed out of place in Fargo on a stormy night. The larger of the two men stepped right in front of him.

"You wouldn't happen to be Charles Baker, would you?" asks the big man in the ill-fitting coat.

Baker finds himself looking at the man's chin. He's not only broad, he's tall. The other guy has fallen in behind him.

"I'm Chuck Baker. What about it?"

The big man flips open a wallet just long enough to flash a badge and a police identification card.

"You're coming with us. Get in the back seat."

With that, the big man grabs Baker by the arm and half-guides, half-pushes him toward the unmarked squad car. He opens the back door and shoves Baker in, while the smaller man gets in the back seat next to him from the other side. The big man shuts Baker's door, then walks around the car and gets into the driver's seat. He starts the Ford and pulls away from the curb. He drives right past Baker's hotel, turns the corner, and heads south on Broadway toward Front Street.

"Where are you taking me?"

"We're going someplace where we can talk," says the big man.

Baker stares at the driver. He realizes he's one of the two detectives Baker saw arguing over the shrouded murder victim in the alley behind Front Street.

"Are you Captain Wayne Thompson of the Fargo Police?"

"Isn't he smart, Phil?" says the driver, glancing in his rear view mirror at the smaller man sitting next to Baker. "Must be a college boy."

"It's just that I saw you in the alley the night Sara Whitlow was killed, that's all."

Thompson turns around and frowns at Baker.

"Well, that's what we want to talk to you about, pretty boy. Seems you think you know a lot about police business."

Thompson drives down to the foot of Broadway and turns left on 1st Avenue South. On his right is a large park. Thompson parks the car and gets out.

"Come on, scoop. Let's take a stroll. It's beautiful this time of night. Nobody in the park but muggers and thieves." Then he laughs.

The three of them walk about 200 yards along a damp path into the park and then stop. The two detectives point at a park bench and tell Baker to sit down. Baker notices the bench is wet from the storm, but he figures the two detectives are unlikely to care if he gets his pants wet. He sits down as instructed.

"I read your article in the paper yesterday morning," says Thompson. "It was the one with your name on it. You did write that story, didn't you?"

"If it had my byline, then I wrote it."

"Good, because I wouldn't want you and me to be talking about different articles. In that article with your name on it, you suggested the Fargo Police had fucked up the arrest of Indian Joe, that about right?"

"No, I don't think that is correct. I said . . .

That's when Thompson cold-cocks him with his right fist. Baker doesn't see the punch coming. But then, he isn't expecting the big cop to hit him. Nobody has hit him in the face since he was a kid and that slug didn't even bloody his nose. He would have had to really think hard to identify the year it happened. But he's pretty sure he'll forever remember the slug he just received, in the summer of 1965 in Island Park.

The blow hit Baker squarely in the mouth and caught the tip of his nose. A big man throwing a sucker punch can produce a world of hurt. But Thompson doesn't just want to inflict pain. He wants the young newspaperman to walk away with permanent reminders of the encounter. So Thompson is clutching what look like brass knuckles in his right hand. The blow chips both of Baker's two front teeth, splits open his upper and lower lips, and breaks his nose. Blood is flowing everywhere. Baker is left semiconscious.

"I was meaning to show you these," Thompson says to Myers, giving him a glimpse of the heavy piece of lead that fits into the palm of his hand and then mushrooms out to form thick bands around each of his fingers.

"Aren't they something? One of my patrolmen took them off a kid earlier this summer. He said his little brother had made them at Agassiz Junior High School. Said he carved out a wooden mold in the shape of brass knuckles. Then he melted down some solder and poured it into the mold. Came up with these homemade brass knuckles. I guess we can't really call them brass, can we? Anyway, I was anxious to try them out. All in all, I'm quite pleased. I think the little juvenile delinquent should get an A for his extra credit work. What do you think Phil?

"Definitely an A student."

Thompson grabs Baker and sits him up on the bench. The blood now flows down his face and runs onto his shirt before dripping onto his trousers.

"Now you listen to me, you pompous little shit. I don't know who you think you are, coming into my town and writing about the Fargo police as if we're a bunch of goddamn idiots. That Indian was guilty as hell and we could have proven it. Now he's in the morgue because someone had the good sense to burn his stinky jeans, and someone else had the good sense to write about it and tell the world where he could be found. So fuck him and fuck you. I don't ever want to read anything in the newspaper again that says anything negative about my department or me, you got me?"

Baker knows he's going to be sick. He bends over and vomits on his pant legs and shoes. He tries to spit, but can't. His tongue is too swollen. The blood and vomit just hang from his mouth in a long string. God, his head hurts.

"Here's how it's going to work from here on out. We're going to run you over to St. John's Hospital. It's about five minutes from here. They'll fix you up. They're going to ask you what happened. You're going to say you don't know. We'll say we found you on the street. We'll say it must have been a mugging. You'll agree with that, okay, scoop?"

Chuck wonders why in the hell he ought to agree with that story. He got mugged by the goddamn police.

Then Thompson hits him hard in his right leg, just above the knee. The pain settles deep in the muscle and it hurts worse than anything Baker has ever experienced before. He cries out and the tears stream down his face to mix with the blood.

"These brass knuckles, or whatever we're going to call them, work really well, Phil. I think we're going to have to get each of us one of these."

Baker puts his head back and wills himself to breath normally. He's terrified he will suffocate. He can no longer breathe out of his nose and the more his tongue swells up, the harder it is to breathe through his mouth.

"Now let me see if we've got this straight. We're going to go to the hospital. You will say you got mugged. But didn't see who did it. That right? Otherwise, I will keep practicing on you with my brand-new brass knuckles until you won't need St. Johns. We will be able to drive you directly to the morgue. So, what's it going to be?"

Baker isn't sure what to say.

His inability to answer earns him another blow right to the same spot on his thigh above his knee. Now he weeps like a baby, pleading with Thompson not to hit him again.

"I got mugged," he blabbers. "I didn't see who did it. I got mugged. I didn't see who did it. Please, don't hit me again. Please."

Then he just sits and bawls, like he hasn't cried in years. He can't stop shaking. He hurts all over and is terrified that this big cop is going to hit him again.

"I think this boy has got religion, what do you think, Phil?"

"Sometimes it takes a guiding hand to make the ignorant see the light," says his partner.

Ten minutes later the three of them are in the emergency room of St. John's Hospital. Captain Wayne Thompson calmly explains to the nurse on duty that he has picked up a young man off the street in downtown Fargo.

"He looks like he was mugged. Can you do anything for him?"

"Oh, of course, she said, let me call a doctor right away."

Thompson looks at Baker.

"You are lucky we came by, scoop, or heaven knows what might have happened to you," says the police Captain, for the nurse's benefit.

Baker just looks at him in horror. He can't stop thinking that none of this would have happened had he just studied harder at George Washington University.

The doctor admits Chuck into the hospital for an overnight stay out of concern that he might have a concussion. Eighteen stitches close the wounds in both the upper and lower lips. The doctor resets the damaged nose, but says Baker will need plastic surgery to make it look normal again. Meanwhile, he predicts, both of Baker's eyes will go black and blue within two days. The two top teeth are loose and the right one is chipped. The doctor wires them to the adjacent incisors, but tells him he needs to see a dentist as soon as he can. Baker looks awful. The nurse says he probably shouldn't plan to kiss anyone for at least a month. Baker figures she says that to cheer him up.

It doesn't work.

Chapter Fifteen

Never Make a Cop Your Enemy

Pinks waits until 11 a.m. Saturday to call Pam with the information on Sara's girlfriend that she had asked for. A few minutes after she gets the information from Jerry, she has Terri Squires on the phone. As Pam expected, the young woman is anxious to talk as soon as money enters the conversation. Pam explains she has a trust fund for Sara that now belongs to Bruce, but she doesn't know how to reach him. She says she's prepared to pay a "finder's fee" of $250 if Terri can give her his telephone number and mailing address. Terri insists on receiving the money first, saying she doesn't trust people much anymore.

"But when will I get it? How do I know..."

"I think I understand your concerns, Miss Squires. I'll wire you a hundred and twenty-five dollars to the Fargo Western Union office this morning, as long as you have the information I need now. You do know how I can reach Bruce, correct?"

"Yes, ma'am." Terri replies. She's beginning to get excited.

"Good. Call me Pam. You just head down to Western Union around noon—that's two hours from now, right? It's just after ten in the morning there in Fargo, right?"

"Yes, ma'am, uh, Pam."

"You should be able to pick up the money sometime shortly after twelve. You have a driver's license with your photo on it?"

"Yes, ma'am, Pam," Terri says nervously to the senator's wife. Her hands are starting to sweat at the idea of having $125 in her purse before nightfall.

"Well, that's all you'll need. Show your license to them and they'll have you sign for the hundred and twenty-five dollars in cash they'll hand you. Now I'll need you to do one thing for me.

"Tell me where Bruce is."

Terri is so excited she wants to scream. She stifles it. Barely. A little squeak comes out.

"You need to call me right away, Terri, as soon as you get the cash, before you buy anything with it. Come right back to your place and call me collect and tell me how I can reach Bruce, because I need to get something in the mail to him today before five. I don't want to wait until Monday to send it. As soon as you get the money, come home and call me with Bruce's information, and I'll send you another hundred and twenty-five dollars. How does that sound to you?"

"Good," Terri says, trying to sound normal. She can't remember the last time she had a hundred dollars cash in her hands.

"Alright then, Miss Squires," Pam says. "I'll expect to get a call from you about one o'clock your time. Have you got a paper and pencil handy? I'll give you my number."

*   *   *

The hospital releases Chuck Baker by noon. It's Saturday. The assault by the Fargo police detective leaves Baker with a bad headache and a sore right thigh, but the x-rays don't show any fractures. The nurse on duty gives him an orderly's scrub top to wear back to his hotel. He appreciates the gesture. He knows his shirt, like his shoes and pants, which she hands him in a paper bag, are still coated in dried blood and vomit. At least he doesn't have to put the shirt back on. She leaves him to dress in privacy. He hasn't showered—his face, neck and arms got wiped off with a wet washcloth at some point, but that's it. He looks awful and smells worse.

To get to his hotel, he tries to walk up 4th Street but finds the route blocked by police barricades. Apparently, some sort of Mexican festival is going on in the north end of the park. Then he tries cutting through the park, but is whistled to a stop by a policeman on a motorcycle. He says the park is closed. Baker explains he's just cutting through, but is told he has to go around. By the time he does, he is exhausted. And he still hasn't made it up the steep hill from 1st Avenue South to Front Street and the start of Broadway.

When he gets to 1st Avenue and the hill, he stops to catch his breath. Despite his condition, the police presence piques his reporter's curiosity. Police barricades block off 1st Avenue east to the river and as he walks up the hill, he can see down the alley to 4th street where a lot of Mexicans are standing around—

right about where he had seen the brown door with the "deliveries only" sign.

A police barricade also blocks off the entrance to the alley. But there's clearly no sign of any crime. It's like some kind of event, but not a festive one. Or even organized, for that matter. Something having to do with lots of Mexicans. He had no idea so many Mexicans lived in Fargo.

At the top of the hill, on Front Street, he sees two more barricades that stop both vehicles and pedestrians from going down Front Street toward the river and Moorhead.

Baker is puzzled. He can see lots of activity within the police barricades, so obviously some people are allowed inside. He stops again to catch his breath. It is a hot day and the breeze isn't its normal, gusty self. A policeman standing inside the barricade sees him and yells, "Hey, move it along." And he does, but concludes the Fargo police are one hell of an unfriendly bunch.

When he gets to his hotel Baker does his best to charge unnoticed through the lobby. But that doesn't work. Hans Stutzman, the Hotel Donaldson manager, spots him as he comes in.

"Somebody needs a bath," says Stutzman, holding his nose as Baker walks by.

He wants to run up the stairs, but quickly discovers the punches to his right leg make that feat impossible. In fact, he can barely hobble up the stairs. When he gets to the top, he nearly trips over Mac and Sam on their way down.

"My God, you must have had quite a night," says Sam, struggling to regain his balance after Baker runs into him. "Anyone looks and smells as bad as you, I'd have to figure you got drunk, got laid, and then ran into the lady's ugly husband

and his two brothers and had to fight your way back to the hotel. That about tell the whole story?"

"Nothing as exciting as that," says Baker. "I got mugged, or at least that's what I'm told I'm supposed to say."

Baker pushes on by and gets his key to his room out of his pocket.

"Wait a minute," says Sam. "What do you mean, you got mugged?"

"I didn't get mugged. I got a goddamn beating by a fucking police detective. He says I have to say it was a mugging or the next time it will be something worse."

Baker pushes his way into his room and shuts the door.

Sam looks at Mac and Mac returns his look of concern.

When Baker comes back out with his toilet kit his two neighbors are still standing there.

"You need to talk to us," says Sam.

"Yeah, okay. But first I've got to take a shower."

"That you do. You smell like a sacrificial lamb at a goat fucking. Why don't Mac and I go downstairs and blow some smoke at the ceiling fan. Come down when you're ready. I'll get Mule to bring some ice for your face."

Forty-five minutes later, Baker comes down in a pair of Levis and a long-sleeve, blue Oxford button-down shirt. He smells better, but still looks like the loser in a street fight that went 15 minutes too long. In the small lobby, Sam and Mac have some ice waiting in a bucket, along with a towel.

"Come over here and sit among your elders," says Sam. "Nobody hears confession better than grizzled old war veterans."

"I've got nothing to confess. I left work last night and was heading back here when this asshole cop grabs me and takes me down to the park at the foot of Broadway. He says he didn't like my newspaper story about the Indian who killed the senator's daughter. He said it was too derogatory about the Fargo police or some such shit. Then he takes out these brass knuckles, only they're made out of solder, and uses them on my face. Then my leg. When he finishes, he says not to say a word to anyone about what happened, and, oh yeah, if I write anything bad about the police again, we'll do this whole routine one more time. Lovely fellow."

Who is the guy, do you know?" asks Sam.

"Sure. He's Wayne Thompson. Big guy, detective captain. He had a little guy with him. I don't know who he was."

"That would be Sergeant Phil Myers. The two of them have been together for a long time."

"All I know is that they're both assholes."

"No question about that. But rough ones. How long have you been in town? Two weeks? In that short period of time you've managed to make enemies with the two meanest cops south of Moose Jaw. Everyone who lives here knows not to cross them."

Sam looks over at Mac. Then he looks back at the young reporter.

"Want some advice?"

"Sure, it's probably too late to ask for it, but why not?"

"Don't write anything criticizing the Fargo Police. And if you get a call asking you to donate to the Fargo Police Benevolent Association, only ask one question: 'How big a check will you take?'"

With that, Sam breaks out in laughter and even Mac has a grin on his face.

"I'm just shitting you about giving them money. But be damn careful about what you write. Thompson is a rogue cop and a mean son of a bitch. But he's tied into the city fathers. From all indications he does their dirty work for them."

"What do you mean by that?"

"I mean, if you piss off somebody important in this town, expect an after-dark visit from Captain Thompson like the one you had last night."

"You mean the guy is an enforcer, like the kind of guys the mobs have?"

"I don't know what kind of guys the mobs have. In this town, important people pay Thompson to do their dirty work. If that's how the mob operates, then sure, I guess you could say it's the same model."

Then it occurs to Baker to ask a logical question.

"Thompson has been all over the killing of the senator's daughter, including screwing up her murderer's trial. Is it possible he's doing the dirty work for some important people in this town?"

The room falls silent. The two veterans look at each other.

Sam finally speaks.

"There are times I wish my partner here would speak up. Are you asking me: Do I think big shots in Fargo had Sara Whitlow killed? No, I don't. Are you asking me: Do I think these big shots might have Wayne Thompson trying to cover up some facts in the case? Yes, I think that's entirely likely.

"But let me add something. I believe the Indian killed Sara. Furthermore, I believe he killed her for no good reason. I don't know who killed the Indian, but if I were to meet the man, I would be pleased to buy him a drink."

Sam struggles to his feet and Mac hands him his crutches.

"Sara is gone, bless her heart, and the Indian is dead, damn him to hell. Life goes on. Now Mac and I are going out to have ourselves a late lunch. Afterwards, we're going to take a short walk to build up a thirst. We might just get as far as the Waldorf down on Front Street. We'd invite you along, but I suspect you're working again tonight, right?"

"Yeah, every weekend. When I was hired, they made a big deal about what a family newspaper they are. I thought that sounded great at the time. Then they explained that because I was single, I would have to work weekends and holidays so the married men could be with their families. Actually, I don't mind. I frankly don't know what I would do on the weekends anyway."

"Be careful what you write, my young warrior. You have a powerful enemy."

*   *   *

At 2:18 p.m., the phone rings. Pam picks it up. "Hello?"

"Mrs. Christenson, I don't have a telephone number for Bruce. He doesn't really have one. He's a truck driver and is always on the move. I have a mailing address, though. Got a pencil and paper handy?"

"Yes, I do, Miss Squires. Go ahead."

Terri gives Pam the Great Northern Construction Company name, and a Post Office Box number in Dickinson, North Dakota. Then she adds: "Write on the back of the envelope, 'Driving truck out of Beach.' That's the name of the little town he works out of, on account of it has very sandy soil. He won't get your letter overnight, but he'll get it eventually."

"Thank you for your help, Miss Squires. Can I call you Terri?"

"Yes, ma'am!" Terri shot back, too enthusiastically.

"Please, call me Pam."

"Oh, yes ma'am, Pam, I will. Thank you!"

"Don't hang up, I need your address too, Terri, so I can send you a check for the other half of the money."

"Oh, yeah, I almost forgot," Terri giggled like a schoolgirl, then gave Pam her address.

"Oh, by the way, Terri, feel free to go into Sara's trailer, if you can. Do you know where Sara and Bruce lived? Do you know anyone who can let you in?"

"Yes, ma'am, I'm actually her neighbor. I mean I was... and I have a key. Do you need it?"

"No, Teri, but I want you to help yourself to anything that's there. I don't think Bruce is ever coming back."

"Thanks, Pam!" says Terri, and then she wonders how charitable the senator's wife would be if she knew Terri had removed everything of value from Sara's trailer mere hours after the funeral.

As soon as they say their goodbyes, Pam goes to her desk in the sunroom just off the kitchen and writes a short letter to Bruce:

Dear Bruce:

Sara is gone, and my heart is still broken, as I know yours is. Thank God that savage Indian is dead. When you said during the funeral you were going to get your revenge, I didn't doubt you for a moment. I cannot ever thank you enough for what you have done. It has provided me with my only relief since Sara's passing.

> Bruce, I want you to leave North Dakota. It is too dangerous for you there. I know you and Sara had planned to start a new life in Arizona. Please do that now. Enclosed is $1,000 in cash. Also enclosed is a check for $10,000. Deposit the check in a bank wherever you decide to live. I hope the money is enough to get you started in your new life.
>
> When you get to where you are going, please let me know.
>
> Love, Pam.

She inserts the letter, along with a check and the cash, into a sturdy but otherwise undistinguished brown business envelope. After she addresses it, she writes AIR MAIL next to the address, then puts double postage on it just to be sure. Finally, she flips the envelope over and writes:

Driving truck out of Beach.

She then writes Teri a check and puts it in a regular business envelope, which she addresses, then licks a stamp and presses it into the upper right corner. She walks out to the garage with the two envelopes, gets in her car and drives directly to the nearest mail collection box less than a half-mile away, beating the 3:30 p.m. pick-up time by 15 minutes.

* * *

That night turns out to be slow at the *Forum*. It's a blessing. Baker isn't feeling great. The pain killers the doctor gave him have worn off and his nose, lips, gums, and head all hurt. So does his leg. He manages to write his local weather story. Before that he took a call from a reporter out in the field who'd covered a beauty contest at a county fair and then called in the facts for the night city desk—him—to write a story. He manages to write it, along with his local weather story.

Then the Fargo police radio squawks and Baker listens, glancing up at the clock. Shit. The last edition will be printed and on its way before he could possibly finish writing a news story about whatever has the police all excited. That was the nature of Sunday newspapers. Most of the Sunday paper's various sections are already printed by early Saturday night. That leaves only the Sunday sports section and portions of the front section—including page one—to be put together late Saturday night.

Everyone connected to the production of the Sunday paper is sensitive to the need for firm deadlines. The various sections of the Sunday newspaper can't be assembled until the last two sections—the sports and the front section, including the front page, are printed and sent to the bindery. In other words, no late-breaking story is important enough to delay the process.

The police radio is coming to life again as more officers sign on. Something big is happening in Fargo. Baker grabs a pencil and paper. The cops are talking in code: "A ten-forty in the alley behind Front Street."

Baker looks in his desk for the sheet that explains what the various police codes mean. He wonders how long it will take him before he has them memorized. A 10-40 is a homicide. The hair on the back of his head stands up. He then hears a policeman say the victim is a Native American.

My God, somebody has killed another Indian.

*   *   *

In the alley behind Front Street, Thompson stands over the body of the dead Indian and watches as the coroner grunts while rolling it over onto a stretcher. "Rigor Mortis has already set in," the coroner says as he stands up and nods to his assistant. The pool of blood has dried. I think this guy was killed almost twenty-four hours ago, Wayne," he says to Thompson as he and his assistant lift the body and slide it into the back of the coroner's vehicle, an old, converted ambulance. "How is it that a dead, bloody body could lay here in the alley all day without anyone noticing it until an hour ago?"

Undoubtedly some Mexicans saw the body of the dead Indian, Thompson thinks to himself. It's the weekend, when they're the only ones on this block—except obviously some Indians—late at night. But neither Mexicans nor Indians have any reason to report the find of a dead body. After all, it's Front Street. Mexicans have nothing to do with Indians, if at all possible, and less to do with the local police. And Indians never call a cop for anything. Why would any of them report finding a dead body? The cops would arrest them on suspicion, and at the very least make the Mexicans' employer come to town to bail them out and hire them an attorney. And Indians sometimes never get bailed out. Best to walk by a dead Indian on Front Street.

"Don't worry about it, Doc," Thompson tells the coroner. "We got it."

That was the end of the investigation.

*   *   *

At the end of a long day of hauling gravel, Bruce sidles into the office and winks at the plain-Jane receptionist. She smiles back at him, and he wonders, looking at her ring, just how married she is.

"A letter came for you today, Bruce," she says in her babyish Marilyn Monroe voice, as she grabs the sturdy brown envelope off her desk and hands it to him. "Looks important."

"Why thank you, uhh... Mary," he says, quickly glancing at the nameplate on her desk to remind himself.

"Actually, I'm Nancy," she says, trying to hide her slight disappointment that he didn't remember. "Mary had to leave earlier so I'm at her desk the rest of today."

"Oh, okay," Bruce says, glancing at the envelope as he starts to tear at it. He immediately stops as he notices the name written atop the return address in the upper left:

P. Christenson

Glancing two lines down, he sees the Washington D.C address and quickly turns toward the door. "See you tomorrow, Mary," he yells over his shoulder as he pushes outside.

He waits until he's safely ensconced in the little hovel of a motel room the company provides him before pulling out his pocketknife and carefully opening the letter.

He reads her letter three times. He fondles the $100 bills at least five times. Then he looks at the front and back of the check at least fifteen times. Ten thousand dollars is more money than he normally earns in a single year. *My God.*

Bruce packs up his gear, puts the check into his billfold, stuffs all but $100 of the cash into the bottom of his ditty bag, and loads his pickup with his paltry possessions. Then he walks over to the foreman and tells the son-of-a-bitch what he really thinks of him and his beat-up gravel trucks. Within an hour Bruce is out of North Dakota and into Montana. He figures he'll take a round-about way to Arizona. He sees no sense hurrying: it is still summer and he knows Arizona will be hot as hell.

As he drives along, he keeps thinking about Sara's friend Terri. He didn't tell her he had left. Damn, he says to himself. She might be nice to have around on a chilly evening in the Arizona highlands. He thinks he can always give her a call when he gets settled in Arizona. Maybe she'll want to come down for a visit.

Then Bruce thinks about Sara's mother Pam. He doesn't fully understand why she detests Indians, but she sure does. Could be because she is a West River girl. That might explain it, he figures. Then a Sioux Indian goes and guts her daughter. That would be enough to cement a dislike for Indians, he concludes. Ten thousand dollars. Holy shit. He lets out a whoop.

He wonders if she has any other Indians she wants dead.

Chapter Sixteen

Beet Growers Flatter Battered Newsman

On Sunday morning Chuck Baker calls David Behrie, the cab driver who brought him to the Donaldson two weeks earlier. He says he needs a ride to the Fargo Country Club and back. Behrie says he normally doesn't work Sundays, but seeing as how he's trying to establish good rapport with a new client, he will do it. Baker arranges to be picked up at 11 a.m., then tells Behrie he'll want to head back to the hotel at 1 p.m.

The cab is outside the Donaldson when Chuck comes down. He is wearing his best go-to-work clothes, complete with a tie. He figures it's Sunday and Fargo's elites probably go to the club directly from church. Besides, if he is overdressed, slipping off his tie will make him casual in a moment.

"What in the hell happened to you?" says Behrie, gawking at Baker's face. The cab driver appears to be dressed for an outdoor barbeque without guests.

"Would you believe I walked into a door?"

Behrie turns around in his seat and stares at Baker.

"No, I wouldn't believe that. But if that's your story, I'll work with you. Geez, that must have hurt." Behrie turns back around in his seat, puts on his blinker, checks his rearview and guns the cab out onto First Avenue, heading west. "When did you and this door collide?"

"Friday night. Well, actually, very early Saturday morning."

"So, you got stitches in the lip, I can tell. Broke your nose, it seems from the way you talk. And I would guess you lost a couple of teeth. Anything I'm missing?"

"Nope, that about covers it. Oh, my right leg is badly bruised."

"You hurt the door any?"

Chuck chuckles softly.

"No, I'm not the kind of guy who goes around beating up on doors."

Behrie turns around and looks at him again.

"I don't know. I think I might have tried to get in a lick or two. You're making me hurt way up here. How many stitches did you take?"

"Can we talk about something else?"

"Yeah, sure. So, what takes you to the land of the rich and pampered on a Sunday morning?"

"I've been invited to brunch. I figure it's one less meal I have to buy, so I accepted."

"If you don't mind, who's your host?"

Chuck pulls a note out of his breast pocket of his blazer. He reads the name to the cab driver.

"Holy shit. You're dining with Andrew Bacevich? Do you know who he is?"

"Well, I know he's a big shot in the sugar beet business."

"He runs the sugar beet cooperative. But that's not the half of it. He's filthy rich, lives in a mansion, and owns half the politicians in the Valley. He'd own them all if he thought he needed them. Nobody in the city councils of either Fargo or Moorhead does anything without checking with him first. He's what I would call the 'silent mayor' of both cities. He's equally tight with the Cass and Clay county board members. So why do you suppose he's buying you breakfast? What do you have that he wants?"

"I don't have a clue. I'll let you know when you give me a ride back to the hotel, how's that?"

"We're just about there. Pretty down here, don't you think?"

Baker notices the homes appear to have gotten bigger and fancier as they drive south on 4th Street. Passing under the new interstate highway, they go by large lots containing homes that would look comfortable in Fairfax County, Virginia. Then the cab sweeps him around a curved driveway that leads to the entrance of the Fargo Country Club.

"See you at one, partner. Have a good time."

"Yeah, thanks," says Baker as he gets out of the cab and goes inside.

His arrival doesn't go unnoticed. People stare at him, then look away. He guesses he would stare**,** too**,** at someone who apparently had gone straight from a Saturday night bar fight to a Sunday Country Club brunch. Besides, he is frowning, but he can't help it. Smiling pulls his stitches and hurts. But the frown compliments his two black and blue eyes and swollen nose, he thinks to himself, unconsciously bringing a little smile. *Ouch.*

He walks in and notices a dining room off to his right. He heads for it, but is stopped at the entrance by an officious-looking hostess in a pink skirt and a blue blazer.

"Good afternoon, sir. Are we here with a member?"

"Yes, I'm here as a guest of Mr. Bacevich."

The name obviously means something to her.

"Oh, yessir. You must be Mr. Baker. We have been expecting you. Right this way, please."

The hostess leads him through the large dining room. It is full of well-dressed, well-fed diners of all ages, from young children to grandparents. The room reeks of money. Typical country-club crowd, thinks Baker. It reminds him of Arlington's Washington Country Club. He figures 95 percent of the members of the Fargo Country Club are Republicans. Probably all supporters of Senator Christenson. His stepfather undoubtedly knows most of them by their first names and just how much each has donated to the senator's last campaign.

The hostess approaches a table for 16, overlooking the 18th hole, clearly the best table in the dining room. A chair is vacant next to a well-dressed gentleman in his mid-50s who rises to his feet when he sees the hostess approach. In a booming voice, he announces to the table, "Ladies and gentlemen, our guest of honor is here."

Baker's a little taken aback by the announcement. He thought he was going to be dining with three, maybe four, men. Here is a table of fifteen people, mostly men, but some women too. They all get to their feet and lightly applaud as he comes up to the table.

The host approaches and grabs him by the arm.

"Come over here. You're sitting next to me. Let me introduce myself. I'm Andrew Bacevich. My friends call me

Andy. I've invited some folks to meet you. They've heard good things about you."

By this time, Baker can feel his face turning beet red. He figures it just makes his wounds look that much worse.

"Ladies and gentlemen, please be seated. I present to you our guest, Charles Baker, formerly of Washington, D.C., and now of Fargo, North Dakota. As many of you know, Chuck— I hope I can call you Chuck—was a reporter at the *Washington Star*, a great newspaper in our nation's capital. He recently left that newspaper to come to our city to finish his degree at North Dakota State University and to work at the *Forum*. We are blessed to have a man of his skill and smarts in our community.

"I invited Chuck to come over and meet with us today so we can thank him for the enormous favor he did us. I'm not even sure he realizes what it is. And that's okay. That's what great reporters do. They just do their jobs. And the readers they write for get all the benefits. Well, in this case, I want him to at least know how much the folks in the Red River Valley appreciate what he did for us.

"I'm going to tell that story. But not right now. Let's give Chuck a chance to eat. And the rest of you, too. Then I'll stand back up here and delight all of you with my storytelling."

That gets a laugh out of the group just as the waiters appear carrying platters of sweet rolls to the table. Andy Bacevich sits down next to Baker and says, "I'm really glad you could make it. Son, I didn't realize you had been in an accident. Are you okay?"

Baker knows that over the coming month he's going to end up explaining many times how his face got reconfigured, so he might just as well try out a plausible lie right here.

"I was mugged, coming home from work Friday night. I don't carry any money on me, so the two guys didn't get anything. When they couldn't find a billfold or even a watch to steal, they got really angry and just started hitting me. When I went down, they finished up by kicking me. The doctor figures I got the facial injuries from a hard boot kick."

The woman sitting on his right has been listening intently and she says:

"That is just awful. I don't think I have ever heard of anyone being mugged in Fargo, have you Andy?"

"No, not that I can recall," says Bacevich. "What did the police have to say?"

"They said they would investigate. I haven't heard anything since."

"If you don't mind, do you remember who in the police department you talked to?"

"Yes, I was assisted by a Detective Wayne Thompson and his partner. I didn't catch his name."

The woman spoke up again, her voice tinged with concern and anger.

"My God, that's just terrible. You've been here, what, just two weeks, and you get mugged? We wouldn't be surprised if somebody from Fargo or Moorhead went back to Washington, D.C., and got mugged. But that isn't supposed to happen to people who come here."

The woman now had her hand on Baker's arm and a knee up against his thigh. It hasn't gone unnoticed by Baker just how attractive she is. He thinks he can detect her perfume through his broken nose, but he isn't sure. He may just be imaging it. Regardless, he just knows she smells nice.

"Oh, by the way," says Bacevich, "I would like you to meet my wife, Sue."

"Pleased to meet you," says Baker. He tries to smile and sure enough, it hurts like hell. He knows he winced and he hopes she didn't notice.

"Likewise," says Sue, pressing her knee and now some of her thigh against his leg. She still has her hand on his arm. Baker notices he can see down her blouse without any difficulty when she shifts positions, which she seems to do constantly. His head begins to spin. He doesn't know how old she is. Older than him, he figures. But a lot younger than her husband.

Bacevich regains Baker's attention. He explains that brunch at the club is a buffet and so they probably should get up and get in line before the food is all gone. His wife admonishes him by saying he knows better than that; the club always makes much more food than the members can ever hope to eat. She tells her husband to go get in line and says the two of them will join him in a minute.

When they're alone, she asks Chuck about his injuries. He tells her what the doctor said. She shakes her head in sympathy. She asks to see his teeth. He feels foolish, but he shows her. She doesn't seem bothered by the carnage. Then she explains that she's trained as a dental hygienist and is used to looking in people's mouths. She says he needs some work done soon, that she can see a couple of his teeth have been chipped. Then she says they should go get in line. As they stand up, they bump bodies. Baker apologizes and she simply smiles and says, "Don't be silly."

As he stands in the buffet line, he thinks this may well be the first time he has ever coveted another man's wife. He realizes he had better get enrolled in college and start finding some girls his age.

When they arrive back at the table, everyone is already eating. Baker starts in gingerly on his plate full of the softest foods on the buffet table. It's the best food he's had since coming to Fargo, and he's torn between the pleasure and pain of eating it. Meanwhile, Mr. Bacevich is now explaining to Baker that everyone at the table is a sugar beet grower from the Red River Valley. They are also, he adds, personal friends of Senator Christenson and strong supporters of his efforts to get the Garrison Diversion initiative through Congress.

"Do you know much about the Garrison Diversion project, Chuck?"

"Very little. I only heard of it once when I was back in Washington and that was from a congressional aide. I didn't follow a word she said about it."

"That's not too surprising. It's a complicated project," says Bacevich, as others around the table pick up on the conversation and nod.

"I won't even begin to attempt to explain its full ramifications here. But I can give you a bottom line from the perspective of the folks around this table. Garrison diversion may well be our salvation. And if that's the case, then it may well be the salvation of everyone in the entire Red River Valley.

"Here's why. You've seen the Red River, haven't you?"

"Not really. I mean, I flew over it when I came into Fargo. But I haven't really seen it."

"There's not much to see. It's barely a river. And yet it provides water for three of the largest cities in the state. As important, it provides irrigation water for some of the most fertile farmland in the entire country. We wring every drop we can out of that little river. But we're reaching the point where we've just about used it up. When that happens, we will face a difficult choice. We either stop growing our towns and cities. Or we tell our farmers to quit growing their crops. Nobody much wants to do either. So that means we need to find a source of additional water. And that brings us to the Garrison Diversion.

"The project has a lot of objectives, all of them good and worthwhile for the state. But the one that interests us most is the one that diverts Missouri River water, from the middle of the state, to the Red River Valley, here on the eastern side of North Dakota. Now that won't happen overnight. It's going to take years before the Garrison dam backs up enough water for it to flow across the Eastern half of the state and into our little Red River. But we can limp along until then, knowing that irrigation water is coming.

"But all of this is in jeopardy because of one pig-headed congressman from Alabama, the Honorable Jeffery Walker. Since 1957 we have struggled to get Congress to authorize the Garrison Diversion project. We have the strong support of our congressional delegation, our two senators and single congressman, but they can't get the necessary votes from the House authorizing committee because of one of its subcommittee chairmen. That would be Congressman Walker. He keeps saying the Diversion is too expensive and the payoff doesn't justify the cost. He also points out that only about five percent of our state's farmland would ever have access to this irrigation water when it begins to flow. Then he argues that the North Dakota farmers who would benefit from the Diversion should pay for creating it.

"The congressman was playing that tune again this year and again, it appeared the Diversion project might not get federal authorization. That is, until your story ran telling everyone about him getting caught with the pecker of that Negro janitor in his mouth."

Bacevich's friends—or are they just sycophants, Baker wonders—laugh at his vulgarity, but not his wife, Sue.

She frowns and says, "Now Andy, don't be crude. There are children in here, and your voice carries."

"Oh, let him talk," says a man seated across the table. "Andy so loves to tell this story."

The whole table is now chuckling.

"No, I won't tell the story. We have the original story teller here in our midst. Let's have him tell the story."

And with that, Andrew Bacevich was on his feet, banging on his water glass.

"Ladies and gentlemen, I present to you the man who brought down the faggot who stood between you and your dreams of plentiful irrigation water. Welcome young Chuck Baker."

Baker realizes he is supposed to stand, so he does, although he's uncomfortable making a presentation to a group of 15 people in a room full of a whole lot more. Diners at a lot of other tables appear to be listening in to hear what he has to say.

"Thank you, Andy, for inviting me to join you today. As Andy told you, I'm new to this part of the country. I see many of you looking at my face. Well, there's a story behind my wounds.

"I was out at the Agriculture College two days ago. I wandered into one of the barns to see if I could spot some farm animals. We don't have many of those in Washington, D.C. I came across this college kid who told me he was an agriculture major learning the proper way to raise mules. Now I have to admit I laughed a little bit. I couldn't believe anyone would go to college to learn to raise mules.

"We got talking and being the reporter, I guess I was interviewing him without really meaning to. I asked him, 'what have you learned here at the college?'

"By then we were in the corral with a bunch of mules. He was brushing one down as I stood patting the mule on its rump.

"'Well,' he said, talking really slow. 'I guess I learned three important things here at the AC. One, you never spit tobacco into the wind. Two, if you're going to raise chickens, you need one rooster for every ten chickens. And three, never pat a mule on the rump.'"

"Well, I laughed and said, why wouldn't you pat a mule on the rump? Just then that mule squared off and kicked me smack in the face.

The whole table laughed. Baker smiled. *Ouch.*

"So excuse my broken-up face. I'm still in the learning phase of my introduction to your fair city," says Baker.

As the chuckles die down, Baker continues.

"In the short time I've been here I have heard great things about the sugar beet growers in the Red River Valley. I know of your contributions to the economy of this region.

"You are correct; I worked for the *Washington Star*. And I wrote a story about a congressman and a black janitor caught on film by the Capital Hill Police engaged in a homosexual act in a bathroom. That congressman was identified as Jeff Walker of Alabama, the ranking Republican on the Interior and Insular Affairs Committee of the House of Representatives.

"The janitor was identified and immediately fired. The Capital Police simply notified the House leadership of Congressman Walker's involvement. Under normal procedures, that well might have been the end of the story. The Congressman would have had his hand slapped and everybody would have gone about their business with the sordid episode permanently under wraps.

"But the *Washington Star* broke the story. Consequently, the congressman has announced his intention to resign his congressional seat and to seek treatment for alcoholism. I saw the police clip of him and the janitor in the bathroom together. At no time did either of them touch a drop of liquor. I for one am not convinced liquor explains the Congressman's behavior in that bathroom."

The guests around table hoot with laughter.

"Now, as Andy explained to me, Congressman Walker was a fierce opponent of the Garrison Diversion project, something I understand is of keen interest to you."

The table broke out in more cheers and whistles.

"You should know that when I wrote my story exposing Congressman Walker"—once again, Baker was interrupted by laughter around the table—"no pun intended," Baker smiled. *Ouch.* "I had never heard of Garrison Diversion. I couldn't have told you what committees the congressman served on or what issues they had under consideration.

"In other words, it was pretty much dumb luck that your nemesis got caught on film with his pants down and I was the one who brought it to everyone's attention with my news story."

With that comment, Bacevich grabs his water glass. "I propose a toast to celebrate the departure of Congressman Jeff Walker from the U.S. Congress."

With all kinds of "hear, hear" and "bravo" and "I'll drink to that" comments, the guests raise their water glasses and drink a toast to the retirement of an Alabama congressman.

"Well done," says his host as Baker sits down. "We ought to get you to do an after-dinner speech for us sometime."

"You've just heard my only speech," replies Baker, draining his drink glass. He's relieved he got through that as easily as he did. He had no idea when he accepted the luncheon invitation that anyone was going to ask him to give a goddamn speech.

"We understand you didn't know you were doing us a favor, but we wanted you to know that what you did really benefited the Red River Valley and the state of North Dakota," says Bacevich.

"How do you intend to reward him?" asks his wife Sue.

"Oh, wait a minute," says Baker. "I am a professional journalist. I get paid to write news stories. That's reward enough.

"Don't be silly," she counters. "You got paid by your Washington newspaper. Now you're in North Dakota. We ought to pay you for helping us out when you didn't even realize you were."

"She has a point," says Bacevich. "I don't want to make you uncomfortable, though. Is there anything we can do that wouldn't violate your professional ethics?"

"No, really, I couldn't take any money or anything," says Chuck.

"I have an idea," says Mrs. Bacevich, "I feel terrible about your injuries. These happened in our backyard. They have nothing to do with your article in the *Star* and they certainly have nothing to do with my husband's business, wouldn't you agree?"

Baker looks at her and says she's right; his injuries certainly had nothing to do with the Alabama congressman or sugar beets.

"Well, then, dear," she says, looking at her husband, "I don't know why we couldn't, as good citizens, volunteer to help this new arrival in our community get his injuries treated. We know a very good dentist who could work with him to do something about fixing those teeth. Once those stitches are taken out, he might need some plastic surgery, too. We know the best doctor in town for that kind of work. He could put

Chuck's nose back where it belongs and make sure his lips are the size he likes. Wouldn't that be something your association could do as a good neighbor, dear?"

"Excellent suggestion, honey. Chuck, we hear you say you wouldn't do anything that constitutes a breach of ethics for you. But allow us to argue that money from a nonprofit service organization that goes to compensate doctors for treating a private citizen who got mugged on our city streets shouldn't constitute any conflict of interest or a breach of ethics for you. We are not going to give any money to you; we simply intend to pay some local doctors to right a wrong committed in our city. I don't see any reason why you couldn't accept that. Can you think of any?"

Baker thinks about it for a minute and for the life of him can't come up with a single objection. Heaven knows, he needs the work done and he sure can't pay for it himself. He hadn't planned to tell his stepfather, figuring he would just mock him for his inability to get along in his hometown.

And besides, the City of Fargo caused the damage. The citizens of Fargo, one way or another, ought to pay to fix it.

"No, I guess I can't."

"Good, then," said Sue. "It's settled."

By the time he's out in front of the club saying goodbye to his new friends from the sugar beet growers' association, he is almost feeling charitable again about his newly adopted hometown. He has finally met some really nice people who seem to care about him as a person.

Sue Bacevich gives him a quick hug and says she will call him on Monday with the phone numbers and names of two doctors.

"I want you to call for appointments right away, you understand? Tell them I referred you. Otherwise they'll both say they're not taking new patients. And when they ask you how you're going to pay the bill, just say Andy is taking care of it. They can call his office to confirm."

Baker turns away with a final wave goodbye and gets into his waiting cab.

"Well, you look like you had a good time. Must be fraternizing with the rich appeals to you," says Behrie as he steps on the gas.

"They're good people," responds Baker. "They kept talking to me all through the brunch, though, so I didn't get a chance to eat much. With my sore lips, it takes me awhile to get food into my mouth. I think I'm as hungry now as I was when I went into the place. But now I've got to go to work. I'll guess I'll just have to get by with a candy bar later."

"Think of it this way; it will keep your weight down," says the overweight cab driver as he heads north into the city.

*   *   *

About an hour later Wayne Thompson gets a call at home. He recognizes the voice on the line immediately. He's surprised to hear from the head of the sugar beet cooperative on a Sunday. He knows it means trouble.

"To what do I owe this surprise?" says Thompson.

"Don't be cute with me, Thompson. I just had a very upsetting afternoon with a close group of friends. My wife is lying down now because she's so distraught. A pleasant young man from Washington, D.C., was our guest at the country club for brunch. But he showed up looking as if he had been in a car wreck. He said he was mugged on the streets of Fargo Friday night and that you are the investigating officer. Is that correct?"

Thompson put the phone down by his leg and looked up at the ceiling and said to himself, "I'm going to kill that son of a bitch."

"Thompson, are you there?"

"Yes, I'm here. Who are we talking about?"

"We are talking about the only person to have been mugged like this in the history of the City of Fargo as far as I know. His name is Charles Baker and he works at the *Forum*. You know damn well who we're talking about. You're the investigating officer. And I want to know what your investigation has learned about this unfortunate affair."

Thompson releases a breath of relief. It's obvious Bacevich doesn't know who beat the hell out of the *Forum* reporter. At least the little shit had the common sense to keep his mouth shut about that.

"I apologize, Mr. Bacevich, you caught me off guard, what with it being Sunday and I'm off duty. Sure, I'm investigating the horrible beating of that reporter. My partner and I were the ones who found him on the street and took him to the hospital. It was a mugging. The kid had no money on him; not even a watch. The muggers—we figure two of them—must have been pissed when they didn't get anything and so they beat him up. The kid had a concussion and doesn't remember anything. We don't have much to go on. We searched the streets for suspects Saturday morning after the incident, but there wasn't anybody out. I don't know what more to tell you."

"I want you to find out who did this. My guests at lunch today were the members of my board of directors. You know who they are. They were upset to learn that a *Forum* reporter can be mugged on a downtown street and his attackers not be arrested. I know this isn't your jurisdiction, but you were the officer on the scene, for whatever reason, so I expect you to follow through. Keep me abreast of any developments. Otherwise my wife is going to nag me to death. She really took a liking to this boy."

"Yes, sir. You'll be hearing from me."

Thompson hangs up the phone after he heard the click from the other end.

Well, that's just great, he says to himself. That little prick has made friends with the most powerful man in town. I should have killed him Friday night instead of just popping him one. Christ, I don't need this shit in my life.

Thompson goes out into his back yard to start the grill. His buddy Phil Myers is coming over after he makes sure the Mexicans have been loaded up and hauled away from Front Street. Thompson is cooking steaks for the two bachelors. He dumps the charcoal briquettes into the grill. Then he thinks about Myers.

I hope he enjoys his steak. Because he sure in the hell isn't going to enjoy the story about the call I just got. I don't know if I should serve that up as an appetizer or a dessert. Nah, no sense in letting it interfere with the dinner, thinks Thompson. I'll get it out while I'm serving drinks.

Chapter Seventeen

Investigative Reporting Key to Degree

Sue Bacevich never did believe Chuck Baker would follow through and schedule doctor appointments to get his face treated. So she called him at the *Forum* and gave him a scheduled time for his upcoming dental appointment. She also told him she had made an appointment for him with the best plastic surgeon in the state, and made sure he put it on his calendar. Then she reminded him that all the costs associated with the work would be picked up by the Red River Valley Sugar beet Cooperative. She closed by saying she would contact him after his first appointment to make sure he was pleased with his doctors.

Baker isn't looking forward to either appointment. But he is going to go. A glance in any mirror makes it abundantly clear that he needs his front teeth repaired, and a lot of help with his damaged nose. Even the three war veterans on his floor at the Donaldson Hotel, no strangers to injuries and pain, wince when they see him.

While fretting about the pending work he's going to have done on his face, Baker continues his job at the night city desk on the morning *Forum*. He also arranges for David Behrie, his personal cab driver, to take him to NDSU to register for classes.

The campus of North Dakota State University isn't particularly interesting, but it does resemble a flatland Land-grant University with its emphasis on agriculture and affiliated sciences. A good deal of the campus is made up of open fields, barns, animal pens, and equipment storage lots. The part of the campus that interests Baker is much smaller, consisting of a few prominent but old classroom buildings surrounded by a hodgepodge of newer structures.

Baker quickly realizes that if the university has a master plan for growth, nobody is paying any attention to it. Placement of buildings in the central campus obviously doesn't suggest adherence to any grand design. He assumes the bone-cold winters, the constant winds, and the abundance of snow all conspire to give preference to the comfort needs of students and faculty—i.e., minimizing the walking distances between buildings—over the recommendations of the university's planning committee.

Behrie drops him off in the back of Old Main, in the heart of the campus. "I think this is where you're supposed to register for classes," he tells Baker.

Baker thanks him and gets out of the cab. One glance at Old Main convinces Baker that it must be the original building on campus, or its runner-up. Baker likes it immediately. Built out of stone, it stands three stories high, has a turret, and looks regal in its setting. With proper maintenance, he figures the building will remain functional for at least a century.

It occurs to Baker that what makes Old Main so attractive is the fact it sits among so much ugliness. Newer campus buildings plopped down around Old Main are cheap looking, uninteresting, and more appropriate for a junior college.

Squatting across the street from Old Main is a large, ancient, wooden structure that would only look at home on an abandoned Army base. The sign in front identifies it as "Festival Hall," although nothing about it suggests festivity.

Baker walks around Old Main and goes in through its main entrance. Following a sign for registration, he walks up a flight of steps to reach a wide central hallway. On the left is a sign announcing the Office of the University President. Flanking it are two offices designated for the comptroller and the university attorney. On the right are two more offices side by side, one for the dean of women and the other for the dean of men. The latter is the larger of the two. Baker doesn't think the assigned spaces have anything to do with sexism. The university's overall enrollment is majority male, thus suggesting the dean of men has a lot more work to do than his female counterpart. Having researched the school a bit ahead of time, Baker wonders if the university could even call itself a co-ed institution if it wasn't for the enrollment of its College of Home Economics and the School of Education.

Further down the hall he finds what he is looking for: the university registrar. The efficient office gets Baker in and out in a hurry. He is told his records have arrived from George Washington University and are already on file. All he has left to do is obtain the signature of the dean of the College of Arts and Sciences acknowledging his transfer credits and he will be, officially, an NDSU student.

Leaving Old Main, he notices its cornerstone. Carved into it is the date it was laid, February 1891. Followed by the date 1893. Baker assumes that the latter date acknowledges when university officials considered the building complete. He follows the sidewalk to the library and onto Minard Hall where he's told he can find the College of Arts and Sciences and its dean, Mark Tallakson.

As he crosses the street in front of Minard Hall he isn't surprised to see it's constructed in the same architectural style as Old Main. He looks for its cornerstone and finds it next to the main door: Built in 1901 as "the Science Hall." Baker can see at least two additions have been added to the original building. Although he can't see the construction from where he's standing, Baker can hear the sounds of still another addition being added to the back of Minard Hall. The university is asking a lot of the old building, Baker muses.

Next door he notices Morrill Hall, another classroom building of roughly the same age and architectural appearance—he's obviously still on the original part of campus.

The dean's office is located on Minard's first floor, where the receptionist tells him Dr. Tallakson is in a staff meeting. Nodding at the suggestion that he make an appointment before showing up next time, Baker then asks where he can find the Agricultural Communication Office, and is directed to the fourth floor.

"Which way is the elevator?" he asks.

"Try the Black Building downtown."

Baker steers his wounded body back to the main hallway in search of a staircase. Actually, it was right in front of him when he entered the building, but he had missed it in his search for a first-floor office. The staircase is made of marble and it looks well worn. Two floors up he stops to get his breath and wonder why he didn't have the good sense to call ahead to make sure someone would be there to greet him.

When he arrives at the office, he's pleasantly surprised to see its occupant sitting at a desk, eating a sandwich and drinking a beer.

Seeing Baker, the man asks, "Would you like a beer?"

Baker immediately realizes he's going to like this guy. "Why yes, I would."

"You look like you could use one."

After accepting a beer from him, the young journalist knows the budding friendship has real potential.

Verne Pease introduces himself as the head of the Agricultural Communication Department.

"Well, I suppose 'department' is a little misleading. The Communication Department consists of me and a couple of part-time instructors from downtown businesses and the university's news bureau."

Baker gets the impression Pease would prefer to have more full-time colleagues with academic training in journalism and communications. Without asking, Baker receives an explanation for the staffing pattern in the department.

"The university likes part-time faculty because they work cheap and don't expect tenure. The dean likes them because there is no end of applicants for the jobs. Seems a lot of people want to teach a college course as long as it doesn't involve advising students or serving on committees.

"Want a tour of the department?"

When Baker says yes, Pease throws out his arms and makes a show of turning in his swivel chair in a circle. That involves a quick look around the office where they are sitting.

"You're sitting in it. I teach many of my classes right here and if I need room for additional space I can generally snag a classroom down the hall. But it isn't easy. The classrooms on this floor are dedicated to the sociology and history departments and they claim they need all of them twenty-four-seven. I've learned it's easier to just use an empty one than it is to fight the bureaucracy and get one reserved for communications. This arrangement requires communication students to be flexible about where to go for classes, but journalists must be flexible and learn to adapt to the circumstances."

Before Baker can ask why the Communication Department has such a low status it cannot even command classroom space for its courses, Pease tells him.

"I don't have an earned doctorate, so I'm nobody, just a lowly assistant professor without tenure," he says. "As such I don't have much clout with the dean and absolutely none with the central administration. In fact, the latter loathe me because I'm also the adviser to the student newspaper and the bigshots on campus don't think I punish its writers enough for their editorial skepticism of the administration."

Both chuckle at that comment, and Baker uses the break in the dialogue to make his own introduction. He tells Pease of his undergraduate experience editing a daily college newspaper at George Washington University. Then he mentions his recent experience as a general assignment reporter for the *Washington Star* and his current position as the night city editor at the *Forum*.

Pease perks up. He spent a couple of years working at the *Minneapolis Tribune* and considers himself a fellow newspaperman. The two talk on for another half hour before Pease asks Baker what brings him to the communication office.

Baker explains how he needs some additional college credit to obtain his degree. Then Baker explains that he has had four years of college course work, but his overall grade point average is too low for him to qualify for graduation. He openly admits that what he needs are some easy courses and high grades.

Pease laughs at that indiscreet comment and says: "You and every other student on this campus." Then he says, "I think I know how I might be able to provide you some assistance.

"Leave me a copy of your transcript from GW and I'll see how close you are to getting a degree from NDSU. I would guess you might want to enroll in a few courses in Ag Communication and perhaps a couple in the other social sciences."

That's when Baker admits he has two other challenges. First, his afternoon and evening work schedule limits him to only morning and early afternoon classes. He concedes his schedule probably complicates matters.

Second, as his transcript will demonstrate, Baker says he has already taken a lot of upper-level courses in sociology and history and wonders if he can find courses at NDSU that don't duplicate what he's already had.

Pease takes a minute before responding. He explains the university offers a lot of upper-division courses in the late afternoon and evenings. Most of these are designed for graduate students who work full time during the day, generally as schoolteachers, and need less-than-challenging coursework to obtain their master's degrees. Without looking at Baker's transcript, Pease says he can't respond to Baker's second concern.

Then he sits thinking for another minute. "There may be a way around both of your concerns. Ever hear of 'independent self-study'? Not waiting for an answer, Pease explains that it's just a way for a student to study on his own, produce an appropriate work product, obtain faculty approval of its quality, and receive academic credit similar to what he would earn taking a classroom course. For example, you might earn three credit hours for taking a self-study course that has you compare similarities between a large urban newspaper and a mid-size regional paper, such as the *Star* and the *Forum*. I'd be happy to sign off on that topic."

He veers off target and spends ten minutes describing the kiss-up university relations department at NDSU and its blind loyalty to the wants and desires of the President's Office. But he eventually brings the subject around to address Baker's needs.

"One thing I can get you self-study credit for is investigative reporting. We don't even offer a regular class on the topic and yet it's the hottest thing in journalism. That and something called 'new journalism.'

"To get the dean's buy-in, perhaps you should investigate some questionable policies or actions here at the university. Let's say the university administration arranges to have dumb jocks get decent grades from cooperating professors who in return receive priority seating at sporting events. I know for a fact this occurs, and I think a guy with your experience could write a pretty good newspaper or magazine story about that practice."

Baker says he's thrilled with the prospect of writing such stories and asks when he should begin to work on them.

"Come back here at this time Friday. By then I'll have a list of possible topics for you. Bring some of your own ideas for stories. Then we'll sign you up for self-study. Oh, in the meantime, get downstairs and introduce yourself to the dean. Tell him what you're thinking of doing in lieu of actual course work. Tell him I've already agreed to be your faculty sponsor. Then see if he'll agree to sign off on the idea. If he sounds interested, tell him you'd be pleased to run your work by him for his review and comments."

Sensing Baker's hesitation in visiting the dean, Pease swings around in his chair and picks up the phone. In a minute he's talking with Dean Tallakson. When he hangs the phone back up, he tells Baker the dean is waiting to see him.

"Oh, you may want to stop by a vending machine in the hallway and buy a pack of gum. No sense in letting the dean know you drink beer before noon."

Baker takes Pease's suggestion and then shows up back at the dean's office with a grin on his face and spearmint on his breath. Dean Tallakson is a tall, fit looking man in a handsome suit and tie. Baker figures him to be in his early 60s. From the academic potpourri hanging on his walls and decorating his credenza, Baker realizes Tallakson has a doctorate in sociology from Pennsylvania State University. Given the academic titles of the books and journals in his bookcase, it's obvious Tallakson's emphasis is rural sociology. Then Baker spots a textbook with the dean's name on it, entitled *Rural Sociology and the Great Plains*, and realizes he has identified the dean's specialty.

Quick as a reporter, Baker opens up his interview with a question sure to get his subject talking.

"I'm from back East, Virginia to be exact. And I'm not sure what people mean when they refer to "The Great Plains." How do you define it?"

Tallakson doesn't miss a beat. "I can see you need to enroll in my course, "Sociology of the Great Plains." You can order the textbook at the student bookstore.

"But to answer your question, you need to understand that the Great Plains is first and foremost a place. Basically, it's a broad expanse of prairie. It lies east of the Rocky Mountains and contains all or part of ten states and two Canadian provinces. It's huge, in other words.

"It's also dry, with less than an average of twenty inches of rainfall a year. That means it's arid and its farmland is marginal and its rangeland not much better. Droughts raise havoc about every twenty-five years and devastating dust storms are commonplace."

Baker is getting the clear impression life on the Great Plains is a struggle for everyone and a complete failure for some.

"Before white settlers arrived, the Great Plains was home to lots of buffalo and bands of Native Americans. Then the railroads pushed across the Great Plains and the buffalo and Indians were driven off the more desirable lands, to be replaced by immigrant farmers and cattlemen. The federal government encouraged settlement of the Great Plains by offering a settler a hundred-and-sixty acre plot of land if he agreed to plant crops and build a home on it. Unfortunately, many of these early arrivals knew little about dryland farming. The exceptions were the Germans from Russia who had experience farming similar land in the Ukraine. But even they were only marginally more successful than the average homesteader when it came to surviving the hardships of living on the Great Plains.

"So the Great Plains is a story of broken dreams. Since 1920 it has lost a third of its population. Several hundred thousand square miles of the Great Plains contain fewer than six people per square mile. To most people's way of thinking, and that includes a lot of government officials, a square mile of land with fewer than six people on it is for all practical purposes 'empty'.

"As a sociologist, I'm particularly interested in examining the impact of population loss on various aspects of life on the Great Plains.

"The population loss hasn't been statewide. Most of our cities are flourishing. But the growth of the cities simply reflects the movement of people from the rural areas to the population centers. Oh, there are exceptions to this rule, and this makes for interesting study too.

"Take North Dakota. As you would expect, the rural counties west of the Missouri River have been shrinking steadily since the Depression. Since the 50s, those with oil or other mineral deposits have staged a comeback. Workers have been flooding into the region to erect oil rigs and lay pipe. But then other oil-producing parts of the world dropped their price and made it less profitable for companies to pump oil out of the Great Plains. Pumping oil is a 'boom and bust' business, and when the pumps are capped, the workers and their families move elsewhere to find jobs.

"Just as an aside, I'm currently working on a paper about the population growth on Indian reservations. For years we've ignored this little-known phenomenon. We all thought the reservations were losing numbers through out-migration and the death of older residents. In fact, the Indian population is increasing, especially on reservations. That's because the Indians are younger than the white population living on the Great Plains. A young population increases its numbers by having babies. Right now, the Indian population is growing three times faster than the general population. And that raises the question I intend to address: how does a small, rural state like North Dakota, with its shrinking and aging white population, coexist with the steady growth of Indians on its reservations?

"Anyway, the Great Plains provides content for study by dozens of rural sociologists. It's just too bad we have to elbow our way to the table through the political scientists, historians, and economists looking at the same data.

"But you didn't come in here to listen to me promote my area of study or recruit you into the camp of rural sociologists. What can I do for you?"

Baker welcomes the chance to get into the conversation. "Well, first, thanks for the very informative discussion of the history of rural North Dakota. I'm sure it will come in handy in my reporting—probably a lot." He then explains that he's just come down from Verne Pease's office and has a request.

"Professor Pease advises me that I should enroll in several independent self-study courses to finish out my undergraduate degree. We both thought it worthwhile for me to concentrate on investigative journalism, given my experience and career goals. And he has agreed to be my faculty sponsor. To get started, I understand, you need to approve my plans to do self-study under the supervision of Professor Pease and to sign off on the topics I intend to investigate and write up for publication in a newspaper or magazine."

"Well, that's a fairly novel approach. You say Verne Pease has agreed to be your sponsor? That will require a lot of work from him and it doesn't reduce his regular teaching load. Do you suppose he understands that?"

"I don't want to put words in his mouth," says Baker, "but that would be my understanding. I will go so far as to say he seems as excited for me to start this venture as I am."

"What do you intend to investigate?" asks the dean.

"Professor Pease and I intend to meet Friday and resolve that matter. We've already kicked around some possible topics and we expect to have more by then. We both figure we'll keep our topics local. I have neither the time nor the budget to roam around the country doing interviews for a story. We've talked about the possibility of looking into issues involving NDSU. With that thought in mind, Professor Pease said you might be willing to suggest topics that you think an honest journalist with no bias could bring to the reading public's attention."

Dean Tallakson gave that thought a minute to digest.

"Pease is probably correct. From time to time I find myself wondering why this university does some of the things it does. For example, the College of Arts and Sciences has the largest enrollment on campus. Yet we seem to play second fiddle to every other college here. I can understand why agriculture, engineering, and even pharmacy get the attention they do. But I don't understand why our sheer numbers don't increase our visibility. Our faculty write scientific papers, edit scholarly journals, and educate dozens of students every year who go on to earn their doctorates. Maybe that's what you should investigate: Why does Arts and Sciences get no respect at a university that sells itself as an agriculture and engineering school?"

Before Baker can respond, the dean sighs deeply and says: "That's all off the record. I don't want an investigation of my pet peeve. First of all, the administration would know where you got the idea."

Baker chuckles.

"And second, I suspect given the politics of this state, the low status of arts and sciences at its agricultural college isn't likely to change."

Baker agrees with the dean. "You're right. It would be hard to write such an investigative piece that didn't just sound like so many sour grapes." After all, if arts and science faculty—even its dean—aren't happy at NDSU, they can always leave. No, Baker thinks, I need a better angle for my investigative piece.

Then Dean Tallakson hands it to him.

"My rant did get me thinking, though, about a topic that might interest you. Actually, I have two.

"The first is in my own field of study, rural sociology. What does a Great Plains state do when it realizes its declining population and the disappearing small towns, farms, schools, and businesses are dramatically changing its character? Many scholars have documented the region's ongoing population loss and the corresponding demise of it socially and economically. There isn't any significant in-migration of population across most of the Great Plains. In other words, the future for states like North Dakota looks pretty bleak.

"But here's what I find interesting. We have a large number of communities in our state that appear to be hanging on when everything says they should be on the verge of going out of business. Nobody so far has been able to explain the persistence of some of our rural communities. But clearly, some are sustainable. But we don't know what enables some rural communities in the Great Plains to persist in this harsh land while similar communities have disappeared.

"Meanwhile, two professors from back East have a different take on the Great Plains. They too recognize the shrinking population. But rather than talk about sustainable rural communities, they argue we should simply grow to accept the continuing decline in our population. Quit fighting it: embrace it, they argue. They want us to create a 'Buffalo Commons.' They want to make more than a hundred thousand square miles of the Great Plains into the world's largest national park. And then pack that park with buffalo and other wildlife and let them roam. Such a park would enable a visitor to see the heart of the continent exactly as Lewis and Clark came across it, a frontier of waving grass and migrant game animals.

"Folks who live on the Great Plains, and in particular those who live in the Western part of the region, are not going to warm to this idea of a national park replacing their towns and farms. But the scholars argue that it's probably going to happen, like it or not, simply because continued cycles of drought, financial woes, and depopulation are going to continue. Our water table is depleting fast, banks are failing, and whole rural counties are emptying out. At some point, in other words, large chunks of the Great Plains are going to form the initial acreage for the Buffalo Commons and its growth will just continue.

"Hear what I'm saying? We have scholars who insist Great Plains residents have got to get their heads around the simple fact that settling the prairies is the largest and longest running agricultural and environmental mistake ever made in U.S. history. And every year the consequences of this mistake just grow sharper and gloomier.

"At the same time, we have scholars who believe the Great Plains is populated with sustainable rural communities. But we don't know why or how they do it. So what are the federal government and the Great Plains states to do? Right now we just seem to be spinning our wheels while we wait for someone to decide what we ought to do: Remain where we are and attempt to emulate the apparent success of sustainable rural communities, or quit struggling and accept the fact we never had any business trying to eke out a life on the Great Plains.

"I can see an enterprising investigative reporter digging into this dilemma. Explain the concept of the Buffalo Commons and sketch out the potential implications for North Dakota residents. It seems pretty logical that people now occupying this Buffalo Commons won't want to see it even discussed. But then the bulk of the state's population lives outside the area where the buffalo will roam . . . people here in the Red River Valley, for example. How might they react to the proposal? How about residents of Grand Forks and Fargo? As potential gateway cities to the park, wouldn't they experience growth and prosperity?

"Look into this notion of sustainable rural communities. Can they co-exist with the Buffalo Commons, or are they potentially the preferred option?

"Anyway, I would readily approve a well-written proposal for such an article. You and Professor Pease can submit it to me anytime."

Then the dean got up out of his office chair and headed for his door. Baker assumed he was taking a bathroom break, but that didn't turn out to be the case.

"Come along with me. I want to show you something. It might well be the centerpiece of another investigative article."

The two headed into the hallway and then up two flights of stairs to the third floor. From there Baker followed the dean down the hall and into an empty classroom. As he stood looking out the window, the dean waved Baker to his side.

"See the construction out here? The university is adding an addition to our building. It will be the fourth in the building's proud reign here as the university's principal classroom facility.

"Now there certainly isn't anything newsworthy about an addition to a campus building; it goes on all the time and nearly everyone thinks it's natural and necessary. I'm in that camp. But this addition has raised some red flags and therein lies your investigative piece.

As the two walked back to the dean's office and returned to their respective chairs, Tallakson continued:

"Here's what makes the addition to Minard Hall interesting: it might well lead to the collapse of the entire building.

"You heard me right. Minard Hall is in danger of collapsing because of this new addition. At least this is the claim of a highly respected NDSU geology professor. He's been in my office three or four times warning me about the problem and saying I need to do something about it. He says his efforts to draw attention to his concern didn't get a warm reception from either the contractor or the university's office of facilities management. So now we're all sitting here waiting to see if the largest building on campus collapses, possibly with us inside."

Baker realizes he's outside his comfort zone. What if the professor is correct? But if everybody in a position to know anything about the construction of the addition disagrees with his analysis and conclusion, what's the story? People with expertise and experience disagree all the time. Does everyone just wait until the building falls—or doesn't—to know where the truth lies?

"Well," Baker says to the dean, "I can't proceed with the project until I talk to the experts myself."

The dean smiles at Baker. "Well, I guess I'll have to approve your independent course of study, then."

The two men get up from their chairs. Baker reaches across the desk, shakes the dean's hand and thanks him for his help.

"I'll be back in a day or two with a written proposal to investigate the potential collapse of Minard Hall."

"I look forward to signing off on it."

As he leaves, Baker's brain is already engaged. It's possible the geology professor will convince him that the building is likely to collapse. It's equally likely the contractor building the addition and the university official responsible for approving the project will say the building is in no danger. That's when the investigation begins, Baker realizes. Will he be able to discover why the contractor and the university are denying a potential calamity on campus?

As he gets into the cab for his ride back to the *Forum*, Baker realizes for the first time he's looking forward to earning his degree from North Dakota State University.

Chapter Eighteen

Anything for a Good Story

Chuck Baker knows his story is going to be tough to write the moment he begins talking to his principal subject.

Professor Allan Nelson isn't sure he should be talking to a newspaper reporter and he's even more unsure about discussing the potential collapse of Minard Hall.

Baker does everything he can to make the man comfortable. Then he discovers the trick is to mention Dean Tallakson's name.

"You mean Dean Tallakson said you should call me? What did he say exactly?"

"He said you are the expert scientist who called attention to the potential problem. Dean Tallakson says before I talk to anyone else, I must talk to you first. He says you're the only one on campus who can explain why Minard Hall might be in danger. And the dean says I can trust what you say. He refers to you as one of the brightest young faculty members on campus, someone who knows his discipline as well as anyone he can think of."

The dean hadn't said any of that. But Baker is pretty confident Dean Tallakson wouldn't take exception to anything he has said to Nelson.

"Well, I'm glad to hear that. But I don't want to get anyone in trouble. I'm not accusing anyone of intentionally trying to damage Minard Hall. I think we have a problem because the right people weren't consulted before the construction began. Then when I pointed out the pending problem, I think everyone involved in the construction thought the project was too far along to change anything. That's what upset me, to be honest with you. I can probably understand why the general contractor doesn't want to interrupt his project and start all over again. But I will never forgive the office of facilities management for ignoring my warning. Are they going to admit later that they had a chance to prevent a disaster, but passed? I'm sure they'll just blame the general contractor and he'll pass the blame on to his subcontractors. Or they'll all say the university should have known about the problem before it let bids."

By now, it's obvious Nelson is ready to tell his story. Baker asks for permission to record the conversation, assuring Nelson that such a procedure protects all parties. He says he'll be comfortable if Nelson wants to record it too. When Nelson says he doesn't have any recording equipment, Baker promises him he'll receive a copy of the *Forum's* recording.

After an hour's long interview, the two agree they've covered the matter thoroughly. Baker asks if it would be okay to call back if he needs to clarify anything. Nelson says that would be fine.

Then Nelson asks Baker a question. "When will the story appear in the paper?"

"I don't make that decision," Baker answers honestly. "And I have to do two more interviews before I can write it. But I think it will be soon." And with that, the two end their call.

Baker goes to work, and manages to get the two other interviews he needs in addition to his normal duties. By the end of his shift he's spent, comes back to the hotel, and slips into bed. He drifts off to sleep drafting alternative leads for the story he plans to write the next day.

The first draft goes smoothly. He's confident he has all the pertinent facts. The only real challenge is laying them out to the readers, so they have a picture in their own mind of the looming threat to Minard Hall.

```
Is the Largest Classroom Building at
NDSU About to Collapse?   'Yes' Says
Professor, 'No' Say Officials

By   Charles Baker
A tenured geology professor at North
Dakota State University says he has
evidence that new construction on one
of the oldest buildings on campus may
cause the entire structure to
collapse.
     The issue surfaced when NDSU began
building an addition onto Minard Hall,
the university's principal classroom
building.  Built originally in 1893,
the four-story-tall building already
had two other additions added to it
over the years.
     The contractor doing the
construction, Wards-Knutson of Fargo,
```

says the building and its addition are at no risk. "The professor may know geology, but he doesn't have a clue about mechanical engineering," said general manager Herbert Goldberg.

Thomas Freeman, director of facilities management at NDSU, also says the professor is wrong. "Minard Hall is old, for sure, but it's tough and resilient. It's handled new additions in the past with no difficulty and we think it will handle the new construction with ease," he told the Forum.

Geology professor Allan Nelson says the issue isn't with the building, it's with the land underneath it. Nelson has built a national reputation because of his studies of land in the Red River Valley within the boundaries of the now-extinct Lake Agassiz.

"The land beneath Minard Hall is made up of water-soaked, slippery clay, the same material that exists throughout the Red River Valley. It's a reminder that the Valley floor was once at the bottom of an enormous lake formed by the melt waters off of glaciers that dotted this part of the continent. A heavy structure sitting on this clay can cause it to slip. And that slippage can bring a building down."

Nelson said studies done after the collapse of large, heavy grain elevators in north Fargo ten years ago concluded the cause was weak clay sliding underneath them.

"The clay-rich sediments from Lake Agassiz are too weak to hold up massive structures," Nelson said.

He went on to say other heavy structures, such as the Municipal Auditorium in downtown Fargo, were built with the knowledge that the ground underneath rests on this same clay. "That's why the Auditorium is supported by dozens of concrete piers that go down through more than a hundred feet of clay to stand on stable ground below."

Nelson said the two new high-rise dormitories erected on the NDSU campus two years earlier also have these same kinds of concrete pilings under them.

He added, "You could call Fargo the "city of stilts" because of the necessary support structures that exist under its large, heavy buildings.

Goldberg said he doesn't dispute the need for heavy buildings to be built on top of concrete stilts. But he added: "Minard is only four stories tall and not particularly heavy. It's full of classrooms and offices, most of which are empty for long periods of the day.

"Keep in mind, this building has been sitting in the same location for nearly one hundred years and has never experienced the ground shift beneath it. Sure, we're adding a large addition to the building. But it sits alongside Minard Hall, not on top of it. The addition isn't going to add any appreciable weight to the original building."

Nelson doesn't dispute Goldberg's argument. But he says it's not directly relevant to the threat he worries about.

"The clays beneath Minard haven't shifted before, that's true. But the conditions have changed. The threat I'm talking about comes from the fact the new addition requires the contractor to dig a long deep hole right alongside Minard. Eventually the contractor will build the footing for the new addition in that hole.

"I've examined the hole," said Nelson. "It is twenty-five feet deep and the bottom rests on damp clay that spreads beneath Minard Hall. What I fear is going to happen is that the clay under Minard, already under considerable pressure from the building's size, is going to slip sideways into that hole before the work on the addition is done and the hole is filled in."

Nelson added: "As the contractor likes to point out, I'm no structural engineer. So I'm not exactly sure what a four-story tall, hundred-year-old brick building does when the clay underneath it finds a place to flow. But I predict a good portion of Minard Hall will be heavily damaged."

Freeman, director of facilities management at NDSU, is neither a geologist nor a structural engineer. He said he didn't want to get into the argument about the threats to Minard Hall.

"All I can tell you is that NDSU followed the rule book after the decision was made to add this new wing to Minard Hall. We had all kinds of engineers involved in the planning of the addition and the review of the construction plans. Nobody flagged any concerns about the ground slipping around under the building.

"We intend to complete the project at cost and within our approved timeframe," said Freeman. "Then if anything goes wrong later we'll pull the engineers back together to see if we can identify the cause of the problem. And then we'll leave it to the attorneys to argue about who's to blame and who's going to pay who for what. That's the way we've always done business in this office."

Nelson sits and sighs. He understands the process. He's worked at NDSU for nearly 20 years.

"I guess what bothers me is knowing that nobody intends to address my concern. It could be done quickly and easily if done right now. I mean,

```
the hole is in the ground.  The clay
is visible.  We have the expertise on
campus to make a judgment call about
the likelihood of slippage occurring.
But I was told this morning that the
contractor intends to dig the hole
even deeper.
     At this point, I guess I agree
with Mr. Freeman:  we'll just wait to
see what happens and then allow the
lawyers to figure out who pays for the
damages.  I just hope we don't have
any loss of life."
     The university president's office
wasn't available for an interview.
But the university relations office
released a statement on behalf of
President Woodrow Yunker.  It read,
"The President's Office has confidence
in its facilities office and its
contractors.  They assure us the
addition to Minard Hall will be done
on time and within budget."
```

Not bad, figures Baker. Now he has to see if it sells.

He grabs the four-page story off his desk at the Donaldson and heads to the *Forum*. He walks up the stairs and spots the object of his search at his desk.

"Mr. Swenson, got a minute for me?"

The managing editor signals for Baker to drop into a seat in front of his desk.

"What can I do for you, young man?"

"I have an article I would like you to read. It concerns the possible collapse of the largest classroom building at NDSU. A geology professor at the university says that the decision to put an addition onto Minard Hall, one of the oldest buildings on campus, is going to cause the structure to collapse. The company building the addition says this isn't true. So does the university's facilities office that is overseeing the work. I think the professor makes a pretty good case for his concern. But nobody is buying it. Everyone seems content to just wait and see if the building falls before looking into the possible cause.

"I should also add that I wrote this article on my own time as an assignment for a class I'm taking at the university. Therefore, I'm offering it to the *Forum* as a freelancer. And I'm not asking for any payment."

Swenson reaches for the copy paper in Baker's hand.

"This your article? Well, sit here while I read it."

Normally Swenson reads draft articles with an editing pencil in hand. Baker notices he hasn't picked up a pencil. Baker wonders if this is how he treats all freelance pieces.

"Interesting story," Swenson says as he lays the copy down. It would be nice if Minard Hall crumbled to the ground before we publish it. Without that climatic ending, all we have is a group of professionals disagreeing about how things ought to be done at their shop. You might notice that we have a lot of that around here, too.

"There's nothing unusual about professionals having differences of opinion. Without the building falling, there really isn't anything newsworthy here. On the other hand, it's an interesting yarn about the interaction between a respected faculty member and the officials hired to run the university. I would think this inherent conflict between academics and bureaucrats is fairly commonplace on campuses, but I don't know that for sure. It's obviously not in any university's interest to have these spats attract the attention of the legislature or the board of higher education.

"Before I make a decision about your piece, I'm going to circulate it around for comment. I for sure want to hear what our higher education reporter has to say. And I need to run it by the lawyers to make sure they don't see a lawsuit coming if we publish it. I'll get back to you."

Baker leaves Swenson's desk and goes back to his own. He thinks the interaction has gone about as expected. Nothing ventured, nothing gained.

Later that afternoon, Swenson stops by the night city desk and tells Baker to drop by when he has a minute. As Baker expects, Jim Rector caught Swenson's comment. The night city editor nods at Baker, telling he can leave his desk to go visit with the managing editor.

"Okay, here's where we stand. Everybody agrees you have an interesting piece. But without the building's actual collapse, there's nothing particularly newsworthy about the story. The lawyers can't come up with any reason to worry about the story, but they say they would be more comfortable if we passed on it.

"So, come back and see me when Minard Hall is a pile of rubble."

Baker is disappointed his story has been rejected, but isn't surprised. Hell, of course the story would be more interesting if the clay beneath Minard Hall brought the grand old building to the ground right away. And Baker agrees that a difference of opinion between professionals is hardly news.

He asks Swenson, "Am I free to ask other publishers if they might be interested in my story? Remember, it's a freelance piece written on my own time."

Swenson sits and thinks about the question.

"No, I guess it would be okay. It's your story. We didn't pay you to write it. And you've given us the option to publish the piece first. Now that we've decided not to do that, I see no reason why you can't peddle it elsewhere."

So that's what Baker decides to do.

He leaves Swenson's desk thinking about the *Minnesota Tribune*. He's heard scuttlebutt around the newsroom about intrusions the *Tribune* is making into the *Forum's* circulation area. That just might be enough to make his article appealing to the out-of-town newspaper, Baker thinks. A lot of *Tribune* readers who live in the Red River Valley undoubtedly attended NDSU. Some readers probably have sons and daughters enrolled at the college. Hell, many of these students probably go in and out of Minard Hall a couple times a week.

As it turns out, Baker's correct: The *Tribune* jumps on his story. It ends up being printed in a Sunday edition as a feature story in its regional section that reaches every subscriber in Western Minnesota and Eastern North Dakota. Baker learns about the story appearing in the *Tribune* from Rector when he walks into the newsroom Monday afternoon, and Rector hands him a copy of the Sunday *Trib*.

"Good story," says Rector. "We should have had it first," he says, intentionally loud enough for the managing editor to hear him.

Swenson doesn't appreciate Rector needling him. His day has already been in turmoil because of the fallout from Baker's piece in the *Minneapolis Tribune*. It began that morning when the publisher's partner, WDAY, the most watched television station in the region, started telling its viewers to watch a "breaking news special feature about a college crisis" during the evening news broadcast. During that segment, the station's top investigative reporter and a film crew plan to interview

Professor Nelson live at the site of the hole. He supposedly will explain on camera how wet clay has the propensity to shift sideways into open holes.

Then Swenson had to deal with his own staff complaints. Reporters and editors dropped by his desk all morning asking why a rival publication carried a feature story written by a *Forum* staff member. They want to know: "Don't we have a policy against that?"

Swenson is forced to write a memo to the staff. In it he explains that Baker's story was written as a freelance article on his own time and without financial assistance from the *Forum*. Swenson reminds his colleagues that the newspaper has a longtime policy of allowing its reporters and editors—under certain conditions—to write for other publications. Then Swenson explains that Baker had given the *Forum* the opportunity to publish the story, but the newspaper declined, for a variety of reasons. At that point, he said Baker asked if he could peddle his story elsewhere and the *Forum* gave him permission to do so. Finally, Swenson acknowledged that in retrospect, the *Forum* might have made a mistake by not publishing Baker's story. And he ended his memo by saying he had made that call.

Swenson's memo pleases Baker. Then too, he's happy to have a byline in the largest newspaper in the Upper Midwest—and to contemplate the $200 check the *Trib* is sending him for it. Not to mention this writing project also brings him a step closer to obtaining his college degree.

His self-congratulatory mood is interrupted by Morrison. "Hey, are you listening to the radio? Sounds to me we have a gun fight going on someplace."

When Baker focuses on the squawk box, he understands what Morrison is talking about. The Cass County Police

Department is attempting to figure out what some commotion out in West Fargo entails. Numerous reports of gunshots in town have reached the county police, but there's plenty of confusion about the cause and the location. From what Baker can detect, at least two state patrol cars are being dispatched to West Fargo.

Baker asks Morrison to explain why the highway patrol cares about a shooting in West Fargo. Wouldn't the town's own police force be expected to respond?

Morrison replies by giving Baker a short history of West Fargo.

"For years West Fargo was little more than an appendage of Fargo. And Fargo never really wanted anything to do with it. The town's primary employer is a foul-smelling, water-polluting meatpacking plant. Plus the place has a lot of animal pens surrounding it holding cows and pigs waiting to be slaughtered. While they're standing around, they shit and piss and otherwise add to the pollution problem. Nobody in Fargo considers the meatpacking plant to be a good neighbor.

"Nevertheless, it employs a lot of folks. And they need homes, schools, and public services. So eventually West Fargo incorporated. But rather than spend a lot of money building its own infrastructure, the town tried to suck off the hind tit of Cass County. For years, the county provided West Fargo with police and fire protection, snow removal, street repairs, you name it. But as the unincorporated town grew, it became obvious to everyone that it needed to manage more of its own affairs. So among other things, the town fathers decided to create a police force.

"Today it consists of a police chief and three part-time officers. That's not enough, of course, to do the job. So the town has a contractual relationship with Cass County and the

State Highway Patrol to provide back-up assistance if needed. I guess that's what we're hearing on the state patrol radio. The local cops must have put in a call for assistance."

Baker looks up at the clock. It's just 10 p.m., early enough to get a local story into the morning paper. He rummages through his desk, searching for the list of local officials who the *Forum* routinely calls for information about their jurisdictions. Sure enough: it contains a listing for the West Fargo Chief of Police, William Pitts. Scratched alongside his name is "Sunny." Baker assumes this is the guy's nickname.

He calls the number and a woman answers, "West Fargo Police Department." When Baker identifies himself as a reporter for the *Forum*, she yells at him: "About time you called. Sunny is out there all alone fighting off a small army of terrorists. Why haven't you gotten him reinforcements?"

Baker grabs a sheet of copy paper and threads it into his typewriter. At the same time, he struggles to put on a headset so his hands are free to pound the typewriter.

"May I ask who I'm talking to, please?" He starts out.

"I'm Ida, Sunny's wife. I guess you could say I'm also the police dispatcher. I've got Sunny on the police radio from his squad car. You really need to talk to him.

Baker says that would be great. But then wonders how he would do that; he can't talk to the police chief through his phone line that's connected just to Ida.

"I really want to talk to him. Can I call him direct? Do you have a number for him?"

"Of course I have a number for him. But that won't do you any good. He's in his squad car and he's talking to me over the police radio. That radio only ties into our other police cars and me."

"Well, do you suppose you could ask him to call me when he has a free moment?"

"Sure, I can do that. But he's in a gunfight. I don't think he's going to walk away from that to talk to a newspaper reporter. You'll need to come out here if you want to talk to him."

"Okay, that makes sense. Can you tell me where this gun fight is?"

"It's at the Safeway. Sunny has the bad guys surrounded. They're in the Safeway, which they were robbing when Sunny arrived. Since he doesn't know what he's up against, he's not going to risk storming the place. Instead, he's been driving around the Safeway in his patrol car shooting at the bad guys through the supermarket's windows."

"Wow. Has he hit anyone?"

I don't think he knows. He says nobody's shooting back at him right now, but he's not sure that means they're down. We're waiting for back-up so we can assault the building."

"Okay, tell Sunny the *Forum* is on its way. Tell him not to shoot me when I arrive."

"Better hurry up. I don't know how long Sunny can keep up the battle. He's running low on bullets."

Baker drops his headset and runs to the back of the newsroom where the photographers work. He had seen one earlier in the newsroom and he's praying he's still in the building.

He is: A young freelancer the *Forum* uses primarily to take pictures of high school sporting events. Baker realizes he doesn't know the guy's name.

"Hey, my name is Chuck Baker and I work the night shift on the desk. I need a photographer for an urgent story I'm working on. Who are you?"

The guy says, "Walt Munstock. I'm working part-time here at the *Forum*. What do you need?"

Geez, thinks Baker, the guy is even younger than I am. What a pair we'll make walking into a gunfight.

"Do you have a car? Can you drive us out to West Fargo right now so we can cover a story about a robbery at the Safeway? As we stand here, the police chief is driving around the building shooting through its windows to keep the bad guys down."

"Sure. Sounds exciting. Let me grab my gear. I'll meet you at the door downstairs."

Baker runs back to his desk and tells Rector what he intends to do. Rector gives him a small smile. It's obvious to Baker that Rector wishes he was a 22-year-old reporter again running to a gunfight.

"Go ahead. Get out there. Call me when you think you have the pertinent facts. If necessary, I'll have Harry take your call and write what you have into a story for the late edition. Are we going to have any art?"

"Probably. I'm taking a photographer with me. And you might ask Harry to pull the mug shot of the West Fargo police chief out of the morgue. He's going to be the main character in my story."

"Okay, go."

Baker grabs a stenographer's notebook and two pens and runs down the stairs to meet Munstock.

"Where's the car?"

"It's outside, with the motor running," says Munstock.

Baker throws the building door open and sees a customized cherry-red '56 Chevy sitting on a chopped frame with oversize tires and dual exhausts. It is the car every high school boy dreams of owning.

As he goes to open the passenger door, Baker realizes it has no handles.

"How in the hell am I supposed to get into your car?" he yells.

"Just give a minute," says Munstock as he slides into the driver's seat. Then he does something that throws open the passenger door. Baker jumps in and Munstock rips away from the curb and down NP Avenue heading west. The speed and noise tell Baker the car has a more powerful engine than the one it rolled off the assembly line with.

Baker is impressed. He asks Munstock if he did his own work on the car.

"Most of it. I attended the Wahpeton School of Science and took a two-year program in auto body repair and refinishing. I brought a used '56 Chevy to school with me and by the time I left this is what it ended up looking like. I'll sell it by the time I graduate from NDSU. Then I'll buy a used Corvette. After I customize and sell it, I'll have enough money to buy a photography studio."

"Well, let's move this machine out to West Fargo as fast as you legally can," Baker says. Then he adds: "I can assure you the *Forum* won't pay for speeding tickets."

When they arrive at the Safeway, two highway patrol cars, two county police cars, and one well-worn city police car are outside with all their lights flashing. Then Baker sees a large man dressed in slacks and a shirt standing by the police cars with his hands handcuffed behind him.

Shit, thinks Baker. We've arrived too late for the action.

Jumping from the car, which he notices has captured the attention of all the police officers standing around, Baker announces that he's from the *Forum* and wonders where he might find Chief Sunny Pitts.

A short, heavy set man with a crew cut haircut wearing a comical looking police uniform steps forward.

"Sunny Pitts. That would be me."

"Chief, can you tell me what's going on here?"

"Well, as you can see, we've captured a man who we suspect was part of a team that tried to rob the Safeway. My colleagues and I are now preparing to enter the store to see if he left any companions inside."

With that, the chief and four officers of the law from Cass County and North Dakota enter the front door of the Safeway. Baker notices that the glass in the door is lying on the ground. The large plate glass windows on either side of the door have several large bullet holes through them. Then Baker notices that every single plate glass window on this side of the building has been shot through at least once.

The store manager, Marvin Flannery, trails the police inside. Baker falls in behind him. The police all have their guns out, ready to use. Anything can happen, Baker reasons, as he looks around to make sure Munstock is ready with his camera.

But a search of the entire building fails to shake out a single bad guy. The police put away their guns and figure the other culprit must have sneaked out while Sunny was shooting through the plate-glass window down at the far end of the building.

Store manager Flannery breaks open a couple of packages of doughnuts and offers them to the officers. They take to them in that natural way cops do whenever free doughnuts are offered. They don't even wait for Flannery to get his coffee machine running before devouring the treats.

That's when Chief Pitts looks up. "Holy shit," he utters out loud. "There's somebody lying on top of the freezer. Look, you can see his shoes."

That gets everybody's attention. The cops all draw their guns and aim them up at the shoes hanging out over the top of the cold-foods display bin with the soles and heels pointing outward.

Pitts, who has the largest gun in the group, owing to the fact he is the only one present who doesn't have to carry a department-issued handgun, fires his weapon twice, in rapid succession.

Baker ducks down, uncertain of what's happening. Did the chief just shoot the guy laying on top of the freezer?

Then, the man on the freezer case jumps to his feet with both hands in the air and yells, "Stop . . . don't shoot." He appears unhurt.

Later, during a wrap-up session, Pitts explains he was aiming at the ceiling. "And I hit it. Both shots."

The guy comes down from the freezer and is immediately handcuffed. At the same time, Flannery announces that the coffee is done and hands out more doughnuts. The assembled police officers appreciate his thoughtfulness.

The bad guy is pushed outside and into a county police car. Because West Fargo doesn't have a place to lock up its scofflaws, the two suspects are hauled to the Cass County Jail in Fargo.

As the police grab coffee cups and reach for the second round of doughnuts, Baker looks over at Munstock.

"Did you get a picture of the guy up there on the freezer case?"

Munstock just stares at the floor. Apparently, Pitts' gunshot threw Munstock off his game. When the loud gun went off, Munstock took a dive to the floor, which Baker realizes is something he probably should have done too.

"Without that picture, I don't have much of a story," Baker complains.

"Okay, here's an idea," offers Munstock. Why don't you climb up on the freezer case and lie down? I'll take a picture of you. When we write a cutline we can say the feet and legs exposed in the picture belong to the bad guy. Why wouldn't that work?

Baker can't think of a single reason, and so he climbs up on the freezer case. The officers standing around wonder what the young *Forum* team is up to, but seeing as they're enjoying their coffee break, they don't stop it.

The store manager might have tried, seeing as how he would be nervous about having a second man in one evening crawl on top of an expensive piece of equipment. But he was over in the bakery section looking for more doughnuts, so he missed his chance to raise an objection.

The two newsmen break the speed limit driving back to Fargo. Both realize they are fighting to meet a deadline, and in the time-honored tradition of newsmen everywhere, breaking laws to meet deadlines is acceptable behavior.

The last edition of the morning *Forum*, the one delivered to Fargo subscribers—as well as those in West Fargo—carries both the article and the photo. Baker is amazed that Munstock was able to take a picture of him lying on top of the freezer case and only reveal his scuffed shoes without socks.

West Fargo Chief Captures Thieves at Local Safeway

By Charles Baker, Forum Staff Writer

A small-town police chief single-handedly broke up an apparent robbery in progress at the Safeway store in West Fargo Saturday night.

West Fargo Chief of Police William "Sunny" Pitts was on routine patrol when he drove by the Safeway and saw its lights on at roughly 10 p.m.

"The store closes for the night at eight p.m., and the cleaning crew is out by nine p.m.," Pitts said, adding that he has never seen the lights still on at 10 p.m. "So I was suspicious."

When he drove into the store's parking lot he noticed the front door was broken. Then he saw someone duck down over by the store's safe. At that point Pitts drew his .44 magnum revolver and began to fire shots into the store.

"I decided not to go into the store on my own, not knowing what I was facing. I called for back-up from the county and state. In the meantime, I did what I could to keep the bad guys inside from escaping."

To do that, Pitts drove his squad car, with its siren running and his roof-top lights flashing, back and forth in front of the Safeway while he continued to fire bullets through the store's large plate glass windows.

"I wanted to keep the robbers off balance and discourage them from firing back at me. I figure I fired at least fifty bullets," Pitts said afterwards.

While Pitts was still firing his gun, reinforcements from the State Highway Patrol and the Cass County Sheriff's Department arrived onsite. Together with Chief Pitts they entered the store with guns drawn and arrested a suspect lying on the floor in front of the safe.

Lying nearby were tools police assumed had been used in an attempt to break into the safe.

The suspect provided no resistance and was led in handcuffs out to a squad car. The police, thinking they might find more suspects, then conducted a thorough search of the store. When they had finished, they came to the conclusion that any other suspects probably had escaped during the commotion caused by the chief's gunfire.

But then Chief Pitts looked up at the top of the freezer case toward the middle of the store and saw a man's shoes and ankles (see accompanying photo).

Pitts fired his .44 caliber handgun twice. It isn't clear if he was shooting at the suspect on top of the freezer or simply into the ceiling to get his attention. But as soon as the pistol went off, the suspect jumped to his feet with his hands up and said, "Don't shoot. I give up."

With their guns drawn, the police ordered the man down. He was handcuffed and led to a squad car. The police then conducted another sweep, concentrating on the top of the various freezer cases located around the store.

At press time, the two men had not been identified. Both are being held in the Cass County Jail while police continue their investigation.

After everyone left the scene, Chief Pitts went back on patrol. He said, "We haven't had that much excitement in West Fargo since a bull gored one of our rodeo clowns two years back."

Managing editor Swenson couldn't believe he was going to write a second memo in as many days discussing some aspect of the work done by Chuck Baker, their new hire. Swenson cited the Safeway robbery story and praised Baker's enterprising spirit, his on-the-scene reporting, and his ability to get a late-breaking story into the final edition. Walter Munstock, a part-time photographer at the *Forum*, was also recognized for his contributions to the story. Swenson wrote that the *Forum* had offered Munson full-time employment.

Nothing was said about Chuck Baker lying on top of the Safeway's freezer case pretending to be one of the robbery suspects, because no one but he and Walter knew the photo was staged. Baker realized the ethics of that stunt probably would be criticized in any modern-day journalism textbook. But he wondered what Professor Verne Pease would think of it.

Chapter Nineteen

Crooks Are Innocent Until Proven Guilty

As his story about the Safeway robbery is becoming the talk of the town, Baker follows his usual Sunday ritual, dropping by the police departments in Fargo and Moorhead to see what he can learn about any noteworthy overnight police work they have done. He normally doesn't stop at the Cass County and Clay County jails. Both staffs are notorious for not finishing up their paperwork during the weekend. Therefore, Baker is in the habit of leaving any county police stories for the dayside crime reporter to gather on Monday.

But the Sunday after the West Fargo robbery, he has a sixth sense that he might be rewarded if he drops by the Cass County Jail. After all, that's where the two desperadoes are being held.

Normally, reporters never have the opportunity to talk with suspects while they're incarcerated. Police jailers and their supervisors see no justifiable reason to allow pushy reporters to talk with inmates, particularly before they're formally charged or have their legal counsel at their side.

But when Baker shows up at the Cass County lock-up, he's surprised when the jailer invites him into the cell block and allows him to talk through the bars to the two suspected West Fargo thieves. The jailer explains to Baker: "I wouldn't normally allow a news reporter near a jail cell, but I'm going to make an exception in your case. The two arrestees say they want to talk to you and I said okay. Just between you and me, I'm letting you talk to them because I liked the story you did on the West Fargo Police Chief. It's about time the *Forum* helped its readers understand the stress and strain of being a small-town police officer in a major metropolitan area."

Although they were all together the previous night in the West Fargo Safeway, Baker and the Carter brothers introduce themselves and agree this meeting is more pleasant than the last.

The interview goes well. Baker is surprised. Both brothers are personable, open, apologetic, and embarrassed. But what really captures Baker's attention is the story they tell about how they found themselves in the Safeway Store with a handful of tools looking at a large floor safe before realizing they had no clue about how to open it.

The interview runs almost two hours. When he finishes, he shakes hands enthusiastically with the two erstwhile crooks and goes back to the *Forum* to write up his story.

Safeway "Crooks" Describe Their Incident As the Culmination of a Really Bad Day

By Charles Baker, Forum Staff Writer

A day after they were apprehended in a West Fargo Safeway Store after dark with a satchel full of tools, two robbery suspects were in the Cass County Jail claiming, "the whole thing was a mistake."

The two brothers, William and David Carter, say they had been drinking most of the day before reaching the Safeway store Saturday evening.

The Carters, William, 22, and David, 20, had started the day in the rented apartment they share in Wayzata, about 30 miles west of Minneapolis. They both work construction and were enjoying their weekend off. After watching a football game on their television set, they decided to go to a nearby tavern and have a couple of beers. As it turns out, they had more than a couple.

Late in the afternoon, they found themselves in the company of two young women, both out-of-work waitresses, or so they said.

"One thing became painfully obvious quickly is that they had no money," said William. We were buying all the drinks for the table."

The four got into a serious conversation that boiled down to two irrefutable facts: one, they had no future in Wayzata and two, things are always best in the West. Buoyed by their quick recognition of these twin facts, the four decided they should leave right then and drive to Oregon. They agreed among themselves that they were leaving nothing of value behind, including personal possessions and family.

"We agreed: anything we find out West is going to be better than what we're leaving behind in Wayzata," said David Carter.

The four went out to the Carter car and the brothers showed it to their two women companions. Neither was impressed. First, the car was a two-door coupe, which meant the backseat would be cramped. Second, it was old, dirty, and full of heavily used work clothes and filthy boots. The two women said they wouldn't even go to a Duluth drive-in theatre in that car.

The two Carter boys were stumped. The rejected car was the only one they had. If they didn't take it, the four of them were basically stuck in Wayzata. Then one of the two women had a suggestion (they will remain unnamed because they are not in custody and neither brother can recall their names).

"The cute one just said, 'Why don't we steal a car?'

Neither William nor I have ever done that and the two girls admitted they hadn't, either. So we were not sure what to do with that suggestion," said David.

Then almost as if fate intervened on their behalf, a relatively new and clean four-door Ford pulled up in front of the bar where they were standing. The guy driving it jumped out, left the motor running, and went inside.

"It's a message from God," one of the girls said, according to the brothers.

"We knew we had our car; all we had to do was get in and take off. So that's what we did," said David.

They drove the car west to St. Cloud. They stopped for gas, used the bathrooms, bought hamburgers, and drove on toward North Dakota. Both women slept most of the way. The two brothers switched off driving, with William at the wheel when they pulled into Fargo.

Hungry, thirsty, and tired, William suggested to his companions that they spend the night in Fargo. None of them agreed. Fargo was too close to Wayzata for any of them to consider themselves separated from their old, boring existences. They wanted to drive on.

"At that point, I said we needed to assess our cash situation. My brother and I have no credit cards, and we for sure knew the girls didn't have any either, so we were dependent on our cash to get us out West. But with both billfolds stretched open on the dashboard, all we could pull together was twelve dollars and change. The girls said they could probably dump their purses and put together another ten dollars. We all realized that twenty-two dollars wouldn't get us to the West Coast, even if we skipped buying beer along the way. We needed a plan."

The two women came up with one.

"They said we should rob a bank," said David. "We laughed at that idea. We're not bank robbers. And besides, it was now Saturday night and the banks were closed."

That's when one of them said, "How about a grocery store?"

"William and I agreed we might be able to handle that," said David. "But we had no weapons. We both wondered if we would be likely to have much luck robbing a store without a weapon."

One of the women then suggested they search the stolen car they were driving. Maybe the owner had a gun or some gear that could be used as a weapon. The four of them opened the trunk and went through a load of stuff that looked pretty much like the contents of any Midwestern car. They found hammers, saws, wrenches, pliers, and an assortment of levels and duct tape. Nothing, in other words, that they thought would convince anyone to hand over their store's money.

"The girls came through again," said William. "One of them suggested we had to find a store with just one employee in it. Then we could flash our hammers and convince him to give us the store cash or we would beat him to death."

David added: "That strategy ruled out King Leo's or Dairy Queens. We needed to find a small store."

They drove by several liquor stores, but most had multiple clerks working on Saturday night and a steady procession of customers. Too risky, the four agreed.

The next thing they knew, they were in West Fargo, looking for gas. Nobody in the car had ever heard of West Fargo.

"We wondered why it wasn't just called the west side of Fargo?" said William.

As they're looking for a gas station, they drove by a large Safeway Store. Nobody in the car thought that would be a reasonable place to rob, but they stopped anyway. The women had to go to the bathroom and everyone agreed Safeway has a reputation for clean restrooms.

When the two women came back to the car, they were all excited. They said the place had just closed. The only person in the store was the manager who had just let them out the front door and then locked it. They watched through the window as he went and cleaned out the various cash registers, putting the folding money into one heavy-duty bank bag and the loose change into another. A third bag contained coupons, best they could determine.

"If we go in right now, we can grab him before he locks up the money," said David.

"Sure," said the girls. "But you've got to move fast."

They were not fast enough. The manager obviously heard the glass on his front door break and got scared. He quickly dumped the bills and coins into the safe and locked it. Then he ran into the back room and bolted out the rear door.

David said, "We knew what he had done with the money because we found the safe locked and next to it a bag full of worthless coupons. Obviously, he had put the money into the safe."

Out of sheer frustration, the two brothers beat on the safe with some of the tools they had brought into the store with them. They were not trying to open it; neither one of them knew how to do that. They were not even sure they had the right tools to break open a combination safe.

While the brothers fretted, the two ladies wandered around the store looking for snacks.

About that time, a police car pulled up in front.

"The cop car spooked us," said William. "The police arrived quicker than we had figured. I'll admit, we all panicked and started running. The girls were smarter than William or me. They ran to the back room and found the door the manager had gone through. And they did the same thing, without so much as a shout or whistle to us," said David.

"Then the cop outside turned on his siren and lights. It was quite a scene. He drove back and forth in front of the store, which didn't make any sense to us," said William.

"But then he started shooting," said David. "That really got our attention. We split up, not on purpose, but we both wanted to stay away from the windows. We didn't know if he had spotted us or what, but we could hear bullets hitting all around us."

That's when the brothers noticed large holes appearing in the store's plate-glass windows.

"They were not small holes. I know enough about weapons to know someone was shooting at us with a high-powered gun," said William.

At that point, they both laid on the floor alongside what they hoped were secure, sturdy aisle dividers.

"I don't think we could have given up if we had wanted to," said David. "I mean, the shots were coming in fast and furious and from all directions. There wasn't any way we were going to be able to approach the door and surrender. The trigger-happy cop would have shot us."

Eventually other police cars showed up, all with their sirens on and lights flashing. The brothers realized their adventure was coming to end.

"We were in different sections of the store. Which meant we each had to decide how we wanted things to end. William decided he would just go back to the safe, lie down, and put his hands over his head while he waited for the arresting officers to enter the building.

David had a different thought.

"It ain't over 'til it's over," he said. "I thought if they break into the store, all commando like, I just might be able to slip by them and escape. I figured William would have the common sense to do the same thing.

We could meet at the car and make our escape."

When the police did enter the store, David said he panicked a little bit. He realized he had to get out of the aisles. He considered hiding in a meat locker or a back room, but changed his mind when he figured those would be the first places the police would search. Then he had another idea: Why not crawl above their sight line and lie down on top of one of the large freezer units that run up and down some of the aisles? So that's what he did.

The police quickly found William lying by the safe and got him into handcuffs. Then they kept searching the store for what they figured was a second suspect. Not finding anyone, they gave up the search.

"I thought I was going to pull this off," said David. I mean, the cops were standing around with their guns in their holsters drinking coffee and wolfing down doughnuts. I just had to be quiet and wait them out."

That strategy became a nonstarter when West Fargo Police Chief William "Sunny" Pitts, who had been the first cop on the scene and had done all the shooting, screamed. He was looking at a pair of shoes and two ankles lying on top of a freezer compartment.

"I heard him yell, but I didn't know it was because he saw me," said

David. But then the idiot shot his gun, twice. I figured he was shooting at my feet, so I jumped up and raised my hands. I didn't want his huge gun to take one of my feet off."

Before the night was out, the brothers had their stolen car confiscated, their clothes exchanged for jail garb, and a decision to make about which of the two bunks in their cell they wanted to claim. If they were waiting for a proper goodbye from the two ladies in their lives, they went to bed disappointed.

The brothers acknowledged they had made a whole series of mistakes and were now hoping to explain that to someone and perhaps catch a break.

"I just hope you say one thing to your readers," said William. "Sure, we came into the store after hours. But we didn't steal anything. Well, okay, we stole a car earlier in the day. But that was out of the local police's jurisdiction. And the owner is going to get his car back. We didn't take anything from the Safeway, not even a donut. We had no weapons. We didn't threaten anyone. And had that first cop not showed up shooting his big gun, we would have just walked back to our car and drove off."

Then David added: "For what it's worth, we just want to go back to Wayzata. We're not cut out for the fast life out West."

> Police said later that they had received a report two young women, who met the descriptions of the two female suspects, had been spotted late Saturday night at a bar near the West Fargo Safeway. Patrons said they left after closing with two men in a car with Montana license plates, heading west.

Baker is pleased on Monday when Sullivan says he likes the story and plans to recommend the Sunday editor run it the coming weekend. "It's just the kind of Sunday feature story we look for," he says, and Baker agrees. It's just the kind of light read you want after church services and before a heavy brunch.

The editor who assembles the bulk of the Sunday paper—with the exception of the front page, regional pages, and sports pages—is thrilled to get Baker's story. He's thrilled because of its length, not its content. In fact, he only read as far into the story as necessary to grasp its meaning so he could write an appropriate headline. As Sunday editor, his job on Friday and Saturday is to wrap stories around the large national advertisements. This can be challenging, which is one reason why Sunday editors, who never have to face a tight deadline, nevertheless develop ulcers trying to find suitable copy to fill their advertisement-dominated inside pages.

Management realizes that readers tend to feel gipped if they open their Sunday paper and find page after page of national ads. Letters to the editor complain about the practice and scream, "Where's the meat?" In response to the feedback from readers, better-managed newspapers throughout the country run their national ads about four-fifths of their intended size. This leaves space around them for a "news hole" the

Sunday editor can fill with the "snackable stories" readers say they want.

Normally, the snackable stories are just AP features and news about faraway places that have no real timeliness. If they don't run this Sunday, they can be saved for next Sunday's paper. Stories about famines in Africa and hungry children in Asia are commonly used as filler—if not exactly snackable – news copy. So are the run-of-the-mill feature stories about political turmoil in the Mideast and government corruption across South America. All snackable, to be sure, but not particularly satisfying. Hardly anyone ever reads one of these stories to the end.

But every once in a while, a good feature story about something in the Upper Midwest comes into the composing room. Such a story has plenty of reader appeal. It's the kind of story that people talk about on Monday over morning coffee and clip to share with former neighbors. Baker's story of the Wayzata boys who robbed the Safeway in West Fargo and now want everyone to just forget it ever happened is a rare, space-filling Sunday story. And it's made even more appealing, at least to the Sunday editor, because of its length. Plenty long to run across multiple pages.

As a consequence of its timeliness, the Sunday editor can push the story up to the front page without much resistance from anyone. At the same time, the Sunday editor will ensure the guy putting the front page together knows he can only have a small portion of the story for page 1. Most of the article has already been set in type and spread out across multiple pages inside. In fact, by Saturday night, most of those inside pages with portions of Baker's story will already have been printed.

Nobody will ever fund a study to see if this procedure— starting a feature story on page 1 and then using the bulk of it inside to fill holes around national ads—draws reader attention to the advertisements. Nevertheless, newspaper ad salesmen say it does. Management will say they know they get fewer complaints about the monotony of national advertisements running page after page when the readers are turning those same pages to continue reading a really good feature story.

*   *   *

The next day, Tuesday, Charles Baker took his sore mouth to the oral surgeon Sue Bacevich recommended. She said nobody could repair busted teeth better than Dr. Tim Canning.

Baker doesn't know about that, but he does appreciate how pleased Canning's office is to learn its new patient has wealthy benefactors; namely, Andy Bacevich, one of the wealthiest and most influential businessmen in the Red River Valley. Dr. Canning says he understands that the Bacevichs have assumed responsibility for any costs Baker racks up as his patient. That leaves Baker to hope that the fancy-titled dentist doesn't take advantage of the situation and do more high-priced work on him than necessary.

The next day, Wednesday, the plastic surgeon accepts his new patient under the same terms and conditions as the dentist. But he begins his work by rebreaking Baker's nose. That catches Baker by surprise. He wasn't prepared mentally to relive the pain, bruising, and black and blue swelling that accompanied his original beating.

The plastic surgeon gives him a prescription for the pain, which he fills on the way in to work. He opens up the bottle as soon as he gets it. They look like horse pills. He swallows one. It takes three efforts at the drinking fountain inside the Drug Store to get all three down.

Twenty minutes later, he staggers into the newsroom. It's late Wednesday afternoon. Swenson does a double-take at Baker's wrapped-up face. "Again?"

"Plastic surgeon," he barely mumbles. "Rebroke it."

Swenson walks over and puts his hand on Baker's chest, stopping him from getting any closer to his desk. "Slow news day. Take it off," Swenson says. "In fact, it's a slow week. See you Friday. Or better yet, don't come in until Saturday. That way I won't have to look at your face again until Monday."

Baker grunts a chuckle, winces, turns around and shuffles back out of the newsroom. When he wakes up fully clothed in his bed at the Donaldson the next afternoon, that's the last thing he can remember.

The next 36 hours are a slow daydream of listening to the radio in his room, downing an occasional half of a pain pill, and repeatedly dozing back off. Finally, by about 3 a.m. Saturday morning, he feels awake and brave enough to unwrap his face. Staring in the bathroom mirror, he looks as bad as he did the day after his beating by the two cops. But he's beginning to feel a lot better.

That Saturday is a slow day at work, thank goodness. Completely routine. Sunday morning, he's finally starting to feel like himself again.

*   *   *

When the Carter brothers of Wayzata enter the courtroom Monday morning to hear the charges filed against them, Baker is there, notebook in hand. The brothers are despondent, and it shows. They stand before the judge with their heads hanging down. At this stage in the procedure, the judge has yet to decide if they'll even go to trial. Nearly everyone in the courtroom assumes they will.

As far as the judge is concerned, the only issue before him that day is to determine whether Cass County has sufficient evidence of a crime.

The judge starts out by asking the Carter boys if they had a chance to read the story in yesterday's Sunday *Forum* about their alleged crimes. He looks down at the two brothers and they both say that they had read the story.

The judge says so has he.

Then he asks, to no one in particular, "Is there anyone in this courtroom who didn't read the *Forum's* story about the Wayzata boys and their Safeway adventure out in West Fargo?" Nobody answers, of course. But a lot of heads are nodding up and down.

"Let me see if I can list the charges filed by the Cass County District Attorney's Office against David and William Carter. They stand before you here today accused of first-degree robbery of a safe inside a Safeway Store. They are charged with second-degree assault on the facility itself, including the damage to the safe, the store windows, the front door, and some of the store shelves and the grocery contents sitting on them. They are also charged with stealing a car and driving it across state lines. Charges are also pending against them for possibly kidnapping two young women from Minnesota and bringing them across the state line into North Dakota.

"The Cass County District Attorney's Office also said in a statement that I have in front of me that it has witnesses from the Cass County's Sheriff Office, the North Dakota Highway Patrol, the West Fargo Police Chief, and the manager of the Safeway store. The District Attorney also said the much-read

Forum article and the police reports of the robbery will collaborate all its charges.

"Let's review these facts.

"First, the alleged robbery. The Carter brothers freely admitted to the *Forum* reporter that they had entered the Safeway Store. I think we can all assume that's an accurate statement. They were later discovered in the store after it had closed. So far we might have a breaking and entering charge to contend with.

"But there doesn't appear to be an actual robbery of anything, including the store's safe. The brothers told the *Forum* reporter they did not know how to break open a safe. And the police report says that none of the tools found onsite would have been of any help to someone wanting to open a combination safe. So, we're back to a simple breaking and entering charge.

"But the district attorney has filed other charges against the accused. He says the store was assaulted. That may be true. Certainly, it's true that the West Fargo Chief of Police assaulted the building. We read in the *Forum* article that he said he probably fired fifty high-caliber bullets into the store through its plate-glass windows. But none of the police reports filed says anything about the Carter brothers doing any harm to the facility. All the police reports credit the West Fargo Chief for shooting out the door and windows.

"What about damage to the safe?" Clearly, the safe contains plenty of dinks and scratches accumulated over the years. But it's an old safe, and the store manager has said he doesn't honestly know how many of them were there before the alleged intrusion.

"What about the shelves and their contents? Again, the store manager says there was minimal damage to the store's interior. And the damage he associates with Saturday night's incident was all caused by the Police Chief's fifty bullets. I'm sure the district attorney will argue that those bullets were fired because the sheriff thought the place was being robbed. But it wasn't being robbed. Would he have fired fifty bullets into the building for a simple breaking and entry? Not likely.

"Which raises the logical question: Should the sheriff have known, before he began firing his bullets into the store, if a crime was being committed? He told the *Forum* reporter that he made the assumption that the store was being robbed because its lights were on. He also said he thought he saw an intruder inside. That intruder could easily have been a teenager trying to steal a carton of cigarettes. That kind of crime happens all the time and hardly anyone ever gets shot for it.

"Then there is the charge of grand theft auto. My clients told the *Forum* reporter that they in fact did steal a car from in front of a bar in Wayzata and drove it to West Fargo. Furthermore, they allowed two young ladies they had met only hours earlier to hitch a ride with them to West Fargo. Nothing suggests the two women were abducted. In fact, they left the Safeway when the police arrived and from all indications later accepted another ride from two strangers heading West. I don't think this court needs to worry about them.

"The gentleman who owns the car from Wayzata is in court here today. He is in town to claim his property and drive it home. He says his car is in fine shape and except for the near-empty fuel tank, it suffered no damage from its adventure. The owner has told court personnel that after reading the *Forum* story, he doesn't intend to press charges against the Carter brothers. He said there are days when he too would like to flee Wayzata and head to Oregon.

The court erupts in laughter. The judge's face hints at a smile as he bangs the gavel.

"Back to the Safeway. Store management said its corporate office does not intend to press charges against the Carter brothers for theft. It says its store manager should not have allowed the two women traveling with the Carter brothers to enter the store after hours to use the bathroom. Had he adhered to store policy, they wouldn't have seen him handling cash. Had they not witnessed this, and told the Carter brothers about it, there is little likelihood that the two of them would have entered the store.

"Finally, besides the broken windows and shot-out door, no damage was done to the building, no money went missing from the safe, and with the exception of the doughnuts the store manager fed the police, nothing went missing off the store shelves. Corporate says its insurance company will cover the cost of replacing the windows and door. And that might not even be necessary. The West Fargo merchants have announced they intend to host a pancake breakfast to honor the police involved with the Safeway incident. Income from that breakfast will be given the Safeway to help it put its store back together. The manager has said that the Chamber of Commerce, of which he is a member, believes the publicity of the crime-breaking prowess of the West Fargo Police Department will probably stem future crime.

"So, as we sit here today, I'm wondering if there really is a compelling reason to ask the County Court to go through the trouble and expense of hosting a trial."

The judge looks over at the state's attorney.

"Do you have anything to add before I issue my ruling?"

The state's attorney hesitated. Then he got to his feet.

"We thank the judge for his summary of the situation involving the Carter brothers and the West Fargo Safeway. We learned some facts that were unavailable to the state's attorney's office when charges were developed against the alleged thieves. Some of these new facts certainly cause us to alter our initial position. For example, we are prepared to drop all charges relating to damage done to the building and its contents. If the owner of the car involved isn't interested in pressing charges against the brothers, then the district attorney isn't going to try them for the crime. Anyone who read the *Forum* story about the alleged thieves will undoubtedly come to the same conclusion we have: the two potential and unnamed female co-conspirators, now nowhere to be found, were not kidnapped by the Carter brothers nor were they forced to do anything against their wills.

"However, the state's attorney believes there is ample evidence, as collaborated by the Carter brothers themselves in the *Forum* interview, that they did break and enter the Safeway store with the intent of stealing funds. We are prepared to move to trial on this charge."

The judge flashed the state's attorney a look of disappointment. Then he looked at the two young men before him accused of breaking and entry with malicious intent.

"In the state of North Dakota, breaking and entering frequently results in felony charges. But not always. To warrant the felony charge, the breaking and entering normally involves serious property damage or somebody getting badly hurt.

"In our situation here today, we have breaking and entry. But no serious property damage nor any harm done to another human being. So I don't believe the charge should be labeled a felony. I remind the state's attorney that the penalties for misdemeanors may include jail time, but generally for less than a year. The penalties can also include some criminal fines. But not always.

"Does the state's attorney still wish to move to trial on a misdemeanor charge of breaking and entering against William and David Carter?"

After a moment's hesitation, she said: "No, your honor. Cass County will drop all charges against the Carter brothers."

With that, the judge gaveled the proceedings to a close and ordered the Carter brothers released.

But he did give them a stern look.

"I recommend that the two of you scrape together sufficient funds to buy yourselves bus tickets back to Wayzata as soon as possible. And the next time someone tells you 'the West is best,' tell them you know better."

Then the judge tells them he thinks he can find them the money they need to get home, probably from the Legal Aid Society. They thank him for all his assistance.

Before the Carter brothers can head over to the Legal Aid Society, they're corralled by several local television reporters. Baker watches from a distance as David Carter reflects on the whole situation. "I thought we had probably made a mistake doing that interview with the *Forum* reporter, but as it turns out, that's what saved us. I guess you could say the truth was our salvation."

William Carter agrees with his brother. And adds: "You know something else? I really enjoyed reading Chuck Baker's story. That guy is one hell of a storyteller."

Chapter Twenty

Arid States Have No Easy Choices

Chuck Baker wakes up in his room at the Donaldson to the pounding on his door. It's 7:30 a.m., early for a fellow who works the night shift at the *Forum* and then has to struggle to switch from work to sleep.

When he opens the door, he sees Sam on his crutches standing in front of him.

"Hey, buddy, want to join the old guys for breakfast at the VFW? Good news for you, you're not a member, so we'll have to pay for your egg."

Baker knows Sam is kidding. He will buy Baker any breakfast he wants, as long as it's less than $2.50, which is pretty much the limit of what Sam, Mac, and Will spend on themselves.

"Sure, how soon are you leaving?"

"Let's gather in the lobby at eight a.m. That'll give you time for a shit 'n' shave."

"Okay, see you downstairs." Baker wonders what triggered the invitation to breakfast. Normally he doesn't see the veterans before lunch. Baker tends to sleep in and even though the fellows are generally early risers, they have little compulsion to socialize much before noon.

Once they assemble in the lobby they exchange their usual greetings, which is little more than, "Hey, what's up?" Mac, true to his normal pattern, says nothing, but he does nod at each of them.

Once seated at a table in the VFW, with each of them agreeing to order the same thing—two scrambled eggs with sausage mixed in, toast, and a cup of coffee—they begin quizzing Baker about stories they've read in the morning *Forum*. He has fallen into the routine of dropping off copies of the newspaper in the bathrooms on his floor, so by the time lunch rolls around, the three veterans are pretty much up on the news as of 11:30 the previous evening. But by now, after living with Baker, they realize there's always more news than the *Forum* elects to provide its readers. Eager to know the inside scoop, they depend on Baker to share what he knows with them. This morning the three of them want to know what's going to happen to the Wayzata brothers.

Baker disappoints them. He tells them he doesn't know.

"The county judge let them off scot-free. He also arranged for the two of them to get enough cash for two one-way bus tickets back to Wayzata. Unless they find themselves again in a Wayzata bar with two ladies looking for an adventure out west, I think we've seen the last of them around here."

While the three vets rehash the newspaper story, Baker glances over Mac's shoulder and notices the television in the VFW is tuned to WDAY. It's announcing a special alert. Then a newsman appears under a banner that reads: "Minard Hall

Collapses." The television has no sound, so he's not sure what the full story is.

He jumps from his chair and runs to the television to bring up some sound out of it. But he can't find a volume control. He looks back at his table for help.

Sam looks over at the server and says, "Hey, how about some sound on the television?"

The waiter looks around. The lunchroom is practically empty, so he shrugs his shoulders and says to Sam, 'Sure thing, buddy. Give me a minute."

By the time the sound comes up, the news bulletin is half over. But pictures of Minard Hall are on the screen. The pictures show Minard Hall some time ago and then the same view of the building following the collapse.

Baker isn't impressed.

"I wouldn't call that a collapse," he says to his colleagues. "The building is damaged, but it's still standing."

Sam chuckles and says Baker reminds him of a Marine Corps major he once knew in Korea. Despite how bad his troops got bloodied in a battle, he always reported that they only sustained a few bruises and were fit for duty.

"I'd say that building has one hell of a bruise and isn't going to be hosting any classes for a good while."

Baker can't tell just how much damage has been done. From what he can see on the screen, a fracture runs all the way down from the top floor into the basement. It looks to Baker as if half of the original building has slumped, breaking it apart from the other half. As a result, the two sides of the building no longer align with one another.

He still doesn't think the word "collapse" is accurate, but the more he looks at the picture on the television, the more he agrees with Sam that the building has suffered major damage.

He doesn't know if the addition suffered any damage because he can't see it in the television shots. And if the news bulletin had any information about injuries, he hasn't heard it.

"Excuse me, guys. I've got to call the *Forum*."

When Baker gets the city desk on the phone, he's told the *Forum* has reporters and photographers already onsite. His services, he's told, are not needed.

Baker goes back to the table and finishes his eggs. In between bites, he tells the veterans about the dangers of digging long, deep holes alongside large buildings sitting on top of moist, slippery clay.

When Baker gets back to his room at the Donaldson, he goes out into the hall to use the phone and calls Geology Professor Allan Nelson. Nobody answers his phone. Next he calls Dean Tallakson's office, but gets no response there either. Not even a recorded message saying the office is closed.

Then it hits Baker. Of course nobody is answering their phones: Nelson and the dean's office are both located in Minard Hall. Feeling stupid, Baker figures out the building has probably been evacuated, assuming anybody was even in the building when the damage occurred. And if they were not present for the building split, it's a sure bet they haven't been allowed in since it happened. Then Baker realizes the Minard collapse, if that's what people are going to call it, probably attracted hordes of police cars, fire trucks, and other emergency equipment. In other words, nobody is going to get close to Minard Hall for a while. He decides he best wait until tomorrow to go see it. In the meantime, he figures he can rely on the *Forum* to have stories and pictures in the afternoon paper.

Back in his room, he realizes he needs to do something to keep his mind off of Minard Hall. Then it occurs to him, he should call Wayne Gautier, the ag professor he met on the plane when he first flew into Fargo. Baker realizes he still needs a few more writing projects if he's to collect sufficient academic credit for his independent-study initiative. Perhaps Gautier can help him figure out this whole Garrison Diversion project. Will it divert adequate water into the Red River? If so, when? And what will be the consequences of such a diversion project on the rest of the state?

Gautier is not in his office, but through the help of a campus operator, is found in a temporary office in the College of Agriculture's main building. His normal office, located in the building next to Minard Hall, is closed "out of caution." Gautier says he remembers the guy on the plane heading to a job at the *Forum* and would be pleased to sit down with him to answer questions about the Red River Valley, as long as they pertain to his area of expertise. Baker laughs and asks Gautier why do professors preface their comments to the media by saying they can only talk about things they absolutely know? Gautier laughs with him.

"In science, you'll find a lot of authorities on a lot of subjects. Name a topic, and I can probably steer you to a professor who's an authority in that field. Name me a professor, and I'm equally likely to know which topics you should talk to him about. But beware of a scientist who professes to know a lot about something he hasn't written a book or a refereed article about. In my case, I can assure you anything I tell you is supported by science. I can also tell you that means a lot of questions you might ask will solicit a 'no comment' response from me."

Baker tells the professor he is happy with that arrangement. Then he tells Gautier what he wants to talk about.

"The sugar beet farmers tell me they're absolutely dependent on the Garrison Diversion for their future livelihood.

They say it's critical that Missouri River water be diverted into the Red River. Then I've heard Senator Christenson's staff explain that the Garrison Dam, which was built primarily with federal funds, has multiple purposes. It's going to prevent floods, provide recreation, and 'oh by the way' divert water to the Red River Valley. But the senator's staff doesn't know what this entails or when it will happen.

"I've also heard that the Canadians are really unhappy with the Garrison Diversion idea and are raising all kinds of hell about the prospect of the Missouri River being diverted into the Red River. For reasons I don't understand, the Canadians fear Missouri River water will somehow taint the Red River, which then flows north into Canada. What's Canada worrying about?

"Final area of inquiry: Will the reservoir behind the Garrison Dam provide a lot of benefits to North Dakota? Will the benefits outweigh the cost to the state from the loss of farmland and the possible submerging of towns and roads?"

Gautier doesn't say anything for a minute. Then he responds.

"I'll talk to you about these issues. Some of them relate to the work my colleagues and I do here at NDSU. We've already published a few papers that answer some of the questions you raise. Because they're in the public domain already, you can quote from them all you want.

"Some of your questions solicit opinions for answers and I don't have any of them to provide. For obvious reasons, I'm going to stay away from political issues related to the Garrison project. That's not to say I think you can separate political considerations from any discussion of the merits of the program. I'm just saying I intend to avoid this conversation if at all possible.

"Before we get together, let me explain some relevant information about North Dakota, its needs and aspirations, and how the Garrison Dam has been sold to address these.

"As you've learned, North Dakota is heavily dependent on agriculture as its principal source of revenue. Understandably, agriculture needs clean water to sustain its productivity. But the state is primarily semi-arid. In truth, some counties in the state are totally arid most the time.

"While North Dakota worries about having sufficient water for agriculture, it also needs water for its growing towns and cities, for industries other than agriculture, and for the wellbeing of its abundant wildlife.

"At the present time, North Dakota is one drought away from a catastrophe. We've experienced droughts before in our history and they've brought us economic calamity, social upheaval, and enormous outmigration of our population. We know we're going to continue to have droughts. We just don't know when. Then too, we know we don't have enough water now. What do we do when the drought arrives? Then the overarching question will be who gets some of the limited water and who doesn't?

"What I'm saying is any time you start a conversation about the distribution of water in this state, you're going to have an attentive audience. But most of them will oppose nearly everything you say, particularly if you offer recommendations. That's because recommendations will have to suggest who wins and who loses in the state's ongoing battle for scarce water.

"Having said all that, when would you like to get together?"

Two weeks later, the two meet in a conference room Gautier reserved in the student union. He explains that he would prefer meeting in his office, but it's a secure facility and it would be a hassle to get Baker in.

"I took your advice," Baker begins the interview, "and have read all the material you sent me. Thanks for that. The information helped me better understand the complexities of what I'm after for my story. I'm almost thinking I'm going to need to sell my editor on a series of stories because I don't know how I can cover everything in one article."

"I was wondering about that," agrees Gautier. "Length could be a challenge for you. Besides, I'm not sure the *Forum* has that many readers interested in your topic. As I said to you in our earlier conversation, it's been my experience that everyone in this state but the dumb and blind know we have droughts and water shortages. Nothing newsworthy in that bit of information. Seems to me you have to write a story that presents the tough choices residents across the state will have to make as the water dries up and the demands for it expand.

"The simple, indisputable fact is water shortages are going to eliminate jobs, reduce agricultural production, and force the state to prioritize who receives the available water. The major choices will be these: agriculture, cities, rural towns, manufacturing, and energy industries, in no particular order.

"The list can always be subdivided. It's not just agriculture. It's the kind of farming. Should wheat farmers have priority for water over sugar beet farmers? Should farmers on semi-arid land be given priority over farmers trying to grow crops on arid land? Should cattle feeding operations be given scarce water while animals raised on small farms go thirsty? Should our distribution of water to energy companies favor oil exploration over strip mining lignite coal?

"Stop, stop. You're writing my story for me. Let's see if I can't organize this just for the sake of discussion.

"First, it seems to me, I have to lay out the problem. I'm saying it's the shortage of water. Okay, that suggests I describe where the water comes from now. The bulk of it comes from our rivers—particularly the Missouri—and lesser rivers such as the Red. It also comes from the sky as rain or snow.

"A problem for North Dakota is the simple fact it doesn't receive enough rain or winter melt off. The state averages about twenty inches of moisture per year. That's not much. But the state average hides an ugly truth: Most counties in the state receive less than the average. For example, in the years between 1889 and 1962, the Western one-third of the state suffered fifty-five years with less than seventeen inches of moisture. The central one-third went thirty-eight years. Meanwhile, the Eastern one-third of the state suffered through only twelve years with less than seventeen inches of rain.

"Prior to the great drought of 1886, thousands of people had come into Dakota Territory to homestead or purchase land for ranching. But then in 1886 the wheat crops ran about one-third less than expected. When the drought persisted for an additional four years, homesteaders fled Western and Central North Dakota. Overall, with the exception of recently added energy workers, the state's population has gone down steadily from its peak in the 20's. Whole counties have been redefined as "frontier" because they contain fewer than six people per square mile.

"Okay, fewer people mean fewer baths, showers, and toilet flushes. That might help preserve the water supply a little. But at the same time homesteaders were leaving, the state's towns and cities were growing. Today one-third of the state's entire population lives in Cass County in the heart of the Red River Valley. North and South of Fargo are two other cities with rapidly growing populations: Grand Forks and Wahpeton. All three of these cities depend on the Red River for their water needs. Yet the Red River is also the source of water for a lot of agricultural interests, particularly wheat and sugar beets.

"Statewide, cities continue to grow as the small towns around them shrink to irrelevance. The municipal water demands grow along with the population. Then too, the cities are host to new businesses and expanding companies, all of which have a need for fresh water.

"Add in the continued demand from the agricultural interests, every cup of water that becomes available is being claimed by someone," Baker summarizes.

Gautier thinks for a minute about what Baker has said. Then he offers an opinion.

"Without question, North Dakota, an agricultural state living with the constant threat of a deadly drought, can mount an argument for the Garrison Diversion. But it's a tough sell. How does North Dakota justify the cost to the federal taxpayers? Then too, how does anyone justify the project to the entire state of North Dakota when Garrison Diversion will benefit only a few counties in the state?

"Take the case of the farmers in Eastern North Dakota. They want more water than the Red River can supply. But to get that water, they want to tap the reservoir (Lake Sakakawea) building up behind the Garrison Dam. There's no natural way that reservoir is ever going to spill water into the Red River. So that's why agricultural interests in eastern North Dakota—particular the sugar beet farmers—want something called the McLusky Canal to be built. And it looks as if Congress is going to appropriate funds this year to start building it. Our senior senator, Tom Christensen, was a prime sponsor and arm twister to get that money approved on the Senate side.

"When funded, water from the Missouri River, now stored behind the Garrison Dam, will flow East through the big ditch. And I mean big—fifty feet wide and twenty-five feet deep. Its proponents claim that once the first seventy-four miles of the McLusky Canal are dug, it will be able to carry nearly two thousand cubic feet of water per second, enough to irrigate two hundred fifty thousand acres. And its fan club says that plenty of water should be left over for municipal and rural water systems.

"But here's the rub," the professor says to his young writing companion. "As of this year, Congress intends to only appropriate enough funds to build that first seventy-four miles of the McClusky Canal. Continued federal funding will be required to finish the Canal so that Missouri River water can be moved hundreds of miles to the eastern half of the state. If it's ever finished, the Canal will run through miles of semi-arid farmland and small towns, but not a single spoonful of water will be distributed along the way. That's right: the benefit of the Canal primarily accrues to farmers in the Red River Valley that already receive more natural moister than the farms the Canal is going to cross over. How does that make sense to anyone other than Red River Valley interests?"

"The thing I've always found fascinating is the ability of politicians, special-interest groups, and federal bureaucrats with their hands on the water-development levers, to argue for a massive irrigation project in North Dakota. Basically, the only argument for it is that the irrigation project will augment local water supplies during extreme droughts.

"To some extent, that's true. But a more honest explanation is that the sugar beet farmers, along with Red River Valley cities and commercial interests, have just about drained the Red River dry . . . and that's even before a drought occurs.

"What studies I've read of the Garrison Diversion tell me is that perhaps as many as twelve hundred farmers will have plenty of water to irrigate their land when all is said and done," says Gautier. "They might never have to worry about another devastating drought. But that means less than one percent of the farmland in North Dakota will benefit from this expensive irrigation project. The other ninety-nine percent of the farmland could easily be just as dry as they were in the thirties."

Baker jumps back into the discussion.

"What I hear you saying is that the Garrison Diversion project could well be a bonanza for farmers in the Red River Valley. With guaranteed irrigation every year, their lands will become even more valuable, yet they'll have paid just a token of the actual cost of getting that water. Meanwhile, the irrigation costs will be paid by others who will see no benefit from the largest federal project in the state's history."

Gautier says it's time the two of them shift over to other winners and losers in the Garrison Division sweepstake.

"I don't think we have to dedicate a whole chapter to the sorry plight of the North Dakota Indians, for the simple reason most North Dakotans have never seemed all that concerned about them. But every once in a while, the good citizens of the state should take stock of what the Garrison Diversion does to Native Americans.

"The construction of dams and reservoirs along the Missouri River was sold to Congress as a way to prevent floods, improve navigation, produce electricity, build recreation facilities, and above all, irrigate the land. All true. But nothing was ever said about the price paid by the Indians who reside in North Dakota.

"The Garrison Dam might well be doing more damage to Indian land than any other public works project in American history. And yet the Indians derive little benefit from it."

Baker agrees, saying he had read recently that the Garrison Dam probably reduced the total land base of North Dakota's five Sioux reservations by five percent or better and forced about one-third of their residents to relocate. Then too, the water building up behind the dams of the Missouri tends to flood the best land on the reservations, those acres that lie near the river bed. Consequently, when they relocate, the Indians are forced to the more barren regions of the reservations."

Gautier agrees. "Relocating takes the Indians away from the trees they use for shelter, shade, and fuel. It also removes their game and other natural food sources. Overall, I think it's safe to say the Garrison Diversion touches every aspect of Indian life, and all it negative."

Baker asks Gautier, "What about the Canadians? Didn't I read somewhere that they've expressed concern about the Garrison Diversion?"

"That's an interesting problem," Gautier responds. I think they fear Missouri River water is going to flow into their Hudson Bay drainage. I'm no expert on the topic of water, but I have a colleague who is and he has written that Canada fears that Missouri River fish species and other biological materials threaten the integrity of Canadian waters. They're worried about how this will affect their fishing industry. And they remind us that we signed a treaty in 1909 promising that any water flowing across the U.S.-Canadian border would not be polluted by either side."

Baker adds: "Wait until the Canadians learn that we ultimately want to extend the McClusky Canal further east through a buried pipeline and dump the water into the Sheyenne

River. That river is one of the largest tributaries to the Red River. It intersects with the Red near Fargo and together they move their mixed water north into Canada."

Both men pause for a breath of fresh air. But they're excited that their writing project has substance.

Baker says he has another subject that he thinks is germane to the conversation.

"We haven't talked yet about the tremendous water demands of the oil, gas, and coal interests. And in that vein, we ought to talk about the threat of hydraulic fracturing to the state's water supply."

Gautier agrees. "We normally don't think of water when discussing the impact of oil and gas extraction. That's understandable; a lot of the water used is invisible to the public eye. Water is used to cool drilling bits, remove mud and other debris from the equipment, and to push the oil or gas to the surface. When the latter operation is done, the wastewater—or 'produced water', as the industry prefers to call it—is no longer fresh water. It's salty and often contains oil residues, drilling fluids, and natural contaminants from the rocks themselves. The amount of wastewater produced by a well can be as much as a hundred barrels of water per barrel of oil. You heard me correctly: For every barrel of oil taken from the ground, the drilling process can generate one hundred barrels of wastewater.

"The industry says this wastewater can be re-used. But that scarcely ever happens because it's expensive to clean. Much of it is simply disposed of. In some cases, the wastewater is stored in surface pits so that it can partially evaporate. In the meanwhile, the air around the pits becomes unbreathable and they tend to leak. In other cases, the wastewater is hauled away by truck and dumped somewhere else, in some cases deep underground. But this risks contaminating the ground water.

"Then you have hydraulic fracturing, a process that's not very widespread yet, but that someday may be, if they make it more cost-effective. This is a process where you force water-based fluids under high pressure underground to "fracture" rock formations and push the oil or gas into a wellbore where it can be brought up to the surface. There the oil or gas is separated for export and processing at a refinery. This process uses an inordinate amount of water, both in the fracking stage and during the process of separating it from the oil or gas."

Baker just shakes his head. Then he says it's apparent they have the material to write an interesting book.

"Let's see if I can produce an abstract for a book and get it approved by my mentors, the dean of the College of Arts and Sciences and my lead professor. Once I have it done, we can see if it will trigger the interest of a publisher. I'm thinking our best bet would be a university-based journal or some small publisher that likes to concentrate on important issues that don't get the visibility they deserve.

"I'll run those by Dean Tallakson and see what he thinks. Then I'll get back to you. In the meantime, I've enjoyed the discussion and I look forward to getting words on paper."

"My experience suggests talking is a lot easier than writing. So now the hard work begins," says Gautier.

As it turns out, both Professor Pease and Dean Tallakson think the proposed writing project is worth pursuing. Pease said, "Okay. We can support this writing assignment as an Independent Study project. Get it done and I'll argue that it ought to receive sufficient course credit to complete your degree. And I for one will be interested to see how an undergraduate and a full professor work together doing a book.

If you're successful, perhaps you ought to team up with me to finish my doctoral dissertation." And then he laughed, although Baker figured he might be halfway serious about his suggestion.

Dean Tallakson simply said he thought the monograph would be sure to provoke comment by small-town newspapers and radio talk shows. Then he encouraged Baker to start writing.

* * *

```
ND Water Shortage to Force State
to Make Tough Choices
```
Abstract

```
North Dakota, located on the Canadian border
between Montana and Minnesota, suffers from
a water shortage.  This shortage is forcing
competing interests to fight for what they
perceive to be their fair share of the
limited fresh water.

Two significant factors drive the debate
over who's entitled to water.  One, the
state annually averages only 20 inches of
moisture.  Two, North Dakota has a history
of suffering badly from multiple-year
droughts.

 But the water shortage varies greatly
across the state.  That is, between the
years 1889 and 1962, the western one-third
of the state had 55 years with less than 17
inches of rain; the central one-third had 38
years; and the eastern one-third had only 12
years.

North Dakota ranks 44th among the states in
population.  But its small population isn't
spread evenly across the state.  The
```

counties with the least rain are the least populated.

The eastern one-third of the state contains North Dakota's largest cities: Fargo and Grand Forks. Both cities are in the Red River Valley, which was carved out of prehistoric glacial lake Agassiz. The valley contains some of the country's most productive farmland. The towns and cities in the valley depend on the Red River for water. But so do the valley's fields of wheat, soybeans, and sugar beets. Some years the Red River nearly runs dry and in many more years it's little more than a meandering stream. Yet the demands on it continue to grow as business and industry expand, attracting continued growth in the two cities and their surrounding suburbs.

For years North Dakota residents believed that the Garrison Dam, the world's fifth largest of its kind, would back up the Missouri River into a huge reservoir that would be their future source of water. The dam, built roughly in the center of the state, was sold to Congress as an effective way to ensure flood control, provide irrigation and hydroelectric power, increase river navigation, and offer recreation. But it was sold to North Dakota taxpayers as a way for them to receive more water for irrigating farm fields.

When construction on the dam finished in 1953, the federal government outlined a 60-year plan to move hundreds of thousands of acre-feet of water through a network of channels, including 3,000 miles of canals, pipes, and drains, plus regulating reservoirs and pumping stations, to provide irrigation to 250,000 acres of North Dakota farmland.

But the plans were scaled back when the Bureau of the Budget in 1960 said the Garrison Project would only provide $.76 in benefits for every dollar invested in it. Then too, the Garrison Reservoir floods 350,000 acres of productive land and only promises to irrigate 250,000. And even this amount of irrigation will only reach six-tenths of one percent of the state's farmlands, leaving the other 99.4 percent just as dry as they had been before the project.

This reality check generated considerable discussion within the state and the U.S. Congress about the possibility the country made a mistake when it encouraged settlers to move into North Dakota at the turn of the century. The state simply doesn't have the water resources necessary to support all its desired activities.

Some scholars argue it may be time to close down large segments of the state and allow the land to revert back to a native prairie. This arid prairie could then become a national park and host buffalo and other native species.

Meanwhile, another heavy user of fresh water has come into the state. Oil and gas interests have been increasing their presence. And North Dakota has welcomed them because of their supposed contributions to the local economy. But only recently have residents become aware of the high-water use associated with the oil and gas industry. The industry uses water pulled from groundwater, rivers, and lakes to drill their wells and pump their product out of the ground. After the industry uses up its existing wells, it pushes fresh water into them to flush out any remaining oil or gas.

This fresh water emerges from the ground dirty (salty and containing fluids and oil residues). While it can be cleaned, it seldom is because of the cost to the industry. Besides, cleaning water requires more clean water.

The amount of dirty water produced by a well can vary from almost none to over 100 barrels per barrel of oil extracted. An average well produces 10 barrels of dirty water for every one barrel of oil it generates.

The industry also is beginning to introduce hydraulic fracturing, or "fracking," into its drilling and extraction mix. Fracking requires enormous amounts of water to be mixed with chemicals and sand to create fractures in the rock and then hold them open to allow the gas or oil to flow into a well where it can be pumped to the surface.

In other words, the oil and gas industry is increasingly using scarce clean water for its purposes. But it's not the only industry in the state to do that.

As one example, sugar beet farmers in the Red River Valley have been using their influence to get water from the Garrison Reservoir pumped through a canal that will end up diverting Missouri River water into the Sheyenne River and from there into the Red River. The sugar beet growers want to ensure a constant flow of water for its irrigation needs. But the river goes on to flush into Canada, creating a diplomatic issue. Although not completed yet, the diversion has caused the Canadian government to accuse the United States of potentially violating an international treaty that says

> neither country will pollute the water of the other.
>
> The book closes with a discussion of the options facing the state and the expected consequences of adopting any or all of them.
>
> *Submitted by Professor Wayne Gautier, chair, Agricultural & Biosystems Department, North Dakota State University; assisted by Charles Baker, staff writer, the* Forum, *Fargo N.D.*

*   *   *

When Baker met with Gautier to share the first draft of the abstract, he explained why he made the professor the lead author and himself the "assistant."

"I figure of the two of us, you're the only one qualified to write such a book. Making us co-authors will simply raise questions about its legitimacy. Identifying myself as the person who assisted in the writing is self-explanatory when the reader sees my occupation. In other words, we combined brains with writing skills. I'm betting the publisher will wonder why more bright scholars don't do that."

Gautier laughs, but says if Baker is okay with the arrangement, so is he. And then he asks Baker to leave the draft abstract with him.

"I'll go through it, make changes I think are necessary, and ship it off to a couple of organizations and institutions that publish such works. Do you want to see my changes before I mail it off?"

Baker smiles and says, "No, I think as the primary author, you should have the right to mail in what you consider to be your best work."

*   *   *

Baker hasn't seen Molly, the gorgeous-but-untouchable copy girl, in the newsroom for a while. She has been ignoring him for the past month or so, but his copy paper drawer is always full and a new glue pot appears on his desk regularly. So he knows she's still working at the *Forum*. Then as he thinks about it, he has noticed that she seems to be spending a lot of her time hanging around the Associated Press office. She doesn't provide the two full-time AP writers with either copy paper or paste, so he isn't sure what attracts her to them. He figures he will have to ask her the next time she comes by.

Later that afternoon one of the writers from the women's section stops by and asks him to come over to her part of the editorial room when he has a minute. About ten minutes later he's at her desk. She gets up from her chair and pulls him into the newspaper's "library" for a private conversation.

Baker wishes he knew her name, but thinks it might be inconsiderate to ask her when it's obvious she knows his.

The women's page reporter asks Baker how well he knows Molly, the copy girl. Baker says he doesn't really know her, except to stay away from her. He said he knows she is the publisher's granddaughter and that she is a rampant flirt around the office.

The reporter frowns. "I agree, she is a flirt. And I'm afraid it may have gotten her in trouble."

"What do you mean?" quizzes Baker.

"Well, she told me she thought one of the AP fellows was particularly cute and friendly. Later she told me she had been seeing him after hours, generally for coffee or an early dinner. But last week she said she no longer wanted anything to do with him. In fact, she said she hated him.

"And then she said something really strange. She said she hated him "for what he did to me." But she didn't explain what that was. That's why I'm coming to you. She said the two of you were friends and I was wondering what you know about her relationship to Mike Nesvold, the AP guy."

Baker says he doesn't know Molly well enough to have that kind of conversation with her. And he adds that he hasn't ever noticed her spending time with Nesvold.

"If they are seeing each other, they do a good job of disguising it," he says.

She responds: "I worry about her. She hasn't been at work for nearly five days and nobody knows why. I've been tempted to go upstairs and ask her grandfather if he knows anything. But I don't have the courage."

Baker tells her not to worry. He tells her he'll see what he can find out and will get back to her.

Later that afternoon, after the AP staff had filed the radio copy for the 6 p.m., news broadcasts, he wonders into the room. Nesvold is sitting at his desk smoking a cigarette and reading AP copy. Baker asks if he has a minute to answer a question.

Nesvold looks irritated at having to do anything for a *Forum* staff writer, but he says, "Sure, what's up?"

Baker tells him he has heard a rumor that he and Molly the copy girl might be an item.

Then he asks his question: "Now she's no longer coming to work. Do you know anything about why that is?"

"What the fuck are you insinuating? Who the hell are you to come into my office and ask such a question? Get the fuck out of here before I throw you out."

Baker turns to leave, but before he does, he says: "Molly has a lot of friends in the editorial office. I hope for your sake she's okay."

Nesvold yells, "Get the fuck out of here."

He says it loud enough so that when Baker returns to his desk a lot of *Forum* staff look over into his corner of the building to see what the commotion is all about. He gets a particularly dirty look from Swenson, the managing editor.

When he sits down, Rector asks him what that exchange was all about.

"Oh nothing, I guess. I asked Nesvold a personal question and he made it clear he didn't want to answer it. I won't ask it again."

And with that, the nightly flow of copy continued.

The next day when he comes to work he immediately notices a difference in the mood of the editorial staff. Nobody is laughing, talking loudly on the phone, or even typing at their normal pace. Something obviously has happened and it isn't good news.

Before Baker even gets to his desk, managing editor Swenson calls him over to his desk.

In an unfriendly voice, he demands to know what had occurred between him and Mike Nesvold the day before.

Baker stumbles over his answer. He tells him it is a personal issue and prefers not to say anything more about it.

"I don't care if it was personal. Either tell me about it or you and I are going to part ways."

Baker recoils from the hostility. He knows he is in trouble; he just can't figure out why.

"You do know that Nesvold killed himself last night, right?"

"What, killed himself? What are you saying? No, I didn't know that."

"Last night, after he left here at around eight p.m., he got into his car and drove at top speed into a bridge support on the

Interstate. The police said there were no skid marks and the car's speedometer froze at ninety-seven miles per hour. In other words, his car was traveling at a high rate of speed when it ran into the concrete column. Furthermore, Nesvold was heading toward Moorhead, although he lives in West Fargo."

Baker sat at Swenson's desk, stunned. He felt nauseous. Could he have been the last person to talk to Nesvold? Was he upset about what I asked him? Baker answered his own question. Yeah, he was upset. But enough to go out and run his car into a bridge abutment? That seemed a little far-fetched.

Swenson then asks the question that's haunted him all afternoon: "What did the two of you talk about?"

Baker realizes he has no reason to keep the conversation secret now that Nesvold is gone.

"I realized that Molly, the copy girl, hadn't been around lately. I knew she had been spending time in the AP office with Nesvold. So I went in there yesterday and asked him if he knew why she hasn't been at work. He exploded and swore at me. He never answered the question and I left it at that."

"That's all you said to him?"

"I think I said something to the effect that Molly has a lot of friends at the *Forum*. And we all are hoping she's okay."

Swenson sits back in his chair and sighs loudly. He picks up his phone and makes an inside call. He asks if he can drop by for a moment. Then he hangs up.

When he gets to his feet, he orders Baker to follow him upstairs to the publisher's office.

Baker isn't enthusiastic about an encounter with the publisher. He has never met the man and has no desire to do so now. But this is a command performance and so he follows Swenson into Tom Tyeman's office. As he is being introduced—without benefit of a handshake—he tries to remember what he has heard about Tyeman. Married the previous publisher's daughter and took over the newspaper upon his father-in-law's death. No journalism experience of any kind. *Typical publisher*, Baker thinks to himself.

Swenson carries the conversation. He tells the publisher what Baker said to him just minutes earlier. Baker notices the publisher's interest peaks when Molly is mentioned.

Tyeman then turns to Baker. "What are you trying to say? Do you think my granddaughter was having an affair with the head of the AP Office?"

Baker shakes his head. "No, I have no idea about the nature of their relationship. Before yesterday, I didn't even know they were friends."

Then everyone sat in silence. Finally, Tyeman says, "You might as well know. Molly is pregnant. I think about three months along. Her mother decided to send her to Arizona to live with one of her aunts. She can have the baby and I guess we'll have to decide at some point what to do about it.

"We've been racking our brains trying to figure out who the father might be. She didn't date, at least that we were aware of. And I didn't think she had established close relationships with any of our male staff members. It never occurred to me to consider Nesvold might be the father.

"My wife told me this morning that Molly had called her from Arizona last night all upset. Apparently, she had been talking to someone she called "a close personal friend." Best my wife could figure, this person had upset Molly during their conversation. I wonder now if that person was Nesvold. And I wonder what he said to upset her."

Swenson says the obvious. "And maybe Molly said something that upset Nesvold too. I mean, Nesvold was married and had two kids. I'm sure he wasn't providing any support—emotional or financial—to Molly. And we have no idea what she wanted of him at this point."

Tyeman says, "We know all we're going to learn, I guess." And then he stands up, signaling our departure.

Baker can't help himself. Later he would explain to himself it's the nature of being a reporter.

"I could ask around to see if anyone knew about the relationship between the two. Nesvold was close to the other AP staff. I would guess they might know something about Nesvold's relationship with Molly. And I would be curious to know if Nesvold left a note for anyone. Maybe his bosses in Minneapolis. I could also call Nesvold's wife and ask..."

"You will do no such thing, goddamn it," Tyeman cut Baker off. "Swenson, is this the caliber of staff you're hiring these days? Muckrakers and yellow journalists? I don't want any stories about my Mollie and Nesvold in my newspaper. And I don't want a word about our conversation here to be repeated to anyone. Am I understood?"

Swenson and Baker nod their heads and turn to leave.

Once in the corridor, Swenson says to Baker: "I knew I was going to rue the day I hired you. And now you've pissed off the publisher. Jesus. Do you suppose we can make it through the rest of the week without you tipping over another applecart?"

Baker responds with a proper, "Yes, sir." But in his heart, he has some doubts.

Chapter Twenty-One

Water Story Sinks Reporter

Baker thinks the *Forum* story of Mike Nesvold's death is a complete whitewash. The word "suicide" doesn't appear. Nor does any mention of an entanglement with the copy girl. The fact his car made no skid marks on the pavement before hitting the bridge abutment isn't mentioned, either.

When Baker checks out the byline, he sees the article was written by Steve Becker. Not surprising. He'd been an AP wannabe for as long as Baker has worked at the *Forum*. Baker assumes he already has his resume ready to submit to the AP when it gets around to filling Nesvold's spot.

What really bothers Baker, though, is the fact Becker also wrote Nesvold's obituary. The obit featured a handsome picture of Nesvold with his family. It also said that he had been on his way to Moorhead on an AP assignment when the accident happened. Complete hogwash. Becker was just making sure that the word reached mother AP that her Fargo correspondent was on a work assignment at the time of his death, thus ensuring a company-sponsored death benefit would go to his wife. The obituary also included positive comments from fellow AP correspondents about Nesvold's work ethic, character, and integrity.

Nesvold was to be buried in his family's plot in suburban Minneapolis. Baker only recognizes one name on the list of pallbearers, Nesvold's fellow AP correspondent from Fargo. But the obituary also has a list of honorary pallbearers, and they include the *Forum* managing editor, editor, and publisher. Baker guesses it's true that a tragic death has a way of zeroing out the deceased's previous sins.

Baker wonders how Molly is taking the death of the father of her unborn child. He would like to ask her. But he realizes that will never happen.

Baker disobeys the publisher's order not to discuss the Nesvold-Molly situation with anyone. He tells the veterans from the Hotel Donaldson all about it. He knew they would enjoy the tale, particularly after he had them read both the *Forum* story and the follow-up obituary. That whets their appetite for Baker's "story behind the story." And he doesn't disappoint. The three of them go back and forth about who's more to blame, Nesvold or Molly; what should Molly do with her baby; and should the *Forum* have allowed Nesvold to sail off into the sunset without any criticism of his behavior? Their answers didn't agree, but it was obvious they enjoyed the conversation.

*   *   *

A couple of weeks later, Professor Wayne Gautier calls with some good news. A publisher of a small, scholarly book company in California has committed to publishing the book based on Baker's abstract. Now Baker knows how he's going to spend his mornings and early afternoons: writing the book. Gautier comes through with a university workspace complete with a first-rate typewriter and a research assistant who, if asked nicely, will fetch him an occasional cup of coffee. The writing goes smoothly as does the interaction with Gautier. The lead author does a great job of presenting the facts and leaves it to Baker to edit and rewrite as necessary.

The two work together on a book title, but agree they're not all that pleased with the outcome:

```
            Water Shortage:
          Not Enough for Those
      Without Powerful Connections
```

The book writing takes four months, and the publisher requires another four to get it into print. Apparently, the publisher had no luck coming up with a snappy title, because it went with the one the authors suggested.

Baker was given all the credits he needed to graduate once the book was accepted for publication. And with the registrar's help, the university agreed that he had sufficient credits and a just-adequate grade point average to graduate at the end of the academic year.

He decides not to participate in a graduation ceremony. He doesn't want to rent a graduation gown or sit for a portrait. Dean Tallakson intervenes on his behalf and has his diploma delivered to the dean's temporary office, far away from Minard Hall, in Old Main, the oldest building on campus. When the dean's secretary called to tell him to come by and pick it up, she prescribed the day and a particular hour of the morning. She said the dean wanted to congratulate him personally for getting through college. When Baker arrived at the dean's office, he's pleased to see his advisor, Verne Pease, and his co-author, Wayne Gautier, sitting around the dean's conference table. In the middle of the table sat a bottle of champagne in an ice bucket. The four men spent the better part of an hour congratulating Baker on receiving his diploma and congratulating themselves for having the insight to identify Baker as a quality student—as long as he didn't take math or science courses.

Baker thanked each of them personally for their assistance and particularly their friendship. Handshakes were warmly received around the table and if a second bottle of champagne had been consumed, hugs would undoubtedly have been exchanged, too.

When the book is finally published, the four gather again. This time Gautier brought the champagne. The two authors autograph their companion's books and try to write something meaningful to each of them. They were not sure how successful they had been at the task, but the recipients seemed pleased.

Gautier says the publisher has already arranged for him to attend book-signing events at bookstores across North Dakota, and adds that the publisher told him they would like Baker to join him for book signings in the Red River Valley, because of the proximity of both NDSU and the *Forum*. Baker says he will attend as many as possible.

Everybody around the table laughs. "What else have you got to do? You don't have any more classes to take and you only work nights!" exclaims Pease. "That leaves you a lot of daylight for book signings."

Baker admits Pease has a point. And he assures Gautier he will accompany him to as many book signing events as possible. "Just remember, you're the one who has to answer the questions."

* * *

A week later Gautier calls and says he was just interviewed by Bruce Strand, a sociology professor from Concordia College who writes book reviews for the *Forum*.

"I think the interview went well, but we'll have to see. He seemed to have a pretty good grasp of the points we're trying to make. He seemed particularly interested in the section where you discussed the sugar beet farmers and their efforts to influence policy. I guess it hadn't occurred to him that they're trying to divert Garrison River water into the Red River to ensure the viability of sugar beet growers."

Baker doesn't know the book reviewer personally, although he has edited many of his reviews after he drops them off on Friday afternoon for Sunday's paper. Baker agrees with Gautier that they ought to expect a positive review.

When he's at work that next Friday night, he's handed the review to edit. But when he sees it's about his book, he passes it over to Harry Morrison and asks him if he would do the honors.

After a light edit, Morrison tosses the review back to Baker. Then the state editor says: "You sure have a way of pissing off important people. Wait until this review hits the street. It might help you sell your book, but it sure in the hell isn't going to make either you or the professor very popular. I wouldn't be surprised to see the *Forum* write a negative editorial about your book."

"Why do you say that?" asks Baker.

"Because you guys gore all the sacred cows in this part of the state. Everybody knows the various interests compete for the limited water. But I've never heard anyone say someone is going to have to back away from the trough to allow someone else to fill up on the available water."

Baker says he thinks that's a little strong, and says he'll read the review for himself.

Trying hard to be nonjudgmental, Baker immediately realizes that the reviewer did the publisher a favor by saying this is a book every citizen in North Dakota ought to read. But then he added: "Read it, for sure; but like it? I doubt it. And that's because few readers will agree with the arguments the author advances.

"The author maintains that within North Dakota, competing special interests are all trying to corner the market on available clean water. Nothing particularly newsworthy about that assertion. But the author goes on to say that this struggle will rip the state apart because the water shortage is so severe that those competing for it will break laws, buy politicians' votes, and discredit their competitors.

"Few readers are going to buy that argument. Yes, there's a water shortage. And without question, the farmers want their share for agriculture and the cities and towns want enough to maintain a certain level of service to their constituents. Business and industry can make a strong case for their share, and nearly everyone will agree that the state has to provide water for the oil and gas industry so it can drill and pump energy resources for the nation. But most North Dakota citizens won't agree that the thirst for available water will drive anyone to play rough with their competitors or deny any of them a fair share.

"North Dakota residents pride themselves on their "can-do" spirit, on their willingness to compromise for the greater good, and for their ability to get along with their neighbors. None of this sentiment comes across in the book. All the author can see is crisis, gridlock, and then probably the need for the federal government to step in and decide who gets water and who doesn't. This isn't an outcome anyone in the state is likely to invite or tolerate."

But at this point, the reviewer changes his tune. He says the author makes a good point about the sugar beet growers in the Red River Valley.

"First, they're growing a product nobody really needs; there's no shortage of sugar in the United States or around the world. Second, if it wasn't for federal subsidies to grow the unmarketable crop, and the federal government's willingness to purchase the surplus sugar generated by the sugar beets, its growers couldn't stay in business. Third, if any argument can be made for one special interest to relinquish its hold on fresh water, it's the Red River Valley sugar beet growers. But as the author points out, the growers are pulling out all stops to get even more water. They want the federal and state governments to finance the tremendous cost of diverting Missouri River water into the Red River so that irrigation for the sugar beets can continue even through a drought.

"If anything can unite the groups seeking the scarce water, it's the argument that everybody would have more if the state and federal governments quit subsiding the sugar beet growers. At a minimum, every politician outside of the Red River Valley should unite in opposition to the sugar beet industry's efforts to divert Missouri River water to the Red River to irrigate their crops."

Wow, thinks Baker. That's strong, even stronger than the book itself. But it's probably correct: the sugar beet farmers have no legitimate argument for taking a larger share of the state's limited water supply. And they might have a difficult time even defending what they now suck out of the Red River.

Baker calls Gautier to read him the review. The principal author agrees with Baker that the review is fair, even if it isn't in complete agreement with the argument the book makes.

Gautier also reminds Baker that they shouldn't expect a lot of readers to agree with their point of view. After all, says Gautier, "We wrote the book because it's obvious to us nobody in this state is coming to grips with the hard realities they face when it comes to the water shortage. Our book's designed to promote a wider, more extensive discussion about the limited water supply while also identifying those special interests that keep going after more of the precious resource.

"Let's face it. We're up against the "Dakota Nice" point of view. This is the simple notion that churchgoing Christians with strong family ties to the state can work out their differences. It's part of the belief structure that says frontier residents have always had it tough, and yet they persevere. So what's a little water shortage? We can work it out among ourselves."

"Good luck with that," responds Baker. "It's that 'Dakota Nice' point of view that has allowed this crisis to drag on without resolution. Being nice doesn't work when the fight is over scarce water, the most basic lifeblood of the Ag economy. The state has a water shortage today and the problem is only going to get worse tomorrow as the demand for it increases."

They end their conversation agreeing that the *Forum's* book review ought to generate good questions for their scheduled book-signing events.

The review appears in the Sunday *Forum*. The very next day, the Valley's sugar beet farmers call an emergency meeting of their cooperative for later in the week. The officers, led by Andy Bacevich, agree that the cooperative needs to get out in front of this challenge to their water rights.

Bacevich's wife Sue weighs in with a suggestion. "Why don't you invite Chuck Baker to this meeting?"

"Why in the hell would we want him there? He obviously wants to throw us to the wolves. Besides, he's done all the harm he can do. The *Forum* management is still with us, I assume, because what's good for sugar beet growers is good for the Red River Valley and their subscribers. In fact, I'm pretty sure we can get the *Forum* to publish an editorial that disowns the book and perhaps even condemns its staff writer's involvement with it.

"No, our bigger problem is that goddamn professor. Our folks checked in with their friends at the university and learned this Gautier guy is well-liked, respected, and considered a first-rate scholar. He's the one that's going to continue to cause us heartburn as he parades around the state giving speeches and signing his book. I frankly don't know what to do about him."

Sue Bacevich thinks about what her husband just said. Then she tells him she agrees with him. Gautier is the challenge; Baker can't do any more harm.

Then she adds, "But I sure wouldn't mind seeing him cut down to size. He's playing in the big leagues with that book and we need to remind him he's just a small-town newspaperman begging for an occasional byline."

Her comment gets Bacevich thinking.

"When you talked to him last time, didn't he say that one of the advantages of going to school while he works is that he avoids being drafted? Hasn't he graduated by now? Shouldn't he be in uniform defending our country? I'm going to ask the fellows at our meeting if any of them are in tight with a member of the Cass County Draft Board. Maybe they need to know about this draft dodger in our midst who hates North Dakota farmers."

She responds by saying she's going to give Baker a call and invite him to lunch. She says she'll find out if he has graduated and what he plans to do about the draft. She tells her husband that information might just turn out to be helpful to them.

Bacevich agrees and tells his wife Baker and the professor have accomplished one thing.

"The fellows and I have already decided that we're going to ask Fargo to quit advertising itself as "Sugar City.""

"Wait a minute, wasn't it your idea to have Fargo tagged "Sugar City?""

"It was. I still think it has a nice ring to it. But that damn book has made a mockery of everything to do with sugar beets. And I don't want to spend any time explaining the virtues of calling Fargo "Sugar City." For all I care, it can call itself "Water Shortage City.""

That afternoon, Sue Bacevich reaches Baker on his phone at the *Forum*. He sounds a little apprehensive when he realizes who he's talking to, but relaxes when he realizes she's not calling to complain about his book. She tells him she's worried they're losing touch with one another and believes they owe themselves a lunch out, her treat, of course.

"The last time I talked to you I believe you said something about a book project. Did you ever get that done? Really? Well, please bring a copy with you to lunch. I want you to sign it and tell me what it's all about. The title sounds controversial, which I guess is the approach publishers take if they want to sell books.

"Why don't we meet at the Graver Hotel lunchroom Thursday at noon. I'll call and leave a reservation in my name. I'm looking forward to seeing you again."

When she hangs up, she turns to her husband. "I have him wrapped around my little finger."

After a brief pause, she smiles and adds, "I wish I could say that about my dealings with you."

The luncheon goes just as she planned. As he gives her his book, he signs it with a friendly, if less than affectionate, greeting, and tells her the book is a gift.

She then asks him about his studies at NDSU and he tells her he has just graduated. He's thinking about a new book project, but he intends to remain at his job at the *Forum*.

Then she asks about his draft status.

"Aren't you reclassified once you graduate from college? I would think the draft board would want to get its hooks into you now that you've lost your student deferment."

Baker says she's probably right. But he's hoping that the Cass County Draft Board has enough volunteers and college dropouts to meet its monthly quota. He makes it clear he's not interested in military service, but will go if drafted.

She smiles at him, but she's thinking: You're out of here, boy. Go play soldier and leave the water fights in North Dakota to the locals to sort out.

That night, over cocktails at the country club, the Bacevichs discuss their day and their common interest in the future of a *Forum* staff writer.

Sue Bacevich tells her husband that Baker is a college graduate and therefore is accessible to the draft board. "They could send him a greeting anytime they want," she says.

"That's good to hear. I found someone who claims he's a good friend of the husband of the chairwoman of the draft board. He says he'll let the husband know what we need and he'll get it done."

They order another round of cocktails and congratulate themselves on their quick progress in bringing Charles Baker to ground.

Sue Bacevich asks her husband what he intends to do about the book's author, the NDSU professor.

"Don't you worry your pretty little head about that," he responds. "I made a few calls this afternoon and I think it's a safe bet that our professor is going to wish he had never teamed up with young Mr. Baker."

One of his calls went to Henry O'Malley, a sugar beet farmer with strong ties to Fargo's veteran community. Bacevich asked him if he knew anyone on the Cass County Draft Board. O'Malley said he didn't, but mentioned he's a close friend of the husband of the board chair.

"What do you want me to whisper into his ear?" asks O'Malley.

"I think the Board should move a *Forum* staff writer to the top of its draft list because he's no longer eligible for a student deferment and ought to do his duty to his country."

O'Malley agrees. Then he tells Bacevich that the chair's husband also works for the *Forum*. I'll check to see what he thinks of your draftable friend. This just might be the easiest thing you've ever asked of me."

It was. The husband of Cass County's Draft Board chair was Michael Sullivan, head night foreman at the *Forum*. He said he thought the best thing that could happen to that snotnose kid Charles Baker was a tour in Vietnam. Sullivan said he would make sure that Baker's name went to the top of the draft list.

Within the week, a letter from the Cass County Draft Board went out addressed to Charles Baker at the *Forum*. The letter read, "Greetings: You are hereby ordered for induction into the

Armed Forces of the United States." The letter told him he had to appear in person within two weeks at the Fargo Post Office, site of the county draft board.

The letter from the draft board sits on Baker's typewriter when he walks into work. He knows what it is before he even opens it. He is paralyzed by the same feeling he had when George Washington University mailed out its grades at the end of the semester a year ago. He had hoped he would never have to feel that way again.

He is surprised to read he has only two weeks left of "freedom." Two weeks seem an insufficient amount of time to get his affairs in order. Okay, he says to himself, I could get my affairs in order in one day. I just don't want to go.

Baker then notices that Sullivan, the back-shop foreman, is standing over him with a big grin on his face.

"Hey, draft dodger, is that a letter from your local draft board? How much time did it give you to report for duty?"

Baker doesn't want to talk about it and tells Sullivan that. He just laughs. And he explains that he only wanted to be sure the letter had arrived. Baker asks him why he was anticipating it. That's when Sullivan delivers his punch line.

"Who do you think is married to the chair of the Cass County Draft Board? Buddy, your next stop is going to be a Vietnam jungle shooting at some little slant-eyed gook. Make us proud."

"Sullivan, go fuck yourself."

That gets another laugh out of Sullivan as he heads back to his side of the swinging door. Just before he does, he turns back to Baker and makes a fist out of his right hand and vigorously pumps it up and down. Baker gets the message: he's being told to fuck himself too.

Harry Morrison, the state editor whose desk is kitty-corner from Baker's, catches the interaction between the two. He asks if he can read Baker's letter. Baker hands it over, figuring it's just a matter of time before everyone at the newspaper knows he's being drafted.

Morrison spends about one minute reviewing the letter.

"Okay, draftee, what are you going to do now?"

Baker thinks for half a minute and then says, "I guess I'll tell the *Forum* I'm leaving. Then pack my bag and report for duty."

Morrison says, "You know, you can take a different course of action. If you just follow the instructions on the letter, you'll end up in the army. But if you can get yourself accepted into the Air Force, Marines, Coast Guard, or Navy before you have to report, you can avoid the draft and be considered a full-fledged volunteer. As a rule, volunteers fare better than draftees. Do you have a preference for which branch of service you would like to join?"

Baker has no clue. "I've never given it any thought," he says, before adding: "I guess I should have."

"Yeah, that might have been smart. But you can begin that thinking process right now. Let's begin with a question. Do you know anything about the U.S. Naval Reserve? You can join up, go to boot camp, and then get tested to see what your aptitude and skills suggest you ought to do for a job in the Navy. If the Navy has a need for such an individual, you're all set. You'll go off to a Navy school and learn how to do your new job. When you finish the training, which can take three to twelve months, you'll get an assignment. You can request a particular assignment, such as serving on a submarine or an aircraft carrier. Hell, you can even request Hawaiian shore duty. But you're not likely to get any of those assignments because they're generally gobbled up by the regular Navy sailors. Reservists tend to get the slim pickings, such as duty on a destroyer escort out of the old Philadelphia shipyard or shore duty in an Alaskan seaport.

"Now if none of that appeals to you, we're back to your letter and orders to report to some crummy Army training base in a godforsaken southern state such as Arkansas or Georgia. When you finish boot camp, you'll go to advanced infantry training to learn to kill with a rifle and a knife. Then within six months you'll be on your way to the jungles of Vietnam."

Baker feels sick to his stomach. But he manages to ask the logical question.

"Harry, haven't I read that it's nearly impossible to get into a reserve unit? I'm told they have waiting lists and I have no time to wait."

"Well, my young draftee, I might be of some assistance to you. Have you never noticed that on some weekends when I come in to work, I'm wearing a military uniform?"

Baker has to think a minute.

"Sure, I guess so. But I can't tell you what branch of service you belong to or what your rank is."

"Well, I'm a commander in the U.S. Naval Reserve. I not only hold the rank of commander, which is the army equivalent of a lieutenant colonel, but I'm the actual commander of the Fargo reserve unit. If you want to join up, I think my endorsement might just be what you need to get past the front door."

"Wow, this is all moving so fast. But if I understand what you're saying, I ought to move quickly to join your reserve unit. Assuming I'm accepted, how soon would you guess before I actually ship out? Look at that . . . I've already got the lingo down."

"You come with me tomorrow morning and we'll get you through the initial paperwork. Then we'll schedule your physical exam. Assuming you pass, we'll stand you before an American flag and induct you into the Naval Reserve. And we'll issue you a uniform and expect to see you at our regular monthly drills. You can remain with our unit for as long as a year before going on active duty. While you're with us, we'll fly you to the Great Lakes Naval Base for boot camp. Then later on we'll send you back for some advanced training in seamanship. During that period, you'll be on board a Navy ship sailing the Great Lakes. When these two assignments are completed satisfactorily, you'll be a seaman first class and ready to report to your active-duty station.

"Keep in mind, during the initial year with us we'll do our best to align your intellect and skills to an appropriate job in the Navy. We have hundreds for you to choose from. You'll probably want to try to get classified as a specialist in journalism. Joe Jones on the *Forum* editorial staff has that specialty and holds the rank of petty officer first class with our reserve unit. He can tell you what it takes to succeed in that rating.

"But there's a rub. The Navy will only train journalists who sign up for a five-year obligation. If you go into the Reserves, bypass specialized training that requires a longer time commitment, you'll ship out as a seaman. But your obligation for active duty will only be for two years. Keep in mind, though, you'll have to join a reserve unit when you return and serve another two years of part-time service. You go that route and it's anybody's guess what you'll end up doing while on active duty. Frankly, the Navy isn't terribly interested in guys who only have a two-year active-duty obligation. I mean, why invest a lot of time and resources in training them when there's a lot of regular Navy personnel with four-year obligations more than happy to get trained. You could end up on a tramp steamer swabbing decks for two years and taking orders from 19-year-old petty officers. Somehow I can't see you doing that."

Baker just sits and shakes his head.

Finally, Morrison says, "Hey, it's time to go to work. Why don't we end this conversation and agree to meet tomorrow at ten-hundred hours at the Naval Reserve Training Center out by the NDSU campus. Can you get your own ride to the center? Wear a sport coat, dress slacks, and a white shirt. You'll want to impress the sailors you're going to meet. Alright?"

Baker thanks Morrison for all he's doing for him and says, "I'll meet you at the Reserve Center tomorrow." Then he sits back in his chair and wonders what he's getting himself in for. Baker can't recall ever meeting a sailor before Morrison—a newspaper-sailor man in a landlocked state.

You can't make this stuff up, he thinks to himself, completely bewildered at the turn of events in his life in just the last ten minutes, since he opened the letter from the Draft Board.

Chapter Twenty-Two

Police Captain Comes to a Crushing Conclusion

When Charles Baker goes to the *Forum* the day after being sworn into the Navy, he finds a note on his desk instructing him to go talk to Swede Swenson, the managing editor. Baker can't believe Swenson already knows he's leaving. Oh well, he says to himself, we have to have this conversation sooner than later.

After he tells Jim Rector the night editor where he's going, he leaves his desk and heads over to the one occupied by Swenson.

Swenson signals him to sit down and then he offers Baker his hand.

Gripping it, Baker returns Swenson's smile.

Then the managing editor says, "I heard today you've graduated from NDSU. Let me be one of the first to congratulate you on that accomplishment. I can only imagine what a challenge that must have been while working full time here."

Then Swenson shoves a letter across the desk to Baker. It's short and Baker reads it in less than a minute:

```
Dear Chuck -

Congratulations on obtaining your college
degree.  In recognition of your accomplish-
ment, the Forum wishes to offer you full-time
employment with the title of Night City
Editor.  Your pay will increase 15 percent
from what it has been this past year.
   Furthermore, because we consider your
initial year of employment to have been
exemplary, your new pay will be made
retroactive to your original date of
employment.  You will receive a check for
this retroactive pay along with your next
regular paycheck.
   We anticipate great work from you and
we're prepared to provide you with
opportunities to increase your
responsibilities and pay.  We recognize
your writing talent and will assist you in
transferring from your current desk
assignment to the general reporting staff
if that's what you choose to do.  However,
we are impressed by your skill and
initiative as a Night City Editor and hope
you will choose to remain in this
position.  It's our opinion that
advancement at the Forum is faster from
your current position than it would be as
a general assignment reporter.
   Again, from the entire Forum
management team, congratulations on
obtaining your degree and welcome to a
full-time job at our newspaper.

Swede Swenson
Managing Editor
```

Baker wants to argue that he thinks he has been a full-time employee at the *Forum* for the past year. But he bites his tongue because the newly announced change in his status comes with more money in his paycheck.

Then he realizes, despite the bad timing, he needs to share the change in his status.

"Mr. Swenson, thank you for that letter. I can't tell you how excited it is to be officially a full-time employee. And I appreciate you making the appointment retroactive to the time I first came to work here.

"But I'm afraid I've got some bad news to share. I'm going to be leaving the *Forum* soon. I've been drafted, and told to report within two weeks. However, this morning I joined the Naval Reserve. As you undoubtedly know, the local reserve center is under the command of my colleague on the desk, Harold Morrison. Thanks to his help, I've been accepted into his unit. I should learn within the next two weeks what my obligations to the Navy are going to be. Harry said I have to go to boot camp and then go on the water to learn some actual Navy skills. The question of when I'll be expected to leave for full-time duty is unknown. It could be anytime from the end of next month to the end of the year. I just don't know yet, but will make sure you are the first person to hear it after I do."

For a moment, it appears that Swenson intends to withdraw his letter. But then he quits reaching for it and sighs.

"Okay, I guess I should have anticipated that outcome. You graduate and the draft board comes right after you. I support your decision to take some control over your life by joining the Naval Reserves. I think any choice is better than going into the army as a draftee. I would have recommended you join the Air Force myself, given my pleasant experiences as an Air Force officer. But I think you made a good choice.

"So, the letter stands. Your pay will go up and you'll receive the retroactive back pay. And as long as you promise to let me know ASAP when you're leaving to serve your country, my congratulations on full-time employment stands."

Baker gets to his feet and shakes Swenson's hand. And he tells Swenson that leaving the *Forum* is going be a lot tougher than it was to leave the *Washington Star*.

"I can't offer you a job now for when you come back from the service, because let's face it, I may have moved on myself by then. But I promise to put a personal letter into your employment folder summarizing what I consider to be your exemplary year of experience at the *Forum*. And I'll recommend that the newspaper hire you back when you complete your military obligation."

Baker thanks him again and returns to his desk. His duties await him.

*   *   *

Detective Captain Wayne Thompson calls NDSU and without identifying himself asks where he can find Professor Wayne Gautier's office. The university receptionist has received many similar calls ever since the collapse of Minard Hall, where Gautier's office was located, so she has no reluctance to give out the information requested.

Thompson is told he can find the professor in a two-story building on the north side of campus sitting among several other new facilities that house federally funded research projects. When he pulls up to the building, the sign on the front door says

"Restricted Area. DARPA/NDSU. Entrance by Appointment Only."

Of all the damn foolishness, thinks Thompson. This is a state university campus and he's a Fargo detective. He pulls the door open and enters. He immediately is confronted by a federal security officer, who demands to know his purpose for entering the secure premises.

Thompson isn't impressed with the officer. He doesn't even carry a gun.

"I'm here to see Professor Wayne Gautier."

"Do you have an appointment?" responds the guard.

"I am not used to making appointments in my business. Could you just tell me where his office is located?"

The guard stands up from his entryway desk. "Sir, if you don't have an appointment, you cannot enter these premises."

Thompson just stares at the guard. Then the detective pulls open his coat and shows his holstered .45 revolver. That normally is enough to end confrontations with officious but weak opponents. But not in this case.

The guard picks up his portable walky-talky and presses the transmission button.

"Officer needs assistance at DARPA front entrance. Forced entry by an armed intruder."

That wasn't what Thompson thought the guard would do. And now he's unsure of what he ought to do next.

"Listen, let's not make a big deal about this," Thompson says, finally showing his badge. "I'm a Fargo police detective. You're a university rent-a-cop. I have jurisdiction here. You're in my city."

The guard stands his ground. "Sir, I'm a federal security officer. I am not a university employee. This is a federal facility and you have no jurisdiction here. Now why don't we both wait for my superior to show up and you can make your case to him."

Thompson isn't used to people standing up to him. And he doesn't like it.

"I'll tell you what, sonny. When your boss gets here, tell him to meet me at Gautier's officer. We can work out our difference of opinion over jurisdiction there." And with that, Thompson pushes aside the guard and proceeds down the main hallway.

At that point, he hears a voice shout: "Stop right there. Put your hands in the air and turn toward me."

Thompson stops and turns. But he'll be damned if he'll put his hands in the air. He finds himself looking at an older federal security officer with a gun in his hand pointing at him.

"I said put your hands in the air. Do it now."

Thompson figures he'll meet him halfway. Rather than raise his arms into the air, he simply sticks them out at his side. But this time two other security officers are in the hallway with their guns drawn.

The lead officer orders his two subordinates to take Thompson's gun out of its hoister. But as they approach Thompson, he lowers his hands and shouts at them that he's a Fargo detective and he's the one to give the orders. "Lower your guns and vacate the premises," he says angrily.

The lead officer says, "I don't care who you are. You have no authority in a federal facility. This isn't the City of Fargo. Now, allow us to remove your gun or we will assume you intend to use it. And that would be a big mistake."

Thompson wonders for a minute what the chances are he could draw and put down all three of the armed federal officers before one or more of them shoots him. Then he has another thought: *Why in the hell make such a big production of this? I've done nothing wrong.*

"Okay, have it your way." And he raises his arms over his head and allows one of the federal cops to remove his gun. The officer also removes the detective's identification and badge holder. Thompson quickly realizes they did not take his back-up piece from his ankle holster.

The lead officer then picks up his walky-talky and asks whoever answers to notify the Fargo Police Department that one of its detectives is in federal custody at the DARPA facility on the NDSU campus. "Tell them if they want him back, they should immediately send out a suitable police authority to negotiate his release. Have them see Lieutenant Steve Schneider of the Defense Civilian Intelligence Personnel System (DCIPS) at the DARPA facility."

At that point one of the guards puts plastic handcuffs on Thompson and leads him down the hallway to a small conference room. He seats Thompson and then takes a chair himself on the other side of the conference table.

Thompson realizes he's in a double bind. For one thing, with his hands cuffed behind him, he can't reach his back-up gun. But given the fact the federal officers know who he is, any further action on his part will just dig his hole deeper with the Fargo Police Department. He sits quietly, thinking his best bet is to invent a good reason for his visit to a secure federal building.

Within a half-hour the door opens and Fargo Police Chief Ward Simpson enters, along with a uniformed policeman Thompson figures is the chief's driver.

After introducing himself to the federal officers in the room, Simpson turns to Thompson and asks, "What the hell is going on here, Captain?"

Thompson puts on his most conciliatory face and responds, "Sir, I'm not sure. I came into the building to see a professor. And the next thing I knew I was facing an armed posse of federal officers who said I was an intruder. I told them that I was a Fargo detective and didn't need their permission to enter a building on the NDSU campus, which is located in the City of Fargo."

Lieutenant Schneider of DCIPS tells the police chief that he might have noted when he entered the DARPA building a sign on the front door that said, ""Restricted Area. DARPA/NDSU. Entrance by Appointment Only."

Chief Simpson says he did.

"Well, that's where the problem originated. Your detective ignored it. Then when challenged by one of my officers, your detective said he didn't have to pay any attention to the sign because he was with the Fargo Police Department. He didn't offer any identification, but he did flash his gun at the officer. When ordered to leave, he pushed his way into the building. That's when my officer, following procedure, called for reinforcements and said he had an armed intruder at the front door.

"When I arrived, your detective reasserted his right to access. That's when I had him disarmed and put into plastic cuffs. I wanted you to have this information before I notify my superiors about my armed intruder. It will be up to them to decide if he should be arrested and tossed into a federal jail."

Police Chief Simpson said he appreciated the professional courtesy extended by DCIPS.

"Allow me to apologize to you and your officers for this intrusion." Then, turning to Thompson, Simpson told him he was suspended from the job as of that moment. Furthermore, he was ordered to hand over his service pistol as well as his back-up piece. And to turn in his police badge and identification."

As he was saying this, the chief's driver came forward and took the back-up piece out of Thompson's ankle holster. Then he scooped up Thompson's id packet and badge along with his regular gun.

Simpson then told Schneider that the Fargo Police Department was going to arrest Captain Thompson and charge him with dereliction of duty and entering a secure federal building without permission, and whatever charges the state's attorney comes up with.

Schneider responds with a smile. "I'm satisfied with that being the resolution of our issue with your detective. You arrest him and I won't. It's in both of our interests to have this resolved by your department."

With handshakes, the two officers of the law depart. Simpson's driver escorts Thompson to his car and places him in the back seat with his handcuffs still on. The driver then hands his keys to the chief and asks him if he would drive their car back to the station while he takes Thompson to the jail for booking. Before they part company, Simpson walks up close to Thompson and says:

"You've really screwed the pooch this time, Thompson. You've been a rogue cop for way too long. At a minimum, I'm going to bust you down to a beat cop. But if I have my way, you'll be thrown off the force, lose your pension, and spend some time in the city jail. Now get out of here."

Thompson says, "I want a lawyer. I want James Foster."

Simpson walks away, throwing Thompson a final thought: "Give your request to the jailer."

*   *   *

The next day Attorney Foster is ushered into the city jail and allowed to stand outside the cell holding Wayne Thompson. He has a single cell for security reasons—his. Half of the other jail inmates would love to get a chance to be alone with their tormentor.

Foster looks at Thompson. He's dressed in jail-issued clothing, which means it doesn't fit well. He stands in contrast with Foster, who in addition to his new haircut and polished shoes is wearing an inexpensive but brand-new suit adorned with an expensive tie. He bought the new outfit to celebrate ten months of sobriety, since the Indian Joe case.

He accepts a folding chair from the jailer and pulls up to the cell bars. After introducing himself, he asks Thompson to explain why he's in jail.

Thompson responds by telling his lawyer exactly what he told his police chief: He was arrested for going into a university office building in search of a professor he wanted to talk to. Then he was confronted by a federal police officer who said he did not have permission to enter the building. And within minutes, he was facing an armed posse of federal officers, all with their guns drawn.

During his long career representing crooks and conmen, Foster had heard a lot of unbelievable stories. He gives Thompson the benefit of the doubt, but knows there's more to the story than he's heard thus far.

"What building were you in and who's the professor you wanted to see?"

Thompson tells him. He also says that he realizes now, in retrospect, that he made a mistake. He should have called and received permission to enter the building. But he says he didn't know NDSU was conducting secret research for the government in secure buildings inaccessible even to Fargo police detectives.

"I wasn't there in an official capacity. I thought any tax-paying citizen of North Dakota could stroll into an NDSU office building without receiving the third degree from some rent-a-cop federal officer."

Foster says that might be a reasonable point of view. But adds, "It falls apart when that taxpaying citizen flashes a gun, provides no identification, and makes it clear he has no intention of obeying the direct order of the guard on duty."

The lawyer then digs deeper. He knows he hasn't yet uncovered the real reason for the cop's visit to NDSU.

"Who was it you were trying to see and what was your purpose for the visit?"

Thompson asks if he has to answer that question and Foster says, "No, you can wait for the state's attorney to ask it at your trial and answer it then."

After sighing deeply, Thompson realizes he just doesn't have a plausible answer, either for his attorney and certainly not for a hostile prosecuting attorney. "You're my attorney, right?"

"Right."

"So you're bound to keep everything between us, unless I decide otherwise."

"Right."

"I'm going to tell you the truth. And then you advise me if it's what I should say in a courtroom."

Foster agrees.

"I went into the building simply to talk to Professor Wayne Gautier. You might have heard of him. He's the guy who recently wrote the book about North Dakota's water shortage."

Thompson said he did know the name and in fact has read the book. Then he asks Thompson what interest he has in Gautier.

"I wanted to ask him some questions. He made some disparaging remarks about sugar beet farmers in the Red River Valley. I thought that highly inappropriate and wanted him to explain to me why he did it."

Foster gave that response a minute to sink in. Then he asked Thompson why he didn't just complain about the book in a letter to the editor or call the author on the phone. "Why was it necessary for you to go see him face to face?"

Thompson gives a grunt. "It's been my experience I get better information when I'm in someone's face."

Foster agrees that's probably true, given his police credentials and physical size.

"Were you trying to intimidate him? That's what it sounds like to me. And I'm pretty sure the prosecutor in your case is going to see it the same way. Were you going to threaten him with physical harm? What was your objective? Did you want him to pull his book off the market or to write a public letter of apology to the sugar beet farmers?"

Thompson said he isn't exactly sure what he wanted. "I would have accepted an apology, but that wouldn't have been sufficient. I guess he would have had to issue a public apology to the sugar beet farmers. Maybe he should have agreed to pull his book off the market."

Foster offers the opinion that Thompson isn't behaving as a normal book critic.

"Were you there representing the sugar beet farmers? Did they ask you to go talk to Gautier?"

Thompson says he doesn't want to get the sugar beet farmers involved in his dispute with the Fargo Police Department.

"But isn't it true you have a reputation in town for having a close working relationship with them?"

Thompson admits that's true. He tells Foster of his role as the lead cop on the Front Street task force. In that role, he said he had a lot of interaction with the Red River Valley Sugar beet Cooperative and in particular, its chairman, Andy Bacevich.

That response confuses Foster.

"I guess I don't know what the Front Street task force is or what it does. Tell me about it."

Let me ask you a question first, replies Thompson. "Do you know about the unwritten arrangement between the sugar beet farmers and the powerbrokers in Fargo?"

Foster says he has no idea what Thompson is talking about.

"So you are unaware of the fact a thousand or so Mexicans are trucked into Fargo every weekend throughout the spring and fall? If so, then you're unaware of the Blind Pig, an illegal bar that operates down on Front Street during the Mexicans' visits. The city fathers and the sugar beet growers have an agreement that the Mexican farm workers are welcome in Fargo as long as the regular citizens are unaware of their presence. In other words, they are ordered to stay out of Fargo business establishments and in particular Fargo's bars and saloons. In return, the city fathers block off a section of Front Street that contains the Mexicans and excludes Fargo citizens. The sugar beet growers also operate an illegal basement bar under Front Street that sells booze to the farm workers. As part of this arrangement, the city provides the Front Street task force. It operates the bar, keeps the Mexicans within a few blocks along

Front Street, and prevents any Fargo citizens from interacting with their weekend visitors.

"I agreed to run the task force in exchange for a promotion to captain and an envelope full of cash once a month. My task force consists of regular Fargo cops and many more part-time officers. The regular cops are assigned to the Front Street unit, under my command. I hire the part-time officers as needed.

"Although I'm part of the police department leadership, everyone knows I have special duty. By that I mean I work Front Street. From April through October no regular police officer is ever assigned a Front Street beat unless he's part of my task force. While I'm working Front Street, I take orders from Bacevich and his sugar beet friends. That makes sense, when you think about it. The sugar beet farmers are the ones who bring their workers into Fargo for the weekends. They provide the workers with a bar of their own, access to a few stores and cafes that cater to their tastes, police security, and protection from the occasional hot-headed locals who don't like their city invaded by Mexicans.

"In return, the City of Fargo gets a rather significant boost in revenue from the Mexican workers. At the same time, we assure Fargo residents they don't have to mingle with the workers, provide for their needs, or even arrest them if they break the law."

Foster realizes this is more information than he can handle sitting outside Thompson's jail cell. So he asks Thompson, "What does this have to do with your attempted visit with Professor Gautier?"

Thompson says he's reluctant to talk about it. But when Foster says he can't represent him if he doesn't have the full story, Thompson relents.

"I was asked by the sugar beet growers to see to it that the professor doesn't say anything more about them. Don't write anything more about sugar beets, don't give interviews and speeches on the topic, and if pressed, say you were mistaken about the water demands of the sugar beet farmers. My visit had nothing to do with Front Street. It had to do with the fear the growers have that their initiative to make Fargo "Sugar City" was going to come back to haunt them."

Now Foster is confused.

"I guess I don't understand why your police chief wants to have your case tried in a Fargo courtroom. Isn't he worried that you might tell this same tale on the stand?"

Thompson agrees that's a good question. "My guess is he's upset that the feds are intruding on his turf and out of anger decided to steal their case from them. But it also could be because he figures in his own courtroom he can control the outcome. In other words, he might be able to cut a deal with me to keep quiet about the relationship between the town fathers and the sugar beet growers. In exchange, the charges against me will be dropped."

Foster wrinkles up his brow. "Your police chief may be making a mistake. If he arranges to have the charges dropped, I believe the feds will step in and claim jurisdiction over the case. After all, they only handed it over to the Fargo Police to save themselves the trouble of trying you. But if the Fargo Police drop the case, I think the federal government might well want to get justice for itself."

That scenario hadn't occurred to Thompson. And the prospects of that outcome worry him.

"I want to be tried in a city courtroom. That's the only place where I know I can work out a plea agreement."

Foster tells him he's probably right about that. But on the other hand, he says, no plea agreement is going to help him escape trial in a federal court.

"Where we have the trial is up to you. I can understand your reluctance to have it in a federal courtroom. The trial outcome could land you in Fort Leavenworth for years. And I can't imagine a police captain wants to mingle with its inmates.

"We could take you to trial in a regular Fargo courtroom. I could tell the prosecutor before the trial that we intend to subpoena the mayor and the head of the Red River Valley Sugar beet Cooperative to ask about the illegal activity on Front Street. I could say my client has a lot to say on the subject. And I could argue that the only reason you're in jail is because the farmers and the city fathers want to keep you from telling all you know. But I'll assure him that I also will subpoena the two authors of the book so they can share their accusations. That ought to be enough to convince the city fathers to drop the case.

"But I warn you, this could end up in federal court. And we have no leverage there."

Thompson says he'll take his chances.

As expected, after Foster calls the district attorney and shares how he intends to defend his client if the case goes to trial, the DA calls back within two hours to say the city is dropping its charges. Foster's client is free to go home.

When told the news, Thompson wants to know if the Fargo Police Department is going to put him back on the job.

Foster says, "I believe they will. From what I understand, you're their Front Street go-to-guy. I think the task of replacing you is more trouble than having you around to remind them how vulnerable they all are to criminal charges."

As usual, Foster is correct. With no great enthusiasm, the police department restores his rank and puts him back in charge of the Front Street task force.

But not everyone on the force is pleased with the decision to reinstate Thompson to his old position. His longtime partner, Phil Myers, is called into the police chief's office and told his promotion to the job as the new Front Street task force captain has been rescinded now that Thompson has reclaimed it. The only encouraging thing the chief says to Myers is that they should be patient: The chief is sure it's only a matter of time before Thompson fucks up again.

*   *   *

The first person Myers calls with his bad news is Andy Bachevich of the Sugar beet Cooperative. Bachevich says he's sorry to hear Myers lost the Front Street Task Force job. What he doesn't say is how disappointed he is to learn Thompson is coming back into the position. The sugar beet farmers have lost confidence in Thompson and thought Myers would be a suitable replacement.

Bachevich asks Myers if he's on a secure phone. When Myers says he's calling from the police station, Bachevich arranges to meet him in half an hour at the Great Northern Train Station. "We'll catch a cup of coffee and talk over our alternatives at this point," the Sugar City tycoon says.

Once assembled, Bachevich has already come up with a plan.

"Hear me out, that's all I ask. But I think I have a solution to our problem. Simply stated, Thompson has to disappear."

Myers is confused. "I agree, but how do you intend to make that happen?"

"You're the one who's going to make it happen. We think it will be a good test of your skills and it will give you an opportunity to demonstrate your loyalty to our common purposes. I think the simple way of carrying out our plan is to lure Thompson into a car and then knock him out. Don't kill him; that's not necessary. Just knock him out.

"The car you'll use is now waiting in a parking garage across the street. Here are the keys." Bacevich slides a simple wire ring with two car keys on it across the table to Myers, then continues: "Call Thompson and invite him to lunch. Then pick him up in the used car. When the two of you are alone, knock him out and place him into the trunk. Make sure he's unconscious. Drive the car to the crusher out by the Glyndon racetrack. I'll alert the crusher that you're coming. Leave the car with him. He might even pay you a few bucks for it. If so, keep the money.

"After you leave—you'll need to arrange a ride back to Fargo—the car will go into the car crusher. It takes about five minutes for the crusher to mash the car into a compact block of iron and steel. Then the crusher guy will load the car onto a flatbed truck and see to it that it's hauled to Garrison, ND where the Corps of Engineers will pay the truck driver a hundred dollars for it. Eventually, the crushed car will join other crushed vehicles to become part of the retaining wall being built around the Garrison Dam reservoir to hold in the Missouri River."

Two weeks later Myers calls Thompson and invites him out to lunch before they go to work. It's the first time the two old friends have done anything social since Thompson came back on the job.

When Thompson slides into the passenger seat of the junker Bacevich gave Myers, he asks, "Where did you get this wreck?"

Myers explains that his mechanic loaned it to him while he's fixing the brakes on his regular ride.

As they pull out of Thompson's driveway, Myers reaches into the space between his door and seat and pulls out a small, heavy crowbar. He slides it into his lap and grabs it with his right hand. Pulling onto the quiet residential street and seeing no cars or pedestrians in front or back of him, Myers swings the crowbar in a motion he's practiced dozens of times the past week. The crowbar strikes Thompson on the left-hand side of his face, throwing teeth, blood, and facial tissue onto the passenger's side window. Thompson's body convulses violently, and Myers slams the crowbar backhanded into the side of his face again. Thompson's body goes limp. Myers pulls into an alley just a block from Thompson's home. Myers then quickly reaches over and forces Thompson's body forward, so it's not visible from the street. Myers wrestles Thompson's gun out of his shoulder holster and his back-up piece from his ankle holster. He drops both pieces on the floor in the back seat. Myers is a little disappointed with the mess he's made, but one look at Thompson convinces him he has performed a successful mugging.

Myers drives the wreck about a mile, to the back of a deserted warehouse surrounded by trees. He and Thompson have used this spot many times before, when doing things in broad daylight they didn't want seen. Myers parks and gets out, comes around to the passenger side and opens the door. He's not sure Thompson isn't already dead, but he doesn't want to know. He pulls Thompson's body out of the front, falling over on the ground in the process. He gets up and drags Thompson's huge frame to the back of the junker. He opens the trunk and tries to get Thompson's body inside, head first, but Thompson's weight gets away from him, and they both flop back down to the ground. After several attempts, Myers is finally successful.

The front of Myers' shirt is now covered in blood from wrestling Thompson's body into the trunk. He takes it off and folds it forward from the sides, wrapping the blood inside, leaving only dry cloth exposed. He looks in the side mirror and uses the shirt and a little spit to wipe his face clean, then his hands. He goes back around to the passenger's side and does his best to clean Thompson's blood off the inside window with spit and elbow grease. Then he grabs the detective's two guns and the bloody crowbar and wipes them down before tossing them into the trunk, along with his bloody shirt.

As he shuts the trunk with Thompson's body inside, he mumbles to himself, "Case closed." It's a line he heard Thompson use many times under similar circumstances, sometimes at this very location. He opens the back driver's side door, grabbing the clean change of clothes he hid under the driver's seat before leaving home just over an hour ago to pick up Thompson. Once he's finally presentable, he heads out to Dilworth, where he locates the "Car Crusher." He's impressed by the appropriateness of the name. For in fact, crushing cars is its only purpose.

When he pulls up, a guy with a name badge that says "Kenny" greets him at the gate. Kenny determines that the car is a fine candidate for the crusher. Then he asks if Myers has taken everything out of the trunk and back seat. He glances in the back seat and finds it empty. Myers assures Kenny that the trunk is empty too; even the spare tire and jack are out. He just hopes that Kenny doesn't check. And he doesn't. What does he care, after all, what people want to see destroyed in their trunks? He knows personally several people have driven up with live animals in their trunks, and lied about it. Others he assumes were hauling stolen property in their boots hoping to see it disappear forever. Nobody pays him to check and frankly he has no interest himself in anyone's trunk contents.

Kenny tells him to pull his car right up next to the crusher. He says "Al" will tell him what to do next.

Al obviously is the guy at the controls of the forklift that places the car into the crusher. After he hands the car over, Al tells him to leave the keys inside. Then he instructs Myers to back out of the way. "These wrecks tend to spit glass and even metal when crushed. You don't want to be standing anywhere close."

Myers agrees that's good advice. Besides, he isn't sure he wants to see his old partner become part and parcel to a car carcass.

He stands back far enough to get a nod of approval from Al. Then the car is lifted off the ground and placed without any concern for damage into the bed of the crusher. Within a few minutes an engine kicks in and two opposing sides of the crusher push in simultaneously. Although he can't see the damage, the loud, screeching noise of metal against metal is such that little is left to the imagination. Then the sides retrack and the other two sides close in do some serious damage to the car. By the time these two sides are pulled back, the car is little more than a large square of metal, plastic, and rubber. Al uses his forklift to haul out a condensed block of formerly functioning car. Myers can see oil and other fluids flow from the metal mess. He thinks for a moment he sees dripping blood too, but decides it may just be transmission fluid.

He gives Al a thumbs up of appreciation and walks to the front gate. He has forgotten to arrange a ride, so he asks Kenny what he ought to do.

"Just stand here," said Kenny, "and wave a five-dollar bill at a flatbed truck driver when he comes out. It shouldn't take you long to get a ride into Moorhead."

When Myers goes home he changes his clothes before going to work. He also calls Bacevich and tells him the chore is done.

Bacevich congratulates Myers for the speed with which he handled a delicate operation. And adds, "After the police chief realizes Thompson doesn't plan to return to work, I'll let him know we think you would be a logical replacement as the Front Street Detective Captain. When that promotion is announced, why don't we meet for lunch? I would like to introduce you formally to the sugar beet growers." .

Chapter Twenty-Three

So Long, Fargo

During his first two-day session at the Naval Reserve Center in Fargo, Seaman Recruit Baker begins to think he just might enjoy a stint in the Navy. He's fitted for a uniform, given multiple military manuals, and shown the proper way to salute. He is also taught the various ranks of Navy personnel, from the lowest—seaman recruit, like himself—to the highest—five-star admiral. And he learns that he doesn't have to salute enlisted personnel, but when in doubt, told "Do it anyway." Baker thinks that's probably a good recommendation.

He spends the two days attending classes taught, for the most part, by senior petty officers. The two exceptions were officers. One was a local Fargo attorney with the rank of lieutenant, teaching a course on how to write a will. Apparently, the Navy wants to make sure it knows where Baker wants to have his last paycheck sent in the event his ship goes down with all hands. The other officer was a medical doctor with the rank of lieutenant commander, teaching a class on personal hygiene. Baker found it curious that his fellow recruits seemed to pay particular attention to the subject of hygiene, as if the information was all new to them. Baker has to admit, to himself, that some of the syphilis information was new to him. And he figures the Navy intentionally wants its sailors with prurient intentions to experience immediate recall of the doctor's slides showing heavily diseased penises.

He has two great lunches, served cafeteria-style. He frankly was surprised to see that the culinary specialists were all reservists. That gives Baker some idea of the extent of job classifications open to him.

He finds himself paying attention to the enlisted men around him and the job classifications they hold. In general, it seems to him that the pudgy, slow-moving, and nearly blind sailors all hold desk jobs of one kind or another. On the other hand, the physically fit, quick-moving, and generally alert sailors have jobs that require quick thinking, physical skills, and seamanship. He tells himself again that he's generalizing from a small sample, but the more he studies his fellow reservists, the more confident he becomes in his initial analysis.

He also gives some thought to who among the men surrounding him he would like to serve with. Although he initially thought he wanted to be a Navy journalist or something similar, such as a yeoman, he has already changed his mind. His *Forum* colleague, Joe Jones, is communications specialist and a first-class petty officer. Baker likes Jones, but figures he wouldn't be much help in a street fight.

Now that he's in the service, Baker decides he needs to be out on a ship's deck doing something that requires him to use his physical skills and swimming ability. He reminds himself that he was a star swimmer on his high school swim team and remains in good physical condition. He also wants to find a job classification that might enhance his resume or at least teach him skills he can use later; the Navy isn't likely to be able to make him a better journalist or a clerk-typist.

On the second day of drill, during a required library session, he digs deeper into the job classifications the Navy offers. After a lot of searching, he finds what he's looking for: Special Warfare Combatant Craft Crewman (SWCC). Their primary duty, best he can determine, is to run around on fast boats inserting special operations forces into combat situations and then extracting them when they're ready to leave. The SWCC team operate small attack craft up and down rivers and along the shoreline. In Vietnam, they also are used to stop the Viet Cong from using the rivers for their purposes.

Baker knows this's the job for him. The qualifications require him to be a good swimmer, have top physical skills, be drug-free, and be of good moral character. No problem on any of those fronts.

He takes the description for SWCC down to the Reserve Office's main desk and asks who he needs to talk to about signing up for his preferred specialist training. He is directed down the hall to an office containing a couple of desks and two second-class personnel specialists. Both swing their chairs toward him and ask him what's on his mind.

After a short discussion, Baker learns nobody in recent memory from the Fargo Reserve Center has ever asked about becoming a Special Warfare Combatant Craft Crewman (SWCC). But his interest excites the two petty officers. They too are curious to learn about the classification. After a few minutes reading manuals, they agree that Baker has the necessary aptitude, education, and probably the necessary physical and swimming skills to qualify for SWCC training.

Baker learns, though, that he might have to alter his plans about hanging around Fargo for a year. The personnel specialists say the Navy Special Warfare Orientation, located in Coronado, California—suburban San Diego, he's told—only conducts two classes a year and the next one is slated to begin in three months. But first he has to complete basic training. They then check the schedule for boot camp openings at the Great Lakes Naval Training Center. Looks promising, they report to Baker. He could potentially leave Fargo within the week and start his basic training. Assuming successful completion, he would have about a week to cross the country and enroll in the Naval Special Warfare Preparatory School.

"Can you be prepared to leave that soon?"

Baker says he doesn't see why not. They all agree that it might make sense to get a running start on his Navy training. He asks the petty officers what happens after he finishes the Prep School.

"Well, from what I'm reading here, you would stay at Coronado and enroll in a two-week orientation to Navy Special Warfare. I guess they want to acclimate new warriors into the Special Forces lifestyle," Baker is told.

"But wait, you're not done. After you learn to grunt like an ape and kill with your bare hands, the Navy wants you to stick around Coronado for another five weeks of what it calls physically and mentally exhausting team-building training. Wait, here's the best part. 'The last few days of this training are what is known as 'The Tour.' That's where you apply your skills, teamwork, and mental toughness under various weather conditions and with limited sleep.' A walk in the park, Baker, for a young stud like you."

By now the two petty officers are in full laughter. Baker doesn't care; that's the attitude he expects from desk jockeys. It reinforces his belief that Special Warfare training is what he wants. And the sooner the better. He figures it's a young man's occupation.

Before he leaves, he remembers to ask a critical question: "How long is my enlistment obligation if I go through this training?"

After referring to the manual again, one of the petty officers says, "Four years. Maybe longer, depending on how much training you require."

Baker guesses the look on his face gives away his disappointment.

That's when the other petty office gives him a brief pep talk.

"Listen, Baker, right now you have a two-year active duty obligation. But then you have an additional four-year obligation to continue in the Navy Reserves.

"During those four years the Navy can call you back on active duty anytime it wants. In the meantime, you'll have to attend monthly two-day drills and ship out annually for a full month of active Navy duty. On the other hand, you give four years to the Navy in Special Warfare and you'll be released to go back to living your normal life."

The other petty officer joins in. "If you stay in our program, you're undoubtedly going to get a shit assignment once you leave boot camp. I doubt if you could even get into a training program that might give you an opportunity to earn a rank above seaman. That means the whole time you're in the Navy, you're the bilge puke. On the other hand, four years in a premier unit such as Special Warfare will ensure you advance in rank throughout your time of service. You won't take shit from any enlisted man and probably not many officers. That's the way to go through the Navy, I can assure you."

He's told not to sweat it now, though. First, he has to get through basic training and then be accepted into the orientation course for Special Warfare. He's advised to go back to the main office and tell the ranking yeoman on duty that he wants to get to Great Lakes for basic training ASAP.

"Ask the yeoman to get you into the training and then provide you with your travel authorization. Meanwhile, go home and get your personal affairs in order."

*   *   *

That night, while at the *Forum*, he asks Commander Morrison if he's doing the right thing.

"If I was your age, and in the best shape of my life, I'd jump at this opportunity. But it isn't going to be easy to qualify. Assuming you do, though, you'll rub shoulders with special forces and in particular, the toughest of the bunch, our Navy Seals. Think of the stories you can write later. And nobody will question your qualifications if you decide to write a book about your adventures."

Baker doesn't tell Morrison, but the thought of authoring a book about his upcoming experience has already occurred to him. In fact, he thinks it's the motivation behind his desire to get started on this new adventure.

The following morning, Baker goes back to the Reserve Center and meets with a chief yeoman who Morrison had arranged for him to see. Sitting in front of his desk, Baker learns that he has been accepted for bootcamp training on Monday of the following week. The chief then hands him his plane ticket to Chicago, a voucher for a cab to take him from O'Hara Airport to a commuter train station on the outskirts of Chicago, and a ticket on the commuter train that runs out to the

Great Lakes Naval Training Center. He also receives a cash allowance for meals and incidentals while traveling. Finally, he's told to swing back later and pick up his personnel file, which he has to take with him and then return it to the Reserve Unit after his training.

Baker asks what he should do if he completes bootcamp and intends to proceed directly to Coronado for Naval Special Warfare Orientation.

"When you graduate from bootcamp, you'll be given the opportunity to meet with Navy personnel who will guide you to your next duty station. They will provide you with the necessary paperwork and travel authorization. Good luck to you, sailor."

Back at the *Forum* that evening, Baker stops by the managing editor's desk and hands him a brief memo saying Saturday is going to be his last day of employment. He tells him he's leaving first thing Monday morning and figures he needs Sunday to pack a bag and store his personal possessions.

"Well, that turned out to be a lot sooner than we thought," says Swenson. "Lucky for us, I figured this might happen. I never did think you would hang around long once you had a chance for a new adventure. I've already hired your replacement, the city editor from the *Jamestown Sun*. He'll report to work the same day you leave Fargo. Hell, you don't even have to train him to do your job. We'll give Commander Morrison that duty."

Later, during a lull in the flow of copy, Baker looks across his desk at Jim Rector, the night editor.

"Jim, I want you to know I'm leaving the *Forum* earlier than I thought. I fly to Chicago Monday morning to enter basic training. Saturday will be my last day. Swenson just told me he has already hired my replacement, a guy from the *Jamestown Sun*. He'll start Monday.

"I hope he picks up the job as fast as you did. Maybe this time Swenson did me a favor. I can only hope so. Are you going to work tonight through Friday night?"

Baker nods his head and Rector adds, "Well, I've enjoyed working with you. I really mean that. Swenson has told me he's offered you a job here once you finish your military obligation. I hope you're planning to do that. This newspaper needs young men like you. In the meantime, best of luck to you."

With that, Rector gets up from his desk and hobbles into the backroom to see how the newspaper is coming together.

Baker thinks that went smoother than he thought it would. He's going to miss the old guy. He's a real pro.

Over the next few days, Baker spends his mornings and early afternoons running around Fargo, saying goodbye and terminating his business ties. He tells the bank to keep his account open because he intends to have his Navy checks directly deposited. He schedules a final cab ride to the airport for Monday morning and arranges with the resident manager of the Donaldson to hold his mail and provide him with storage space for his personal possessions.

He calls his stepfather, Jerry Pinks, at his congressional office in Washington, D.C. When he's put through to the minority staff director of the Senate Appropriations' Committee, his stepfather comes on the phone and says, in an irritated voice: "About time you called. You have your mother worried sick. Are you in trouble again? Get fired from the *Forum* or mugged by the sugar beet farmers?"

"Love you too, Jerry. No, nothing like that. But I do have some news. First, I graduated from NDSU. No, the university did not award me academic honors. But I did get a letter from the college president saying he was pleased I'm leaving his university. Second, I got my draft notice. Consequently, I'm leaving Monday morning to enter basic training at the Great Lakes Naval Training Center. I'm hoping to train to become a Naval Special Warfare Combatant Craft Crewman. That would undoubtedly place me on a swift boat in Vietnam working with Special Forces. If I get the training I want, I'll have a four-year obligation. You can assume I'll be out of your hair for a long time."

"Your mother will be pleased to hear you've graduated. You might send her your diploma so she can really believe you did it. Besides, she'll want to frame it and put it up on the wall. Congratulations from me too, especially for your willingness to serve our country."

"Tell Mom the diploma will be in the mail this week. And Jerry, you haven't commented on our book, *Water Shortage*. Have you had a chance to read it?"

"Actually, I've skimmed it. That was enough for me. Let's not part company with our last conversation being about the lousy book you helped write. Can we agree on that? But I want to add, I do appreciate that you sent me a preview copy so I was forewarned. That was helpful."

Baker says he'll always send him advance copies of his books.

Pinks asks his stepson if he plans to return to Fargo when he's out of the service.

"I don't really know. The *Forum* has made it pretty clear that a job will be mine when I come back. That makes me feel good. I've enjoyed my relationship with NDSU and some of its faculty. If I want an advanced degree, I have no doubt that I would be accepted into graduate school in more than one subject area. And then—you'll get a kick out of this—I've really enjoyed living in the Donaldson. Some of my best friends in Fargo live there. I'm going to miss them and if I come back, I'm sure I'll want to move in with them again."

Pinks remains quiet for a moment. Then he says, "Tell you what I'm going to do. As your graduation gift, your mother and I are going to give you the Donaldson to own and operate when you come back to Fargo. I'll keep it running until you return. But when you get back, it'll be in your name to do with what you want. I've always thought it's nicely located to take advantage of the downtown renaissance Fargo is planning. I can see you turning it into a showcase property. And it could easily become the best place in town to hang your hat."

Now it's Baker's turn to be quiet. "I don't know what to say, Jerry. That's the most generous thing you've ever done for me, and I couldn't be more pleased. I would love to rebuild the Donaldson into a showcase property. And even as I sit here, I think that prospect will bring me back to Fargo for sure. Thank you, Jerry. You've given me something to think about when I'm touring Vietnam's waterways on a swift boat."

Baker then asks Pinks if he should notify the Donaldson staff of the pending change in ownership and Pinks says no, "Let's leave matters as they are for now. It's hard enough to get them to respond to my instructions. If they think I'm no longer the owner, they'll ignore me completely."

That gets a laugh out of Baker, but he concedes that Pinks has made a good point. He promises he won't say anything to the staff.

The next morning, he joins the fellows for breakfast at the VFW and all four of them, per custom, order exactly the same thing: two eggs, toast, bacon, and black coffee. He offers to buy, but is refused. Sam says it's their treat. But it's the last one he's going to get. And they all laugh.

They tell him they'll miss him when he goes off to the service. Then Sam and Will remind him he's joining the worst branch of the service.

"I can't believe you passed up the army and the marine corps to be a swabbie," Sam says. And then he grills Baker about what the hell a Special Warfare Combatant Craft crewman actually does.

Baker explains the position for the second time to the three veterans. But he thinks they know exactly what he'll be doing. And every one of them realizes Baker is going to go in harms' way. They don't want to scare him, or suggest he change his mind, so they just kid him about his choice.

Will wants to know if he plans to return to Fargo. Baker had been anticipating that question and he's pleased to tell them that he's not only coming back to Fargo, but back to the Donaldson. In fact, he plans to move back into his current room.

That gets a rise out of his neighbors.

"Fellows, the advantage of Baker coming back is that we don't have to train a new resident in how the bathroom rotation works," says Sam.

Baker then lowers his voice for one of his patented story-behind-the-story tales.

"Listen, this is just between you and me. When I come back, I've been told by the owner I'll have the chance to make some changes in our current residence. I plan to spruce it up and make it the showcase property in downtown Fargo. But I also intend to keep this gang together. I'm thinking we ought to convert our single-occupant rooms into two-room suites, complete with our own bathrooms. While I'm gone you can give some thought to how they might look. Interested?"

The three veterans make it clear they're not enthusiastic about changes in their abode. Or the monthly rent they pay now.

Will says the idea of a showcase property bothers him. "I would hate to think we're going to have hoity toity residents move in with us old veterans."

After smiling at the veteran's comment, Baker says he just might have to reserve their floor for them and a few other veterans they invite in and let the stuffed shirts rent rooms on the other floors.

"Keep in mind, you're going to have an in-suite bathroom. So there's absolutely no reason we'll have to mingle with the undesirables living in the building. And I wouldn't worry about a rent increase. We'll charge the other guests enough to subsidize the cost of housing for the veterans. Leave it to me; I'll work something out."

Sam gets serious for a moment.

"Chuck, we're sure going to miss you. Is there anything we can do for you before you leave?"

Baker smiles. He has been hoping such a question might arise.

"I've got one request. I've told you about this union hack at the *Forum* who orchestrated the draft board's efforts to nab my ass and put me in the army. Don't get me wrong: I'm okay with going into the service. I know my obligation. But boy do I resent this guy for pulling strings to ensure my name is on top of this month's list of new inductees. So I wouldn't be all that upset if somebody brought this guy down a notch or two."

Sam asks, in his same serious tone, "Do you have something in particular you wish us to do to him?"

"Actually, Sam, no I don't. I would never ask you to hurt somebody just because he pisses me off. But I have thought of something short of physical punishment that might do the trick. And it plays to your strengths as former commandoes."

Baker hands Sam a slip of paper containing a car description, complete with a license plate number.

"I know this guy loves this car. It's an old vintage Buick. He's had it for years, but he keeps it in really good condition. Well, I wouldn't be all that offended if he had to replace it with something new."

Sam smiles and looks at his companions. "Oh, I think I have just the idea. Leave it to us."

Baker smiles and says, "be careful and don't get caught. He parks his Buick in the same place outside the *Forum* on the nights he's working. After about 9 p.m., the foot traffic all but disappears and only an occasional car or truck passes by. And whatever you do, wait a week or two. I'd like to make sure the number one suspect is in basic training at the Great Lakes."

Two weeks later to the day, a printer yells across the back shop. "Hey, Sullivan, come over here and look out the window. I think your car is on fire."

And so it was, burning intensely, right down to the rims.

*   *   *

Behrie the cab driver is outside the Donaldson Hotel as requested for the early Monday morning run out to Hector Airport. When he gets into the cab, Baker apologizes for asking for a ride at the ungodly hour of 4:45 a.m., and Behrie replies that he wouldn't do it for anyone but one of his regular clients.

Baker's driver already knows about his client's change in draft status. After glancing at Baker's skimpy throw-away bag, he realizes his customer is leaving for military duty.

"Where to today, boss?"

"Chicago and then on to the Great Lakes Naval Training Center about halfway between Chicago and Milwaukee. At least that's what I've been told. I've never been in that part of the country. I'm heading to boot camp and then a career—at least for a couple of years—in Uncle Sam's Navy. You'll have to carry on here without me, but take some solace knowing I'm going to be on the front lines to make sure you're safe from all enemies, domestic and foreign."

Behrie chuckles. "Yeah, I'm already feeling safer."

When they get to the airport, Baker slips his driver an extra $20 for a tip and tells him how much he's appreciated having access to his cab for the past two years.

"Hey, I'll miss you too. You're not the city's biggest tipper, but you're one hell of a lot more interesting passenger than my normal rides. When you get back in town, call me if you need a cab. You know the number."

"You can count on it, my friend. Oh, don't bother; I can carry my own luggage." They are both laughing as they depart—Baker, into the airport, Behrie, back toward Fargo.

When the DC-3 lifts off and banks over the City of Fargo to begin its journey to Minneapolis, Baker realizes that he's not flying the most direct route. United Airlines, he knows, flies directly from Fargo to Chicago. But the Navy put him on a connecting flight to Chicago with a long stopover in Minneapolis. Baker sits in his window seat and simply sighs. He's going to have to adjust to the Navy's way of doing business.

Just then the clouds part and he can see the sun rise. He notices how its rays play off the reflective windows of several downtown buildings.

He snaps down his window shade to keep the sun out, and closes his eyes.

Then he finds himself humming the words to Woodie Guthrie's Dust Bowl tune, "So Long, It's Been Good To Know Yuh." Baker knows the tune, but not the lyrics.

"So long, Fargo. See you on down the road."

*   *   *

Far below, rapidly fading into the distance behind Baker, Sam Bodini is just getting into bed with the sunrise, having put in a full weekend behind the bar at the Blind Pig. He's not happy that sonofabitch Thompson has disappeared. Bodini figures his friend skipped town with a suitcase full of money earned from his various illegal operations. With Thompson gone, seemingly never to return, Bodini is forced to do business with Thompson's sidekick Myers. He has turned into a real asshole now that he's in charge, taking a twenty percent cut right off the top of everything. And he collects in person every weekend.

Across town, Detective Myers awakes with a start, having dreamt about the teeth and blood of his colleague Thompson hitting the car's side window for the third or fourth time this week. Then he thinks about the $5,000 in cash Bacevich slipped him in an envelope at lunch yesterday, "in recognition of all you've been doing for Sugar City and the farmers, Phil." He reaches for the new prescription of Valium on his nightstand and trembles two of the pills out of the bottle with shaking hands. He pops them, grabs the half-glass of water he left on the nightstand, and drinks them down. Then he falls back on his pillow and tries to drift back into oblivion. He's not on duty for another eight hours.

High above the green banks of the Red River, Andrew Bacevich is sleeping soundly in his bed. His wife Sue is sitting in her favorite kitchen nook, overlooking the Red, cradling her first cup of coffee, as the sun starts to peak above the horizon in the distance. She'd heard that Baker would be leaving town today for his stint in the Navy. She wonders if Baker has figured out it was her doing that got him into uniform. She smiles at the thought. Either way—whether it never occurs to him or someday he begins to put the pieces together—she thinks it's kind of funny.

Maybe Andy ought to start calling her "The Sweetheart of Sugar City," she chuckles to herself.

Acknowledgments

This book would never have been completed had it not been for the fact my brother Mark called to tell me the novel he'd recently written was selling like hotcakes. My brother is a great lawyer and a skilled politician, but I'd never thought of him as an author. Then I read his book and found myself saying: This is a good read.

When I called Mark to tell him how much I enjoyed *She Has the Right of It: An Irish-American Story*, he asked: "Don't you have a book in the works?"

Not really. I'd started a novel ten years earlier, but allowed other projects and foreign travel to take precedence. I figured my writing days were done. But now my younger brother, with scant writing experience, had produced a novel. For God's sake, I snorted to myself, if he can do it, so can I. I returned to my manuscript and produced a final version of my story. That's why Mark gets my initial acknowledgment.

After I had finished my writing, I went back to Mark and asked him how he got from typed manuscript to a printed book. He helped out again by introducing me to Marc de Celle, author of a regional bestseller, *How Fargo of You*. Marc is also an editor and illustrator, and with his guidance, my so-called "finished" manuscript underwent another edit and some revisions suggested by a review from a flock of early readers. Then it went to the printer and emerged as a full-fledged book. So Marc gets my second acknowledgment.

I also wish to acknowledge my daughter, Lara Lynne Hollenczer. She co-authored my last book, a scholarly tome about conducting effective public relations. But she assured me I could just as easily write a gritty novel.

I must acknowledge the important contributions my wife, Marcie Dianda, made. I figured she was supportive of my writing project because she assumed it would keep me out of bars and away from casinos. Nevertheless, she read every chapter as soon as I finished it, offered helpful comments, and encouraged me to keep writing.

Finally, I want to acknowledge Fargo, North Dakota. I spent my formative years in Fargo and still call a cadre of fellow graduates of Fargo Central High School my best friends. My memories of Fargo enabled me to write this novel. I will always think of it as home.

About the Author

Edward Joseph Schneider is named after his father and his father before him. For one family, that's clearly two Edward Joseph Schneiders too many. And being the youngest of the three, with absolutely no say in the decision, he was labeled "Joe" and told to stick with it. No family member, friend, or work colleague has ever called him anything else.

Various officious government agencies, however, refuse to recognize his name preference. So his driver's license, military ID, and Social Security card identify him as Edward Joseph Schneider. Consequently, others have taken a similar, bureaucratic approach to identifying him. Publishers being among the most officious of the bunch. His writing in the field of education, including six published books and monographs, list him as either Edward Joseph Schneider or simply E. Joseph Schneider.

But because he is self-publishing his latest book, he decided he could damn well decide to author it as Joe Schneider.

Joe spent his career as a newspaperman, a university faculty and staff member, a national trade association executive, a congressional lobbyist, a book author, an education consultant, and a mediocre tennis player and an even worse pickleball contestant.

He has been married to Marcella R. Dianda for 34 years and all his friends and family members say he's lucky she's still hanging around with him. His daughter, Lara Lynne Hollenczer, gave him two grandchildren, James Joseph and Elizabeth Gray Hollenczer. Much to his chagrin, they live on the East Coast while Marcie and he reside outside Portland, Oregon.

A Blind Pig in Sugar City is Schneider's first work of fiction. It features events and places Schneider experienced personally. But it's not autobiographic. The story's main character, Charles Baker, reputedly graduated from North Dakota State University, worked the night shift at the Fargo *Forum*, and was a member of the U.S. Naval Reserves, which parallels Schneider's experiences. But that's the end of the similarities. Baker only resided in Fargo for two years. Schneider lived in North Dakota until he left at the age of 23 to accept a job offer on the West Coast. But he drifts back to North Dakota regularly to bond with family members and maintain lifelong friendships with classmates from Fargo Central High School.

www.ingramcontent.com/pod-product-compliance
Lightning Source LLC
LaVergne TN
LVHW041653060526
838201LV00043B/424